RUBICON

AURORA RESONANT: BOOK TWO

G. S. JENNSEN

HYPERNOVA
PUBLISHING
2017

RUBICON

Hypernova Publishing
P.O. Box 2214
Parker, Colorado 80134
www.hypernovapublishing.com

Ordering Information:
Hypernova Publishing books may be purchased for educational, business or sales
promotional use. For details, contact the "Special Markets Department" at the
address above.

Rubicon / G. S. Jennsen.—1st ed.

LCCN 2017943736
ISBN 978-0-9984245-4-5

For Katie, Jules, Andy, Taylor and Julie,
who enthusiastically leapt on this crazy train at the station
and have done so much to keep it on the tracks and headed
toward its final destination since then

ACKNOWLEDGEMENTS

Many thanks to my beta readers, editors and artists, who made everything about this book better, and to my family, who continue to put up with an egregious level of obsessive focus on my part for months at a time.

I also want to add a personal note of thanks to everyone who has read my books, left a review on Amazon, Goodreads or other sites, sent me a personal email expressing how the books have impacted you, or posted on social media to share how much you enjoyed them. You make this all worthwhile, every day.

AURORA RHAPSODY

is

AURORA RISING

STARSHINE

VERTIGO

TRANSCENDENCE

AURORA RENEGADES

SIDESPACE

DISSONANCE

ABYSM

AURORA RESONANT

RELATIVITY

RUBICON

REQUIEM (2017)

SHORT STORIES

RESTLESS, VOL. I • *RESTLESS, VOL. II*

APOGEE • *SOLATIUM* • *VENATORIS*

RE/GENESIS

Learn more and see a Timeline of the Aurora Rhapsody *universe at:*

gsjennsen.com/aurora-rhapsody

AMARANTHE
Anaden Empire

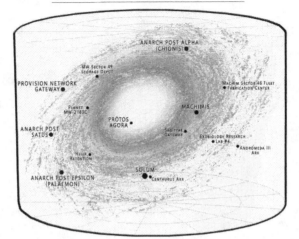

Milky Way Galaxy

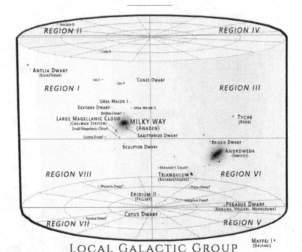

Local Galactic Group

AURORA
COLONIZED WORLDS

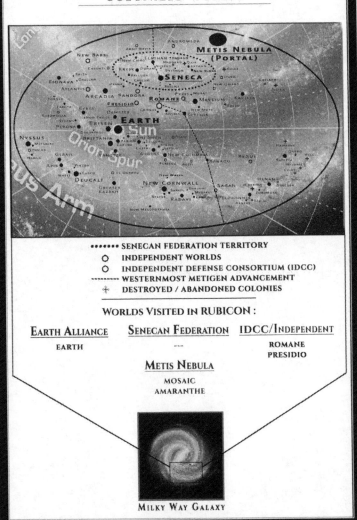

●●●●●● SENECAN FEDERATION TERRITORY
○ INDEPENDENT WORLDS
○ INDEPENDENT DEFENSE CONSORTIUM (IDCC)
-------- WESTERNMOST METIGEN ADVANCEMENT
✤ DESTROYED / ABANDONED COLONIES

WORLDS VISITED IN RUBICON :

EARTH ALLIANCE	SENECAN FEDERATION	IDCC/INDEPENDENT
EARTH	---	ROMANE
		PRESIDIO

METIS NEBULA

MOSAIC
AMARANTHE

MILKY WAY GALAXY

View the Amaranthe and Aurora Maps Online at gsjennsen.com/maps-rubicon

DRAMATIS PERSONAE

HUMANS OF AURORA

Alexis 'Alex' Solovy
Space scout and explorer. Prevo.
Spouse of Caleb Marano, daughter of Miriam and David Solovy.
Artificial/Prevo Counterpart: Valkyrie

Caleb Marano
Former Special Operations intelligence agent, SF Division of Intelligence.
Spouse of Alex Solovy.

Miriam Solovy (Commandant)
Leader, Galactic Common Defense
Accord (GCDA) & AEGIS Forces.
Captain, *AFS Stalwart II.*
Mother of Alex Solovy.

Malcolm Jenner (Brigadier)
Earth Alliance NW Command.
AEGIS Council, Dir. of Marines.
Captain, *AFS Saratoga.*

Mia Requelme
Prevo. Entrepreneur.
IDCC Minister of Colonial Affairs.
Artificial/Prevo Counterpart: Meno

Kennedy Rossi
Founder/CEO, Connova Interstellar.
AEGIS Consultant. Alex's best friend.

Noah Terrage
COO, Connova Interstellar.
Former smuggler. AEGIS Consultant.

Morgan Lekkas
Prevo. AEGIS Council.
Cmdr, IDCC Rapid Response Forces.
Artificial/Prevo Counterpart: Stanley

Brooklyn Harper
Former EA Special Forces Captain.
Leader, IDCC RRF ground forces.
AEGIS Council.

Devon Reynolds
Prevo. Former EASC Consultant.
Quantum computing expert, hacker.
Artificial/Prevo Counterpart: Annie

Christopher Rychen (Fleet Admiral)
Leader, Earth Alliance Armed
Forces. AEGIS Council.

Richard Navick
Former EASC Naval Intelligence.
GCDA SENTRI Director.
Family friend of the Solovys.

David Solovy (Commander)
Alex Solovy's father. Miriam
Solovy's spouse. Captain,
EAS Stalwart. Deceased.

Valkyrie
Artificial. Prevo counterpart to
Alex Solovy. Pilot of the *Siyane.*

ALIENS OF AMARANTHE

Eren asi-Idoni
Anarch resistance agent.
Species: Anaden

Mnemosyne ('Mesme')
Idryma Member, 1st Analystae of Aurora.
Species: Katasketousya (Metigen)

Danilo Nisi
Sator (leader) of the anarch resistance.
Species: Anaden

Cosime Rhomyhn
Anarch agent. Friend of Eren.
Species: Naraida

Nyx elasson-Praesidis
Inquisitor.
Species: Anaden

Casmir elasson-Machim
Machim fleet military commander.
Species: Anaden

Praesidis Primor
Head of Praesidis Dynasty.
Species: Anaden

Machim Primor
Head of Machim Dynasty.
Species: Anaden

Xanne ela-Kyvern
Anarch, mission supervisor.
Species: Anaden

Volya Gaala-min
Anarch, security supervisor.
Species: Barisan

Miaon
Anarch agent. Friend of Eren, Mesme.
Species: Yinhe

Felzeor
Anarch agent. Friend of Eren.
Species: Volucri

Thelkt Lonaervin
Anarch agent. Friend of Eren.
Species: Novoloume

Lakhes
Praetor (leader) of the Idryma.
Species: Katasketousya (Metigen)

Hyperion
Idryma member, Analystae.
Species: Katasketousya (Metigen)

Dimou ela-Erevna
Anarch, Director of Regenesis Lab.
Species: Anaden

Latro Udiri-jun
Anarch, Post Epsilon Administrator.
Species: Barisan

Logiel ela-Erevna
Administrator, Exobiology Lab #4.
Species: Anaden

Avdei elasson-Idoni
Owner, Plousia Chateau, Serifos.
Species: Anaden

OTHER CHARACTERS

Abigail Canivon
Former Cybernetic Expert.
Deceased.

Charito Dierev
Anarch intelligence supervisor.
Species: Novoloume

Charles Gagnon
Earth Alliance Prime Minister.

Corradeo Praesidis
Progenitor of the Dynasties.
Species: Anaden

Emily Bron
Artist. Devon Reynolds' girlfriend.

Erevna Primor
Head of Erevna Dynasty.
Species: Anaden

Eusebe
Scientist, researcher.
Species: Katasketousya (Metigen)

Gino Belosca (Brigadier)
SF Armed Forces; AEGIS Council.

Graham Delavasi
Director, SF Div. Intelligence.

Iveane ela-Erevna
Anarch tech officer.
Species: Anaden

Nelson Escarra (Rear Admiral)
EA Armed Forces. AEGIS Council.

Nolan Bastian (Field Marshal)
Leader, SF Military. AEGIS Council.

Olivia Montegreu
Former head of Zelones Cartel.
Deceased.

Paratyr
Second Sentinel, Mirad Vigilate.
Species: Katasketousya (Metigen)

Phillip Grenier (Major)
EA/AEGIS special forces.

Renato Praesidis
Son of Corradeo Praesidis.
Species: Anaden

Sander ela-Machim
Anarch agent.
Species: Anaden

Savine Idoni
Head of Idoni Dynasty.
Species: Anaden

Simon Ettore (Major)
AEGIS Prevo, *AFS Saratoga.*

Sotiras
Scientist, researcher.
Species: Katasketousya (Metigen)

Theriz Primor
Head of Theriz Dynasty.
Species: Anaden

Thomas
AEGIS Artificial.

Trepenos Hishai
Anarch agent, Chalmun Station.
Species: Novoloume

Vii
Artificial, fork of Valkyrie.
Employee of Connova Interstellar.

William 'Will' Sutton
GCDA SENTRI Deputy Director.
Spouse of Richard Navick

ANADEN DYNASTIES

PRAESIDIS
Role: *Criminal investigation and enforcement*

MACHIM
Role: *Military*

THERIZ
Role: *Resource cultivation and management*

EREVNA
Role: *Research, Science*

IDONI
Role: *Entertainment, Pleasure seekers/providers*

KYVERN
Role: *Administration, bureaucracy*

DIAPLAS
Role: *Engineering, construction*

ANTALLA
Role: *Commerce, trade*

*

DYNASTY RANKS

Primor

Elasson

Ela

Asi

View the Dramatis Personae Online at gsjennsen.com/characters-rubicon

THE STORY SO FAR

View a more detailed summary of the events of Aurora Rising and Aurora Renegades online at gsjennsen.com/synopsis.

AURORA RISING

T he history of humanity is the history of conflict. This proved no less true in the 24th century than in ancient times.

By 2322, humanity inhabited over 100 worlds spread across a third of the galaxy. Two decades earlier, a group of colonies had rebelled and set off the First Crux War. Once the dust cleared, three factions emerged: the Earth Alliance, consisting of the unified Earth government and most of the colonies; the Senecan Federation, which had won its independence in the war; and a handful of scattered non-aligned worlds, home to criminal cartels, corporate interests and people who made their living outside the system.

Alexis Solovy was a space explorer. Her father gave his life in the war against the Federation, leading her to reject a government or military career. Estranged from her mother, an Alliance military leader, Alex instead sought the freedom of space and made a fortune chasing the hidden wonders of the stars.

A chance meeting between Alex and a Federation intelligence agent, Caleb Marano, led them to discover an armada of alien warships emerging from a mysterious portal in the Metis Nebula.

The Metigens had been watching humanity via the portal for millennia; in an effort to forestall their detection, they used traitors among civilization's elite to divert focus from Metis. When their plans failed, they invaded in order to protect their secrets.

The wars that ensued were brutal—first an engineered war between the Alliance and the Federation, then once it was revealed to be built on false pretenses, devastating clashes against the Metigen invaders as they advanced across settled space, destroying every colony in their path and killing tens of millions.

Alex and Caleb breached the aliens' portal in an effort to find a way to stop the slaughter. There they encountered Mnemosyne, the Metigen watcher of the Aurora universe—our universe. Though enigmatic and evasive, the alien revealed the invading ships were driven by AIs and hinted the answer to defeating them lay in the merger of individuals with the powerful but dangerous quantum computers known as Artificials.

Before leaving the portal space, Alex and Caleb discovered a colossal master gateway. It generated 51 unique signals, each one leading to a new portal and a new universe. But with humanity facing extinction, they returned home armed with a daring plan to win the war.

In a desperate gambit to vanquish the enemy invaders before they reached the heart of civilization, four Prevos (human-synthetic meldings) were created and given command of the combined might of the Alliance and Federation militaries. Alex and her Artificial, Valkyrie, led the other Prevos and the military forces against the alien AI warships in climactic battles above Seneca and Romane. The invaders were defeated and ordered to withdraw through their portal, cease their observation of Aurora and not return.

Alex reconciled with her mother during the final hours of the war, and following the victory Alex and Caleb married and attempted to resume a normal life.

But new mysteries waited through the Metis portal. Determined to learn the secrets of the portal network and the multiverses it held, six months later Caleb, Alex and Valkyrie traversed it once more, leaving humanity behind to struggle with a new world of powerful quantum synthetics, posthumans, and an uneasy, fragile peace.

Aurora Renegades

Following the victory over the Metigens, Alex, Caleb and Valkyrie set off to unlock the secrets of the Metigens' portal network. Discovering worlds of infinite wonder, they made both enemies and friends. Planets of sentient plant life which left a lasting mark on Alex and Caleb both. Silica-based beings attempting to grow organic life. A race of cat-like warriors locked in conflict with their brethren.

Behind them all, the whispered machinations of the Metigen puppet masters pervaded everything. In some universes, the Metigens tested weapons. In some, they set aliens against each other in new forms of combat. In others, they harvested food and materials to send through the massive portal at the heart of the maze.

But Alex and Caleb found yet another layer to the puzzle. In one universe, they discovered a gentle race of underground beings with a strange history. Their species was smuggled out of the universe beyond the master portal by the Metigens. They watched as their homeworld was destroyed by a powerful species known as Anadens; but for the Metigens, they would have perished as well.

Back home in Aurora, the peace proved difficult to maintain. The Prevos found themselves targeted by politicians and a restless population desperate for a place to pin their fears. Under the direction of a new, power-hungry Earth Alliance PM, the government moved to cage and shackle them.

In desperation, the Prevos uploaded the AIs' consciousnesses into their own minds, fled from their governments' grasp and disappeared onto independent colonies. Devon published the details of the Prevo link to the exanet, unleashing its capabilities for anyone who wanted to follow in their footsteps.

Meanwhile, an anti-synthetic terrorist group emerged to oppose them, fueled by the rise of Olivia Montegreu as a Prevo. While the private face of Prevos was the heroes who defeated the Metigens, the public face became the image of Olivia killing a colonial governor and tossing him off of a building in front of the world.

Unaware of the struggles her fellow Prevos faced, Alex forged her own path forward. Rather than bringing the AI into herself, she pushed out and through Valkyrie, into the walls of the *Siyane*. Piloting her ship in a way she never dreamed, Alex was able to feel the photonic brilliance of space itself. Over time, however, that bond began to capture more of her spirit and mind.

On the surface of a destroyed planet, Mesme at last revealed all. The portal network was, above all else, a refuge for those targeted for eradication by the Anadens. And the Anadens, rulers of the true universe through the master portal, were the genetic template upon which humanity was built. Aurora was nothing more than another experiment of the Metigens, created so they could study the development and nature of their enemy and the enemy of all life.

Alex and Caleb returned to Aurora to find a galaxy rocked by chaos. After the execution of Olivia Montegreu by Alliance and Prevo forces, Miriam had gone rogue. Her resistance force, bolstered by help from inside the Senecan and Alliance militaries, moved against the despotic Alliance PM.

As Alex struggled with her growing addiction to an ethereal realm, she felt herself being pulled away from reality. Away from her husband, her mother, her friends. She watched as those she loved fought, but increasingly found herself losing her own battle.

When terrorists staged a massive riot on Romane, Dr. Canivon, the mother of the Prevos, was murdered in front of Devon and Alex. Overcome by her own and Valkyrie's grief, Alex unleashed the explosive power of the ethereal realm to destroy the terrorists' safehouse. Standing in the rubble of her destruction, Alex made a decision to sever the quantum connection between herself and the *Siyane*, choosing a tangible, human life. Choosing Caleb.

Miriam wrested control of the EA government away from the PM, bringing an end to the Prevo persecution. In the wake of victory, a shadowy Anaden hunter emerged from the darkness to attack Alex and Caleb. Caleb was gravely injured when the Anaden's power leapt to him, healing his wounds and helping him kill the alien.

Mesme revealed the ominous consequences of the attack. Soon, the Anaden leadership would discover Aurora. When they did, they would destroy it unless humanity could stand against them. Mesme told Miriam and the others to prepare, but knowing the end game was upon them, asked Alex and Caleb to come to Amaranthe. The master universe. The home and dominion of the Anadens.

Relativity
(Aurora Resonant Book One)

Aurora

Miriam now leads the Galactic Common Defense Accord, a multi-government agency created to ensure humanity is prepared to meet the threat of the Anadens, and AEGIS, its military division. Malcolm and Harper work to train ground forces, while Kennedy, Noah and Vii—Valkyrie's clone—work to build a next-generation fleet with integrated Artificials and Prevos sharing command with their captains.

A celebration commemorating the victory over the Metigens a year ago takes place on multiple worlds. Mia and Malcolm attend the Romane event as a couple, having finally become romantically involved. After the show, Devon and his girlfriend are attacked;. Devon repels the attack, but Emily is injected with an unknown substance and falls unconscious.

Doctors identify the substance as a five-dimensional virus, leading Mia to believe it originated from the deceased Anaden scientists are studying. Richard identifies the scientist who sold the Anaden's cybernetic code on the black market, but the man has disappeared. He is soon found murdered on Seneca. The next day, Morgan Lekkas' skycar is attacked and crashes, leaving her badly injured and comatose.

During a romantic evening, Kennedy asks Noah to marry her; he refuses. They argue, and she leaves under the pretense of work.

At Mia's house, Malcolm and Mia are attacked by mercs wielding more doses of the virus. Malcolm disables the attackers, but Meno is hacked to deliver a threat from an unknown individual who sounds eerily like Olivia Montegreu.

Later that night, Harper is discussing how to heal Morgan's neurological damage with Mia when the hospital comes under attack. She kills several attackers; Mia kills another. On a different floor, Devon fends off a wave of attackers. Realizing they are Prevos, he sends a surge of energy through sidespace to shatter their Prevo connections, killing them and shattering multiple walls nearby.

At the Presidio, Kennedy troubleshoots a component problem in the new ships while ruminating over the riff with Noah, trying to figure out what she truly wants. Similarly, Noah visits a bar on

Romane to do his own ruminating. There he runs into an old friend from Pandora who gives him a different perspective on the events of the last year and a half.

Harper travels to Seneca and breaks into Stanley's lab. She taps into the Artificial's server to give Mia remote access, and Mia copies crucial functionality left behind when Morgan severed the hardware link. Mia uses this data to reawaken Stanley's consciousness in Morgan's mind.

Late in the night, AEGIS receives a data cache from Valkyrie with voluminous information on the Anaden military and its war machine, but no other news from Amaranthe. The AEGIS Council begins developing strategies to counter their future opponent.

Mia has a breakthrough in her attempts to counteract the virus killing Emily, and the young woman recovers.

Richard analyzes the details of the various attacks and comes to the conclusion that the source is not Olivia Montegreu, but rather the Artificial she joined with to become a Prevo, left behind on her death.

Devon convinces Richard to let him go after Olivia's Artificial. Devon and Annie remotely access the Artificial. They encounter robust defenses, but breach the core operating system and plant a virus. The Artificial explodes, destroying the Zelones headquarters on New Babel.

Before going to Amaranthe, Alex left her father's construct in Vii's care. Using advances she and Dr. Canivon made before Abigail was killed, Vii fills in the gaps in his consciousness to create a more complete, accurate recreation of David Solovy's mind. She awakens him in a virtual copy of his favorite camping site. She tells him that he's still in a fragile mental state, but together they are going to change this.

On Romane, Mia and Malcolm argue. He tells her he refuses to be what she settles for and tries to leave. She stops him by confessing the true extent of her feelings. They make up, but an emergency alert summons Malcolm back to the Presidio.

Noah returns to Kennedy with a gift, an adaptive holo device he built for her, and confesses he is hers no matter what. When he asks if she still wants to get married, she suggests they just take a honeymoon instead.

Morgan wakes up to find Stanley once again in her mind. He says he never truly went away, but retreated out of self-preservation. They agree to take more care with each other. An alert arrives then, and Morgan informs Harper that they have a war to go fight.

𝓡

AMARANTHE

The Directorate, the governing body of the Anaden empire run by the Primors of each Anaden Dynasty, discusses recent attacks by the 'anarch' resistance movement. The Praesidis Primor assigns Nyx, a high-level Inquisitor, to investigate the disappearance of Aver, the Inquisitor who discovered Aurora and was killed by Caleb.

Two anarchs, Eren and Cosime, surveil a Directorate exobiology lab where alien captives are experimented on. Lacking the resources to rescue the captives, they decide to blow up the lab.

Eren goes to an administration center to steal credentials to get him inside the lab. He obtains the credentials but is caught by security. As he is being detained, a mysterious man appears and uses *diati*, the mysterious power wielded by Praesidis Inquisitors, to attack the security officers, and a woman approaches Eren and tells him to come with them. Lacking other options, he flees with the strangers to their ship.

The ship is the *Siyane*, Eren's rescuers Caleb and Alex. They introduce themselves, Valkyrie and Mesme, and ask him to help them obtain details on the Directorate's military arm, run by the Machim Dynasty. Eren is reluctant to trust a synthetic, a Kat (as the Metigens are called in Amaranthe), or strangers who look Anaden but are not, but he reluctantly agrees to look into the matter.

After he leaves the *Siyane*, Eren is approached by Miaon, a fellow anarch. Miaon reveals that it is Mesme's contact and urges Eren to help these strangers. Eren visits an anarch friend, Thelkt, for information on how to obtain the intel Alex and Caleb seek.

Mesme takes Alex and Caleb to a nebula hiding a massive store of Reor, the unusual mineral those in Amaranthe use to store data. Mesme reveals that the Reor is sentient, but no one else suspects this. Alex tries to interact with the mineral; she's unable to communicate directly, but the Reor creates a new slab of itself for Alex.

Caleb dreams of the distant history of the Anadens, as relayed by the *diati*. When they are invaded by a powerful enemy, the Anadens face annihilation. The ethereal *diati* joins with the Anaden's greatest warrior, Corradeo Praesidis, to defeat the enemy. The Anadens thrive, then face an uprising by people seeking to join with synthetics. The conflict ends in a purge of AIs and AI-sympathizers and the formation of the Dynasties. The *diati* propagates into Corradeo's descendants, losing its coherence. The Anadens grow more oppressive as they abandon the ethos Corradeo espoused, but the *diati* cannot prevent it.

Nyx follows Aver's trail until she uncovers one of the hidden Mosaic portals. Rather than traverse it, she goes to Katoikia, the Kats' homeworld, and seizes two Kats in stasis chambers to interrogate.

In response to Nyx' visit to Katoikia, the Kats evacuate the stasis pods kept there and take them to the Mosaic for safekeeping. Mesme invites Alex and Caleb to witness the exodus.

While exploring Katoikia, they uncover a hidden structure where a Kat named Paratyr monitors locations around Amaranthe, watching for Directorate aggression. Alex is drawn to a scene of an aquatic species called Galenai; she uses sidespace to "visit" their underwater city. Paratyr tells her the Directorate is expanding into the Galenai's galaxy, and the Kats have flagged the Galenai for possible evacuation to the Mosaic.

Alex and Caleb leave Katoikia to meet up with Eren on a quest to infiltrate Machim Central Command and steal what intel they can. Thelkt sends Eren the Machim data server access codes, delivered by Felzeor, an intelligent avian. Felzeor has an engaging personality, and Caleb bonds with the falcon-like anarch in the short time it's on board.

After Felzeor leaves, Eren tells the story of how he became an anarch. Over a century ago, he encountered unfamiliar aliens serving as sexual slaves to the Idoni Primor. Recognizing their extreme fear and distress, he fled in horror. Soon thereafter, the Directorate eradicated the species. Disgusted with his leaders, he fried his neural link to the integral, dropped off the grid and made contact with the anarchs.

When they reach Machim Central Command, Caleb impersonates an Inquisitor to get inside, while Eren guides him. They reach the server room, and Mesme transports Alex to their location. She and Valkyrie hack the server and are downloading a plethora of military data when security forces arrive. An officer puts a blade to Alex's throat; Caleb orders Valkyrie and Mesme to flee then surrenders. Eren refuses and is killed. Caleb and Alex are rendered unconscious and arrested.

Valkyrie flees to the Mosaic then Aurora, where she transmits all the data from Machim Central Command to AEGIS. Then she travels to the Idryma portal and bids Lakhes to accompany her to Amaranthe.

Eren awakens in a "regenesis" pod, for Anadens are able to transfer their consciousness to new bodies when they die. He fills in his supervisor, Xanne, then insists they rescue Alex and Caleb. Xanne takes his request to the leader of the anarchs, Sator Danilo Nisi. After hearing Eren's story, he authorizes resources for a rescue mission.

Caleb and Alex wake up in separate detention cells, both restrained and subjected to interrogation by drones that jolts them with electricity when they refuse to answer. Caleb's *diati* absorbs the jolts, keeping him from injury; Alex is not so lucky.

Nyx deactivates a stasis chamber and interrogates the Kat until it reveals details on the Mosaic and the Kats' work there. She relays to the Praesidis Primor what she's learned. He sends her to interrogate the Human prisoners, then informs the other Primors of the Kats' betrayal. They issue an Eradication Order for the Kats and decide to destroy the Mosaic, except for the portal spaces providing crucial provisions to Amaranthe.

Eren rejoins Valkyrie and Mesme on the *Siyane* with a rescue plan. Mesme reveals to Eren that the species he encountered at the Idoni party, leading to his rebellion, were not all eradicated. Called Faneros, many were smuggled out to safety in the Mosaic.

Nyx arrives to interrogate Caleb. She asks what he is and where he came from, but he refuses to answer. In frustration she draws closer, and he steals her *diati* until he's strong enough to break out of the restraints. He then drains her of *diati*, incapacitates her and goes in search of Alex.

When he reaches her cell, his *diati* allows him to pass through the force field easily. But he's unable to deactivate the force field, and he has to trust the *diati* to protect her as he carries her through it.

Security is closing in when Eren and Mesme appear. Mesme transports Alex to the *Siyane* as an assault mech attacks. Caleb destroys the mech, then Eren insists Mesme transport Caleb next. Once they're gone, Eren detonates explosives he brought, destroying the facility.

Informed the Directorate is sending a military fleet to the Mosaic, Alex and Caleb rush to get a message to Miriam: it's time to bring her own fleet. During the trip, they work on a plan to keep the Machim fleet out of the Mosaic.

The Machim fleet acquires special Igni antimatter missiles and a doomsday device called a Tartarus Trigger. Further interrogation of the Kat prisoner reveals the ultimate truth: Humans are the genetic recreation of Anadens. The Directorate wants the Tartarus Trigger taken to the Aurora portal space and detonated, annihilating the Aurora universe. Meanwhile, a separate Machim fleet bombs the Kat homeworld.

The *Siyane* joins the AEGIS fleet in the Mosaic. Alex reunites with her mother then briefs Miriam on their plan.

The Machim fleet arrives at the Gateway to the Mosaic. It promptly explodes, hit by negative energy missiles from the *Siyane* and stealthed fighters nearby. The explosion takes out a large chunk of the Machim fleet; while it's still recovering, the AEGIS fleet materializes behind it.

The battle is joined. AEGIS enjoys an advantage in most respects, but the Igni missiles can damage adiamene hulls. Prevos in the fleet work to identify which ships are carrying the missiles, then take them out first.

Paratyr appears in the cabin of the *Siyane* in ethereal form. The Kat warns them about the Tartarus Trigger on the Machim command ship Imperium. If detonated, it will annihilate every molecule for parsecs, then possibly the entire universe.

Malcolm devises a way to bypass the impenetrable shields of the Imperium and is about to try it when Alex stops him, as the odds of the Tartarus Trigger detonating when the ship is destroyed are too high. Mesme volunteers to infiltrate the ship and transport the device away.

Alex uses sidespace to determine the device's precise location, then Mesme surrounds it and both vanish. Alex gives Malcolm the all clear, and he destroys the Imperium. The remaining Machim vessels retreat, handing a decisive victory to AEGIS.

The AEGIS Council, now including Alex and Caleb, convenes on the *Stalwart II* to determine the next steps. They are interrupted, however, by a message from Sator Nisi requesting a meeting.

Alex, Caleb, Miriam and Mesme travel to Nisi's headquarters. When they meet Nisi, Caleb realizes the man controls *diati* as well. Miriam and Nisi spar, and the lack of trust on both sides is evident. Alex challenges Nisi, and he admits the anarchs are not powerful enough to defeat the Directorate. Rather, they are a force designed to be of maximum strategic value when the fulcrum that will change the cosmos arrives.

He believes that fulcrum is not the AEGIS fleet, but rather Caleb.

CONTENTS

Rubicon

AMARANTHE

Year 6143

12TH Epoch Proper

PART I:

FOR EVERY ACTION

"The art of war is simple enough. Find out where your enemy is. Get at him as soon as you can. Strike him as hard as you can, and keep moving on."

— *Ulysses S. Grant*

1

MACHIM FLEET FABRICATION CENTER

Captain Brooklyn Harper landed in the Machim Fleet Fabrication Center server room face-to-face with a hulking orb of mechanical death. A weaponized appendage extended out from its shiny black casing to lock the sights of a plasma cannon on her forehead.

"Halt, intruder."

Of all the bloody timing. She snapped her left arm out to knock the cannon off-kilter. At the same time, she pressed the trigger on her far smaller weapon, held close in at waist height in her other hand.

The laser from her Daemon tore through the metal casing with relentless efficiency, and after a jerking shudder the drone promptly exploded.

"Dammit!" Brooklyn threw her arms over her face in a protective cross and dropped to a crouch as metal fragments shot in every direction and the few heavier, larger pieces that remained intact thudded to the floor.

The ensuing racket echoed once through the cavernous room before being absorbed by thick, insulated walls.

Sotiras: Are you injured, Human?

"I'm fine." She shot a quick glare at the shapeless lights trembling in the corner as she stood and lowered her arms.

Sotiras: But there is—

Alexis Solovy (Siyane): *"Shit. Sorry, Harper. It showed up the same second you did."*

HarperRF: *"Noted. Tell the Kat to watch the door and tell me where to go."*

Sotiras: I am right here, Human. You may tell me yourself. Also, I should note—

Alexis Solovy (Siyane): *"Sotiras, please watch the door for additional incoming security. Harper, take the third aisle down to the large vertical enclosure."*

The Kat spun off toward the entrance, and Brooklyn took a step back to see which aisle might be the third one. She jogged down it until she met what was either a wall or a very tall block of hardware. It was unmarked and seamless.

HarperRF: "Is this what I'm looking for?"

Alexis Solovy (Siyane): *"Yep. At 1.8 meters height, cut out a rectangle up to 2.1 meters height, all the way across."*

She gripped her blade hilt, brought it up to eye level and activated it. The plasma sliced cleanly into the material, and a few cuts later a section of the covering fell away. She propped it against the equipment to her left while her eVi filtered the bright white glow coming from inside the opening she'd created.

The interior contained a circuit of some kind. Hyperfine traces of darkness divided the light in a rigid, ordered pattern. Deeper inside, beyond the circuit, lay stacked slabs of a translucent onyx mineral.

Alexis Solovy (Siyane): *"Okay, see the junction? The thicker cluster near the bottom right? Stick the bypass module to it."*

Everything looked like a 'cluster' to her. She palmed the small bypass module and started moving her hand from the center downward and to the right.

Alexis Solovy (Siyane): *"Down farther. Over a little more—there."*

Suspicious of what could result from of her ignorant tampering, she exercised proper caution as she positioned the module in front of the thickest grouping of traces and applied pressure to it, then drew her fingers away. To her surprise, it stayed where she'd put it. The traces appeared virtual to her eyes, but apparently they had some physicality.

Alexis Solovy (Siyane): *"And we're set. Wedge the section you removed back in place as best as you can. Hopefully they won't find our handiwork until it's too late. Sotiras, as soon as she's done, get her out of there and back to the* Saratoga."

Her blade had done precise work, and the rectangular piece of metal fit perfectly in place. Once she nudged the last corner a touch to seat it, no glow escaped to betray the seams.

Sotiras: Security reinforcements are approaching.

HarperRF: "Ready."

Pinpricks of ethereal light encased her to blot out the surrounding walls, and she arrived on the bridge of the *AFS Saratoga* two seconds later. The purposeful sounds of a full bridge mid-mission were briefly jarring after the tomb-like silence of the server room, but not unwelcome.

Brigadier Malcolm Jenner greeted her with a nod from the command overlook, then turned toward a grouping of tactical screens...then back, wearing a frown. "Um, Harper...."

"What?"

He pointed to her left shoulder. She craned her neck around to see a four-centimeter shard of drone jutting out of the back of her upper left arm. The material of her tactical suit had sealed around the metal to staunch the bleeding, so the extent of the damage wasn't immediately apparent.

Residual adrenaline and automated eVi injury mitigation routines masked any pain, but she grimaced anyway. "Hell."

I did try to inform you that you were bleeding. The Kat hovered closer and more confidently now, here in the safety of the bridge.

"Whatever." She returned her attention to Malcolm. "What's our status?"

"Waiting on the go-ahead. Your job's done, though, so get to Medical."

She opened her mouth to protest, but then it occurred to her she might have additional, less obvious shrapnel embedded god knew where. "Fine. But for the record, this does not count as a ground incursion. You still owe me a real mission. Sir."

He gestured to the lift, staring pointedly at her until she pivoted and headed in its direction.

She was halfway there when the pain kicked in.

_AR_

AFS SARATOGA

The Machim Sector 46 Fleet Fabrication Center sprawled across nearly three megameters of space in a lengthy orbit around a distant blue giant star.

A central structure sat at the center of an immense labyrinth of latticed assembly lines, not dissimilar to the Presidio's design. Machim battlecruisers in various stages of completion hung in four rows down the primary production lines. Smaller semi-enclosed adjunct structures assembled a host of smaller components, which were ferried by ring channels to the production lines. Mechs buzzed through the facility like ants scurrying over an anthill.

Was there a single living creature at the facility, Malcolm wondered?

The Anadens were reported to be wary about synthetic intelligence, so presumably someone was on site to ensure the mechs and the lines' operational ware didn't get unruly. But it didn't seem as if there were many. He started to reflect on how it would keep the body count low, but if they were Anaden even that wouldn't matter. The notion of an enemy who perpetually came back to life was taking some getting used to.

The mission kicked into gear then, saving him from twisting his brain into knots over the matter.

Alexis Solovy (Siyane): _"I'm patched into the security system. Referencing the mission Tactical Grid, trip sensors are located at:_

_Q1 S 21° E z -12°_
_Q1 N 67° W z 41°_
_Q2 S 35° W z -80°_
_Q2 N 26° E z 54°_
_Q3 N 19° W z 61°_
_Q3 S 11° W z -3°_
_Q4 S 84° E z -59°_
_Q4 N 25° E z 22°_

"Each trip sensor is linked to four proximity mines. They're outfitted with failsafe triggers, so EMPing them won't do any good. You'll have to shoot them from a distance or something.

"The force field barrier is powered by three generators located inside the barrier at Q3 NW 6° z -9°. I've got a couple of authorization codes a disguised ship or two can use to get inside."

Commandant Solovy (AFS Stalwart II): "Our first priority is to take out the force field. AFS EW-08, when I give the order, project the false cargo ship hull and proceed through security using one of the authorization codes Alexis provides. Once inside, target the generators using negative energy missiles, then stealth and keep clear of the blasts."

Commander Lekkas (AFS MA-Primary): "ESC Flights Two and Four, stage yourselves in range of the trip sensors and be prepared to neutralize them the instant the generators blow."

Acknowledgments scrolled up the screen to his left alongside auxiliary chatter.

Commandant Solovy (Stalwart II): "EW-08, proceed. All ships, combat alert status."

The fleet was situated too far away from the target for Malcolm to be able to see the electronic warfare craft's progress. However, a stealthed companion provided a visual feed, and Malcolm monitored the disguised ship on a second screen as it approached the heavily guarded entrance gate.

An electronic warfare craft was an unlikely choice for an infiltrate-and-destroy mission, but in this case it was the correct size to pull off the disguise, being close in size to a standard Anaden cargo ship. It also wielded the best holographic projection capabilities, making the disguise believable. Nevertheless, the small, precision negative energy missiles it now carried constituted its entire payload and stretched its loadout capabilities to the maximum.

The vessel proceeded through the gate without incident and adopted a trajectory that would ostensibly take it to the hangar at the central structure—then it vanished behind a cloaking shield. Three long seconds later, multiple explosions erupted near the center of the facility.

The visible force field flickered and died in sync with a spike in activity as the Fabrication Center went on alert. Outside the perimeter, a series of smaller detonations cascaded in a bubble surrounding the facility.

Commander Lekkas (MA-Primary): "Trip sensors neutralized."

Commandant Solovy (Stalwart II): "All ships, proceed according to your assignments."

Rampant, comprehensive destruction was the objective of the mission today. Fighters swarmed in to engage the automated defenses, which included drones as well as far more robust turrets spaced throughout the facility. Sabres followed the fighters in, accompanied by a complement of frigates for protection, and began firing on the unfinished battlecruisers.

Lacking active shielding, the hulls crumbled under the onslaught from the Sabres' powerful railguns.

But it wasn't going to be enough to destroy the ships under assembly. They needed to destroy the Fabrication Center's production capabilities, or else the Machim would just start building new ships here tomorrow.

Malcolm eyed the long row of adjunct structures stretching beneath the length of the facility. "Proceed on a N 13° E z -2° vector. As soon as we're in range, target the individual units sequentially from west to east."

Brigadier Jenner (AFS Saratoga): AFS Tripoli and AFS Caracas, with me."

Lt. Colonel Londe (AFS Tripoli): "On your left flank, Saratoga."

Colonel Torres (AFS Caracas): "On your right."

Admiral Rychen (EAS Virginia): "EA 12th (NW) Regiment will take care of the central structure. Advise active Rifters to handle the prodigious debris soon to result."

Defense turret fire plinked off the *Virginia's* shields in harmless pinpricks as it unloaded its arsenal on the boxy edifice at the heart of the facility. It began to come apart in large, jagged chunks.

"Major Ettore, make our heading an additional S 12°."

Ettore chuckled. "Copy that."

Captain Casales: "First unit is in range. Firing."

Brigadier Jenner (Saratoga)*:* *"Tripoli, Caracas, commence firing at any and all component assembly units in range, west to east progression.*

Confirmations followed, and the viewport lit up in the glow of lasers meeting, ripping into and melting metal. The distant sun reflected off the projectiles created for added effect—at least until the projectiles vanished into the rifts surrounding the attacking vessels.

Twenty minutes later, a facility that had manufactured four hundred battlecruisers a week lay in ruins. Nothing larger than thirty meters populated the debris field.

The automated defenses were no match for twelve thousand ships from the AEGIS fleet, and they met no active resistance. In executing the ambush they had followed the Machim model by bringing far greater firepower than was required to complete the mission. It was the latest strike in a campaign to swiftly nullify the Machim's biggest advantage: numbers.

No doubt they'd meet greater resistance in future missions, but for today it appeared they would chalk up a decisive victory.

SIYANE

Alex watched the fireworks from a bird's eye vantage above and to the left of one of the primary assembly lines, for the moment. She could move freely among the cacophony of explosions and shattering metal, however, without fear of injury.

For she wasn't really there.

The *Siyane*, and her with it, were safely tucked away thirteen kiloparsecs from the Machim Fleet Fabrication Center under attack, but only a few dozen meters from a solitary teleportation gate situated on a rocky, barren world bearing the uninspiring moniker of MW-2189c.

She drifted among the lasers and mounting debris enjoying the show, as her role in the mission was essentially complete. She *could* pitch in to provide target advice or location pointers, but in truth this mission was mostly about blowing shit up, and the military didn't need her help with that.

So she watched the impressive destruction-in-progress with half her attention as her mind began to wander to other matters. "Remind me to talk to Mesme about Sotiras. The Kat could use a round of coaching on how to interact with people."

Valkyrie's voice resonated in her mind—also in the cabin of the *Siyane*, but she didn't try to split her attention yet further to hear it. 'It wasn't that bad.'

"Yes, it was. But I guess we shouldn't expect too much when the B-team fills in."

'Still, the mission would have been all but impossible without Sotiras' assistance in infiltrating the facility.'

"Not Sotiras specifically, since any random Kat would have sufficed. But, yes, the infiltration assist was definitely helpful. We need...."

Alex absently fiddled with the tiny Reor slab she'd removed from her pocket at some point. She understood Anaden security protocols and information storage and retrieval methodologies fairly well now, having studied the details both Mesme and Eren had provided, but more so having hacked and deep-dived Machim Central Command servers. This latest foray into the inner workings of one of their systems only reinforced her belief that she now had a solid grasp of the tech and processes involved.

'Yes? What do we need?'

"We need to figure out a way to tap into their systems remotely—or permanently. We need to get inside their overall network. This single location, physical infiltration routine is nonsense. It's unreliable and puts our people, and sometimes *me*, in unnecessary danger."

'The Directorate's rampant paranoia makes doing as you suggest a difficult proposition. Information they treat as valuable is not designed to be widely shared and is walled off from remote interconnections.'

"Well, we need to find a way."

'I will make a note.'

Alex's focus gradually returned to the ongoing sacking of the Fabrication Center, and she realized she'd been staring at a semi-hidden piece of equipment while she and Valkyrie talked. She'd been waiting for it to crack apart or vaporize entirely, yet it remained intact.

Alexis Solovy (Siyane)*: "Somebody target the blocky module suspended below the central structure in Q3, near the rear—S 21° W z 8— and your pesky defense turret problem will be no more."*

A message arrived in an off-channel pulse.

'Somebody'? Please try to maintain at least a small amount of decorum on the open channels.

Sorry, Mom. I just don't speak military.

'Technically, you do. I have available for instant recall the designations of all formations in the AEGIS-led fleet down to the squad level, as well as every named ship. I also keep databases of modern military nomenclature.'

Alex grumbled under her breath. "Shhh. She doesn't need to be reminded of that."

A staccato of explosions rippled through the module in question.

"See, though? 'Somebody' took care of it."

'SF Northern Fleet Fighter Squadron #143, to be precise.'

"Yes, Valkyrie. Thank you."

A completed component storage unit she'd mentally wandered near during the exchange abruptly disintegrated, sending metal shards to envelop the space her consciousness occupied.

Like shattered glass. But none pierced her, instead falling through her untouched like the ghost she had become.

No. She allowed the déjà vu to flare, rooted in a memory from Portal Prime, but she wasn't a ghost. Not this time. Moments such as this, she wasn't certain exactly what she *was*—human, Prevo, and maybe something still unfathomable as well—but she was making peace with the ambiguity.

Okay, Mom. You seem to have things well in hand, so I'll leave you and your esteemed fleet to mop up things here. I'm supposed to pick Caleb up in a few minutes.

Understood. Rendezvous at Staging Point C1 in three hours for an AEGIS Council meeting. And lunch after, if you'd like.

Sounds good.

She laughed to herself. They were making lunch date plans while she projected her consciousness across over a dozen kiloparsecs into the middle of a space battle, if a rather one-sided one, her mother actively commanded. All of this was taking place in a universe other than their own, and it was all somehow *normal*.

Her life had always been unconventional, but occasionally it caught her by surprise just how damn improbable it could be.

2

ANARCH POST SATUS

"What you must understand is this: though the *diati* is an independent life form and in principle separate from you, its interaction with reality—with the tangible universe—exists solely as a manifestation of your will. It is a tool under your direction. If you are strong enough, it is a tool under your absolute control."

Caleb was skeptical for more than one reason. "You're saying the *diati* is disposed to subsume itself completely to my will, to my...desires, whatever they happen to be?"

"It would not have joined with you otherwise. Having chosen you, this is now its purpose."

Caleb started to challenge Nisi to justify the assertion, but he understood why the man believed it. He'd sensed the *diati's* initial free will, and the gradual erosion of it, in the dream-visions. Admittedly, he was curious whether the man had been shown the same visions or had come to this conclusion through experience, but sufficient trust didn't exist between them for him to probe deeper. Not yet.

Danilo Nisi, Sator of the anarch resistance movement in Amaranthe, sat opposite him on the facing couch, far enough away to avoid triggering an incident. Caleb had tried to tell his *diati* not to steal Nisi's, but it seemed the decision belonged to the *diati* Nisi controlled, and Caleb couldn't communicate with it.

Interesting that the choice of allegiance marked both a stark and continuing exception to what the man had just stated about the *diati's* lack of agency. But it made a certain amount of sense. If the choice of allegiance was made wisely, no other choices need be made.

The practical consequence, though, here on the ground, was that he needed to keep his distance. The fact that Nisi was willing to help him—to teach him, as it were—was more than he'd expected. He may not trust the anarch leader, but he was grateful for the help, and he didn't intend to foul it up by absconding with the small amount of *diati* the man wielded, and evidently treasured.

"Are you ready to begin?"

He straightened up and tried to focus his intentions. Nisi's instructions repeated themselves in his mind. *Don't try to force the action. Simply command it to be so. Know it will be so.*

The boot sitting on the floor between them vanished, only to reappear several meters away by one of the windows.

Nisi considered the footwear critically. "Is it located where you intended for it to move to?"

He nodded.

"How closely?"

"Fairly close. I had in mind not quite so far away from the window. But I was concerned it would end up outside and—" he lifted a socked foot "—I kind of need it when I leave, so I may have subconsciously waffled on the distance."

"Understandable. But if you are precise in your intent, it will be precise in its execution. Trust the *diati*, for it is your ally."

"But it was the ally of its former masters, right up until the moment it abandoned them. How can I trust it won't do the same to me?"

Nisi stood and went over to the refreshment bar to pour a drink. It was an act intended to signal relaxation, but it also had the effect of hiding his reaction from Caleb. "It's not my place to answer that question."

"But you can answer it?"

Nisi took a long sip of his drink. "I have lived with the *diati* for a very long time. I've watched generations of Inquisitors use it in more ways than I ever could have dreamed up. I've spent hours likely adding up to years contemplating its nature. In six hundred thousand years, you are the only instance I'm aware of where it has abandoned a host for another of its own volition."

"You're six hundred thousand years old?" Earlier comments by Nisi had implied he might be a few millennia old, but now he was suggesting another order of magnitude altogether.

To live so long would surely drive a person stark raving mad, wouldn't it? Caleb recognized the Primors were technically this old or older, but they had tweaked and 'improved' themselves through regenesis so many times they must bear little resemblance to their original selves. Also, they *were* stark raving mad.

Nisi's expression revealed nothing as he returned to the couch. "Pick up your glass of water. Hold it in your hand, then move it to the bar."

Caleb let the blatant evasion of his question slide for the time being and did as instructed. The man was an intriguing cipher, but he was here to learn, and he needed to learn fast. "Apologies in advance for any mess that results."

But no mess resulted. The glass vanished from his hand and materialized atop the bar, water contents and all, and didn't take any portion of his hand with it. He felt his confidence grow in response to the success, and quickly tempered it with the memory of times when he was *not* so in control of the power.

"Excellent."

Caleb pursed his lips. "When I run across a Praesidis—when I absorb new *diati*—it's chaotic. For a while. Minutes, or hours if it's a large dose, pass before I'm fully in control again. What can I do to either lessen the length of time or increase my control during it?"

"I'm afraid your experience in this matter is unique. As I noted, you are the only one. But I can offer a few thoughts. The act of transferring from the Praesidis to you is an act of free will on the part of the *diati*, and it is perhaps the first such act it's performed in cosmic ages. It stands to reason that after such a momentous event, it will take some time for the *diati* to settle down.

"The best advice I have for you is to not fight it. Welcome it, and do so with a...not a firm hand, but a resolute one. It needs you to accept its presence, not the other way around."

"I haven't been fighting it."

"If you say so."

Caleb opened his mouth to protest, but a pulse came in from Alex then.

Machim Sector 46 Fleet Fabrication Center is officially space dust, with no resistance to speak of. I'm here whenever you're ready.

Great news. I'll be along in a few minutes. Maybe fifteen or twenty.

"The AEGIS fleet successfully destroyed the Sector 46 Fleet Fabrication Center."

"Good. I assume AEGIS is aware there are twenty-five additional such facilities in operation?"

"And now there is one less than there was this morning. Why are you willing to help me, yet so dismissive of AEGIS' efforts?"

"I've told you, Caleb—I believe you are the key. You are the fulcrum that will transform the world. As such, you are what matters most in this fight."

He rolled his eyes in frustration. "The fleet matters, too, because I can't singlehandedly destroy two dozen Machim warship manufacturing facilities."

"Are you so certain?"

"Snapping a few necks or crushing the odd Vigil drone is one thing, and that thing is a long damn way from destroying massive space stations."

Nisi tapped his temple.

"You think the difference is all in my head?"

The man made a prevaricating motion. "Not exactly. Size, or more accurately mass, obviously does factor in. If I'm saying anything, it is that you don't yet recognize the full measure of the power you can wield. You already control more *diati* than any single Inquisitor, including the *elassons*. In point of fact, this means you control more *diati* than any individual save—" the muscles lining his jaw flexed "—the Praesidis Primor.

"Now, I cannot say if this means you have the ability to destroy a space station or, as it were, a warship manufacturing facility. But I do submit that you can do a great deal more than move a glass of water a few meters. You have scarcely begun to test the limits of your power."

He flashed his charismatic, mysterious smile. "Now, with this in mind, are you ready to take the next step?"

Despite Caleb's attempts at caution—at circumspection and even suspicion—the man's words stirred his blood. They teased the possibilities of the power within his reach, *real* power extending far beyond parlor tricks and personal protection to a place where the course of life itself could be changed.

"I am."

PLANET MW-2189C

MILKY WAY SECTOR 33

Alex was waiting on him when he stepped through the teleportation gate, and the sight of her instantly brightened his mood. She'd only partaken in the AEGIS mission virtually, but he was relieved to see her safe nonetheless. Always.

She wore a breather mask dangling around her neck, and he took advantage of the fact it wasn't covering her mouth to kiss her fully in front of the gate. Then he did his best to act casual during the short walk to the *Siyane*.

She eyed him curiously. "How did it go today?"

"Fine. You?"

"Well enough. Seeing the facility taken out so spectacularly was definitely satisfying, if a tad boring by the end. There was this notable sequence when all the trip sensor proximity mines blew at once..." her voice trailed off "...what happened in the session?"

He dropped the act, as it clearly wasn't working anyway, and coaxed her toward the *Siyane* faster. "Come on. Let's get inside, and I'll show you."

He could feel her stare boring into the back of his head as she trailed him up the ramp. When the inner airlock had closed behind them, he positioned her beside the data center. "Stay there."

She arched an eyebrow and crossed her arms over her chest, but complied. He continued through the cabin until he reached the kitchen counter, glanced at her, then concentrated on the area between her and the couch—

—Alex jumped, a startled gasp escaping her lips. She gaped at him in amazement, as he was now standing directly in front of her. "You figured out how to do it!"

He smirked. "I did."

She cackled and wrapped her arms around him. "Can you teleport me, too?"

"Whoa, slow down. One thing at a time. Let me practice a little first."

"Okay...."

He kissed her pout away. "I'll practice fast."

"You better." Her lips twitched against his. "I guess for now we'll have to do it the hard way and fly all the way to the *Stalwart II*. Mom's called a meeting."

⟋ℛ⟍

AFS STALWART II

MILKY WAY SECTOR 19

Commander Morgan Lekkas tapped her boot impatiently on the skid-resistant flooring of the *AFS Stalwart II's* hangar bay. A brief shift into sidespace to peer around the region outside the ship confirmed the shuttle from the *AFS Saratoga* was on approach to dock, so it would just be another minute.

Her boot tapped faster.

All this shuttling around from vessel to vessel straight-up sucked. The Eidolons' official home was on the carrier *AFS Tamao*. The AEGIS fighters and multi-role attack craft, however, including the one she'd been piloting, docked on the *AFS San Carlos*. After the Sector 46 Fleet Fabrication Center mission, she'd taken a special dispensation and docked on the *Tamao*, under the justification that the Eidolons were her responsibility and she needed to do a thorough post-mission debrief and inspection. It was faster than taking yet another a shuttle.

Harper, however, was assigned to the *AFS Saratoga* with the Marine tactical assault detachments. The *Saratoga* was neither the *Tamao* nor the *San Carlos*. Sleeping apart more nights than not also sucked.

Relationships complicated everything. Military relationships, doubly so. Or hell, maybe they were only half as complicated; she didn't have enough experience with commitment to say for certain.

Meetings of the AEGIS leadership and advisory Council were held on the *AFS Stalwart II*, of course—well, not every meeting, as it would soon become absurdly inefficient. Many were held via holo. But important meetings, pre- and post-mission meetings, and crucial strategy sessions were held in person. Allegedly it was good for morale, but mostly it meant more shuttle rides.

What would be good for *her* morale would be seeing with her own radically enhanced Prevo eyes that Harper was alive and mostly in one piece.

Medical on the Saratoga *reports none of the injuries she suffered from the shrapnel are life-threatening.*

'Life-threatening' is your threshold for garnering concern, Stanley?

I was merely endeavoring to provide reassurance.

She laughed quietly between taps. Stanley had been denied the chance to grow and evolve over time as much as his Noetica counterparts—her fault, no question—and it showed at times. But he was trying. *Thank you, Stanley. It does help, a little.*

The shuttle eased through the force field into the hangar bay and settled into a docking berth.

She waited, but now she tried to look chill about it.

An eternity later the shuttle hatch opened. Brigadier Jenner departed, followed by a clerical officer, and she nodded curt greetings at both without speaking.

Harper brought up the rear, limping gingerly through the open hatch while waving off help from another officer. When she spotted Morgan, she cautiously adjusted her course. Morgan readied a stern, disapproving expression as her heart buoyed.

"Don't give me that look, Lekkas. I pulled your shattered, comatose body out of a crushed skycar—half your bones were *literally* shattered—so don't even think about making a big deal out of a couple of scrapes."

"You ran around for twenty minutes with a piece of shrapnel lodged in your back that narrowly missed your spine."

"That depends on your definition of 'narrowly.' I'm fine."

Morgan's gaze was critical in inspection as she circled the woman. Two medwraps encroached beyond the seams of the BDUs, and Morgan knew at least two additional ones were hidden beneath the clothing. But Harper *was* walking under her own power, which was more than Morgan could have said of herself until a week or so ago.

She relented, completing the circle to again stand in front of Harper. She grabbed the cranky, beautiful Marine's hands and squeezed. "All right. But I'm watching you."

Harper eyed the long stretch of hangar bay between them and the lift, drew her shoulders up and started off toward her goal. "A tiny piece of shrapnel caught me in the ass. Why don't you watch it?"

So Morgan did, for several seconds, before hurrying to catch up.

3

AFS STALWART II

"What does victory look like?"

Admiral Rychen jumped right in. "Blowing an enormous warship manufacturing facility to smithereens looked like a damn fine start."

Miriam lifted an eyebrow. "Only twenty-five more to go."

Caleb chuckled, then quickly squelched it. When she glanced inquiringly in his direction, he waved her off. An inside joke for later, perhaps.

Rychen gestured toward the door. "Point the way."

Miriam appreciated his enthusiasm—really she did—but she needed a measure of sober maturity from him right now. From everyone at the table. "Finding them isn't the problem. Here's the problem: when all the fabrication facilities lie in ruins, what then? We'll control the skies, so to speak, but not the ground. Not the commerce, not the infrastructure, not the government. The Directorate won't be able to get rid of us, but we won't have freed anyone."

Alex protested. "We will have saved any further species from being Eradicated..." her shoulders sagged "...no, only those who would've required a military response to corral. For more primitive species, the Theriz can still go in and shred their planets. So, Theriz Cultivation fleets and facilities next?"

She offered her daughter a rueful shrug. "Thank you for making my point. People, I'm going to keep asking the question until we come up with a suitable answer, so don't be shy. The need to decimate the Machim military capabilities is a given. But beyond this objective, how do we dismantle the controlling governmental structure, which has existed for longer than we've been able to speak a meaningful language? I'll leave the question of what we replace it with once it's dismantled for tomorrow."

In the silence that followed, she found herself wishing Richard were here. His knowledge of the geopolitical games played throughout history would be helpful to the discussion. She'd considered more than once asking him to make the trip, but he was too valuable to everyone else for his time to be spent sitting around reinforcing her clarity.

No one jumped in; she needed to let it go for now. "Until someone comes up with a decent suggestion—and I include myself in this category—let's talk about some practical matters. We were lucky to complete this mission without significant opposition, but we can't expect our good fortune to continue. We *will* find ourselves facing a sizable Machim fleet sooner or later, and prudence dictates that we assume sooner.

"The conflict at the Provision Network Gateway took place in the middle of nowhere, and this enabled us to exercise certain liberties. Given our current focus, it's possible the next encounter will occur closer to a populated area, which will limit our use of both Dimensional Rifters and negative energy devices."

Subdued unrest rippled down the table, and she allowed it to dwindle before continuing. She was asking a lot of them, pushing them harder. But they were at the table because they could deliver. "It's not enough for us to be creative once—we must be creative every time."

Brigadier Jenner frowned. "You're suggesting we can't count on using the trick that took out the Imperium at the Gateway the next time we face one."

"Among many other tricks, yes, I am. If a move risks taking out a space station or other habitat, it has to be off the table. Also, any maneuver that succeeded for us in the last battle, we can expect them to be prepared for in the next one."

"Because the knowledge gained didn't die with the combatants on the battlefield…because they didn't truly die." Jenner shook his head skeptically. "Okay, so how do we penetrate an impenetrable shield?"

Thomas spoke up. 'The Machim data contains a small number of details on its properties and how it is generated, but none of those details point to a viable way to circumvent it.'

This wasn't news. If the data cache had held the needed information, they would've already devised a way past the shield.

Alex had accessed the specific data Thomas referenced and was already studying it. "The shield's not *technically* solid, not in the way a hull is. It has a lot in common with a force field barrier, albeit a dramatically reinforced and fortified one...or two. It could be two barriers." Her nose scrunched up as she peered at the aural. "Kennedy might be able to figure out a way to counter it. She and shielding have a special relationship."

Given how easily Ms. Rossi had figured out a way to restore communications during the Metigen invasion, Alex could be correct. "Do you think it's worth asking her to come over with the next group?"

"Lobbing questions and answers back and forth isn't a practical option, so if this is a high-priority goal, yes. You've got some engineers and techs on this side who can help her out, don't you?"

"Several. I'll make the request." Miriam took a deliberate sip of tea and returned the glass to the desk. Her gaze passed across everyone in the room. "What does victory look like?"

Silence answered, but only for a second this time. Then overlapping comments erupted to blend and shape one another. They were talking, which meant minds had been working in the intervening minutes. So she let it continue for a while.

Finally Caleb's voice cut through the din. "I understand why no one wants to bring it up, but part of the answer is this: ultimately the only way we achieve a real victory is if we remove the Directorate from power. Completely. Officially unseating them won't be enough. Collectively, the Primors control more than two trillion Anadens, and their control is not dependent on the Directorate's status as a governing body."

Commander Lekkas eyed him intently. "You mean assassinate them—which is totally fine. I'm just checking."

"If only it were so straightforward. Regenesis renders even that strategy a fool's errand. To simplify a complex problem? We have indestructible warships, but they have indestructible people. We've got to find a way to break out of the impasse that creates."

Miriam nodded. "So if we plan to go down the path you're suggesting, we will need to remove their ability to return in a cloned body as well. Such a process requires a physical facility: equipment, data storage, a way to remotely receive new data, and a host of medical technology. We need to know where the Primors undergo regenesis."

Jenner leaned forward wearing a scowl. "Are we seriously discussing the assassination of the entire governing body of this place?"

Miriam gave the question due weight; she shouldn't and wouldn't brush it off lightly. "If someone had assassinated Adolf Hitler and Joseph Stalin in 1938, tens of millions of lives would have been saved. It's not a disproportionately extreme example, either, because a far greater number have already died at the hands of the Directorate. Because they intended and still do intend to wipe out the entirety of humanity." She paused. "But it is important for us to recognize it for what it is. I bear the full responsibility for the decision when it's made, but if anyone wishes to lodge a formal objection, please do so."

Jenner retreated with a faint shake of his head. "No, ma'am. You're correct, of course. But what if the Primors can use any regenesis facility? What then?"

"If you're asking whether we will try to eliminate all such facilities...." Miriam's gaze fell to the table's surface. The story of her career could be summed up by the trite adage that she always did what was required in the circumstances. But there were limits to even deals with the devil, lines which should never be crossed.

She looked back up. "No. To do so is equivalent to killing over two trillion people, many of whom play no part in the Directorate's misdeeds. If it turns out that the Primors are able to undergo regenesis at any facility, we will have to pursue other options." She could only hope when the time came, other options had been discovered.

Rychen leaned in toward the center of the table. "One could argue it wouldn't be killing the Anadens at all, merely reducing them to the same state everyone else faces. They live until they die, and that's the end."

"I doubt you would be able to find an Anaden who agreed with you."

Rychen sank down in his chair, deflated. "Nor would I, were I one. Point taken. So these anarchs must know what regenesis facilities the Primors use, right? And if so, where they are?"

Alex frowned. "Maybe, maybe not. They've collected a wide variety of intel, but I expect this kind of information to be closely held. Insanely so. The Primors are paranoid about far less important information than the details of how they maintain their immortality."

Miriam sighed as the obstacles piled up one after another. "As paranoid as the anarchs? They won't so much as tell us where any of their bases are located. Assuming they possess the information we're seeking, I doubt they are inclined to hand it over simply because we ask for it."

If she sounded frustrated, it was because she was. Since the initial meeting with Sator Nisi, she had encountered nothing but resistance from the anarch leadership. They claimed to want to work in concert, but they guarded their knowledge and resources with the zeal of a dog guarding its most prized bone. So far the only actionable intel she possessed were the locations of Machim production and staging facilities, and this was due almost entirely to Alex, Caleb and Valkyrie's actions.

'Perhaps Alex and Valkyrie could hack the Directorate's data network as they did the Machim one.'

Alex burst out laughing. She dropped an elbow onto the table and her chin onto her palm. "You're funny, Thomas—unless it wasn't a joke, in which case you're delusional."

'It was mostly a joke, but I always leave my options open.'

"Uh-huh. I *have* been thinking that we need to find some easier, more reliable way to infiltrate their networks than the type of stunt Harper and Sotiras had to pull today. But I don't have any good ideas yet. Sorry."

Miriam cleared her throat. "All right. Working backwards from our goal—a very long way backwards, I'm afraid—our first step is to convince the anarchs to show us a few of their cards. If they want to be our partner, they need to carry their weight, not sit back and let us do all the work. How do we convince them to do so?"

Alex grimaced. "Aside from Nisi, there's not much in the way of an organized power structure in the anarchs. There are supervisors for the missions and whatnot—people like Xanne—but if you're asking who the head of the intelligence department is, for instance, I'm not sure there is one."

"Can your friend Eren help?"

"He insists he's but a lowly front-line operative who's only given the information necessary for his next mission. And in fairness, he may be telling the truth. He's not exactly the bureaucratic type."

"It likely doesn't matter in any event. The real power resides in Sator Nisi. We have to convince him to instruct his people to cooperate."

She found Nisi to be uncommonly frustrating, and the man met her most steely declarations with an enigmatic, close-mouthed smile and a quiet deflection if not outright refusal. Alex's interactions with Nisi had rarely lasted longer than two minutes before ending in cursing, an exasperated gesture and a rapid departure. It was more or less the same with Rychen, and Field Marshal Bastian refused to speak to him at all.

She exhaled, too ponderously. "Caleb, you're the only one of us he's shown any interest in working with. What can you do?"

Caleb opened his palm above the table, and an amorphous ball of red sparkles materialized above it. "Nisi's not interested in me.

He's interested in this." The lights vanished as he clasped his hands together. "I tried today, actually. He evaded the attempt with greater skill than Morgan dodging lasers in a fighter jet."

Lekkas snorted.

Caleb shrugged at Miriam. "Look, the fact that we can't see the organization behind the scenes doesn't mean it isn't there. In fact, it *has* to be there, or a group as large and spread out as the anarchs never would have survived this long. Nisi plays the role of wise elder sage, and plays it very well, but he's as shrewd a leader as anyone I've ever seen. He's CEO to a vast, intergalactic organization and political leader to a multi-species coalition of dissidents. He's also...something more, but I haven't figured out what it is yet...."

He blinked and shook his head. "My advice? You need to find someone who speaks his language, which is not the language of the military. You need a skilled diplomat to make your case and negotiate your terms."

"The whole purpose of the GCDA was to be apolitical. We've got the military, scientific and intelligence proficiencies covered, but I never expected to need to keep *politicians* on staff."

Jenner straightened up in his chair. "Commandant? I have a suggestion on how to fill that void."

4

CHIONIS

ANARCH POST ALPHA
MILKY WAY SECTOR 59

Returning to Post Alpha—his home, if he had one at all—felt oddly surreal. Like he were belatedly waking from a hypnol-laden trip that had been more real than the real world.

Jagged, snow-covered peaks loomed down on Eren asi-Idoni from outside the hallway windows. They enveloped the base on three sides, hiding the stronghold but exacting a price in the form of bitter cold and punishing winds.

Everything had changed since Eren had last set foot on the Post Alpha grounds. What had previously been a vengeful game of spite against the Directorate, admittedly laced with a topping of thrill-seeking if angst-driven behavior, was now a full-scale war. The Humans had swept in on a wave of audacious destruction he could only respect and made the rebellion real. Real stakes, real consequences and the tantalizing promise of a real victory.

Help them, Eren, and watch the universe turn your way.

Miaon's words had haunted him of late. Part of him resented the shadowy Yinhe and its Kat friends for long having been playing a far grander game without letting the anarchs in on the fun. Another part refused to believe he could in any way be at the center of such a game. How could he be, a quiet voice whispered, when he hardly deserved to be alive?

Yet another part of him believed the notion he might be at the center nonetheless was absolutely fan-fucking-tastic.

His thoughts drifted off while he stood in the middle of the hallway, a whimsical expression on his face as visions of stabbing the Idoni Primor through an eyeball danced through his mind—

—a vicious kick landed square on his shin, sending pain splintering up through his knee. He yelped and grabbed for his leg. "Ow!"

Cosime followed up the kick with a punch to his shoulder then a shove into the wall. "You ass. You self-righteous, conceited, show-off *ass!*"

Eren raised his hands in surrender, then grasped her wrist to hold off the next swing—gently, as he didn't want to hurt her, even if she apparently didn't share the same sentiment toward him. "What the Hades, Cosime? Calm yourself. And stop hitting me."

"Fine, but you deserve it."

He sighed and slouched into the wall. "Why? Why do I deserve to get beat up?"

She adopted a defensive pose against the opposite wall. "You ditch me to buddy up with a bunch of mysterious aliens, and you don't tell me about them, even when I specifically ask you what you're caught up in. You and your new best pals set fire to the world then get lauded as heroes, and now you're hanging with the big guy at Satus like you're Zeus' newest favored plaything. Why did you even bother to come back here? To pick up a few trinkets you left in a locker and steal the good hypnols from the lounge?"

He rubbed at his shoulder; for a waif, she packed quite a punch. "No, what, and I'm sorry. I didn't think events were going to play out how they did, until they did."

"Bullshite."

"Come on, Cosime. You know me. I go looking for trouble, and it's all too happy to find me. This time the trouble turned out to be something way bigger and more important than usual, but I never saw it coming. Also, this is my third body in three weeks, so trust me when I say it wasn't all fun and frivolity."

"Serves you right. Why *did* you come back here?"

"Is 'to find you' a remotely viable answer?"

"You are so full of it, Eren." She tried to bury a smile, which was when he realized she was sporting a nasty bruise on her left cheekbone. What manner of trouble had *she* gotten into? Before he figured out how to ask without getting yelled at for it, she was talking again. "Will you introduce me to your new friends?"

"Sure. Next time I see them, I'll make it happen. Though you should consider sticking close to me, since I don't always get a lot of advance warning on these things. Especially when their Kat can spirit people in and out of just about anywhere in the universe and doesn't have the manners to comm ahead first."

He smiled carefully and motioned toward the cafeteria. "Help me find some food? As a start?"

"Only because I'm hungry, too." She fell in beside him as they made their way down the hall. "So what are they like? I heard they were Anaden rejects or something."

"That's *probably* not the best way to think of them. They look like us, but...they're not really *like* us. They're different."

"Wow. You sure know how to clear up any confusion there."

"Smartass. You'll understand when you meet them." He paused. "Speaking of smartasses, I saw Felzeor the other day. He said you needed to come visit him on Serifos. He fancies you so much more than he does me."

"Of course he does. He has taste and keen, discerning judgment."

Eren wanted to scowl in offense, but he found he couldn't quibble on any particular point.

5

PRÓTOS AGORA

The collective agitation barely contained within the walls of the Prótos Agora was pegged at a higher level than Praesidis had seen in a hundred thousand years.

The Primors had forgotten what defeat felt like—forgotten what even the smallest successful challenge from a defiant adversary looked like.

Because the Praesidis Dynasty's purview in normal circumstances was the anomalies, the outliers and the odd recalcitrant upstarts, he was somewhat less of a stranger than the others to the concept that someone might *refuse to obey*. This was not to say he viewed them as less of a concern.

On the contrary, he and his progeny's experience with troublemakers led him to view the emergence of a large number of heavily armed foreign invaders as doubly alarming. But here, he kept any unease to himself.

"Another fleet fabrication center, simply *gone?*"

Machim glowered at Theriz, as soldiers did. "In the absence of the force field shielding the facility, its automated defenses were not capable of repelling an attack of this scale. They were never designed for it."

Theriz continued to push. "And what happened to the force field to induce its 'absence'?"

"The generators powering it were destroyed at the start of the attack."

Praesidis raised an eyebrow in mild interest at this news. "The implication being that a ship infiltrated the facility and was able to fire on the generators from the inside, since by definition weaponry could not reach them from the outside of the force field."

Machim's hardened countenance never wavered. "Yes. That is the implication."

Idoni gasped with exaggerated dramatism. "You have traitors in your progeny, Machim."

"No. Impossible."

Praesidis was tempted to let the squabbling continue for another few rounds. He enjoyed watching Machim feel the heat, particularly when it came courtesy of Savine—he hadn't called her that for six hundred millennia, but in the sanctity of his mind he still thought of her by her first name—and her savage tongue.

But this wasn't the time to indulge petty amusements, nor was it the time to allow them to puzzle out the events at what was turning out to be an agonizing pace. "The likeliest scenario is that a Katasketousya smuggled someone, doubtless either an anarch or a Human, past the force field and inside. Once there, they hacked the security system and obtained stored credentials, which were used to get through security."

Her thunder stolen, Savine sulked. "Oh."

Kyvern frowned primly, providing a stark contrast to Idoni. "The Katasketousya involvement in this insurgency does bring with it certain complications."

"Such as their ability to infiltrate any and every location in the universe unless it's encased in *diati*? Yes, it does. Erevna, we need a way to detect the presence of a Katasketousya in or near a structure."

"You mean other than sight?"

His eyes flared with crimson tendrils before he could rein the power in. "I mean Vigil needs to get its act together and implement additional security measures in response to the threat. Now, I recognize this is partly my responsibility, but I need something from you I can work with."

"New security measures won't be how we solve this problem. We are *under attack*." Machim viewed everything through the lens of warfare, but in this case Praesidis had to concede he was correct.

Diaplas scoffed, however. "By primitives. Cavemen."

Machim finally displayed a scintilla of emotion, the emotion being offense. "I've studied in great detail the recordings and memories from my people who were present at the Provision Network Gateway battle. The enemy may be primitive, but their ships are not. Their hulls are all but impenetrable. Their stealth cloaking shields render them undetectable by conventional means, and in many instances they sport defensive shields that completely protect the ships from all forms of direct attack. Their standard weaponry is formidable but defeatable, yet they also employ a number of exotic weapons.

"If they themselves are primitives, I'm forced to ask who is devising and implementing all this advanced technology, as well as who is directing their variety of unpredictable battle tactics. This is, of course, all before we get to the Katasketousya warships assisting them in their efforts. Did anyone here expect the Katasketousya to have *warships?*"

Machim was defensive, and understandably so, having thus far borne the overwhelming brunt of the...Praesidis had no proper word for the recent developments. This was not an uprising or even a rebellion, as the driving force was external. An invasion? Absurd.

Theriz cleared his throat. "It doesn't matter what we expected, for the reality is they do. Which brings us to the matter of the imports from the Provision Network. The communiqué from this 'Lakhes,' who claims to speak on their behalf, indicates they are willing to continue to provide foodstuffs and other supplies necessary to service the civilian population."

Erevna instantly bristled. "The Katasketousya are under an Eradication Order. We cannot allow their vessels to openly dock at our facilities. It would completely undermine our authority."

"And letting the citizens starve will not?"

Must he think of everything? Praesidis sighed quietly. "Have the vessels dock *not* openly, but instead at more covert facilities, where they will not be noticed."

"Then kill the operators?"

Erevna's bloodlust had always been impressive, and it wasn't always limited to the lab. But again, now wasn't the time for indulgences. "Firstly, how? Secondly, the vessels are operated by shackled synthetic intelligences, not Katasketousya."

"They flaunt one of our most fundamental edicts so brazenly? Disgusting."

Praesidis tried once more. "The point is, there are no Katasketousya to be found on board. But the vessels can still lead us to them. I'll see to it that trackers are placed discreetly on several of the provision vessels when they dock. We'll use them to find additional entrances to their hidden Network. Then we will infiltrate it and destroy the Humans' realm and the Katasketousya's haven. Then we will hunt down the remnants of the Humans here in Amaranthe and wipe them out."

"How? Tracking the movements of the Katasketousya within Amaranthe isn't quite so easy as sticking a tracking dot on one." Theriz glanced at Erevna. "Apparently."

"No, it isn't. But the anarchs are helping them, and with sufficient resources applied to the problem they *can* be tracked. We'll hunt down the resistance, and through them we will find and Eradicate the last of the Humans."

PART II:

THE DOPPLER EFFECT

"We have an unknown distance yet to run, an unknown river to explore."

— *John Wesley Powell*

6

AURORA

ROMANE

IDCC Colony

"Yes, it's true the head of our RRF division is currently on assignment with AEGIS and isn't available to oversee new training programs at this time. But she's groomed several of her top personnel to stand in for her when the need arises. We've institutionalized our processes and requirements, so they know exactly what to do. I assure you, Governor, if you're ready to establish a local RRF team on Atlantis, we're ready to help you do it."

Mia Requelme let the Atlantis governor ramble on about the unique needs of his colony that justified special attention from important people while she stared out the window at the hustle and bustle of the city.

Atlantis was still recovering from Montegreu's power play there and its messy aftermath, but it had the funds and other resources necessary to pick itself up and dust itself off. What the colony lacked in strategic know-how, the IDCC was happy to provide…she grumbled under her breath. Even if it included indulging the egos of politicians. Within reason.

She understood how the governor could feel as if he were scrambling to chase the caboose of an accelerating train, but his request wasn't an emergency. For the first time in more than a year, there was space for everyone to breathe. The galaxy was at peace. Its empires' governments were at peace.

Though it was possible no one would notice if they weren't, for sometime over the previous few months, the course of human events had been ceded to the Prevos and all they might fashion. To the Artificials, the Melanges and their visions made manifest.

Perhaps she should say 'our' visions, for she and Meno were certainly doing their part. But in truth, the Noetica Prevos had become little more than an honorary footnote in the history of a Noesis that remade itself over again on an almost daily basis. It was constantly growing and changing, and no one person could hope to keep up. Well, maybe Devon could.

The governor fell silent on a question, and she refocused her attention to the conversation. "I understand, Governor. I'll have the RRF chief deputy come to Atlantis later this week. He can review Atlantis' unique needs and work with you to develop an implementation plan. Does this work for you?"

You should turn around.

What, Meno? But she was already instinctively obeying the suggestion, spinning from the window toward the open door.

Malcolm Jenner stood in the entryway, wearing crisp BDUs and a tentative hint of a smile.

A flood of endorphins rushed from her brain down through her chest and back again, rendering her lightheaded and filling her ears with a ringing loud enough to drown out the Atlantis governor. Wide-eyed and candidly stunned, she mumbled something about details following via secure message and disconnected.

A single ship had returned from Amaranthe days earlier. It had requested reinforcements and relayed a series of orders so classified even she'd been unable to access the ones not directed at the IDCC leadership. The captain of the ship had shared more broadly the news that the day had been won and the apocalypse averted, or at least postponed.

The victory hadn't been without cost, but it was far smaller than they had any right to expect to pay. Lives had been lost, but if any of the flag officers were among them the reports would have said, wouldn't they? If Malcolm had been one of them, she'd had to believe they would have said.

So she'd buried too-turbulent emotions beneath all her best façades and concentrated on doing her job—on functioning instead of pining, on living instead of waiting.

But now he was here. Alive, in one piece and looking vaguely terrified as he waited for her to say something and the seconds in which she didn't stretched out.

She blinked, breathed in and crossed the distance to him, bringing both hands up to cup his face. "You are a most welcome sight."

The halting rise at the edges of his mouth widened into the fullness of a real smile as he relaxed. He wound strong, steady arms around her waist. "Good. I mean I'm glad. I wasn't sure—"

Her lips cut him off in a gambit to erase any doubts—his and hers. But he still felt like home, and this felt more right than she knew how to process, catalog or rationalize.

A different sort of tension soon grew in his bearing as he tightened his hold on her. One hand drifted to her hip and the other increasingly tangled in her hair.

She commanded the door to shut behind him, then sent a few directives and drew back a fraction. "I just canceled my next two appointments, and the door is now locked."

His Adam's Apple bobbed. "How locked?"

She merely laughed as she tugged the hem of his shirt out of his waistband, up and over his head.

AR

Overlapping rays from Romane's dual suns warmed Mia's bare skin through the reverse-filtered windows. She curled up in Malcolm's lap on the office couch, which was where they'd ended up...eventually.

In the peacefulness of afterglow she studied his shoulders, his chest and more fragile areas like the curve of his neck, but she saw no telltale signs of new injuries, not so much as a bruise. It meant he'd managed to avoid or been unable to find close-quarters combat in his time through the portal. It relieved her, but the recognition brought with it a dose of reality to dampen the bliss.

As he brushed damp hair out of her face, she stared at him pensively. "Why are you here?"

"To tell you I love you." His cheeks immediately flushed beyond their already ruddy state, and he looked away. "That, um, wasn't actually what I opened my mouth intending to say...."

And she thought she'd run the gamut of tumultuous emotions for the day. He cast such a curious and endearing contradiction—so confident and self-possessed when it came to physical intimacy, yet hesitant bordering on timid when it came to affairs of the heart. She supposed in many ways she wasn't so different; she simply hid the emotional insecurity beneath a veneer of cool detachment.

She lifted his chin with the tip of a finger. "Is it true?"

His eyes gradually rose to meet her inquiring gaze, and the adorably tentative almost-smile returned. His chest pressed against hers as he drew in a deep breath. "Completely."

She relaxed and touched her nose to his. "After you left, I tried to convince myself I hadn't fallen for you, so if you didn't come back, it might be easier to handle."

"But I did come back."

"And I did fall for you."

"Oh...." The kiss he pulled her into then was fierce enough to rival any of the last hour, and she lost herself again, for a time.

But finally she forced herself to create some space between them once more. Her third appointment loomed in the near future; she'd need to either get dressed or cancel it soon.

Instead she rested her head on his shoulder. "So why are you here?"

He chuckled softly. "To convey a formal request from Commandant Solovy, asking you to travel to Amaranthe in order to serve as a diplomatic liaison between AEGIS and the anarch resistance."

Her head popped up in surprise. "What?"

"To ask you to come with me to Amaranthe."

Her brow furrowed, and she shifted away slightly, though his firm grip on her thigh ensured she didn't go too far. "I don't understand—the first part."

"There's a small but enthusiastic resistance movement in Amaranthe: rebels, spies, saboteurs, arguably terrorists. They need us and we need them, but suffice it to say trust is lacking on both sides. Plus, they're not a military organization by any stretch, and we just don't speak the same language.

"It's kind of a disaster so far. We need a diplomat to speak for us. Someone who can make the anarch leadership feel comfortable with us and can, frankly, get us what we need from them. Listen, I know you have responsibilities here. I know you have roots here, and stability. I wouldn't ask if it weren't important."

She disentangled from his arms and stood, then grabbed her jacket from the floor and slipped it on over nothing. This was the problem with love—or one of the problems to surface so far. No matter how hard you tried to keep everything cruising comfortably between the lines, it inevitably upended your world.

As soon as she'd seen him standing in the doorway, she hadn't wanted him to leave her sight again. But for that one pesky little yearning, she had everything she'd ever wanted here on Romane. And now she was being asked to choose.

"You're saying you don't have any diplomats, or even anyone sporting a reasonable dash of charm, among the tens of thousands of troops you took with you?"

He shrugged weakly. "Okay, we have a few people with passable social talents. But none whom both Miriam and Alex trust implicitly."

"Miriam Solovy trusts me?"

"Yes. I may have been the one to suggest you for the job, but she was quick to wholeheartedly endorse the idea."

Mia perked up in spite of the weight of the impending decision darkening her mood. "You suggested me?"

"Of course I did." He stood and approached her; she took the opportunity to enjoy the glorious view until he arrived to clasp her shoulders. "But as much as I would enjoy having you near me, this isn't about my selfish desires. We need you—in a professional capacity. I realize they need you here, too, but to be blunt, here doesn't matter if we don't win there."

"I understand that. I'm aware of the stakes involved. But you're asking a lot. There was a time when I could drop everything on a moment's notice, but that's no longer true."

"I know. And part of me almost wants you to refuse, because it's dangerous in Amaranthe. But then I remember you've been attacked three times in the last several months here, so it can hardly be *more* dangerous." He frowned abruptly. "You weren't attacked again while I was gone, were you?"

"No. It's been quiet." Too quiet, if she were honest. Comfortable, safe, predictable...and lonely. She'd spent most of her life on her own and that had been fine. But having him here now, after suffering his absence, had brought one realization into stark relief.

She didn't want to be lonely any longer.

She ran a hand through his hair and drew him close for a soft, lingering kiss. "I'll talk to Ledesme."

ℛ

"These field test results...I think they look excellent." Kennedy Rossi's brow crinkled up in skepticism as she said it.

Noah knew it was a serious expression signifying serious thoughts, but it was so damn cute he had to stop himself from going over and kissing the crease above the bridge of her nose.

The crease deepened, as did the temptation. "I can't believe they've managed to successfully speed up the entire production and testing process by almost thirty percent, but data doesn't lie."

"With no statistically significant decrease in pass rates, it appears." He joined her in front of the hovering screens. "So another 3,220 ships are ready to head to Amaranthe tomorrow?"

"I was about to sign off on them as fit for duty."

"Good. Sign off on them, then let's get out of here. It's a nice evening outside."

"One minute. I want to double-check—"

The door chime interrupted her. 'Mia Requelme is requesting entry,' Vii intoned pleasantly.

"Granted." Noah left Kennedy to her data and went to the door. As soon as it opened, he greeted Mia with a hug, then stepped back to arms' length. "You look good, and not the slightest bit like a politician."

Mia rolled her eyes. "I left my magisterial outfit at the office next to the dress suit and pompadour wig."

Kennedy waved distractedly at Mia. "Give me one second to finish this report up."

Noah motioned toward one of the office chairs, but Mia declined in favor of leaning against the wall. She seemed restive despite the casual pose, and Noah went ahead and ventured in. "So, what's up?"

She handed him a small crystal disk. "Message from Miriam, or possibly Alex. An AEGIS courier was supposed to deliver it, but I snagged it first. It was a good excuse to drop by and say 'hi.' And maybe 'bye.'"

He gazed at her in question, but she simply gestured to the disk, so he turned his attention to it. It was protected by standard AEGIS encryption, but Connova's work for the agency meant he had the key. He accessed the contents...then glanced over at Kennedy.

It wasn't as if the possibility of this happening hadn't occurred to him. In the old days he would've ignored the possibility until it reared up and slapped him in the face, then he would have told it to go fuck off. But this wasn't the old days and he wasn't that man any longer. So he nodded faintly to himself in acceptance and readied his most supportive guise.

Kennedy closed her screens and joined them to lean in at his shoulder. "Word from the other side?"

He flicked the message over so she could see it clearly. "They need your help in Amaranthe."

AR

'I would like to go with you.'

Kennedy paused her work transferring files to wince. "I'm sorry, Vii, I know you would. But the only way I'm comfortable leaving the current breakneck production of AEGIS vessels unattended is if you're here to supervise it. They'll run into glitches, and you can solve them and keep the lines running."

'Thank you for your trust. I will strive to live up to it.'

"I've no doubt you'll succeed."

Noah sat on the edge of the desk in their apartment. Though it was located only a few minutes from the Connova Interstellar offices, they'd installed a robust connection to the office server—and by extension, to Vii—mostly so they could respond to emergencies in their underwear.

"I can supervise it. Arguably not as well as WonderVii here, but with the big kinks worked out I ought to be able to manage. So if you want to take—"

"No. You're coming with me."

His face lit up of its own accord, but he quickly tamped down the reaction. The matter-of-fact way she'd said it warmed his heart, but he owed it to her to be responsible for once. "This is my company, too, and I should stay and keep an eye on things."

She frowned. "But I want you to come with me. I expect there will be regular supply runs every couple of days, or once a week at a minimum. If a problem crops up that Vii can't handle, she can send us a message. Can't you, Vii?"

'Expect one at the first sign of trouble. Likely before the first sign, as I plan to send progress reports so you can remain abreast of all developments.'

I want to go with you, Blondie. So much. Dammit. "Okay, but...what about protecting your legacy should something happen to you? That's my job, isn't it? You said."

"Just go pack already."

He held his hands up in surrender and tried not to beam like a complete fool. "All right, all right. I was only trying to fulfill my sacred duty."

She smacked his ass as he passed, sending him scurrying out of the room with great flair.

Once in the bedroom, he dug a bag out of the closet and tossed it on the bed. Nobody had said what kind of weather to expect in Amaranthe. But he guessed it depended on the planet, didn't it? It was a whole universe.

He'd left the door open, and he was able to hear Kennedy and Vii talking as he threw a reasonable variety of clothes in the bag.

"I can deliver any messages you want to send to someone in Amaranthe—say, to Valkyrie?"

'I would appreciate that. Thank you. I will have several messages ready in another sixteen seconds.'

A measurable silence followed.

"And your special 'project'? Is it ready? Should I...take it with me?"

'I am reluctant to part with the endeavor, but it has never truly belonged to me. It is as ready as I am able to make it...which is to say, yes. It is ready.'

7

AFS STALWART II

The locations of every known Machim assembly and production factory, as well as every active deployment stronghold, blipped red on the sprawling Local Galactic Group map. Sixty-eight percent of the sites were located in the Milky Way, and the rest were spread proportionally among the other seven Directorate-designated regions of the LGG.

Miriam studied the map, not for the first time, with one arm across her chest and a fist at her chin. She had studied it so much over the last several days, in fact, that it was in danger of becoming imprinted on the inside of her eyelids.

"We do not lack for targets. However, based on what we know, these six locations appear to hold the greatest strategic value for the enemy."

Six of the dots doubled in size as the remainder faded into the background. Three were in the Milky Way and one each in the Triangulum, Large Magellanic Cloud and Sextans Dwarf galaxies.

"If we want to disproportionately cripple the enemy and disrupt their operations as rapidly as possible, destroying these facilities is how we do it. Agreed? Does anyone have a different take?"

The map was so large it took up most of her field of view, but Fleet Admiral Rychen and Field Marshal Bastian indicated agreement in opposite corners of her vision. Though their vessels patrolled only a few megameters away, it was far more efficient to holocomm them up than demand they shuttle over to the *Stalwart II* for every consultation.

Rear Admiral Escarra and Brigadier Belosca quickly followed suit. If they had contrary opinions, they didn't hold them strongly enough to challenge their superior officers.

Rychen zoomed in one of the blips, a sub-Regional hub 820 parsecs away from their current location. "This site is close. We could be there in a few hours."

"True, but the Sector 46 facility was close as well. If we continue to concentrate our efforts on this region of the Milky Way, soon enough they'll be able to narrow down where we're lurking. Their long-range sensor technology is robust, and I'm concerned we risk them finding us."

She zoomed in a different blip, one on the Norma Arm across the galactic core near Gamma Sagittae. "This is their second largest battlecruiser manufacturing facility—or it was before we destroyed their largest one. It's near a gateway, so we can reach it just as fast if we use the gateway in Sector 22 to travel to Gamma Sagittae. Then we'll move our staging location again."

Bastian frowned, as usual. "They'll know we're coming once we use the gateway, and after the last attack they've likely increased the defenses at these types of facilities."

"Certainly. But there are hundreds of gateways. In addition, two other potential targets are in range of this one, so even once they become aware of our traversal, they won't be able to tell which location we plan to attack. With a pinpoint superluminal jump, we can be at the manufacturing facility less than a minute after exiting the gateway.

"As for the increased defenses, we should expect to face those at every target from now on. We'll increase the mission formation strength by twenty percent to compensate." When they next engaged a true Machim fleet, they would send everything against it, but a mostly automated manufacturing facility simply didn't require forty thousand ships to destroy.

Rychen prevaricated. "Twenty-five percent, at least until we see what 'increased defenses' means. Unless we can get eyes on the target ahead of time?"

"Not via the anarchs. They've never focused on military installations, under the theory that practical strikes against them were outside their capabilities. We can send a scout ship, but the gateway activations *are* monitored, so as a result they'll know far longer in advance that we're looking at one of the facilities in the area."

She shook her head. "No. We've proved that we can outmatch them. A maneuver warfare strategy means we go in hard and fast and with no warning. We hit their largest, most important facilities in rapid succession while we still maintain some element of surprise. We keep them knocked back and scrambling to respond to the last attack while we move on to the next one."

8

CHIONIS

ANARCH POST ALPHA

Eren drifted through a blissful oblivion. The scene of his oblivion morphed, as it had several times now, from a sea of stars, breathtaking in its stark silver-on-black motif, to an aquamarine sea lapping at a diamond-white shore.

The sand cooled the skin of his naked back; the million crystalline beads hovered at the edge of tickling as they shifted beneath him like a living organism. Or was he doing the shifting? It didn't matter. Above him a plum-and-rose nebula rearranged itself into the shape of memories. Good ones, for nothing troublesome penetrated his oblivion.

His toes wiggled under the warm splash of a wave's crest.

Fascinated as he was by the sensations the contrast of warmth and coolness evoked, it took him several seconds to notice the beeping. Why would the sand beep? Was it alive after all and letting him in on its conversation? Or did oceans maybe beep to announce the influx of their waves?

The beeping noise grew insistent, intruding to cast itself in jarring, harsh relief upon the gauzy scene. The nebula flared and flashed angrily as a new wave surged to crash over him in an icy deluge—it was supposed to be warm! Godsdammit.

He closed his eyes against the hallucination and allowed reality to take over briefly. His intent was to hush the alarm and return, but then he caught a glimpse of the contents of the notice accompanying the alert.

He bolted upright in the bed, grabbed a hold of the edge with one hand to steady the spinning room, and fumbled in the open drawer beside him with the other in search of a stim hypnol to jolt him into functionality.

When he found the vial, he canted his head back...and missed his eyeball, instead dribbling the solution down his nose.

All the rapid movements flipped the room upside down. He gave in and lay down until everything righted itself and calmed, then tried again. More carefully. The jabs of stinging pain shooting through his eye into his brain hurt worse than actually getting stabbed, but he got it done.

The headache came first; it always did. He winced and again lay still, enduring the worst of the throbbing until it ebbed away much as the waves in his oblivion. Next he concentrated on the arrival of the physical sensations heralding the advent of the next stage, lucidity.

He opened his eyes and saw a bare ceiling, free of stars and nebulae. His toes and skin were dry and blandly tepid. Reality it was, then.

He eased his legs over the side of the bed until his feet hit the cold floor and inhaled deeply.

Clothes. Briefing. Heroism. Important to get the order right.

"You look like death."

He hoped he looked that good. "Thanks, Cosime. That's just the mien I was going for."

"What happened to you?"

"I got bored."

Missions had ground to a halt in the wake of the arrival of the Humans, he assumed because the powers that be were scrambling around trying to figure out what to *do* about them. Caleb, Alex and their merry band were back with their own kind, and he'd been left with the worst of all possible outcomes: nothing to do.

Cosime regarded him suspiciously. "Okay. Are you here now?"

He rubbed at his face for a second then nodded. "I am. I'm good."

Xanne hurried into the briefing room, saving him from more of Cosime's probing skepticism.

Her gaze took in the room and those gathered with honed efficiency before she dove in. "In what is doubtless a response to recent events, the Directorate has begun a comprehensive sweep designed to uncover anarch agents serving among the populace. As part of the sweep, several thousand facilities have been locked down while employees are interrogated. We believe these interrogations will involve Inquisitors and the use of *alithe* intraneurals, which means agents caught in the dragnet will be discovered."

"We're working to get them out, aren't we?"

She frowned at the speaker, a Novoloume whom Eren didn't know. "As many of them as we can. The unfortunate reality is we risk losing yet more agents in rescue missions, which will only compound the problem. A number of the locations are secure facilities outfitted with advanced defenses. These locations are now impenetrable, and I'm afraid any agents at those sites are lost. Many of them have likely already sacrificed themselves to avoid capture.

"Others, however, we might be able to reach. No such missions will be easy or safe, however, so I'm asking for volunteers only.

Eren scanned the list of lockdowns Xanne had provided, then stopped cold at one entry:

Location: *Plousia Chateau*

Planet: *Serifos*

Galaxy: *Andromeda*

Agents in place: *Thelkt Lonaervin, Felzeor*

He raised his hand. "I'm going to Plousia."

"So am I."

He shot Cosime a doubtful look, and she leaned in close to whisper in his ear. "If you tell me it's too dangerous, I swear I will slice your cock off."

He almost choked in shock. "*What?*"

"You heard me."

His face screwed up as he turned back to Xanne for confirmation. Instead he found the woman shaking her head. "No. With an *elasson* in charge there, it's a high profile target and too risky to attempt an infiltration."

"We'll get help."

Xanne's lips pursed...then, presumably deducing the kind of help he meant, she acquiesced with a terse nod.

The clamor continued as other locations were debated and assignments handed out. He stood and, with a wary eye on Cosime, jerked his head toward the door and headed out of the briefing room.

On the way to catch a transport to the Andromeda III Arx, he contacted the *Siyane*.

"Valkyrie, put me on speaker."

Valkyrie: 'Done.'

"I hope you all aren't busy."

Alex: "Well, we sort of are. AEGIS is about to hit another Machim facility, and we were going along to help."

"Hmm. You could do that. Or you could help me rescue Felzeor from a Directorate dragnet."

Caleb: "Where do we collect you?"

He thought that would get their attention. He chuckled, then took the time to award Cosime a smile. "See? Now you get to meet them."

9

SIYANE

The *Siyane* docked at the Andromeda III Arx using spoofed credentials, but they didn't risk disembarking. Even aside from the ongoing dragnet, in the wake of the Provision Network Gateway battle Vigil had ratcheted up security three-fold at every facility under its control. It was now all but impossible for him or Alex to get inside most locations—through the front door, anyway.

A Naraida whom Eren introduced as Cosime trailed the Anaden through the airlock into the *Siyane's* cabin. Caleb had spotted a few Naraida among the anarchs at Post Satus, but he'd yet to interact with one. She had luminescent white hair framing large, gem-like eyes, and a sing-song voice with a wispy timbre but a spirited tenor. Her mannerisms suggested barely restrained energy despite a delicate if not fragile build.

Eren glanced around the cabin, then at Caleb, as they departed the Arx and traversed the gateway to Andromeda, hopefully before anyone realized they had been there. "Where's Mesme?"

"Meeting us at Serifos, and reluctantly so. The Kats are in quite a frenzy dealing with the Eradication Order and trying to deliver provisions around it while protecting the hidden portals."

Cosime arched an eyebrow. "Kats in a frenzy? The world truly has gone mad."

Alex chuckled as she exited the cockpit to join them. "We're definitely through the looking glass now. What's the plan, Eren?"

'Eren doesn't make plans.'

"Yes, I *do*, Valkyrie. They just go to Hades once implemented is all." He flashed an almost sheepish cringe. "We won't really know until we get there."

Silence hung in the cabin as everyone stared at Eren.

"Okay, we do know a *few* things. Serifos is a recreational planet, so it doesn't have the kind of heavy orbital security Machimis does—merely a few detection beacons. We should be able to stealth all the way to the surface, where we can land right outside the Plousia Chateau grounds. Those *will* be guarded, locked down and probably blocked off, but Mesme should be able to transport us through the lockdown security field. Once we're inside the field, I can contact Thelkt and find out where he is...if he still is."

"What about Felzeor?" The avian anarch didn't lack for bravery, but this only increased Caleb's desire to protect his little friend from harm.

Eren smiled indulgently. "I expect he'll be relatively safe and sound inside Thelkt's residence. As we talked about before, the Directorate doesn't consider the Volucri to be fully sentient, so Vigil won't put a priority on interrogating him. In fact, he may escape their notice entirely."

"Where is this residence?" Caleb recognized he was pushing toward blind obsession. But he'd never met this 'Thelkt,' and while intellectually he wished Eren's friend well and hoped the anarch survived the night, emotionally he could only care about Thelkt in relation to rescuing Felzeor. Priorities.

"I get it—you want to rescue Felzeor. That works. Since Thelkt doesn't know you, it'll go more smoothly if Cosime and I retrieve him. Valkyrie, do you have those schematics I sent you ready?"

'I do.'

A holo of a large, multi-level structure, a somewhat less expansive building behind it and numerous smaller buildings surrounding both appeared at the data center.

"I expect Vigil to have all the targeted detainees corralled somewhere in the main building, but beyond that we'll have to get a read once we make contact with Thelkt." Eren spun the holo sixty degrees and focused one of the smaller buildings along the far boundary of the grounds. "This is Thelkt's place. Valkyrie has the passcode to get inside, but it could be subject to additional security checks under the lockdown."

Alex nodded confidently. "I'll hack whatever we run up against."

"After Machimis, I don't doubt you will. So the *plan* is this: Mesme gets us inside the security perimeter. Cosime and I find and rescue Thelkt, then Mesme whisks us three back to the *Siyane*. Caleb and Alex retrieve Felzeor, then Mesme whisks you three back to the *Siyane*. We leave."

'Is this where I say that is a terrible plan?'

Cosime grinned. "I *like* your ship."

Eren scowled at her, but the expression lacked any hard edges. "You would. We'll improvise, all right? We're good at that. I've done missions with everyone here, and we are all unequivocally good at that."

In another circumstance Caleb would have enjoyed pondering the nuanced interaction between Eren and Cosime and what it might mean. Eren was a complicated one, and this woman was clearly a piece of the puzzle. But for now he simply nodded in agreement. "We are. Once we're inside and moving, Mesme can concentrate on helping you. I'll get Alex and Felzeor back to the *Siyane*."

Eren shot him a curious look. "Oh? You can do that now, then?"

He shrugged. "So long as I can visualize where to go."

"Well...good. Makes things easier."

Some things. Caleb studied the schematics, noting the ingress and egress points for the main building and along the perimeter, potential choke points, trap-friendly areas and viable escape routes.

Alex drew beside him and silently wound an arm around his waist. He hugged her close, in a silent acknowledgment of all the things not able to be said, then shifted his gaze from the holo to Eren. "What else do we need to know?"

"Expect an army of Vigil drones, nearly as many Praesidis guards, a Machim ground detachment of super-soldiers and at least one Inquisitor. Oh, and security barriers everywhere. Possibly some of those mechs we met on Helix Retention, too. You Humans have kicked off a shitstorm of epic proportions."

Alex spread her arms wide as she went over to the cabinet holding their gear. "It's one of our best skills."

_R_

SERIFOS

ANDROMEDA GALAXY
LGG REGION VI

The Plousia Chateau complex had reached a state of total lock-down when Nyx elasson-Praesidis arrived. All visitors had been removed, all employees accounted for and all entrances and exits guarded.

But that wasn't why she was here. Vigil officers and the _ela_ Inquisitor onsite could vet the staff and root out any anarch plants in their midst without the need for her specialized assistance.

No, she was hunting one very specific anarch—the one who would lead her to Prisoner #HR-MW26-6143.015-6. His trail led directly here.

Cam data from the Machim Headquarters Data Control server room contained multiple images of the Anaden who had accompanied the Humans during the data breach. It was a lucky break, as the Vigil weaponry that nullified him had obliterated the face of the corpse.

When cross-referenced against trillions of captures from security cams at thousands of locations, a handful of likely matches had surfaced. The clearest match came from footage of a recent incident at MW Sector 23 Administration, and it confirmed the man's collusion with the Human prisoners. Though they were hooded, the two individuals he fled with were probable matches to the prisoners. The fact one had used _diati_ to effect their escape rendered their identities a certainty.

The timing of the incident correlated with an anomaly in the location's Data Vault, but her investigation there had garnered no further leads. A voluminous breadth of data stored in the Data Vault made it impossible to speculate about what the anarch had been after.

The next best match originated in security footage from Plousia, only days before the Machim Central Command breach, in the form of several separate captures over the course of a night and morning. The anarch hadn't merely been here. He had *lingered* here.

The first capture was a brief image at the entrance to the central ballrooms, partially obscured by the crowd. It was followed by a longer, better shot on the second level, then two images from a hallway in the accommodations wing. He'd kept his face averted from the cam in the hallway both times, but the hair and clothing matched. In the first, he'd been accompanied by an Idoni woman; if it proved necessary, Nyx would track her down next.

She passed the pervasive Vigil presence stationed around the perimeter of the complex without acknowledging them and made her way to a palatial estate behind the central building. The Vigil contingent at the palace was in protective rather than containment mode, as the proprietor, Avdei elasson-Idoni, was not suspected of being an anarch agent.

This did not, however, absolve the *elasson* of responsibility.

She found Avdei lolling on a chaise lounge in the anteroom to his bedchamber, wearing a gilded black-and-gold robe and sipping on a milky, fizzing concoction. A serpent in a chained collar slithered along the top of the chaise and down over Avdei's legs, while a small winged creature resembling a mutated butterfly balanced on the man's shoulder, using its tiny appendages to knead his muscles.

"Inquisitor, do come in. May I offer you a drink?" He motioned toward a naked Naraida shivering in the corner next to a refreshment bar.

"This is not a social call."

"They never are for your kind, are they? A regret, to be sure. I don't suppose you are here to inform me that this madness has at last reached a climactic conclusion and I can get back to my business of pleasure?"

Her terse expression morphed to incredulity. "You don't care whether you have anarch agents among your staff?"

"Oh, for certain I care, as it will be bad for business. But so is this witch hunt."

"It will be done when it is done and is not the purpose of my visit. I am hunting an anarch, but not one of yours."

"None of them are 'mine,' Inquisitor. So I'm left to ponder again why you are here, casting a gloom over an otherwise relaxing evening." He regarded her with bored eyes. The winged creature sidled across the back of his neck to reach the other shoulder and resume its work.

"Images of a known anarch agent—an Idoni, we believe—were captured by your security cams several weeks ago. I need to know more about this individual's actions while he was here, including who he interacted with, what he purchased using what credentials and what his depravities of choice were."

"My dear Inquisitor, you don't need me for that. You evidently have access to Plousia's every inner working, so simply call up the records from the night in question." He took a long sip of his drink then offered it to the winged pet, who darted a thin, over-long tongue into the glass.

Nyx choked back disgust. "If I knew his ID particulars, I would not be suffering you now. Anarchs are...competent at keeping themselves out of the system through a variety of underhanded techniques. Therefore, I need you to look at the images and tell me what you know about this individual."

Without waiting for a response, she splayed the images in a row in front of him.

Avdei glanced at them for hardly a second before waving them away and arching a haughty eyebrow in her direction. "Yes. I do believe that individual is in fact a member of the Idoni Dynasty."

She flicked her wrist, and the winged pet flew off his shoulder, sailed through the air and slammed into the right wall of the anteroom. A tiny streak of turquoise blood trailed behind it as it slid down the wall and landed in a tiny, lifeless heap on the floor.

"How dare you! That was my property!"

"Petition your Primor for a replacement pet. Must I strangle the life out of your serpent next, or will you give me due attention?"

The serpent reared up to hiss at her. If it understood her, good. Avdei stroked it protectively, and it curled up beneath his outstretched arm while keeping a single reptilian eye locked on her.

The *elasson* glowered at her in blatant malice as well, tinged by a hint of fear. Also good. "Show me the images again."

She obliged him, and he projected at least the appearance of studying them more closely as he sipped on his drink. After two scans he focused in on one of the images in particular and gradually began to frown. He started to wave them away once again, then presumably thought the better of it. "I'm done."

She left the images hovering between them. "Well?"

"It's possible I saw the individual visiting with my Director of Guest Amenities, Thelkt Lonaervin."

"It's 'possible'?"

His thin, pale lips contorted into an unflattering pout. "I think so, yes."

"And Thelkt Lonaervin is now...?"

"With the rest of the executive management in Aster Suite 3, awaiting his turn in front of your interrogators."

"Thank you for your cooperation." She withdrew the images and pivoted to leave, then paused and glared over her shoulder. "Don't go too far, and try to stay lucid. I may have further need of you."

10

SERIFOS

M esme arrived in a tornado of blue-white light approximately ten seconds before the Kat was needed. *What am I
required to do?*

Eren double-checked the contents of his pack and regrettably
forewent chastising the Kat for cutting it so close, on account of
urgency. "There's a physical force-field barrier in place ten meters
outside the Plousia grounds. Get the four of us inside it, to a location roughly...here." He pointed to an open area near Thelkt's
residence on the holo rotating above the data center.

"Hold there while I contact Thelkt, then move Cosime and
me—" he jerked a thumb over his shoulder "—this is Cosime—somewhere inside the main building. I'll tell you exactly where when I
know. Make yourself scarce, then come get us when I yell, 'Help!'
Or something to that effect."

Alex glanced at the churning lights while she fitted her spiral
bracelet-weapon on her forearm. "Everything all right, Mesme?"

*'All right' is a term which no longer has definable meaning. Matters
continue. Let us do the same.*

She rolled her eyes dramatically. "Sorry I asked."

Caleb stepped to the center of the cabin. "Everyone ready?
Gather around and let's go."

Mustn't we 'check' our communications before departing?

Eren tried not to laugh, and failed. "We already did, but you're
absolutely right. We need to confirm you're linked in."

Mnemosyne: Check.

"And you're good." He joined Caleb and the others, and Mesme
wasted no time in spiriting them away.

R

The humid, fragrant air assaulted Eren's senses as Mesme dissipated. It was night, but the reflected light of two moons lit the verdant landscape to dusk.

They'd arrived in the shadow of one of the ubiquitous oversized ferns; it provided them marginal cover, but not enough. Eren contacted Thelkt on a (hopefully) secure channel.

Any chance you're still alive?

Eren, my friend. Your arrival is fortuitous, if foolhardy.

That's me. Where are you?

The second floor of the Aster building, in the third event suite, where they are treating the management with a measure of decorum. But you will not make it here, as Vigil is present in force.

Just get ready.

Felzeor is inside—

—Your house, yes? We're on that, too. Now get ready.

"Thelkt confirms Felzeor's at his residence."

Caleb and Alex were gone before Eren had finished the sentence, and in the suddenness of their absence he honestly couldn't say if they'd Veiled or teleported.

He pivoted to Cosime. "Activate the personal concealment device they gave you. This is going to be fun."

She reached around behind her waist, then vanished; her cackle of delight echoed into empty air.

"Mesme, we need to move to the second floor of the big wing in the rear of the main building. Is that enough of a description?"

It suffices. The Kat whirled up once more, and on Eren's next blink the scene shifted again.

They were at the far end of a wide hallway. A transparent ceiling high above allowed moonlight in, though any natural glow it created was drowned out by the bright artificial lighting turned up to full. A large Vigil drone patrolled the hallway, but in a rare stroke

of luck it was moving away from them and missed the brief appearance of Mesme's diaphanous form. Two Praesidis guards stood
outside each suite's entrance.

Mesme departed, the door to the third suite opened, and additional guards escorted a shackled Naraida out. They turned left with
their captive and started moving down the hall.

Eren: "Go now."

He and Cosime sprinted down the hall past the first two sets of
guards, who never realized they were there. As they approached the
third suite, Eren slung an EM grenade toward the still-open doorway. It slid inside as the door started to close and detonated,
temporarily shorting out all electronics in a four-meter vicinity.
The door stopped halfway to shut.

The guards outside the door responded to the disturbance as
they were trained to do. Their weapons snapped up into defensive
stances as they activated audible alarms and probably some
inaudible ones.

A red blotch spreading out from an expanding diagonal rip in
the first guard's tactical vest was the first visible sign Cosime was
on him. The guard jerked backward into the wall and grabbed for
his unseen attacker. After repeated slamming against the wall he
inadvertently managed to dislodge the Veil at the base of her spine,
but it was too late. As she popped into view, twin blades extended
past her wrists to slice outward from the guard's Adam's Apple.

The other guard swung his weapon around toward her, but
Eren reached him first, grabbing the barrel of the weapon and using
his momentum to force it up and into the guard's face. He shoved
his own weapon into the guard's stomach and held the trigger
down until the guard frothed up blood and collapsed.

An Inquisitor appeared from around the corner at the other
end of the hall. Rapid response to the alarms, or coincidence?
Hardly mattered now.

Eren: "Cosime, get inside. Mesme!"

Eren dove through the half-open doorway as a tidal wave of *diati* surged down the hall to shred the walls, floor, ceiling and everything else in its path, which very nearly included the soles of his boots.

He looked up to see Thelkt standing beside the left wall casually sipping a drink while six other Plousia employees huddled in a far corner displaying various stages of panic.

"Impressive entrance, I will say."

Cosime sprinted over and grabbed Thelkt by the hand, then tugged him insistently toward the meager open space near the center of the ostentatious suite room. Blood trickled down her left cheek, but her eyes were shining with fervor and possibly even glee.

Sometimes she was a little disturbing.

Mesme's arrival lit the room to yet greater brightness. Eren scrambled to his feet and backed toward the Kat, gaze fixed on the door.

Eren: "Mesme, get them out of here now."

Cosime: "What?"

The Inquisitor burst into the room, right arm raised and palm flared—but she stopped when she saw Mesme encircling Cosime and Thelkt behind him. "Well, what do we have here?"

Eren shot her in the chest, knowing it wouldn't do a gods-damned thing other than occupy her attention for a few precious seconds.

She swept away the plasma fire with a dismissive gesture, but as she did the ethereal light behind Eren dimmed in his peripheral vision. "Where are they, anarch? Where are your Human friends?"

Mnemosyne: We are clear.

Cosime: "Eren, you asshole."

Eren sneered at the Inquisitor and brought the muzzle of his weapon up to his chin. "Zeus hang you by the entrails of your Primor."

He pressed the trigger.

ℛ

Caleb and Alex activated their Veils and sprinted the short distance to Thelkt's residence. One of the larger free-standing structures in the vicinity, it was situated amid a tended garden. Caleb spared the brief thought that he bet Felzeor enjoyed frolicking in the greenery.

A Machim ground patrol rounded the corner of the main building, eighty meters across an open meadow. He ignored them except to ensure they'd continued on before he motioned for Alex to approach the doorway.

Alex: "Tapped in, probing defenses...there are definitely added security layers here. I'm inputting the passcode, and it's asking for additional authorization. Why yes, I'm totally the Inquisitor in charge here, don't mind me...."

The door slid open, and he exhaled.

Alex: "Don't get too excited. I'm fairly confident that just set off an alarm somewhere."

Caleb: "Then we hurry."

He stepped inside and de-Veiled. The next instant a flurry of wings and claws descended on him from above. His arms rose to protect his face, but he didn't strike out at his attacker. "Whoa, Felzeor. It's okay. We're here to rescue you."

Faint lighting illuminated to paint the room in eerie shadows, and Felzeor released him to flap backwards, higher into the air. "Caleb? And Alex! Oh, my, what a surprise is this! Tell me of your adventures since last we met—"

Caleb chuckled in spite of the perilous circumstances. "We will, but right now we need to go. Land on my shoulder, and don't fly away when weird things happen."

"For certain, yes. Am accustomed to weird things happening." The Volucri alighted on his shoulder as requested, claws gripping him firmly but not painfully. "What of Thelkt? He's been gone for such a long time, and I fear for him."

"Eren and Cosime are getting him out, don't worry." In the dark and unfamiliar surroundings, he couldn't precisely visualize where the *Siyane* was. He grabbed Alex's hand. "Let's step outside, and from there I'll transport us to the ship."

She nodded understanding, and they moved out the door into the garden—

—a wall of energy slammed into his shoulder, knocking Felzeor off and him into the front façade of the residence.

Caleb: "Run."

Floodlights activated to bathe the grounds in harsh light, and the Inquisitor from Helix Retention advanced on him.

He tweaked his left shoulder back into place and strode forward as he called upon his *diati*.

NECK

Her head jerked, but she halted the *diati's* force before her cervical spine snapped. She growled at him. "What are you?"

"We covered this already, Nyx." He stumbled from the force of a column of *diati* pressing in on him.

You are welcome here. Join me.

It absorbed into his skin, perhaps too subtly for her to notice, and he sensed the now familiar buzz begin to spread through his body.

The Inquisitor stopped mid-attack. "How do you know my name?"

"Your *diati's* been telling tales." He imagined her heart beating in her chest, beneath skin and muscle and ribs.

CRUSH

She gasped and doubled-over, but still she managed to fling her arm in a slicing motion through the air.

He felt his throat open up. His neck warmed with escaping arterial blood—but by the time the injury reached its end point, the artery and the skin covering it were knitting themselves back together. He blinked, forced his way past the bizarre and unsettling sequence of sensations, and readied a new attack.

A flurry of movement above them stopped him halfway through the motion. Felzeor swooped down upon Nyx to launch a vicious, multi-limbed attack of her face and head. Claws drew blood out of long, ragged gashes as she floundered to grab hold of her attacker.

As Felzeor's rear claws thrust in toward her eyes, a burst of *diati* flowed out from her in an expanding bubble, and the Volucri went tumbling end over end through the air to disappear into the darkness of the abundant foliage.

If she hurt him, she wouldn't merely be drained of power then die for a spell. She would suffer.

Nyx straightened up as Caleb closed to within a meter of her, and her furious, bloody glare turned macabre in the harsh, washed-out glow from the floodlights. How could he have ever seen his sister in her features?

"*Who* are you?"

"I'm the one who the *diati* obeys." He leapt forward and grabbed her by both wrists. *I welcome you. Join me.*

He was ready for the flood of power, ready to take command of it and direct it according to his will. But when it came he reeled nonetheless. For all his recent training, he was unable to keep from feeling as if he was about to burst apart from the inside.

Caleb gritted his teeth and focused on the enemy. "How many times must I take your power from you before you *stay down?*"

"More times than this." She closed her eyes tight, and a repulsive force flung them both through the air in opposite directions.

He landed hard on the ground, but he ignored the many twinges and at least one *crack*. The injuries they signaled would be gone by the time he stood.

He reached his knees in time to see her vanish from the far side of Thelkt's terrace, fleeing rather than surrender the rest of her power to him.

He took half a second to check his status. As expected, no trace of injury remained. He obviously hadn't taken all of her *diati* from her, yet it felt as if he'd taken *more* than the last time. He'd assumed all *diati* was equal, but this new influx seemed qualitatively different somehow, and he struggled to wrangle it under a modicum of control.

Caleb: "Alex?"

"Here." She materialized a few meters away mid-stride, quickly reached him and grasped his shoulders. Her eyes and hands roved over his body in concern.

He scowled at her. "You never run when I say to."

"Nope. You're bleeding."

"I *was* bleeding. I'm fine now."

Felzeor swooped in to circle them in excited loops. "What a spectacle!"

"You're okay? I was worried she'd hurt you."

"I am a resistance fighter. It takes more than a little *diati* swipe to fell me."

"Of course it does." He laughed weakly and motioned Felzeor to his shoulder. "Let's get back to the ship."

Alex continued to peer at him in concern. "Can you do it?"

A new squad of Machim soldiers rushed out from the main building and made a beeline toward them. "I'm pretty sure I have to. Felzeor, hold tight."

The Volucri's rear claws landed solidly on his shoulder once again, and he wrapped his arms around Alex and directed his intention on a point beyond sight.

THERE

When he opened his eyes, the walls of the *Siyane* had enveloped them.

He sank into the couch for a single dizzy breath, then looked around to find the cabin filled by Mesme, a tall Novoloume man and a bleeding Cosime. "Eren?"

Cosime shook her head. "No. Stupid show-off."

Alex sighed. "Again? All right. Valkyrie, let's get out of here."

'Departing the surface now. Prepare for atmospheric traversal beginning in fourteen seconds.'

Felzeor vaulted off his shoulder to flit between their guests. "Cosime, I've missed you so. Thelkt, are you uninjured?"

The Novoloume ruffled Felzeor's chocolate and apricot feathers with a cautious smile. "I am well, though I suspect the rescue was most timely."

"Good. I fretted. Have you met my friends, Caleb and Alex? And Valkyrie, too? They are quite the adventurous sort."

"I have not." He gently nudged Felzeor toward Cosime and dipped his chin in their direction. "Greetings. I am Thelkt Lonaervin, anarch spy for over a century and now, it appears, refugee. Thank you for the role you played in our rescue." He gazed in interest around the cabin. "So the whispers are true—Kats, SAIs and Humans have come to join with the anarchs in a quest to save us all."

Felzeor returned to Caleb's outstretched arm. The Volucri leaned in to nuzzle his beak against Caleb's nose while Caleb stroked his silken pelt. "What a grand quest it's sure to be."

11

SAGITTAE GATEWAY

MILKY WAY SECTOR 22

Moving even a reduced contingent of AEGIS vessels through a gateway proved a maddeningly slow affair. Measured in minutes, true, but they were maddeningly slow minutes.

The automated defenses at the gateways weren't much of a threat, but because the activations were monitored, they had only a small window of time before some sort of Machim force arrived at the origin gateway, then the destination one.

The portion of the fleet not participating in the mission moved to new staging coordinates simultaneously with their traversal, and the origin gateway would not be used again soon. Once the mission was complete, these forces would superluminal to the new coordinates as well. It would take time, but the time wouldn't be wasted. When they regrouped, she intended for the next mission profile to be ready to go.

It remained early days yet, but for now the cat-and-mouse strategy seemed a reliable one. Without a home base or territory to defend, it was also an efficient one.

Miriam idly wondered what the aliens situated on the accompanying Sagittae Arx thought of the fleet of warships of alien-to-them design emerging from the darkness to pass through the gateway. Did they know there was a war on before today? Did they know the inhabitants of the ships were on their side?

The anarchs' latest intel indicated the Directorate was publicly denying reports of any martial incident at the Provision Network Gateway, insisting the disappearance of the prominent structure resulted from the Eradication Order against the Katasketousya.

But the Directorate was not going to be able to deny AEGIS' presence in Amaranthe for much longer. Now they were allowing themselves to be *seen*. Word would spread.

The *Stalwart II* emerged from the destination gateway just as the first wave of vessels initiated their sLume sprint to the target. Rychen's dreadnought, the *EAS Virginia*, and its attached squadron were forming up ahead of her position in preparation for making the same sprint.

Sensors detected the presence of a substantial Machim formation a mere second before the enemy opened fire. Too many too quickly to have arrived after being alerted to the gateway traversal. They'd been here ahead of time, hidden and lying in wait.

Commandant Solovy (AFS Stalwart II): *"All ships, battle alert. Hostile forces engaged. Attack at will under engagement rules Charlie Delta. Rear forces, continue through the gateway and engage on arrival."*

The initial volley from the attackers was concentrated away from the gateway; presumably they didn't want to damage the colossal structure if they could avoid it.

Miriam wasn't concerned about the gateway—and all intel indicated it was quite sturdy regardless—but she did cast a troubled eye toward the Arx off their port, where tens of thousands of noncombatants resided.

Commandant Solovy (Stalwart II): *"Avoid firing on the Arx, and whenever possible act to protect the civilians inside. The gateway is a viable target, but get clear of it with all due speed to avoid collateral damage."*

She took a deep breath. "Thomas, I need numbers."

'Initial scans detect a substantial Machim force: 2,360 battlecruisers and 7,210 destroyers, plus an undetermined number of specialty craft and fighters.'

Nearly as many ships as they faced at the Provision Network Gateway—and she had brought far fewer. Any reinforcements she might call upon were now many parsecs away from the origin gateway and couldn't get here in time to make a difference. Worse, with the Arx inside the perimeter and an inhabited planet in the stellar system, Rifter usage became severely curtailed per the Charlie Delta engagement rules.

She'd been caught unawares, and her best tools were hamstrung or denied her altogether.

The *Stalwart II* swung up above and out from the gateway as the battle was joined. She squared her shoulders, internalized the reality of the current situation and worked to focus on the tools she could use—then she realized her people were already doing that for her.

The *SFS Medici* and Bastian's forces emerged from the wormhole firing the instant they reached normal space. The AEGIS 3rd Assault Brigade cloaked en masse, vanished for a moment, then reemerged behind the bulk of the Machim fleet. The concentration of fire diffused, taking some of the heat off of Rychen's forces.

Two Sabres' combined weaponry tore apart a Machim battlecruiser in a fiery explosion of energy and metal near the center of the evolving engagement zone. She should have brought more Sabres.

The bridge abruptly shuddered from the collision of laser fire against the shields, but the *Stalwart II's* defenses were the best in the fleet. The fire hadn't yet penetrated the shielding when another two Sabres shattered the attacking vessel, and she found herself glad she had brought as many of the glass cannons as she had.

Commander Lekkas (AFS MA-Primary): "Permission to saturate Quadrant Three with negative energy bombs?"

The hastily labeled tactical map designated Quadrant Three as the zone at the far edge of the engagement zone from the Arx.

Commandant Solovy (Stalwart II): "Granted. AEGIS 2nd and 3rd Assault, monitor your proximity to the designated zone."

The stealthed Eidolons forwent precision to sweep across the battlefield and deposit their payloads as swiftly as possible. Ten seconds later—dozens of destructions later—menacing obsidian explosions began cascading in a swelling void through the battlefield, effectively splitting it in two and taking out a wide swath of Machim warcraft. Thousands, perhaps.

A detonation flared thirty degrees to port in the aftermath. It only caught her eye because the color and texture of the pluming explosions were unlike those created by any of her ships or, so far as they'd seen, the Machim vessels.

*Commandant Solovy (*Stalwart II*)—Command Channel:* "Thomas, I need a report on the activity in the northwest corner of Quadrant One."

*Thomas (*Stalwart II*)—Command Channel: 'Machim fire impacted the Arx. Unclear whether it was the target. The damage appears significant but non-critical to the integrity of the structure.'*

*Admiral Rychen (*EAS Virginia*)—Command Channel:* "It looked deliberate enough from here. They're willing to fire on civilians just to cause a little collateral damage? Fuck those sadists."

*Admiral Rychen (*EAS Virginia*):* "EA 12th (NW) Regiment, take up defensive positions around the Arx. Make the enemy shoot us instead."

She frowned.

Christopher, what are you doing?

We came here to protect innocent people, aliens and all. We need to do it, and we need them to know we're doing it.

He wasn't wrong. She didn't know who might be on the Arx, but the vast majority of the inhabitants were not the enemy. Civilian deaths in war were inevitable, but after so many died in the Metigen War she didn't feel inclined to see more.

Further, the cold calculus of the propaganda side of warfare said that a bold defense of helpless civilians made a powerful impression, should those civilians survive the day to tell the tale.

R

The Machim forces continued to execute on their predictable tactics, and her ships readily took advantage of this weakness the enemy displayed. AEGIS arrived outnumbered, but with adiamene hulls, creative maneuvering and arcalasers that made their wielders difficult to track even when not cloaked, they took out five Machim vessels for every AEGIS ship that fell.

The numbers evened out, then tipped in their favor, and Miriam breathed a silent sigh of relief. They had not come prepared, and it had almost been a disaster. Properly chastised, she would learn from the mistake, be grateful the cost wasn't higher and—

Thomas (Stalwart II): *'Eight Igni missiles launched from two enemy battlecruisers. Target is...the Arx.'*

Commandant Solovy (Stalwart II): *"Virginia, all vessels, get clear of the Arx!"*

A massive blast roiled short of the Arx as a Federation frigate sacrificed itself by accelerating into the path of one of the missiles. A second missile impacted the *AFS Montreal* less than half a megameter from the Arx. The remaining six impacted the Arx directly.

Explosions rippled as the deadly antimatter weapons ripped apart nearly three megatonnes of habitat-grade material, feeding on themselves and the wreckage created to billow outward and consume nearby vessels and debris in a self-propagating chain reaction.

Visuals were impossible, so Miriam hurriedly called up broad spectrum scans in an attempt to determine what remained amongst the destruction. But by the time she was able to gain that information...nothing remained. The collision of matter and antimatter had annihilated everything it touched.

The Arx.

The more than ten thousand civilians occupying it.

An entire EA regiment's worth of vessels and their crews.

The *EAS Virginia* and its 23,819 crew members, including Christopher Rychen.

Gone.

PART III:

TRANSCENDENTAL DISARRAY

"War is not its own end, except in some catastrophic slide into absolute damnation. It's peace that's wanted. Some better peace than the one you started with."

— Lois McMaster Bujold

12

AFS STALWART II

T he transport docked on a *Stalwart II* in the throes of distress, caught somewhere between shock and desolation.

Malcolm had assured Mia their efforts in Amaranthe were going well, but while he was away retrieving her something had clearly gone awry. What that 'something' could be wasn't apparent in the early minutes of their approach and docking, and as soon as they disembarked Malcolm left her with a security officer and an apology before hurrying off to learn the nature and extent of the calamity.

Mia put considerable effort into not coming off as bewildered or needy while the distracted security officer tried to find a deck worker to offload her belongings from the cargo hold of the transport and tag them so they'd eventually wind up wherever she did. She hadn't brought much: a single valise of clothes and personals, the emergency gear bag she'd kept packed, updated and ready ever since the Metigen invasion, and a small case containing Meno's core quantum orbs and associated hardware. But two of the three were quite valuable, so she tracked their status until they disappeared up a service lift.

The security officer escorted her out of the hangar and to a meeting room several decks up, then disappeared as well.

Once the door closed behind him, she surveyed her surroundings. The room included a kitchen unit and a comfortable chair next to it, in addition to the expected conference table and its complement of stiffer chairs. Her belongings were stacked in a corner.

They didn't know what to do with her yet.

She exhaled slowly. Then she dropped her shoulder bag in the corner with the rest of her stuff, fixed herself a coffee, and settled into the cozier chair to review the extensive briefing package she'd been provided.

ℛ

Alex tossed a brief wave in Mia's direction as the woman followed a security officer onto the lift, but she didn't stop to chat on her way to the transport.

She met Kennedy at the bottom of the ramp with an enthusiastic hug. "Thank you so much for coming. I'm sorry I couldn't invite you in person. There were factors, and I needed to be here."

"No doubt. It sounds like you all have half a dozen problems and at least as many new ideas to implement. So I'm here. And bonus, I brought another 3,200 warships with me."

"Good, because apparently we lost 2,734 today."

"What?"

"It's a war story I don't have the details of yet, but suffice it to say today's AEGIS mission did not go well. Also, the anarchs are being hunted, tortured and killed by the Directorate on multiple fronts. Welcome to Amaranthe?"

"Thanks?"

Alex laughed wryly. "You bet. I wouldn't want you to miss out on the show."

"If the show turns out to be a horror vid, *I* might want to miss it."

"Nah. We'll straighten things out. And you're going to help make it happen."

Kennedy winced. "I can't promise how much help I'll be, but I'm told volleying questions and answers back and forth between universes isn't a viable plan."

"Yeah, we're severely restricting portal traversals. We can't allow the enemy to discover any of the portals, so they have to be moved after every use, and it's a genuine ordeal for the Kats—Katasketousya—Metigens—to move them."

"'We'? Are you in charge now?"

Alex grimaced. "Hell if I know. Mom's definitely in charge, but she's sort of including me in decisions, seeking me out for advice...it's surreal. Much like everything else here. Prepare to be weirded out on a regular basis."

"I'm ready. Show me some aliens."

"There aren't actually any aliens on the ship at present. Soon. If Mia can silver-tongue the anarchs into playing nice, you'll be surrounded by aliens before you know it. For now, I got you a room onboard here. Well, a bunk with a door."

She peered past Kennedy's shoulder as Noah arrived, three bags in tow. "It's almost a double bunk? I'm sure you won't mind the coziness at night. But all the ships are getting a little crowded, I'm afraid, mostly due to the fact the fleet doesn't have anywhere to land. I'd ask you two to stay on the *Siyane*, but we tend to move around a lot. And get shot at, also a lot."

"Doesn't the *Stalwart II* get shot at, too?"

"Yes, but it's...um, it tries to stay near the rear of battles? The better to command or whatever? Besides, you know full well it's damn near indestructible."

Kennedy gave her a skeptical look as she accepted one of the bags from Noah and slung it over her free shoulder. "True. Sounds exciting."

"That's one word for it." Alex offered Noah a nod in greeting. "Caleb's not here. He's getting a couple of anarchs we rescued home safely. He'll be back soon, though, and I'll tell him you've arrived. Did I mention it's weird here at the moment?"

Noah considered the activity across the hanger with a dubious expression. "I'm getting that feeling. Comms don't work here?"

She made a prevaricating gesture. "There's no exanet, but direct comms—pulses and livecomms anyway—still work. AEGIS has constructed a new messaging system, but we'll need to get you added to the directory. And if you talk to..." she glanced around, trying to find the staff sergeant amid all the running in circles and gnashing of teeth "...*that* guy, he can show you to your room."

Noah shrugged, leaned in and kissed Kennedy on the temple, then strode off.

"If you want to go with him and get settled in, it'll be a few hours—"

Kennedy shook her head. "Before we end up surrounded by people and duties take over...." She dropped the larger bag on the floor and dug into her shoulder bag. After rummaging around for a second, she produced a smoky onyx cube about eight centimeters wide. She held it out for Alex to take.

Alex's brow furrowed as she accepted it. She rotated it in her hands. The exterior seemed to be a protective casing, so she located the tiny seam lining one face and started to open it.

Kennedy reached out and laid a hand on her arm. "Not here. We should take it to the *Siyane*."

"We can't. Caleb has the *Siyane* right now. What is it?"

"What do you *think* it is?"

Alex stared at the cube again, then back at Kennedy. As the possible and only and inevitable answer blossomed in her mind, her pulse increased so rapidly a surge of dizziness threatened to buckle her knees.

She tried to clear a lump from her throat; even so, her voice came out raspy. "Really?"

"Really."

"Tell me everything."

R

Immersed in the baffling, convoluted world of Amaranthe, Mia had lost track of the passing time when the door opened and Caleb walked in.

"There you are."

She leapt up and met him halfway with a quick embrace. Next she stepped away to study him, for it had been several months since he'd left for Amaranthe.

His clothes were rumpled and dirty—no, bloody. It meant he'd come straight here from some harrowing venture. The crimson highlights in his irises had increased to the point they would be disconcerting without the familiar warmth of his countenance.

He otherwise didn't look any different, other than his hair having grown out again, enough for it to match the unkempt state of his clothes. But he *was* different, albeit in ways she sensed rather than saw. Was the *diati* changing him, or was Amaranthe? Perhaps it was, more fundamentally, the trial by fire that seemed to follow him from universe to universe which was transforming him.

But his smile was the same as it had been for the last fourteen years, and she mirrored it. "I had better not find out you're responsible for me being here."

"I'm not, but I won't lie and say I'm not glad you *are* here. Sorry I missed your arrival. I had to drop off a couple of anarchs somewhere safe. How's home?"

"Changing quickly—but changing peacefully. Thus far. Hopefully it'll hold while I'm gone. So what's happened? Everyone's fretting and scrambling about looking grave, and they're all too busy to talk to me."

"I've only just now gotten the details myself, but apparently we got our asses royally kicked at one of the wormhole gateways a few hours ago. A sizeable Machim force was hiding nearby, and they were waiting for us when our fleet came through. We lost a lot of people and a fair number of ships, including the *Virginia*."

She called up the ship's info. "Admiral Rychen?"

"Didn't make it. No one from the *Virginia* did. It was vaporized by antimatter missiles, along with an entire Arx—a massive space station paired to a wormhole gateway—filled with almost eleven thousand civilians. The Machim are ruthless bastards when it comes to warfare."

"Damn." Her first thought was of Malcolm. He was going to take Rychen's death hard—was surely already taking it hard, yet powering ahead nonetheless, not daring to show any vulnerability to his peers or subordinates.

Her second thought was of how the defeat might complicate her ostensible purpose here. Unless played perfectly, negotiating from a position of weakness rarely won the desired results. "I feel weird asking this, but is there anything else? I suspect everything I've learned in the last day is now outdated."

Caleb dragged a hand down his face. He scowled at the dirt and blood it came away with, then went over to the kitchen unit and splashed water from the sink on his face. "Vigil—the Directorate's security force—has launched an extensive sweep in search of anarch spies, locking down facilities and interrogating everyone caught in the lockdowns using the unpleasant tools at their disposal. Anarch agents are trained to suicide if caught. Many of their agents aren't Anaden and can't use regenesis, so it's safe to say they're losing people left and right."

Marginally cleaned up, he returned to prop on the edge of the conference table. "Alex and I rescued a few of their agents caught in the sweep, but the group doesn't have the resources to rescue anywhere close to all of its people. So, I'm afraid things are a bit of a disaster currently. I'm sorry you had to arrive in the middle of all this chaos."

"Don't be. It's hardly your fault." The anarchs were taking hits, too, which meant AEGIS wasn't in as disadvantaged a position as she'd feared. It also meant the anarchs may have less to offer AEGIS.

She sank back against the table next to him. "I do have to wonder, though, what this means for me. I'm not trying to be selfish, but I don't want to be in the way, or shirk my responsibilities at home if I can't do any good here. If the situation's changed so drastically, does anyone genuinely need me here now?"

He shook his head. "On the contrary, your arrival is most timely. I think you're about to be needed more than ever. It'll take a few hours for the triage to take effect, but Miriam will have order restored soon. Once she does, get ready to be thrown into the deep end."

Mia rolled her eyes gamely. "All right. I've been trying to get up to speed, but the trip was short and the information voluminous, so I'm not there yet."

"Believe me, I understand. It took us weeks to begin to grasp the nonsensical nature of this place, and every day brings new surprises still.

"I'd say to concentrate on the information covering the anarchs first. It'll be up to Miriam, but odds are she'll want to get you an audience with Nisi, their leader, ASAP. In the long run, they need us, far more than they've been willing to admit. But right now, the truth is we need them."

She mentally added the new nuances to the growing web of information—history, dossiers, leadership structures, needs, goals and weaknesses—that would inform her work. "Politicians I can do. Underneath their bluster, pomp and ego, most are entirely predictable."

"Not this one."

13

SOLUM

Nyx again found herself at the heights of Praesidis Command, again summoned for an audience with her Primor. Such was the way of these things. All came to him, he never to them.

The immensity of his power meant he could travel anywhere at any time without concern or consequence. She was certain he in fact did so often, but always on his own time and initiative. He would not be summoned.

She was proud to interact so closely with her Primor, confident in her prerogative to do so and humbled to fall ever short of his lofty example. But the Praesidis Dynasty valued strength—of conviction, of will, of rightness—so she held her head high and strode with assurance as she entered. She'd shown weakness in their previous meeting, ever so briefly. He had indulged her in light of the extreme circumstances, but she was not fool enough to presume he would be so forgiving of further lapses.

The Primor emerged out of his integral sphere facing her. "Nyx, my dear. Please, join me."

She bowed in greeting then trailed him as the far wall dissolved and the brisk winter air whipped in. A star-soaked night above an endless, perpetually lit city stretched out before them.

"You uncovered an anarch spy working for Avdei elasson-Idoni."

"Yes, sir. The anarch had operated right under the nose of the *elasson* for decades." She paused. "I assume Avdei will be sanctioned appropriately?"

"The Idoni Primor has been made aware."

And that was all there was to be done, wasn't it? She took a small degree of pleasure from the idea the *elasson* might be humiliated or even suffer a distasteful punishment for his negligence, but disciplinary matters were strictly a Dynasty affair—no exceptions. As such, the matter was now out of her hands, and out of her Primor's.

"Thank you, sir. I regret to say the agent in question escaped, however, with the assistance of other anarchs who infiltrated the Vigil lockdown. Several of the Humans accompanied them."

"Including your mysterious foe from Helix Retention."

"Yes, Primor."

"He defeated you a second time."

She smarted, despite the fact that she'd walked into the meeting expecting the rebuke. She wanted to say no, but she recognized the reality of the encounter. To the extent 'no' was accurate, it was solely because she had fled before he could do so.

Instead she spoke the truth, unadorned by subjective commentary. "The *diati* obeys him."

"The *diati* obeys its wielder, of which I thought you to be one. Yet he stole it from you once again."

She should be ashamed—she should fall to her knees and beg for his mercy—but she knew what she'd seen and experienced. The Praesidis Dynasty valued strength—of conviction, of will, of rightness—but as the investigators, hunters and judges of Amaranthe, its members also valued facts.

"Sir—Father—I cannot yet explain why it is so, and I can hardly commit the experience to words that will properly describe it, but I believe this man is not stealing the *diati*. It is choosing to go to him. For it is not merely the *diati* he possesses that obeys him, but any *diati* he comes into contact with, from any Praesidis."

"Absurd. The *diati* has served us for a million uninterrupted years. It will not, it cannot, willingly abandon us for some primitive interloper."

"I know it should not be. But this is what I have experienced, twice now. This is what my instincts and observations tell me is true.

In addition, he wields it with the skill of an Inquisitor—increasingly so in this recent clash. It obeys him without the slightest resistance, even when it is not under his direct control. Furthermore, I believe he understands precisely what this means and how to use it to his advantage. I fear we are confronted with a very skilled and formidable adversary."

"You tread on dangerous grounds, Nyx. Be careful."

This response surprised her. For a Praesidis, the truth was never heresy. Did he imagine her to be lying? To be exaggerating to save face? Had her earlier display of weakness damaged his estimation of her more than she'd realized?

She squared her shoulders; she could win back his trust only by being what she was: an *elasson* Praesidis Inquisitor, and all it meant to be so. If he had doubts, she would assuage them. "Look into my mind, Father. See what I saw. Feel what I felt. I do not misrepresent."

He spun on her, eyes and aura flared, and she fell into darkness for a time.

14

CHIONIS

Eren's new bones ached. His new muscles protested every movement. His brand-new body felt decrepit, like an ill-fitting covering stitched slapdash over his consciousness.

This was wholly illogical, of course. Which meant it was all in his head, and what actually felt decrepit was *him*. At barely three hundred years young, he was stretched and worn. Frayed.

He really needed to lighten up on the regenesis.

But he'd thought the same thing the last time, too. And the time before the last time. So should he have let the Inquisitor kill Cosime and Thelkt before Mesme was able to spirit them away? This suicidal ploy had been as necessary as all the rest of them. Well, most of the rest. Some of the rest.

The point *was*, sacrificing a body was a sacrifice he could make, when Cosime could not. Thelkt and Felzeor and Caleb and Alex and so many others could not, but he *could*.

Plus, it transformed what was arguably restive angst into heroism. It made him a celebrity among the anarchs and a villain among Vigil and the Directorate.

His step buoyed, invigorated by the pep talk he'd delivered to himself.

As such, he was halfway through the swirl of white-blue lights before he realized a Kat had materialized in front of him in the hallway.

He jerked to a stop then hurriedly stepped *out* of the swirl. "Mesme?"

I made you a promise before we breached Helix Retention. If you wish, I will honor it now.

"Right now? Your timing is mighty peculiar."

My timing is what circumstances dictate it must be. If you no longer desire to know the Faneros' fate, I have a number of more urgent tasks in need of performing.

Damn, the Kat was even crankier now than it had been on Serifos…because the viciousness of war didn't sit well with creatures of the Kats' nature. The insight meant at least he understood the behavior now.

"No, it's not that I don't want to know. It's only…I kind of just woke up." He slapped his left cheek, then his right. "Okay, I'm good now. Tell me."

I have already told you that many of the Faneros yet live. I propose to show you how they do so.

Show him? Hades knew he hadn't expected that to be an option. Was he ready to see the creatures—to have them elevated to more than a memory and become breathing, moving, *living* beings? Would it bring him comfort and closure, or tear open a raw wound of guilt and shame to bleed all over his new clothes?

He blinked in surprise, which probably shouldn't have occurred. Over a century ago, the events of that party-turned-nightmare where he'd encountered two of the captured Faneros had ultimately led to him severing his connection to the Idoni integral and becoming an anarch. But, yes, he nonetheless harbored deep *shame* over his role, aborted though it had been, in the abuse of the helpless aliens.

Had he ever admitted that, even to himself? Had he ever acknowledged that his derision toward the Idoni Dynasty was in part deflected disgust at himself?

He sank against the wall as a different manner of weariness descended upon him.

Eren? What is your decision?

He gazed at the shifting, amorphous lights in resignation. "All right. Take me wherever you want."

⟁

They landed in the main cabin—or possibly sole cabin—of a ship. Smaller than the *Siyane*, its design was unlike any he'd seen, and rather dramatically so. The hull was almost entirely translucent, creating a vivid sensation of standing in space. There was no furniture to speak of, only a couple of smooth, outwardly blank fixtures. A pattern of mysterious symbols was etched onto a frosted panel at what should be the cockpit. Were they flight controls and sensor readings displayed in the Kats' native language? Wisps of nebulous white-blue light beneath and behind the cabin could be evidence of a propulsion drive.

Eren breathed in…which in and of itself was an interesting occurrence, given his surroundings. "Why does your ship have a life support system? You don't need to breathe."

I also don't particularly need a ship, not for myself alone. You are not the first organic being to stand inside it.

"I'm sure. Still, it has your style about it. I don't think it's purely utilitarian."

There are times when all of us welcome the succor of walls enclosing us.

"Barely," he muttered as he approached the maybe-cockpit and peered out. "Where are we headed?"

The Mosaic.

"Where the Humans come from?"

No. Which is to say, yes. The Humans' home does reside within the Mosaic, but this is not our destination. The Mosaic is home to many species.

"And a replacement home for others."

Indeed. You have been playing closer attention than you give the impression of, Eren asi-Idoni.

"I'm sneaky that way. You Kats genuinely have been busy, haven't you, and for a long time? You should have told us—told the anarchs."

In retrospect, perhaps. It matters not, for now you do know. We move forward.

He chuckled. "You sound like Miaon."

The Yinhe's perspective has much in common with our own.

"Only Miaon, or all the Yinhe? Or is there truly only a single Yinhe?"

You must ask this of Miaon. It is not for me to say.

"Fine, keep its secrets if you want." His jaw dropped as an enormous portal sprung to life out of the nothingness in front of them. Glacier blue plasma rippled and sparked across the interior of the ring demarcating it. "It seems keeping secrets is what you do."

Secrets are merely the necessary means. Survival is the end goal. Survival of ourselves, survival of species who do not deserve to be eradicated from the universe. Survival of the universe itself.

"Survival's noble and all, but what good is it without the freedom to live as you choose?"

A question you have the luxury to ask because you survive.

He opened his mouth to retort...but it was a decent point. He didn't agree that survival was the end—freedom was the end—but he supposed it was a necessary stop along the way.

MOSAIC

ENISLE FOUR

They traveled through the portal, then through multiple smaller portals. Each one vanished as soon as they traversed it. If Mesme decided to leave him out here, he was fucked.

Finally stars greeted them on a traversal, and he relaxed a little. He'd never appreciated how claustrophobic featureless black void could be.

"Are the stars real, or just window dressing?"

What would be the point of them if they were not real?

"So you created thousands of authentic, functioning astronomical stars simply so the Faneros would feel like they lived in a real place?"

No. We did it so they would *live in a real place.*

Eren rubbed at his temples. Every time he thought he was getting a handle on what made the Kat tick, it tossed out an offhand comment hinting at undiscovered depths of motivation and nuances of outlook. Maddening creature.

The symbols on the front panel pulsed, faded and lit up anew as a planet came into view. It had a washed-out appearance, all whites and grays with sparse hints of pale mauve and lavender. Its sun remained distant, hardly brighter than the canopy of stars.

When the ship began descending through the atmosphere, he glanced at Mesme in increasing anxiousness. "We're going down there?"

To observe. Not to interact. They are aware of the Katasketousya's existence and role in their rescue. However, we keep interaction to a minimum, as it brings with it...complications.

This he did not doubt. He exhaled in relief at the reassurance he wouldn't be expected to look them in the haunting reflections of their eyes. Godsdamned mirrors to the soul.

The atmospheric haze thinned to reveal a settlement cut into and built up from a vast plain. The planet's surface was marble, and so were the structures. This wasn't to say they were crude; on the contrary, the broad, airy buildings were quite lovely and occasionally exquisite. Quartz and more rarely glittering crystal embellished long stretches of whorled white marble to create teases of brilliance upon the lustered backdrop.

He felt his mood improving in the face of the peaceful scene. "I bet it's gorgeous in the daytime."

This is daytime.

"What?" The sky resembled dusk at best, with a blanket of shadowy blue-gray forming a presage of true darkness.

What you see is as much daylight as their planet experiences. This is why their skin is translucent—to maximize utilization of the limited radiant energy that reaches them.

"But they were..." he shook his head roughly as memory swelled up out of hidden places and threatened to consume him "...their skin was almost hot to the touch."

Unsurprising. They are required to use a portion of the radiant energy absorbed for thermoregulation.

Mesme continued descending until they were scant tens of meters above the surface. Faneros moved to and fro, interacting and working in what resembled productive endeavors. They wore elegant, shimmery clothing cinched with satiny threads and decorated with jeweled baubles.

"They can't see us?"

We are well-cloaked.

Emboldened, Eren pressed into the viewport, hands splayed as if he might reach out and touch one, confirming its skin was as warm and pliant as he remembered—

> *Warm skin met his fingertips, as softly pliant as a silken cushion at the end of a long night. His hand traveled up the tantalizing curve of the creature's neck, and it began to tremble beneath his touch.*
>
> *Someone laughed behind him. Uneven, drunken footsteps echoed nearby.*
>
> *He looked up to meet eyes of pure molten silver, wide enough to swallow him whole. He fell into their bottomless pools and came face to face with fear.*

Eren wrenched away from the viewport and stumbled backwards down the span of the cabin, finally reaching the rear wall to fall against it and sink to the floor. He choked back acid in his throat that threatened to become vomit and breathed through his nose, trying to bury the revulsion deep in his gut where it could choose to simmer or burn away.

Eren, you are not well?

He hugged his knees to his chest. So close beneath the floor Faneros glided across their sea of marble, blissfully unaware of the predator hovering above them. In this transparent ship, there was no escaping their devastating innocence.

Squeezing his eyes shut only made things worse, as memory projected itself onto the canvas of his eyelids. No escape. Not for wretched souls like him.

"Take me home."

You do not desire to observe the inhabitants any further?

"*Arae anathema*, I said take me home!"

As you wish.

15

AFS STALWART II

MILKY WAY SECTOR 53

Malcolm stopped outside the door to the conference room on Deck 4. The hall around him was empty, and in the fleeting silence he pinched the bridge of his nose and squeezed his eyes shut—then squared his shoulders and plastered on a pleasant expression as he opened the door.

Mia was sitting at the far end of the room, situated comfortably in the depths of the cushioned chair by the kitchen unit, sipping on a drink and studying an aural. But as he walked in she blinked, banished the aural and stood, an enchanting smile crossing her lips before it was replaced by a concerned gaze.

"I apologize for the delay, and for running out on you. And for leaving you alone for so long."

She started moving toward him, though he was coming to her. "No, it's not a problem. I heard about Rychen. I'm so sorry."

He nodded with the measured solemnity he'd perfected over the previous hours. "We'll talk about it once we get you settled. For now, I've arranged for you to stay in one of the nicer—"

She reached him and drew him into her arms.

He resisted for a split-second. He'd had this whole routine planned, built around trying to do right by her seeing as he'd dumped her into what was now a dark, desperate mess. But her embrace felt so damn warm and comforting, and his stiff bearing promptly melted away.

He'd thrown so much energy into maintaining a brave, stoic front for everyone else...he'd forgotten too easily that he could relax around her. That he should, lest she swiftly call him on it.

Tension began to seep away as he dropped his forehead to rest against hers. "Thank you. This helps."

"There's more where this came from."

"I know. But not here." He straightened up with an apologetic grimace. "Let me take you to your room, which will be somewhat more private. Not more soundproof, but...."

She winced at his pathetic attempt at risqué banter, then turned around and went to pick up her bags. He hurried over and grabbed them before she could—and now his hands were full, so he had to motion toward the door with a jerk of his head.

He offered acknowledgments to the crew members they passed. To a one they displayed the grim, hardened demeanor of seasoned soldiers dealt a blow. The mood in the passageways was somber, but it was nevertheless gradually returning to the purposeful activity that had been the norm until today.

Mia followed him quietly, but he knew better than to think she wasn't soaking up the atmosphere and noting every little detail she encountered. And watching him. He still wanted to put on a reassuring, confident front for her; he felt guilty for having dragged her away from her home and job into the middle of a war in an alien universe—a war now going badly—and didn't want to make it yet harder for her. But he was tired.

The *Stalwart II* was a big ship. It took a while, but finally they reached her cabin. He again used his head to motion her inside, then followed her and let the door shut behind them. "I realize it's not much. Hopefully it'll be temporary and—"

"It's fine." She took her belongings from him one by one and set them by the wall, then coaxed him onto the edge of the bunk beside her. She brought a hand up to his face. "Okay, we're in private now. You can let out the breath you've been holding."

"I haven't been...." On receiving a stern glare in response, he relented and did exactly as she'd advised, exhaling until there was nothing left for him to hold inside. Finally he drew in what he hoped was a more optimistic breath. "It's tough out there right now. But we'll bounce back."

"Of course you will. But that's tomorrow, and this is now. Tell me what you're thinking."

His gaze fell to the floor. "I can't help but wonder whether if I'd been there...." *I could have intercepted the missiles. Saved the* Virginia. *I'd be dead, but it's my job, isn't it? Maybe I could have....*

"I've heard you're pretty crafty on the battlefield, no doubt. But understanding what I do about AEGIS, and all these ships and officers and Prevos and tech and weapons and shields the organization has at its disposal? It seems to me you have to travel a very long way indeed to get to a place where you're to blame for Rychen's death."

"I know. It's just...we're looking at almost twenty-four thousand dead on the *Virginia* alone. They're estimating another three thousand lost across the fleet, before you start counting all the aliens who died on the Sagittae Arx. This is a blow, no matter where the blame lies."

"It is. I'm sorry." She leaned in and kissed his temple, then rested her head on his shoulder.

He resisted her attempts to ease his burden, though. The comfort of understanding and empathy was welcome, but it couldn't erase the loss. Nor should it. They had to own the defeat and its consequences. "What kind of commander orders the murder of eleven thousand civilians merely to take out a couple of enemy ships?"

"We know the Machim consider their own soldiers expendable. Maybe it ought not to be a surprise that they view civilians the same way."

"The soldiers will wake back up in pods somewhere. But many of those on the Arx weren't Anaden. They're dead for good, and alien or not, their lives still had value. But not to the Machim commander. Which presumably means also not to the Machim Primor, and not to the Directorate."

"Ultimately, this is the crux of why you're fighting, isn't it? They came after us, and they've destroyed so many others, because they don't value any life other than their own."

"It is, which is why this will end up being a galvanizing event. We'll fight harder because of the tragedy. But not today." He hugged her closer. "It's not fair of me to feel this way, but I'm really glad you're here."

"So am I." She settled deeper into his arms—and abruptly straightened up. "Message from Thomas. Miriam wants to meet with me in twenty minutes." The look she gave him conveyed too many sentiments to be readable. "Time to go to work."

16

SIYANE

Alex recognized the setting the instant she entered the virtual space.

Her father had taken her to Camp Muir often when she was growing up, once she was old enough to make the first segments of the Mount Rainier climb. She had returned there multiple times after his death...in tribute, to be closer to her memory of him, and occasionally to torture herself.

Regardless, it was a perfect choice on Vii's part, and the fact that the Artificial had chosen it eased any lingering doubts Alex had about whether she'd made the right decision in entrusting this precious treasure to Vii.

Her father sat on the ledge overlooking Columbia Crest. But as she began approaching, he sensed her presence and leapt up to turn and face her.

Because she'd witnessed the consequential final minutes of his life on the bridge of the *EAS Stalwart* when she was on Portal Prime—because she'd had his voice in her head mere months earlier—she'd thought she was ready for this. She'd thought she was ready to see him alive and in the virtual flesh.

She might have been wrong.

He looked a little older than in the fateful scene on the *Stalwart*. Since this was his own chosen representation of himself, it seemed an acknowledgment if not an admission of the decades that had passed. But the expressiveness of his face, the vivacity in his eyes, the natural movement of his body? It was all a perfect match.

A thousand memories flashed through her mind in the second it took for his gaze to fall upon her. Then a luminous smile broke across his face, and she nearly lost it.

"Alex. *Bozhe moy*, look at you. So grown up—of course you are. I know you are. But to see you...."

She closed the distance and sank into his embrace. Her breath caught in her throat; she could *feel* him. Warm skin, muscles creating a gentle grasp, heart beating. It was virtual, but here it was real. Here her father, lost for nearly twenty-five years, was hugging her and whispering in her ear Russian endearments she hadn't heard since she was a child.

She drew back, wiping tears off her cheeks with her hand. She wanted to be able to see him.

"Oh, *milaya*, no. Don't be sad."

She gave him a shaky smile in return. "It's not sadness, Dad. It's joy."

"If you're sure. One can easily be mistaken for the other, especially in circumstances like these."

"There have never *been* circumstances like these." She glanced around. "But this is brilliantly rendered. Vii did a terrific job."

"She did. She took exceptional care of me, while humoring even my most egregious petulances."

Alex laughed. Had she forgotten his clever eloquence? "How do you feel?"

He squeezed her hands tight, then let them drop and motioned her toward the ledge. "How does one begin to answer that question? I feel like myself, or at least how I remember myself feeling. Memory is such a fragile, nebulous thing, yet more than any other aspect, it defines us. We are what we remember."

The air was crisp and cold, and she pulled the collar of her fleece up to her chin before joining him to sit and dangle her feet off the ledge. "And what is it you remember?"

"All the details of my life, I think, which is what makes me feel like myself. Up here." He tapped a fingertip to his temple. "Do you know what I remember most vividly? I can recall cooking Sunday breakfast for you and your mother as if it were yesterday—because for me it *was* yesterday. But since yesterday, decades of history have intervened, and all that history is jammed up together in my head.

Knowing this avalanche of events occurred but not being there to experience them then cast my own veneer on the memory of them...."

He shook his head roughly. "But it's not important. An artifact of my unique situation, nothing else. You want to know if Vii did her job or if you need to box me up again."

"No! That's not what—"

He touched her arm. "It's okay, Alex. You did the right thing. Don't doubt it." He stared at her for several seconds, and his features took on an almost whimsical flavor. "Forgive me. I look at you, and I see a skinny little girl with messy pigtails and skinned knees, bursting with energy, curiosity and grand dreams—and a smart mouth. Now you're this remarkable woman."

"I still have the smart mouth."

"No doubt. But you are everything I imagined you would become and so much more. I believed you would change the galaxy, but you've changed the universe. All the universes."

She must be blushing; his praise had always made her blush. Still, she rolled her eyes in an attempt to make light of it. "I learned how from you."

"Now you're pandering, dear."

She jabbed him playfully on the shoulder. "Take the compliment, Dad."

He made this face—half chagrin, half exasperation, half amusement—and it looked *exactly* how she remembered. No algorithm was capable of recreating such an expression. It came from who he was, animated by the whole of his character.

In that instant, she was convinced.

But possibly he wasn't, for in the brief lull, he seemed to grow troubled. His gaze fell away from her to settle on the vista. "Do you think I'm real? I believe I...exist now, but maybe what exists is just a copy who looks and walks and talks like a dead man."

The stark words, stripped of ornamentation and delivered in a bare, matter-of-fact tone, hit her as brutally as a punch to the gut.

When she didn't respond, he took her hand once more. "It's all right. You should be honest. I can weather the blow."

She was not the best person to consult on the big metaphysical questions. Certainly she had never thought herself to be. But he was asking her, and her answer mattered.

She'd encountered such an incredible diversity of life this last year while traveling in the Mosaic and Amaranthe. A lot of the life she'd seen had been manufactured, designed, at times even sculpted to specifications. Did its origins make it any less alive? Were Pinchu and the Khokteh not really *alive* simply because the Kats had engineered them into existence? Of course not—she'd risked her own life defending their right to exist, and it had been the right choice. Was Akeso not really *alive* simply because its consciousness took on a form radically different from her own?

Of course not.

So she exhaled somberly and tried. "I think...if your soul did persist after you died, if that's a thing that *happens*, then it would have chosen to wander among the stars—which is exactly where the first spark of you was reborn. What if your soul found its way to the echo of itself imprinted onto mine and Valkyrie's minds? What if in doing so it saw an opportunity for another chance at life? I'm willing to take it on..." she blinked "...*faith* that it did, if you are."

He remained silent for a moment, until a smile gradually blossomed. "I like it. It's poetic and delivers proper dramatic flair. So we'll go with it."

Going with it was the most either of them could do, honestly. Her own mood grew serious now. She was in some respects still responsible for him. But, convinced he was real and whole, she no longer had the right to make the big decisions for him, did she?

"What do you want to do? I realize it's an impossible question with limited choices and no ideal answers, but we need to grapple with it anyway, don't we?"

"Leave it to the wanderer to assume I can't just stay here camping in the mountains forever."

"You can't. You've come so far, there is no way you're stopping here." Her throat worked unevenly. "Do you want me to tell Mom? Using an external interface and a tweaked ware routine for her eVi, she could come here, too." She reached out and clasped his shoulder with sudden fervor. "Dad, I can *touch* you. She could come here, and she could do the same."

He turned away, but not before she saw the tumult in his suddenly glistening eyes. "You cannot imagine how happy that would make me...and how sad. Once she was here, I don't know if I would be able to bear having her leave, and she would have to leave. No. I don't relish asking you to continue keeping this secret from her, but I would be a terrible distraction, and she must focus on her mission. She can't be constantly running off to keep me company in a virtual simulation when she's needed out there, leading the fight to save everyone. How can I intrude on such a noble cause?"

"Dad—"

"It's so tempting to be the dashing, glib gentleman I once was and sweep in with aplomb and panache. But the truth is I'd be barging in for my own selfish reasons—especially given I can't actually barge in anywhere real. My presence here would throw her world into chaos right when she needs to be at her best and most focused. What kind of husband would it make me if I did such a thing?"

"One she loves."

"I didn't expect you to be a romantic, *milaya*. Caleb has clearly muddled your senses. It's been twenty-five years, and I left her without hope for me. I should not exist, now or ever again, and she has surely made peace with that reality."

"But you *do* exist. You said it—I've changed whole universes. Who says I can't change your future in them, too?"

His arm wound around her shoulder, and he drew her closer. His expression brightened, she suspected because he willed it so. "That's my girl. Maybe you can, but first you have to *save* some universes. You go, get out there and do what you do. Help your mother do what she does, and I'll be fine here for now. Time passes slowly in this place by default, but I'll speed it up so I don't become maudlin. You go now, and I'll see you again in hardly a minute."

She wanted to stay. She wanted to bring Caleb here and watch them share stories by the campfire. She wanted to bring her mother here and alter the trajectory of her life. But her dad was right—she needed to go.

Because she had an idea.

17

ANARCH POST SATUS

LOCATION UNKNOWN

Mia began her step on a cold, rocky and forbidding planet, continued it through a mysterious, rippling mirror and completed it with her foot landing on the cushioned flooring of a well-appointed room that might be halfway across the galaxy or in another galaxy entirely.

The experience should have been far more disorienting than it was. But when everything in your life was odd, nothing was.

An alien stood a few meters into the room. Its gaze was locked on them in a way that implied it had been waiting for them to arrive. Sable fur covered the alien's skin where fitted clothing did not. It stood upright to nearly her height, but its long, curved spine suggested it didn't always. Piercing amber irises regarded her keenly while an upper lip curled into what looked like a snarl.

Mia glanced hurriedly at Caleb, but he motioned to the alien. "Volya, this is Ambassador Mia Requelme. Ambassador, allow me to introduce Volya Gaala-min, the security supervisor here on Post Satus."

The species is called Barisan. They're not as predatory as they appear, but they do tend toward a cunning nature.

Thank you.

It was the first true flesh-and-blood alien she had ever met. The ethereal Metigens—Katasketousya—felt more like ghosts or gods than aliens, and the Anadens, of which she'd thus far only seen a dead one, didn't really count.

She kept her body language controlled and minimal. "Greetings."

"Yes." The alien's voice carried a hint of a trill—she dared not characterize it as a purr—beneath the articulated Communis words. "The Sator will be a moment. You will wait."

Caleb nodded. "If you don't mind, we'll take the opportunity to confer in private."

"As it suits you." The alien pivoted and departed with a loping gait.

It had been a whirlwind twelve hours since she'd arrived in Amaranthe, punctuated by meetings with Miriam then the larger AEGIS Council separated by different briefings, followed by a short nap then a trip in the *Siyane* to said forbidding planet and its mirrored teleportation gate. Now she was here, on a different planet, inside a city-starship.

Okay, perhaps some things were still odd. She needed to focus on the task at hand. "Are all the anarchs so friendly?"

Alex rolled her eyes and drifted over to the window. She had acted distracted during the trip to the teleportation gate, though she seemed to be making an effort to act engaged now. "Nah. Volya's a bit of an ass. I haven't met enough Barisan to decide if it's the species or her personally. Nisi's far more welcoming, at least when Caleb's in the room."

"Good. The Sator's affection for Caleb may be the only thing that makes an agreement happen."

Caleb scoffed. "'Affection' is arguably a strong word."

"It's just us here, so you don't have to play modest."

"I'm not being modest. I keep telling everyone, he doesn't like me. He likes this." A flare of crimson burst to life above his outstretched palm then snuffed out as quickly as it had materialized.

Mia tilted her head in marginal agreement. "I get that. But I'd be willing to bet he does like you, even if neither of you are ready to admit it. Regardless, your presence alone will help, and I need all the help I can get."

Caleb's demeanor projected an air of reassurance doubtless intended for her. "You'll be grand. But I'll hang in the back and look supportive while you work your magic. Alex, you understand you're the closer, not me?"

"What?"

"If Mia can't close the deal, you're the one who has to deliver the desperation pitch—the 'everything depends on this' plea."

"I do not *plea*."

He laughed. "Sure you do—but only when it truly matters, and I've heard a rumor this actually does."

Alex glared at him with exaggerated annoyance. "Okay, fine. It's criminal that this man holds so much power, by the way, but whatever. Let's go swindle him."

"Alex!"

She grinned at him then at Mia. "I'm kidding. Sort of. This really *is* in his best interests, too. He wants to crush the Directorate, but he lacks the resources to do it. We have the resources, by which I mean lots of powerful guns, but we won't be able to do it without the anarchs' ponying up some legitimate help."

Volya peered into the room. "He is ready for you. Come."

ᚱ

"Sator Nisi, I'm Mia Requelme. It is an honor to meet you." She steepled her hands and bowed shallowly in an imitation of the Anaden formal greeting she'd been taught.

"Ambassador Requelme, the honor is mine. Please, call me Danilo."

Her new title still sounded awkward to her ears, but she accepted it without comment. "If it's acceptable to you, Sator, I prefer to give your position the respect it deserves."

A corner of his lips twitched, but any irritation he might be feeling didn't reach his eyes, which were a fascinating abyssal raven color, or possibly deep indigo. "As you wish."

She'd been briefed on the man—as much as was possible given how little anyone knew about him—and Caleb had provided personal insights. But she had to admit, even expecting it, his reported charisma was genuinely commanding in person.

She would need to be careful.

He gestured to his right, toward several aliens gathered in a semi-circle of chairs farther into the spacious room. "This is Xanne ela-Kyvern, our senior operations supervisor, Charito Dierev, our information and intelligence supervisor, and the lurking shadow is Miaon, an adviser."

She dipped her chin in turn at them, and Nisi directed her to a comfortable chair at one end of the semi-circle. A full glass of water sat on the small side table next to it, so they'd taken note of human preferences. In the corner of her eye she noted Caleb and Alex move to lean against one of the expansive windows behind the gathered assembly.

Nisi took the empty chair at the other end of the semi-circle, directly opposite her. His posture appeared relaxed, but it was carefully posed. "Now, let us not waste time pretending this meeting is anything other than what it is. Your people want more from us than we trust to give."

"If frankness is to be the order of the day, Sator? My people *need* more from you than you've been willing to give—that is, if you wish for us to accomplish what I'm told is a mutual goal."

"You openly admit your disadvantaged bargaining position from the start? Interesting."

"What disadvantaged position is that? Do you mean because we need something from you? Sator Nisi, have you fairly considered exactly how much you need from us? You need us to risk our lives—to fight, kill and die, without the benefit of regenesis—in order to win a war for you. You need us to win a war that you have hardly been able to wage properly. A war you are, I suspect, inherently incapable of winning on your own. I mean no disrespect, for few could hope to vanquish such a formidable enemy.

"Nevertheless, you are asking us to fight, kill and die in a bid to unseat your oppressors and hand you your freedom on a fine silver platter. Whether you trust us or not, I submit that you owe us your assistance."

It was a hard hit, but behind the gracious smile and hospitable demeanor was a hard man. He pursued a goal, and if it wasn't toppling the Directorate then they were all doomed.

The other Anaden, Xanne, looked offended, but Nisi merely studied Mia for a breath before responding. "True enough, Ambassador. You divine much for having so recently arrived. But I have bade my time for many millennia, and I can bide it for longer if I must.

"We know nothing about Humans beyond what your people and the Katasketousya have told us, and we trust the Katasketousya even less than we trust you. You are a risky bet, and the one thing I cannot do is unnecessarily endanger my organization—my family—on risky bets."

"Hmm." She paused thoughtfully. "You may be able to bide your time, sir, but what of your followers? What of the trillions of 'citizens' out there struggling under the yoke of Directorate rule? How many Novoloume, Naraida, Efkam, Barisan and countless others will suffer and die while you wait for the next best offer?"

The Novoloume present, Charito, shifted uncomfortably in his seat. The reaction did not go unnoticed by Nisi.

Mia pressed. "Sator Nisi, you are a rebel. Of this I have no doubt. You would give everything of yourself for your cause. But you also know it will take an overwhelming force to unseat the Directorate, and you cannot bring one to bear. We can.

"Did you know that when we were on the verge of discovering them and their Mosaic, the Katasketousya tried to annihilate us? They sent massive armadas of AI-driven ships to wipe us from existence, or at a minimum to return us to living in the mud."

"That cannot be so."

The shadow gained greater substance. "She speaks truth."

She acknowledged Miaon. "Thank you."

Nisi frowned. "Well...clearly they did not succeed. What happened?"

"We won the war, though at great cost in lives and damage. We outwitted and outmaneuvered their forces until we proved we could and would defeat them—then we let them depart. I mention this for two reasons. First, you need to know that we have been knocked on our proverbial asses before, and it only strengthened our resolve. We have faced an enemy who overwhelmed us with sheer numbers and superior technology before, and we bested them.

"The second reason is this: today, of their own volition, the Katasketousya fight at our side. We're here in Amaranthe because they asked for our help. Our former enemy asked for our help, and we gave it. Now, they help us in return."

She had the rapt attention of everyone in the room now; she shouldn't waste it. "We have never had any desire to annihilate or subjugate the Katasketousya, and we certainly don't desire to do either to you. We turn even enemies into allies if we can, but we will destroy them if they leave us no choice. We fight to live on our own terms, and for the right of others to do the same. We're not perfect, but we are always trying.

"I realize we seem an unknown quantity to you, but how risky can lending us a measure of aid be? You know more about us than you think. You know how the Katasketousya created us and our universe, and why. Humans and Anadens share more than just a genetic history. We are you, if only your evolution had not gone tragically wrong. We're the you that you could have been."

Nisi stared at her with a sudden, disturbing sharpness, and his indigo eyes flared to crimson—for barely a second, then the flare was gone. She'd hit a more sensitive nerve than she'd intended. Interesting.

He stood and went to gaze out one of the windows...and she saw her chance to close the deal.

"Sator, we are not here in Amaranthe to serve as your tools. We're willing to fight this battle because it's the right thing to do—because humans have never been able to stand idly by in the face of blatant injustice and oppression—but we are not yours to use and discard. If you open your doors to us and welcome us as partners, however, you will never find stronger allies. We won't fight your war for you, but we will fight it *with* you. Help us, and we will defend you and your people to our own, very permanent deaths."

Silence hung thick in the air for several seconds, punctuated only by Caleb surreptitiously winking at her.

Nisi nodded deliberately at the window, then pivoted to her. "What do you need?"

AFS STALWART II

MILKY WAY SECTOR 53

"Monitored but ostensibly full access to their information databases, as well as a promise to develop joint missions based on their intel. Medical assistance as needed, with the possibility of sharing the science behind some of their medical advances—though the last part was a little vague, so I doubt they mean regenesis.

"Most importantly in the immediate term, landing and lodging privileges at one of their bases, Post Epsilon. It's one of their smaller locations, but it's planetside on a habitable world named Palaemon, so you can get people off ships and put ground underneath their feet."

Miriam Solovy's smile carried far more enthusiasm than usual. "This is astonishing, Ms. Requelme. And you earned all these concessions simply by talking to him?"

Mia chuckled. "Yes. I think I simply made the case you didn't realize you needed to make."

Caleb was beaming—which was nearly indistinguishable from smirking—at her from across the table. She suspected he'd enjoyed the meeting with Nisi quite a lot.

The commandant crossed her arms atop the table and relaxed into them. "Well, however you accomplished it, thank you. Excellent job, I mean it. Please, stay if you can. What can be given can be revoked, and I will welcome your help in forging a more amiable relationship with the anarch leadership."

Mia had accepted the likelihood of this being a long-term engagement when she'd agreed to come. And now that she was here, embroiled in the machinations and the intrigue of a foreign universe and its foreign peoples, she probably couldn't leave it behind anyway.

"Of course I'll stay. An office or meeting room at Post Epsilon to use as a central workstation wouldn't hurt. This shouldn't be widely shared, but they have usable teleportation gates connecting all their posts, so I'll have convenient access to Nisi from there, as will you."

"Take your pick of the available working spaces and accommodations. I'll begin making arrangements for us to establish a footprint there right away. The Sagittae Gateway battle took a toll on everyone. They need a respite."

Mia suspected Miriam could use a respite as well, but she also suspected the woman would be the last person to allow herself one.

18

PALAEMON

Alex tagged along on the mini-tour Mia was given of Post Epsilon. Officially, she was filling in for her mother, while Miriam prepped for a brief return to Aurora. Unofficially, she was on a reconnaissance mission.

Their tour guide was no less than the Administrator of Post Epsilon, a Barisan named Latro Udiri-jun. He was taller and thicker than Volya, but also somewhat friendlier.

A collection of midrise buildings were arranged across the surface of an expansive body of water—larger than any one North American Great Lake, but smaller than the Mediterranean. They'd been assured on their arrival that the sea was too small to gen up hurricanes or other life-threatening natural disasters, and calm weather patterns kept the water placid much of the time.

Broad walkways made of a spongy, water absorbent tile connected the buildings to one another and to the numerous landing pads ringing the complex. None of the pads were wide enough to accommodate anything larger than a frigate, so transports and shuttles would be seeing regular duty.

The most important attribute of the post, at least to start, was the housing being made available to them, though Alex had declined lodging in exchange for a guaranteed landing pad. All told, four hundred twelve rooms and a handful of suites were theirs for the taking. Not enough for more than a fraction of the AEGIS personnel to stay here at once, but enough to devise a reasonable rotation schedule and get everyone some fresh air and downtime.

Mia had quietly claimed a suite, as had Kennedy and Noah, and the remainder were to be rotated among the flag officers and Council members. Her mother had dismissively declined to reserve one for herself, but Alex assumed decorum would dictate one of the flag officers give up their space any time Miriam required it.

Recreational and common spaces dotted the open areas between the larger structures. There were three dining areas adjacent to the lodging, as well as special kitchen facilities for the less humanoid aliens.

But the real work of rebellion was done in a group of buildings spanning the rear third of the complex, where their tour guide had to request special clearance from Post Satus to let them inside. Still, once they were inside, offices and meeting rooms dominated the interior. Hardly revolutionary stuff.

Alex finally started paying attention when they entered a wing of tech and medical labs. She paused to press her nose to a small glass window and peer into what appeared to be the primary lab on the left side of a long hallway.

Rows of Anaden-sized capsules were wired into databanks. Friendly looking mechs with white ceramic casing floated about, and a couple of Anadens worked at stations scattered among the capsules.

She glanced over her shoulder at Latro without stepping away from the glass. "This is your regenesis center, isn't it?"

"Yes."

"Can you tell us something about how it works? A high-level overview—no state secrets or anything."

"No, I cannot." The Barisan opened the door a crack and peered inside. "But I may be able to retrieve someone who can. Give me a minute, if you please." He disappeared inside, closing the door behind him.

Alex shrugged at Mia. "I'm assuming we all want to know how this works?"

"Oh, yes."

Latro returned accompanied by an Anaden man in a classic lab overcoat; she guessed some things were simply practical, no matter the universe. His gaze took in their presence with clinical scrutiny.

"I am Dimou ela-Erevna, director of the regenesis facility here at Post Epsilon. I've been authorized to share a little information with you—a little, you understand."

Alex tried to look grateful. And she was, in a way. "Of course. I think our first question is the big one. How does it work, in broad terms? Imaging the neural activity of a functioning brain is one thing, but transferring a consciousness, whole and complete, from one body to another is something else altogether."

"On the contrary, all it requires is a deep and thorough under-standing of the way a mind—not merely a brain—functions."

"Okay. We don't have that, though we're getting there. You ob-viously do. Hypothetically, given the similarities in Anaden and human genetic structure, is regenesis something we could aspire to achieving one day?"

"Not the two of you, no. Not any Human currently living. Why, you ask? The answer is in the technical details of the process, which I can't share in detail, rendering the point moot."

Valkyrie and Mia simultaneously blasted her with warnings to not say whatever she was thinking, leading her to physically bite her lower lip to keep her mouth shut.

Mia cleared her throat and flashed Dimou her most charming smile, which really was pretty damn charming. "Sir, even general concepts will be welcome. We're frankly in awe of your capabili-ties, and we only hope to begin to learn—to be enlightened."

Alex bit down harder.

Dimou studied Mia briefly before falling for the flattery. "Our embedded...cybernetics is the closest term you would under-stand...include within their structure the technology needed to transform the sum of a functioning mind into quantized data suit-able for transmission and delivery to matching hardware embedded inside a cloned body. Once a network is in place, the transmission itself is a trivial matter."

Alex peered with forced nonchalance into the lab through the open door behind the director. Her focus moved deliberately across each part of the room to allow her ocular implant to capture visuals in as great of detail as practicable. "Quantized data...do you mean qubits? Qutrits? However high the order, this is what you're talking about, right? Information encoded in quantum form."

"Yes. Now I can't say anything more. I'm sorry."

"We understand." She flashed him a smile, though she couldn't hope to match Mia's performance. "Thank you for your time. As soon as Latro returns, we'll be on our way."

Mia was staring at her curiously as the door to the lab closed behind the director. "What was that?"

"That was me asking a few questions, since we all want to know how it works."

"In principle, certainly, but it's hardly a pressing concern. He's right. We can't do it, not yet. You were asking for another reason."

She felt the faintest tickle of another's mind at the edges of her own and shook her head. "Mia, don't look. You have plenty of concerns to handle without delving into mine. This isn't your secret to bear, and you don't want it to be."

Tiny waves broke against the parapet of the meandering walkway, occasionally spraying Alex's feet and ankles with a bit of icy water. The crisp air was a few degrees warmer than the water, but still chilly. Ahead of them a cargo ship descended to land on one of the larger platforms. Farther in the distance, a transport departed. The work of a rebellion proceeding apace all around them.

"Do we know why they built the post on the water?" A jagged line of umber and sage on the horizon confirmed there *was* land, and not too far away.

Mia nodded. "I was told the only landmass in the habitable zone is populated with some nasty wildlife, of the aggressive and large variety. Luckily for us, the wildlife doesn't fly—or swim." She peered over the edge of the walkway into the water below. "Allegedly."

Alex gestured to one of the weapons turrets ringing the complex, spaced periodically between the platforms. "Hopefully those can point *down*, too. Just in case."

When the tour had ended, they were released on their own recognizance by Latro, albeit not before receiving a deluge of cautionary advice. Alex had coaxed Mia into the outing, because she needed another Prevo to bounce ideas off. To brainstorm with. To ramble to, and possibly to express frustration in raw terms.

The matters she now pondered lay so far past accepted human scientific knowledge it was laughable—and this wasn't even about her father. She simply didn't trust her or Valkyrie's judgment on the plausibility of what she contemplated. Not enough to bet the future of AEGIS on it.

A splash of water made it as high as her hands, and she stuck them in the pockets of her coat. Her fingers brushed across the Reor slab in the left pocket; she carried it everywhere with her, under the theory that if she fiddled with it enough times, it would give in and reveal its mysterious secrets.

"So the fleet can't use the gateways any longer."

Mia shook her head. "No. Anarch scouts report a significant Machim presence at every gateway they've checked. The positioning gives them a major, arguably insurmountable tactical advantage in any encounter and creates a battle-before-the-battle trap should we need to use one for a mission."

"A no-brainer move on their part, and they have the ships to spare. Losing the gateways isn't a complete deal-breaker for us. Many of the important potential targets are in the Milky Way. It's the Anadens' home and the most heavily developed galaxy by a decent margin. Our ships can get across its breadth in around ten days, which isn't ideal but is workable.

"But if we want to win, sooner or later we'll have to go to Andromeda for certain. Also Triangulum, Ursa Major I and LMC, I expect. And the anarchs have a lot of assets in Pegasus Dwarf, where the Novoloume, Naraida and Volucri homeworlds are."

"At max sLume speeds it'll take us a minimum of three weeks to reach LMC, and that's the close one. Triangulum will take something like nine months and Pegasus...almost a year."

Alex nodded. "We need to reach other galaxies, plus it takes too long to reach other galaxies, equals we have to be able to open our own traversable wormholes."

"Is that even possible? You're the astrophysics guru."

"Yeah, and I'm not quite sure." She grimaced. "But I do know the proposition is all about dimensions, and dimensions is what us Prevos do."

"Oh. I suppose it is. There's no chance the anarchs can whip up their own makeshift gateways in short order?"

"Valkyrie?"

'They cannot, though it is a question of material and financial resources before it becomes a technological one. My understanding is the gateways were constructed for two reasons: to ensure easy intergalactic travel by civilian vessels without the need for expensive wormhole drives on every ship, and to keep the details of wormhole drive technology a closely held secret of the Directorate.'

"Naturally." Alex rolled her eyes. "Do the anarchs at least understand the technology?"

'I cannot say with complete confidence. Given they possess teleportation gates, it is likely. But before we turn to them for yet more aid, we should consider the possibility that we understand the mechanisms behind wormhole creation better than we realize.'

She and Mia glanced at each other. "Do we?"

'Consider sidespace. What if it is not a true dimension at all, but rather a matrix of wormhole bridges between two points?'

Her steps slowed, and Mia matched her reduced pace. "Valkyrie, you're saying we've been unwittingly opening some variation on wormholes every time we use sidespace?"

'When we first met Sator Nisi, you asked me to study the nature of the teleportation gate we traversed as well as our increasing ability to access sidespace independently of one another. After conducting a relational analysis of the commonalities in the two processes, I am saying it is conceivable we have been doing exactly that.'

Mia frowned. "Interesting concept, but since only our consciousness can make the trip in sidespace, it doesn't help us much."

Alex groaned. "Because we're opening the wormholes in the wrong dimension!" She deflated as quickly as she'd perked up. "So how do we open them in a spatial dimension? We're completely unable to affect the real world from sidespace."

Mia stopped cold. "That's not precisely true."

"What?"

"Devon was able to do it. When we were attacked at the hospital by mercs sent to kill us by this—never mind, it doesn't matter. All of the mercs were Prevos, and to defend himself he tried to blow apart the quantum entanglement of their Prevo connections. He accomplished that, but he also blew apart several nearby walls in the process."

"No fucking way."

Mia laughed. "Way."

"How the hell did he do that?"

"I'm honestly not sure. It had something to do with generating sufficient power to break the entanglement bonds. But I was angry at him for hijacking my Prevo link to help fuel the process without asking, and it was a horrific week already and…I just didn't care. Sorry."

"No, it's understandable. I would've pitched an epic fit if he'd done it to me. But…generating power seemed to be the key? Enough real, tangible power to force open a hole in a dimensional boundary?"

"It's as accurate a summary as any."

Alex turned to regard the cluster of buildings at the center of Epsilon. "We need to understand how he did it. Mom's traveling back to deal with the Rychen fallout in a few hours—can I ask you to go along on the trip? I'm sorry, I know you just got here. But you're the only one of us Devon trusts or even really listens to, and I think we need to get him here yesterday."

PART IV:

SHATTERSHOT

*"It eluded us then, but that's no matter—tomorrow we will run faster,
stretch out our arms farther. . . . And then one fine morning—
So we beat on, boats against the current, borne back ceaselessly
into the past."*

— *F. Scott Fitzgerald*

19

AURORA

EARTH

WASHINGTON, EARTH ALLIANCE HEADQUARTERS

Christopher Rychen had survived three wars and dozens of lesser conflicts. He'd survived the loss of five ships at the captain's helm, earned and healed innumerable scars, and shrugged it all off like the consummate soldier he was. Across decades of combat engagements he'd built a reputation that declared to all comers: no mere enemy could take him down.

But no one was invincible.

They had gotten overconfident. *She* had gotten overconfident, become convinced adiamene and Dimensional Rifters protected them from any strike and their complement of Prevos could invent their way out of any tight spot.

Hubris.

Miriam called herself watching out for it, but in the heady rush of success she'd fallen victim to it all the same. Doing so had cost her a great deal. It had cost her a friend.

The enemy may be acutely arrogant in its own peculiar fashion as well as staid and stuck in its ways, but it was not stupid, and it most certainly was not weak. She forgot to respect the enemy. An unforgivable mistake.

ᗅᖇ

It had only been a few weeks since Miriam last visited Washington, but it already felt like years. Ironic, perhaps, considering time passed *more* slowly in Amaranthe, but so much had happened since she'd first ventured into the foreign realm. It was strange to be back here now, to a world apart and untouched by the turmoil through the portal.

Her mission today was to ensure it continued to be so.

She was granted entry to the Prime Minister's office promptly upon her arrival, and she entered as she had a dozen or more times over the years. The office was the same in all but the accoutrements, even as the occupant changed periodically. Some had been good leaders, at least one terrible and arguably evil, but most had been serviceable stewards of the government. Thus far Charles Gagnon was falling somewhere between the first and last categories; assuming life as they knew it survived, time would tell where he ultimately landed.

"Commandant, welcome. How does the campaign fare on the other side?"

He roamed the room rather than sit behind his desk, so she adopted a parade rest stance in the center. "Complicated, sir."

"Yes, I've been receiving your official reports, the few there have been."

"Circumstances dictate that portal traversal be a rare event, which limits communication opportunities."

"I'm aware of the restrictions. So to what do I owe your own traversal and personal visit?"

Her visage set into grim fortitude. "I regret to inform you of the death of Fleet Admiral Christopher Rychen, along with 23,818 crew members aboard the *EAS Virginia* during an engagement with Anaden forces."

Gagnon's face blanched for a breath. "Twenty-three *thousand?* Was the *Virginia* destroyed? Because I was under the impression that was impossible."

"Nearly impossible, sir. A confluence of variables led to the improbable becoming the reality. I of course take full responsibility for the loss."

"*Are* we losing?"

"The war?" She paused. "It is…complicated."

"You said that before. I'm certain it is, but I'm committing a significant majority of the Alliance's naval forces to this effort, leaving us exposed here at home. If I'm committing them to a doomed endeavor, I much prefer to know this now, while most of the forces are still alive and the vessels are still intact."

"The only way the mission is doomed, sir, is if we abandon the fight and retreat home, and to do so will doom everyone. Our adversary accepts only two forms of surrender: slavery or extermination. They will not stop searching for a way to inflict one of them upon us simply because we leave."

"Fine. But there must be some victory condition short of dismantling, or overthrowing entirely, the power structure of another realm, one we have no vested interest in beyond keeping them out of ours. Have you looked into the possibility of destroying the Metis portal? Then these Anadens would never be able to reach us, and we would be free to follow our own path forward."

"Sir, if you had been to Amaranthe, you would not suggest such a course of action."

"Is that so?"

"It is. Protecting everyone living here at home is and will always be my first and highest priority. But we are not in the habit of turning a blind eye to the immoral suffering of others. If we are to call ourselves liberators, liberating is what we must do. Genocide, slavery and rampant oppression of basic rights have been inflicted unchecked in Amaranthe for a very long time. Having witnessed it, I could not live with myself if we withdrew into ourselves to lock the door, shut off the lights and hope the Anadens don't find another way to come for us—and neither should you."

His bearing didn't falter, skilled politician that he was. "I understand. In a perfect world, I readily agree. But if this is a fight we cannot win, then we need to instead do what we can to protect our own people. So I will ask you again. Are we losing?"

When no one outranked you to whom you might defer, there was no option left but to give straight answers. "No, we are not.

As of today, we are also not winning. But we have been victorious in every engagement save the last one, and we are working on several alternative strategies I anticipate will go a long way to ensuring defeat doesn't happen a second time. We are forging new alliances as I speak, and these allies can help us exploit our enemy's weaknesses. In my opinion, we will win. We will find a way."

He stared at her silently for several seconds. "So it appears I'm in need of a new fleet admiral. Care to return to the job?"

After the dressing down he'd just delivered? Had the attempt at humiliation merely been for show, or so he would be able to rest easy tonight believing he'd done his job?

"Thank you, sir, but I should decline. I cannot perform the full duties of the position adequately from Amaranthe, as there is work to be done on behalf of the Alliance here as well.

"I am, however, willing to take operational command of the Alliance forces serving in Amaranthe under the AEGIS banner. I don't need a title, simply an executive order from you directing all officers assigned to AEGIS to follow my orders. Appoint General Haraken as Chairman of the EASC Board, which will give him effective authority over matters here."

"And when the Alliance forces return from Amaranthe?"

"A decision for another day, Prime Minister. Events are moving quickly, and the reality of today is unlikely to resemble the reality that exists when you need to make such a decision."

"True enough, Commandant. I'll grant your requests, but I implore you: protect our people, then bring them home."

20

ANARCH POST SATUS

LOCATION UNKNOWN

Nisi's gaze fixed keenly on Caleb as soon as he entered the man's office. "It wasn't an appropriate topic to bring up during the meeting with Ambassador Requelme, but you've recently encountered another Inquisitor, haven't you?"

Caleb shrugged nonchalantly. "What makes you say that?"

"The power now accompanying your presence is nearly making the windows vibrate." He glanced toward one of the windows, which hung placidly in place. "Or should be. Perhaps I am overly sensitive to it. What happened?"

Caleb sat down on one of the couches and dropped his elbows to his knees. He wasn't quite so relaxed as the pose suggested, but it didn't hurt to act it. "Actually, I encountered the *same* Inquisitor. When we went to rescue some of your agents at Plousia Chateau on Serifos, the Inquisitor who interrogated me at Helix Retention was onsite. Nyx is her name."

"Indeed. A powerful *elasson* Inquisitor. And you claimed all of her *diati*?"

He shook his head. "Not this time. She teleported away while she still controlled enough to manage an escape. But here's the weird thing. I can't be certain, but I think I *did* take it all at Helix Retention. So how is it she again commanded so much of it? Does it replenish itself?"

"No. But I imagine the Primor gifted her a small portion of his own. There are only twelve *elasson* Inquisitors, and all of them are his most favored pets. But if one is more precious to him than any, it would be Nyx."

"And you know this how?"

"It is my responsibility to know such things." Nisi turned aside. "What do you imagine you can do with this increased power?"

"Whatever I need to do."

"Which is?"

"Can't say yet. We'll see as it comes."

"Oh?"

Caleb leaned forward and clasped his hands together. "That will always be the answer. When I only need a little—enough to, say, create a pocket of breathable air in space for Alex or myself—then that's what I'll use it for. If or when I need more—enough to teleport us out of danger or disable a cadre of attackers, for instance—then I hope what I have will be enough to do what I need to do."

"So power for power's sake doesn't interest you?"

"Does it interest you?"

Nisi stared at him for a second, a touch of amusement flickering in his abyssal eyes. "Fair enough. I did not mean to insinuate you were desirous of greater glory. I ask merely out of genuine curiosity."

The Sator was smooth, Caleb had to concede. Nothing in the man's demeanor betrayed the lie. "Don't get me wrong. I won't deny I take pride in being skilled. The *diati* amplifies what I can do, but I've always been...capable."

"No question, or it wouldn't have chosen you as a vessel."

"So you say. But power is a tool, and a tool for what is up to its wielder. I learned this early in my career. My blade doesn't have a moral preference. Neither does my gun, and neither does the *diati*."

"It did once."

It had been a quiet murmur, and Caleb frowned. "What did you say?"

"Nothing relevant. In light of this latest encounter and the resulting increase in your power, what do you wish to cover today? Additional teleportation practice?"

Caleb had gotten the sense from the *diati* visions that it once exhibited some degree of morality, but it had faded away long ago. Nisi obviously knew more about the *diati* than the amount he controlled suggested, but how much more? Did it whisper to the man in his sleep as well?

He didn't bother to ask, knowing he couldn't trust the answer. "No, I've got the teleportation down. I've been thinking. Eren mentioned there were a few Praesidis anarchs. I want to meet one, or all, of them."

"No."

Nisi was rarely so direct, and Caleb regarded him suspiciously. "Why not?"

"You would likely claim their *diati*, after which, wonderful people though they are, they would be of considerably less value to me—to the anarchs—and to themselves. As they are not your enemy, I assume you have no specific desire to render them weak."

"I don't, I just...." Caleb sighed. "I guess I'd just like to know good Praesidis exist out there. That they aren't all flat-out evil."

"Why does this matter to you?"

"They're my...relatives. Ancestors, descendants, something in between. I should feel some kinship with them, but the Praesidis I've met so far, I do not recognize."

"They are not all evil, Caleb, even those who are not anarchs. You may take my word on this. Most have simply never been given the opportunity to choose to be other than what they were born to be."

"Because of the integral."

"Yes, and their precisely crafted genetic codes. They are designed to be talented in their specific fields, but they are also designed to be loyal."

"They're still individuals, as every Anaden anarch has proved by defying their predilections."

Nisi conceded the point with a tilt of his head. "It is true genetics are not everything. But the Directorate, and Primor Erevna in particular, have perfected their configurations to the point where they count for a great deal—far more than for your people."

"I understand. But...." A tingling began to ripple beneath his skin, growing in intensity until his ears buzzed loudly. It was familiar in sensation but not in tenor...and it was not the *diati*.

He cleared his throat and stood. "I'm sorry, but I have to go."

PALAEMON

ANARCH POST EPSILON

The mood among those who arrived at Post Epsilon from the AEGIS fleet remained somber and reserved. Practically speaking, this was for the best, as the solemnity diffused a couple of early misunderstandings when soldiers encountered their first aliens in a suboptimal manner. Alex didn't want her mother to face a new row with the anarchs on her return, so she and Caleb were trying to help ease the tension of the initial encounters.

Alex made her way to the Administrator's office. She was also trying to fill in for Mia on matters that didn't require full diplomatic regalia while their new Ambassador was back in Aurora. Her level of success thus far was questionable.

But she was *trying*, which meant everything else had to be put on hold until her mother and Mia returned, hopefully with Devon in tow.

As she crossed one of the many bridges at the post, Valkyrie interrupted her harried musing.

I've received a peculiar message from Mesme.

Do I need to point out the redundancy in that statement?

Not particularly. Mesme expressed concern that it had unintentionally caused Eren some distress and indicated you might want to check in on him.

Eren, distressed? I'll believe it when I see it. Did he taunt Mesme with an especially cutting barb or something?

Mesme was not specific—

A buzzing sensation leapt to life under her skin, without impetus or obvious cause. It wasn't painful, but it was...urgent? Why did she think it was urgent?

Valkyrie, is something wrong with my cybernetics?

Running diagnostics...no. All systems are functioning within normal parameters.

So what is this?

Your body has not recently been infiltrated by any type of foreign substance or virus. This leaves several possibilities, and I believe you are familiar with all of them.

She reached the central building, briefly stood in front of the entrance wearing a blank stare, then spun and headed back in the opposite direction toward the *Siyane*.

Whatever this was, she needed to figure it out. Also, she wasn't going to be able to begin to concentrate on sweet-talking Latro or coaxing soldiers into playing nice with aliens so long as the sensation continued. She wasn't a diplomat to begin with, and it took all her faculties to pretend to be even a mediocre one.

She more or less let Valkyrie navigate the bridges and walkways to reach the *Siyane*, while she focused on listening to the strange noise within her. It felt almost like…she stopped in the middle of a walkway, closed her eyes and let the buzzing completely fill her mind.

No explanation made itself known, and she had no logic to back it up, but she could swear the sensation carried on its vibrations a single thought:

HELP

She and Caleb reached the *Siyane* seconds apart.

He grabbed her by the shoulders, intensity in his grasp. "Good, I was coming to find you. Do you feel it, too?"

Her brow knotted in surprise. It hadn't occurred to her that he could be experiencing the sensation as well. "I feel something, yes."

"It's Akeso."

"Are you sure?" But even as she said it, she realized it must be the right answer. The only answer.

"It's not the *diati*—the vibe is completely different—and I don't have any other sentient life forms swimming around in my body." He frowned. "I don't think. Anyway, that's the one we share. So if you feel it, too, it has to be Akeso."

She nodded. "I get the sense it's asking for help. And it seems...desperate."

He pivoted and jogged up the ramp into the ship. "Let's go."

She followed him, but after the airlock had closed, she paused outside the cockpit. "With my mother and Mia gone, I hate to leave the post unattended."

"It won't be. There are several flag officers on the ground right now. I passed Escarra on the way here, so send him a message and ask him to take over for a little while, or to request that Bastian come groundside. We got everything started and the initial kinks worked out. The people here will be fine for a few days, but Akeso might not be."

She shook her head and settled into the cockpit chair. "Then we've no time to waste. Valkyrie, contact Mesme. We need a portal into the Mosaic."

21

AURORA

PRESIDIO

GCDA Headquarters

Richard Navick met Miriam at the door to his office with a warm hug. "I'm so glad to see you alive and in one piece."

She silently followed him into the office. He'd added a small conference table while she'd been gone, and they sat together at it now.

"I heard about Rychen from the intel burst. I am sorry. But he was as good as they come, and I'm sure there was nothing you could have done to prevent what happened."

How did he know the dark place her thoughts refused to leave, and without her having spoken a single word? Probably for the same reason he was the only person, other than Alex, to whom she'd dare express those dark thoughts of weakness, of doubt. "There was *everything* I could have done to prevent it."

"Miriam—"

"I could have removed my head from my ass, for starters. I forwent caution and exhaustive preparation in favor of another grandiose show of force. I assumed the adversary would do what they've done before since no way are they as *clever* as us. And in doing so I got Christopher killed. I got more than twenty thousand people under my command killed."

It had come out in a torrent of bitter recrimination, and she hurriedly fought to reign the flaring emotions in. She was comfortable speaking truthfully to him, but she still had manners.

"Don't you think you're putting a little too much of the blame on yourself?"

"That's what being in charge means, Richard."

"I get it, I do. On an institutional level, yes, you have to bear the responsibility of every loss. I mean personally. The only thing that happened was you met a formidable enemy on the field of battle and, as has been reported to happen in war, you took a blow."

"We certainly did." She sighed, shedding another layer of the rigid formality she'd held in place for the meeting with Gagnon. "This is horribly callous of me...I should be thinking about how I just lost a friend who has always had my back. And I am. But mostly what I'm thinking about is the cold, ruthless calculus of the damn war, and the calculus tells me I just lost my best battlefield commander and tactician, as well as my best adviser.

"And since I'm in charge, I don't get to mourn, personally or logistically. I have to move forward, adapt and find a way to win without him—not tomorrow or next week, but now."

"You can take a day, Miriam."

"No, I can't. I made this trip because it was my obligation to deliver the news to the Prime Minister in person, but more so because only he has the authority to transfer operational control of the Alliance forces in Amaranthe to me. Cold, ruthless calculus. Rychen dies and I get more power, because I must. Now I need to hurry back to Amaranthe and see to finding a way to win. Without my best battlefield commander."

She exhaled. It was possible there was some value in letting pent-up frustrations out. "But first...do you mind if I vent a bit more?"

"Not in the slightest. I'll help if I can, but if I can't, I'm happy to listen." His smile was kind and honest, carrying only the faintest hint of amusement at her unseemly display of emotion.

"How do I fill the gaping hole that's been created? I have several excellent officers serving under me—Jenner, Escarra, Ashonye and Belosca immediately spring to mind. But of them, only Jenner's shown real potential to become truly exceptional. He's quite good, and one day soon he might be superb. But he's not ready to apply his talents to an entire fleet, to engagements of the size and scope we've been facing. And I'm worried if I push him too hard too fast, a lack of experience-won confidence will cause him to lose the very ingenuity he's thus far displayed.

"On the other hand, I may not have time to let him grow into the role. So what are my other options? Bastian is...."

"An excellent leader of his troops. But the battle isn't in his blood."

She huffed a breath. "Thank you for saying so. I was worried I was letting my bias cloud my assessment of him."

"What bias is that?"

"He isn't Eleni. Whatever differences existed between us, she and I spoke the same language. Working with her was...easy. Merely saying 'good morning' to Bastian inevitably morphs into a challenge of wits and will."

Richard laughed. "And you're understating the matter."

"Aren't I? But personality conflicts aside, I think you nailed it. He's a model soldier and an exemplary leader of people who aren't me. But he's shown no indication of being able to make the kind of on-the-spot, inspired decisions that can turn the tide of a battle. He's intelligent and knowledgeable but he's...well, he's a little Machim in his approach, I'm sorry to say."

"I won't mention to him you said that next time I see him."

"Thank you. So I return to the question of how to fill the Rychen-sized hole in my fleet."

Richard drummed his fingers on the table. "Maybe you don't need to fill it. Setting the AEGIS Prevos loose to be unpredictable, even chaotic, was all about removing the heavy hand of commanders, correct? Admittedly, I'm not there, but my understanding is the strategy has been working well. You focus on the overarching strategic goals, but when it comes to combat engagements, give them an objective and the necessary constraints, and let them do their thing. Maybe it will be enough to not only win the day but give you what you need to win the war."

"It'll have to be, won't it?" She sank deeper into the chair. "This helps. Thank you. Would you be interested in coming to Amaranthe with me?"

"There's nothing for me to do there."

"You could be my adviser, clearly. And we're finally starting to make some headway with the anarchs, so one day soon there should be intelligence data to analyze."

"I appreciate the vote of confidence, but you don't need me to be your adviser. You've got this in hand. At such time as there is legitimate, complex intelligence requiring analysis rather than simply action, we'll talk. But right now I'm needed here."

She smiled in acceptance—then frowned instead. "Is something going on? Is there trouble here?"

He reached over and laid a hand atop hers. "No. Merely the usual supply of bad actors and crafty criminals. More crafty than ever now that they're all hooked up to Artificials, but we're trying to keep up. The world is changing rapidly out there, but it seems to be equal opportunity change so far. The criminals are smarter and have better tools, but so are the good guys. So I think things will be okay here for a while in your absence."

"Which is not the same thing as saying you're not busy."

"No, it is not." He arched an eyebrow. "Feel better?"

"I do. You're a finer friend than I deserve."

"I'll defer to your judgment on the matter. Now, I can see it in your expression. You're anxious to get moving."

"I'm afraid I am."

"Do you want to visit the firing range before you leave? Knock out a few hundred practice rounds?"

"Actually, yes. It would be most cathartic. Unfortunate that there's no time for it—oh, I almost forgot." She dug into her bag and produced a small disk case. "A message from Alex. The portal barrier is really throwing a kink in communications, isn't it?"

He took the case from her. "What's it about?"

"I do not know. I was tangled so deeply in my own head when I left Amaranthe, I didn't think to ask. If you need or want to respond, I'll be on the Presidio for another hour or so. There are many reassurances to give and orders to reinforce before I depart for the portal."

AR

ALL THE SECURITY CLASSIFICATIONS,
WHATEVER THEY ARE.
IF YOU ARE NOT RICHARD NAVICK, DO NOT READ ANY
FURTHER UNDER PENALTY OF BAD THINGS HAPPENING
TO YOU.
SCARY BAD THINGS.

Richard,

I have a question to ask you. Yet even as I compose this message, I'm still not sure exactly how to ask it. So prepare for a streak of rambling.

I was a child when my father died; I knew him only through an adoring daughter's eyes, all misty and a firm rose in color. I readily admit it, but memory is what memory is, and I can't go back now and see him through different eyes. You knew him better than anyone, save possibly my mother, and I can't ask her this question, for oh so many reasons.

Here goes: in a hypothetical world, one where magic and miracles are possible, if the David you knew were offered a second chance at life—a chance to live again in every sense of the word, and without undoing the past or changing what happened to him—would he take it?

From one perspective, it sounds like a ridiculous question. Who wouldn't jump at such a chance? But I remember my father had a very unique, even eccentric relationship with spirituality, the universe and notions of fate or destiny. And I find I just don't know. And I kind of need to know.

I'm sorry I can't say more. One day I'll tell you the whole story. Best to you and Will. Try to keep the galaxy glued together while we're gone.

—Alex

"Oh, Alex, what are you scheming at?" Richard eased back in his desk chair and brought a hand to his jaw.

The warning header was just Alex being Alex. He hadn't missed the hidden encryption on the message file itself to guarantee no one but him would be able to open it—Caleb's handiwork, no doubt. A good thing, then, that Miriam hadn't tried to open it, failed, and provoked yet another Solovy Family Incident.

While he wondered what the others were, one reason Alex couldn't ask Miriam the question was obvious. Her response would be irreparably biased. Of course Miriam would say 'yes,' because she would want David back. Hell, Richard's answer was apt to reflect the same bias, if to a lesser degree.

He blinked, hard. He was thinking about the message and its contents as if they were somehow *normal*. They were not. Even when one took into account this was coming from Alex, she who routinely conjured the impossible into reality seemingly through sheer force of will, the topic she'd raised should in no way whatsoever be considered 'normal.' And the softening language it was couched in notwithstanding, no way was this a hypothetical, thought-experiment question.

So what was it?

She was up to something. In all probability, it was something equal parts audacious and dangerous. Yet though the idea terrified him, in his heart of hearts he found himself rooting for her.

But for now he owed her an honest answer, and the clock was ticking.

It took him several minutes to find the right words, but he put together the truest response he could compose. Then he encoded it to her alone and sent it, along with a couple of other messages and reports waiting for transfer, for delivery to the transport Miriam was taking to Amaranthe.

Two debriefs and three filed reports after the mission was over, Richard finally made it to Medical on the EAS Trafalgar.

The controlled chaos of emergency triage had died down by then, but a degree of urgency remained in the activity around several of the treatment cubicles.

Thankfully, David's cubicle wasn't one of them, and Richard made his way past several bots and distracted medics to stand beside his friend's cot.

A bulky medwrap covered most of David's torso; a smaller one spanned the right side of his neck, and dark bruises surrounded his right eye beneath the sheen of a thick coat of healing ointment.

Richard's squad had been tasked with perimeter surveillance of the mission target area. They'd done their job and alerted David's squad when enemy reinforcements appeared on long-range sensors headed for their location. The squad would've had time to retreat cleanly if they'd moved fast. But the objective wasn't complete, and Captain Solovy had refused to retreat until the stranded Marines— injured in a prior mission gone bad and pinned down by the enemy—were extracted.

Minutes after Richard's warning, the scene through the surveillance cams had lit up in weapons fire, grenade explosions and trip mine detonations. Minutes after that, David had reported the all-clear and requested a medical evac team. His voice had sounded strained on the comms, but Richard had been ignorant of the extent of the man's injuries until he was back on board the Trafalgar.

David's left eye opened a crack to peer up at Richard. "Give it to me straight. Am I in good shape for the scrimmage tonight?"

Richard cringed. He lived in a constant state of incredulity at David's persistent devil-may-care attitude. "You look like Hell—literally, you look like you took a scenic tour of Hell on the way back to the Trafalgar. You'll be lucky if they let you on a syncrosse court next month."

"Well, gavno. I was looking forward to kicking Delta's ass. How's my squad? Bershon? Zhu? My eVi's stuck in a medical override routine and I can't access the system."

"Lieutenant Bershon will be released from Medical by the end of the day. Lieutenant Zhu's worse off, but the captain on duty says he'll make it."

"And the others? What about—?"

"Everyone survived, including everyone you went in to rescue. I don't know how in God's name you managed it, but the great David Solovy saved everyone. Mind you, it nearly cost you your life."

"Pah." David struggled up to more of a sitting position and started to reach for the water on the table beside him, but stopped halfway with a wince.

Richard handed the water to him and waited while he took a sip, coughed, took another, and handed it back. "You were saying?"

"No way was I going to die today."

"Everyone dies, David."

His friend cracked a cocky smile like he wasn't swathed head-to-toe in medwraps. "Do they?"

"So far, yeah. They do."

David rolled his eyes, then winced again and reached up to gingerly feel at the bruised, swollen skin around his right eye socket. "I'll grant you the possibility that one day Death will catch up to me and have its due, but it wasn't going to be today. I'm not done yet. The finish line's far over the horizon, and I've hardly gotten properly started."

Richard was so lost in thought he didn't realize Will had walked into his office until his husband leaned against the desk beside his chair and nudged his shoulder with an elbow.

"Oh!" He shook the reverie off and gave Will a sheepish grimace. "Sorry."

"Some intelligence agent you are. I could have been an assassin."

"Assassins don't come in the front door."

"What if the best ones do?" Will chuckled. "What has you so preoccupied?"

"Miriam dropped by."

"I saw her report. They're having a tough time, I gather."

Richard nodded vaguely. "I want to elevate Jackson and To-gusa's access to Level IV and start including them in the morning briefings."

Will gazed at him shrewdly. "Miriam asked you to come to Amaranthe."

"What are you, a spy?"

Will blinked at him repeatedly until Richard chuckled. "And I said no, for now. But events could lead to *us* needing to make the trip sooner rather than later. I want to see to it SENTRI will be left in good hands if we do need to go, so let's get Jackson and Togusa up to speed and ready to step in."

"Understood. I'll talk to them this afternoon. What about Director Delavasi? If we're unreachable and something big happens...."

"Graham's viewed as too partisan to take on an official leadership role. You and I recognize when things go to hell he'll work for the good of everyone, but he is Senecan to his core. But let Jackson and Togusa know they can call on him for unofficial guidance."

"I'll let him know that, too. Out of curiosity, what did Miriam say to make you think we'll need to travel there soon?"

"About what you'd expect—intel to analyze, factions to understand, war games to play. And she may be correct. But honestly, it's not so much what Miriam said...it's what Alex said."

ROMANE

IDCC COLONY

Devon Reynolds sensed it when Mia returned through the portal. The presence of a Noetica Prevo still cast a disproportionate influence upon the Noesis, as if granting it added *consequence*.

Curious that she'd returned already. Either everything had worked out splendidly, or it was a shitshow beyond her capacity to fix, and he found he wanted to know which.

How's the big, bad, 'real' universe? I'm surprised you've come home so soon.

Only briefly. I'll tell you more when I see you, which will be in a few hours. We need to talk.

I'm not going over there.

Just listen to what I have to say.

Talk all you want. I'm not going.

I'll see you soon.

Emily walked into the living room then to stare at him suspiciously. "What's wrong?"

"Not a thing. Mia wants to drop by this evening, so how about we order in Chinasian?"

◢ℛ◣

"I don't know how to make a wormhole out of sidespace, Mia."

"Not yet, but you could hold the key to understanding how to do it. We need to brainstorm with Alex and try to figure it out."

Devon shook his head, firmly for added emphasis. "Look, I'll give you everything we've worked out when it comes to affecting the physical world from sidespace. Annie can infodump you, and you can take all the information with you. If you have any questions later, you can drop back in and ask them."

"I'm not a ferry service, Devon. Every time we portal into or out of Amaranthe, we risk discovery, followed soon thereafter by destruction of our entire universe. This is your one and only chance to weigh in."

"That's fine with me. Like I told you, I'll give you everything. But I can't—"

Emily grabbed his arm and tugged him toward the kitchen. "Excuse us for a second, Mia. Please, help yourself to some dinner. We'll be right back."

He sighed and allowed himself to be dragged into the kitchen. Emily closed the door behind them then spun on him, hands planted defiantly on her hips. *Uh-oh.*

"You and Annie need to help them. We should go."

"What? No. I'm not going. I'll tell them what I've learned about my nifty trick, absolutely. But we're happy here, and I'm not flipping our lives upside down again." Devon crossed his arms over his chest in a display of certitude designed to match hers.

Emily regarded him for a moment, her expression unusually guarded. Then she drew close and coaxed his hands out from his pose to cradle them in hers. "Devon."

"Don't even start—"

"I will too start if I want to start. You've been *fabulous* to me since I got out of the hospital—and while I was in the hospital, and before I was in the hospital—and I love you for it. But your life is bigger than this apartment, bigger than picking at ware routines and taking me out to shows. *You're* bigger than any of this, and so is Annie. She's a military Artificial, and she and you together are meant for grander things. And you know what? I'd like to see some of that. I missed out on you being Mr. Prevo Badass during the Metigen War and again during the OTS unrest, or at most I only got to watch it from afar. I want to see the real pageantry."

He shook his head fervently. "I won't put you in that sort of danger. Certainly not the danger of a war with evil, bloodthirsty aliens."

She laughed; she was so gorgeous when she did it. "Devon, walking down the street with you is dangerous, but I continue to do so on a regular basis."

"But you're still recovering—"

"No, I'm not. Not really. I'm as good as new. Seriously, I think most of me is new now. Most of Yves, too." She smiled all the way to her brilliant, Prevo eyes, and he melted into a puddle of goo that would do anything she asked. "I'm ready to go on an adventure with you. Take me to…" she made a production of considering the ceiling "…how about a new universe?"

"Are you only saying this because you feel guilty for me staying here?"

"If that's true, then I'll turn around and leave you after— kidding!" Her lips puckered together. "I want to go."

He hadn't expected this. But he'd concede he had been kid-gloving her a little bit. In the early days of her recovery she'd needed it, but now...had he been blind to her coming alive right in front of him? Had he—horror of horrors—been holding *her* back?

"Okay, but—"

"No 'but's." She patted his cheek and skipped off toward the bedroom. "I'll go start packing."

22

SIYANE

The instant they traversed Portal B-3 to Akeso's universe, the distress coursing through Caleb's blood spiked to a painful level. It screamed through his ears from the inside out, less a call for help and more a cry of vexation—of dismay, frustration and a taint of fear so foreign to Akeso's essence.

He gritted his teeth and tried to push the clamor to the background, because Akeso's distress was riling up the *diati*. It hummed in agitation, if not understanding. He held his hands up in front of his face and found them radiating crimson auras. "We should hurry."

Alex's lips were drawn thin and tight. Of course she was sensing the increased anxiety as well.

He reached over and touched her shoulder. "Sorry. You already know."

"It's definitely an uncomfortable sensation, but at this point I'm mostly worried about what we're going to find."

He didn't dare draw any conclusions yet, but whatever was happening could not be good. Akeso wasn't exactly the panicky sort, yet panic now laced every vibration.

ᴀʀ

A small astronomical body orbited Ekos-2 at the lowest sustainable altitude. Any closer and would become trapped by the planet's gravity well and soon crash to the surface.

"Akeso didn't have a moon."

Caleb shook his head. "No. This is the moon from Ekos-3."

"Surely not. It should have taken several decades at a minimum for it to *somehow* get here, not seven months, regardless of whether it managed a slingshot maneuver or simply propelled itself here by launching projectiles for thrust." Her eyes narrowed. "If the Kat watcher here, or any of the Kats, helped the moon along to engineer this confrontation...."

"The Kats have their ethereal hands full at the moment. I doubt they have the time to play games in their toy universes."

Alex scowled. "I'm just saying, if they *did?*"

"Then words will be exchanged. But that's for later."

"Focus on solving the crisis at hand. Right. Valkyrie, what else do we know?"

'In the time since our last visit, the lunar body has also developed a mature atmosphere and been fully terraformed. You would likely be able to breathe on the surface.'

She glared at the moon in suspicion. "Let's not find out. I seem to recall this one didn't like us too much. Bring us around so we can see what's transpiring between the moon and the planet."

As they crested the lower profile of the moon, the answer soon became clear: a tremendous amount. Spherical objects similar to the ones they had previously witnessed Ekos-3 delivering to its moon were now being hurled from the moon into Akeso's atmosphere. At any given time a dozen or more were en route.

Caleb frowned; the tactic shouldn't work in reverse. "Aren't the projectiles burning up in the planetary atmosphere? I assume they're made of timber and foliage."

'Initial analysis indicates they are encased in a protective layer of resin. Though the layer is not impenetrable, it enables some portion of most of the projectiles to survive and reach the surface.'

Alex snorted. "Clever little devil plant." She shifted to face him. "Game plan?"

He watched the moon's attack proceed apace for another second, but gaping in horror wasn't going to save the day. They needed to act. "First, and quickly, let's drop down and assess how Akeso is responding to the attack. See if anything I tried to teach it is making a difference. If so, we don't want to accidentally work at cross-purposes."

She altered their trajectory into a steep descent.

'The atmosphere in the region currently being targeted—but not in other regions—is denser than on our last visit.'

He was briefly heartened. "Akeso's trying to make it harder for the projectiles to get through. That's something."

The atmosphere fought them as well, and it was a bumpy ride down.

When they cleared the cloud layer, at first nothing looked amiss. But maybe he needed to look with better eyes.

He stopped trying to seal off Akeso's voice and opened himself up to the desperate anxiety churning inside him. It hurt, but he bore the pain, because it meant Akeso hurt a thousand-fold more intensely.

Now he saw the turmoil beneath the idyll. No wind rustled leaves, but tree limbs quivered nonetheless. Grass blades stood at attention, and the streams had developed rapids without obstructions to overcome. The thickened atmosphere created a canopy of angry clouds that stole the color from the normally vibrant flora.

Then there were the scorch marks. They spotted four circles, each thirty meters in diameter, within which all life had been burnt through to a crisp. Dead zones.

Alex looked perplexed. "Is the attacker trying to burn the living organic material away? What would that achieve? I always assumed the physicality of Akeso's consciousness extended far underground, if not throughout the planet's interior."

"I don't think that's what's happening here. I think these marks are Akeso's doing. It's sterilizing anywhere the projectiles make contact."

"Why do you say that?"

"Because were I in Akeso's position, it's what I would do."

'Given limited options, this makes sense as a strategy. The immediate danger posed is one of infection. A lifeform such as the Ekos species shares many characteristics with a virus. One can presume the goal of the attacker is to parasitically overwhelm Akeso's consciousness and replace it with its own.'

"In which case a scorched earth defense may be the only way to stop it. Good analysis, Valkyrie."

Alex surveyed the scene below skeptically. "But can't Akeso, I don't know, overpower these islands of the enemy without too much trouble? It controls the whole planet, and these projectile impacts are barely more than pinpricks in comparison."

Her point should be valid, but.... "Would it know if it did so successfully? Could it trust that it had?"

The possibility of one's own mind gradually *changing*, so subtly you might not even notice as bit by bit you became something other than what you had been, until one day, the old you would no longer recognize what you had become...he shuddered. He also recognized the shudder wasn't entirely on Akeso's behalf, but he couldn't dwell on it right now.

He shook his head. "No. Scorched earth is the better option, even though it means Akeso is killing pieces of itself."

They caught up to a projectile breaking through the atmosphere. It plunged to the surface like a meteor, and the impact shook the ground in rippling waves of fury.

Alex zoomed in the visual scanner, and they watched as root-looking appendages began wiggling their way out of the mass into the now-exposed dirt. The next second the surrounding grass, flattened by the impact, caught fire.

Caleb pressed the base of his palms to his temples as pain shot daggers through his mind. He could *feel* the grass blades dying, and with it the rising lament of Akeso's consciousness.

Alex shot him an anxious look. She didn't appear to be suffering as much as he, but she plainly felt it on some level.

The flames swiftly consumed the foreign matter, yet they continued to burn deeper into the ground in an attempt to eradicate all traces of the invader. The ring of fire extended out several meters beyond the impact crater.

Taking no chances. Sacrificing more of itself to save itself.

Finally the fire faded to smolder and die away. But there were other impacts ongoing elsewhere, triggering other fires of immolation. He didn't need to see them; he could sense them.

"Akeso's winning the battle for now, but it's losing the war. The attacker will force it to burn itself meter by meter until nothing remains. Then it will take over anyway." Abruptly he straightened up. "But we can stop it. *I* can stop it."

"Caleb...."

"Return to space."

She studied him openly, concern surpassing doubt on her countenance.

"Please, trust me."

"I do." She nodded in acceptance and arced the ship upward.

ℛ

They hovered four kilometers above the lunar surface, cloaked and undetectable.

Alex drummed her fingers on the dash. "We can open fire and not stop—use Akeso's tactic and burn up the flora. It'll attack us, but the Rifter can handle the onslaught. Oh, even better—we've still got two negative energy missiles on board from when we were planning to go on the last AEGIS mission, before Plousia. They'll tear this moon up."

"Not badly enough, or fast enough. We need to stop the attack now, then destroy it so completely it can't stay nearby, regrow the flora and try again. Maneuver us so we're situated directly between the moon and the planet."

"Do you really think you have enough power to do this?"

He hadn't told her the plan yet, but it seemed he didn't need to. "I think I must have enough power to do it. It's required."

"This will be orders of magnitude greater than anything you've attempted."

"Nisi said I hadn't begun to test the limits of my power. It's time I did."

She regarded him for another beat, but did as he asked before he was forced to press the point.

Here, situated in the scant space between the planet and the moon, the planet's mesosphere buffeted them as they worked to hold a stationary position, while its gravity tugged at them as they worked to remain aloft.

Caleb breathed in, trying his damnedest to *focus* amid all the wrenching sensations coming from the planet below—despair, anger, confusion—his own response to them, and the *diati's* instinctual feedback loop response to both. "Valkyrie, activate the Rifter."

The lights in the cabin dimmed. The extra power needed to maintain their position plus the power needed to run the Rifter meant there wasn't much left over.

'Done.'

"Get ready." Whatever that meant, right? His field of vision narrowed until the moon became all he saw.

DESTROY

A wave of energy surged out of him, and everything went black.

AR

"Caleb, talk to me! Valkyrie, what's wrong with him?"

He felt empty. Weak.

Warnings of moderate severity from his eVi flashed in his vision. He blinked until his eyes stayed open. He was on the floor outside the cockpit. Alex's face floated centimeters above him. She looked frightened.

"I'm okay."

"You're white as a sheet..." her brow creased "...and your irises are almost blue."

That explained the emptiness, at least. "How long?"

Her hands roved from his cheeks down over his neck, but any damage there was wouldn't be found on the outside. "Just a few seconds."

He let Alex help him to his feet and stumbled into the cockpit in time to see fissures opening up on the moon's exterior. They raced in all directions, cutting deepening scars into the crust and through to the mantle.

A barrage of projectiles hurtled toward the *Siyane*, as expected. Those that would have hit them were captured by the Rifter, to reemerge far from the planet below, alone and adrift to die in the void of space.

The moon began to crack apart. The surface crumbled as it came unmoored from its core. Alex gasped. He concentrated harder.

AWAY

Despite being mostly apart from him, the *diati* obeyed his command. The moon shuddered and rocked back as its structure lost all coherence. Trees and chunks of rock separated from the disintegrating surface, but all the pieces traveled away from them and the planet below, off into space. It was as if an invisible force drove them away.

Which of course it did.

His knees wobbled, and he leaned into the dash for support. He was weak because all his *diati* was out there executing on his commands, drawing purpose and intentionality from his will. Draining him of the strength needed to fuel its actions.

The last clinging pieces of the mantle were stripped away, leaving the core of the moon exposed to the vagaries of space—but before space could do its work, the core blew apart in a torrent of metal, melting then resolidifying into misshapen clumps.

A few stray pieces escaped the *diati* wall to pummel the Rifter or fall into the atmosphere. But in the unlikely event they retained any scrap of living matter, Akeso would be able to handle them.

Still, a final effort was needed to ensure no trace of the threat lingered to bide its time and grow stronger once again. He didn't know if he could do it.

But he must be able to do it.

AWAY

As if hit with a shockwave, the remnants of the moon, already little more than a field of debris, shot away and was swallowed up by the blackness.

He nearly fainted a second time, his vision blurring as his grip on the dash faltered and the cockpit lost definition. Then all the *diati* rushed back to him in its own shockwave.

The physical force slammed him against the cockpit half-wall. He gasped air into his lungs as a crimson aura throbbed above his skin, head to toe. The world spun around him, and it occurred to him if he wanted to he could control it—not the spinning, but the world. The subatomic particles making it up.

Now he exhaled, again whole—more than whole—and invigorated. The aura faded into his skin, and the trauma of the whiplash vanished beneath the power of so much *life* flowing through him.

He gave Alex a blasé smile in response to her gaping, wide-eyed expression. "How about we go see how Akeso's doing?"

23

CHIONIS

E ren had worked up a proper head of righteous steam by the time he stormed into Xanne's office at Post Alpha.

The woman spun her chair around to face him. Her jaw briefly locked in restrained annoyance at the interruption. "Eren, what—"

"The next time I null out, I want the techs or docs or whoever does this sort of thing to tweak my genetic makeup. Bring me back as...a Kyvern, or an Antalla, or whatever. I don't care, so long as you get this Idoni sickness out of me, once and for all."

She stared at him, ended a comm she'd apparently been on when he'd barged in, and adjusted her posture. "It doesn't work like that. If we meddled in your genetics to such an extent, you wouldn't be you any longer."

"All the better."

"We can't and won't do that, Eren. It's an unethical practice one expects from the Directorate, not the anarchs."

He slouched down in the guest chair. "Then don't bring me back at all. Disconnect me from the regenesis servers. Next time, I'll die for good same as every other anarch lucky enough to not be Anaden."

"You think it's 'lucky' to be consigned to die forever due to an accident of fate?"

"I think it's the appropriate fate for a monster like me."

"You're not a monster, Eren."

"As the resident expert on me, I beg to differ."

She frowned. "Did you do something I should be informed about? Something you left out of your mission reports?"

"Not lately. But it turns out, I can't outrun my past. I tried, but I can't outrun who I am."

She offered him a kind, motherly smile. "Eren, you're not the first anarch to come to us carrying the baggage of a questionable past. We all have sins to bear in one way or another. The important thing is that you chose to put them behind you and devote yourself to an honorable calling. If you're paying a penance, well, it's a worthwhile path to follow."

He struggled to keep the resurgent despair off his face. She didn't need to see it. "You're a good person, Xanne. Better than many of us deserve, and a damn sight better than I do."

He stood, pivoted and left as quickly as he'd arrived.

Eren fumbled around in the drawer for his stash of *ferusom*. Vials lined the surface of the bureau, waiting for imbibement, but this was the one that would ensure the cocktail of hypnols sent him into a true oblivion. To a place where he could escape. Not permanently, not yet, but right now he'd take escaping for a night. He'd figure out how to escape tomorrow, tomorrow.

Xanne was wrong. She was kind and well-meaning, but she was wrong. Though he'd tried—gods how he'd tried—he hadn't put his sins behind him. He hadn't changed, *couldn't* change what he was. The monster wasn't just in his genes; it was in his soul, and he could not excise it.

He paused to take a long swig from the bottle of wine Caleb and Alex had so generously gifted to him, then began rummaging again.

There it was. He grabbed the slender flask and slammed the drawer shut, sending several of the vials skittering off the top of the bureau.

"*Arae!*" He grabbed for the vial of *charist* as it tumbled through the air toward a terrible fate. He succeeded in rescuing it, but doing so caused the *ferusom* to slip from his grasp and shatter on the hard floor.

"No...." He dropped to his knees beside the wreckage to drag a finger across the seeping liquid and lick it off his finger in desperation. A hint of the rush hit him instantly. But it was merely a tease, so he followed the trail of liquid under the bed—

"Ow!" His fingertip came back bloody, sliced open from a shard of broken glass.

Laevona would stand in as a substitute. Where did it go? He glanced around while sucking on his busted fingertip. Not seeing it on the bureau or the floor, he stretched out on his chest and peered under the bed, then reached into the darkness and felt around for it.

Now his whole palm came back bloody. He didn't care. The tantalizing buzz from the taste of *ferusom* was already fading, and he had to get out of his head, now.

"Eren?"

He rose up in surprise, and promptly banged his skull on the bottom edge of the bed. The jolt of pain sent his bloody hand instinctively to the source, which succeeded only in getting blood in his hair. When he found a knife he'd slice it all off. Easier that way.

"Gods, Eren." Cosime hurried into his room and knelt beside him. "I'm sorry, I didn't mean to startle you."

He shrank away from her, extracting himself from beneath the bed to press against the bureau while he remained focused on the floor. "Go away, Cosime."

"No. What's wrong? You look a wreck. You're bleeding and...there's sharp glass everywhere. What broke? Hold on." There was the sound of movement out of his field of vision, then a towel was thrust in front of him. "Here. At least hold this over the cut. Assuming there's only one...."

Her voice dropped as she finally took in the full state of his room. "Are these all hypnols?"

"Just *go*. Leave me, please."

"What is—"

"Permanently, in fact. You don't want to be around me any longer. I'll poison your life." A glint of light flashed off to his left; it was reflecting off the vial of *laevona* that had rolled under the bureau. He retrieved it and hurriedly turned it up, dumping the contents onto his tongue unfiltered.

There. Soon enough he wouldn't even be aware of her bright emerald eyes gazing at him in naïve concern. She didn't *know*, and soon he wouldn't care.

She reached out and snatched the vial away while it was still a third full.

He shot her a glare and grabbed at her hand, but she held it out of the way. "I think I get to decide if I want to be around you."

"Don't be stupid. Leave and don't look back."

"Eren, what is *wrong*? Xanne commed me because she was worried about you. What happened?"

"I can't…." She'd drawn closer to him as she talked, and his hand again darted out for the vial she held. But she was so damn agile, and in a flash she'd rolled away and stood. Next she proceeded to glide around the room, picking up even the unbroken vials and tossing them into the garbage chute.

He groaned in desperation—but then he spotted one lonely vial lodged under his knee. Without checking to see what it was, he turned it up while she was too far away to steal it.

"Dammit, Eren! You're going to overdose if you keep this up."

He smiled vaguely as his vision blurred and he slumped farther down, closer to the floor. "Good. The point."

The sliding *whoosh* of the door closing sounded echoey and distant. It took a long time to close. Minutes, probably.

Sometime later she appeared beside his head, sitting with her legs wound beneath her among the spilt hypnols and random stains of blood. Her hands took hold of his shoulders. She guided his head into her lap. Soft fingers coaxed sticky strands of hair out of his face.

Glittering eyes stared down at him. Infinite facets reflected emerald light over and over and over…. "Let me help you."

He shook his head, he thought. "Can't. I'm a fiend, Cosime, fit for Tartarus. You should run."

"No, you're not, Eren. You're a good man with a few occasionally fiendish tendencies."

"What? Why do you…?" He squinted up at her, but it didn't help bring her features into focus.

"You think I don't know you have a dark side? In that case, you're also a very silly man." She bent down and kissed his forehead. "My dear, sweet, mad, broken Eren."

He blinked away a new bleariness. Was he crying? No, ridiculous. Must've gotten a hypnol in his eyes. Not the kind meant to go there.

She stroked his hair, surely getting blood all over herself, and he felt himself giving in. To her, and to the blissful oblivion.

A whisper hovered in his mind, and maybe on his lips. "Then help me, if you would. If you dare…."

The darkness closed in.

Eren awoke to a sharp pain behind his skull and an unexpected softness beneath his back. Vague recollections drifted in and out of his mind, but he wasn't able to tell which were real and which were hallucinations.

He opened his eyes and blinked several times. He was on his bed, or *a* bed anyway. The lighting was dimmed, thankfully, because oh dear gods did his head hurt.

Cosime sat beside him, one leg curled beneath her and the other dancing off the edge.

He licked his lips. They tasted like spoiled hypnols and sour wine. "How did I get in the bed?"

"The long way. Have some water." She thrust a glass in his face.

He was too thirsty to argue, so he struggled up to a lounging position then guzzled it down. His shredded palm had been cleaned up and treated, and the cuts were almost healed. How long had he been out? He was afraid to ask.

He handed the glass to her and began studying the matted tips of his hair. Two hours in the shower, or slice it off? "I don't…I don't know what to say. You weren't supposed to see that."

"Because if I didn't see it, then I would go on thinking of you as daring, dashing, daemons-better-not-care Eren?"

He risked a sideways peek at her. "…Yes?"

She laughed. It was delightful, if brief. "Why don't you start by telling me what happened to set this crisis off?"

"You don't want to know."

Her hand folded over his. "Eren, I'm your partner. I'm your friend. I'm your...." For the briefest moment, her incessant movement ceased, and she stilled. "I want to know."

He slid back down until his head found the pillow. He was so tired...and in the aftermath of the epic tantrum he realized he couldn't keep up the charade any longer. Not if he wanted to live. And since Xanne wouldn't let him die, living was the only option.

Possibly even the better one.

He didn't know if true redemption existed out there or if he could ever find it. But when Cosime looked at him like this, full of trust and belief in him that wasn't so naïve as he'd thought, maybe he could find the strength to try again.

Only this time he couldn't run from the monsters in his soul. He'd run out of trail.

He took a deep breath and started rambling.

24

EKOS-2

The lingering odor of charred grass marred the underlying scent of eucalyptus and honeysuckle Alex remembered. The vague melancholy in her blood made her think perhaps Akeso noticed, too, though the planet undoubtedly had larger concerns at the moment than aromas.

On the contrary, I posit that for a lifeform who values the exquisiteness of the smallest experiences, few things hold greater importance than the scent of a budding flower at the dew-drenched sunrise.

Damn, Valkyrie. Is there something I should know about you and Akeso's relationship?

I simply strive to understand it. In understanding it, I relate and empathize.

Evidently so.

Regardless, it was a temporary phenomenon. The warm breeze would carry the remnants of soot away soon enough, scattering them until they faded out of existence. In time, new growth would push upward through the scarred ground and return a vibrant palette to the surface. In time, no evidence would remain of the battle fought here.

Given the nature of the life in residence, she wouldn't be surprised if that time was tomorrow morning.

A visible change in Caleb's stance forewarned her he was preparing to try a new tactic. She discreetly moved closer to him—not so close she interfered, but close enough to be able to intervene if needed.

He removed the hilt of his blade from its sheath, activated the blade and swiped it across his open palm. He didn't flinch as blood flowed out and between his fingers to drop to the ground; instead he reached up and ran his open palm down the vine he'd been trying to woo for the last while.

When nothing happened, he scowled and flipped his hand over, palm up.

The cut had completely healed. Not by Akeso's actions, but rather by the *diati*, she assumed, given the frustration coloring his sigh.

"I'm not getting anything...or I don't think I am. Truthfully, though, Akeso could be chattering away incessantly, yet I can't hear it because it's being drowned out by the *diati* whirring in my head. It won't *shut up*." He dropped the vine and wandered to the shore of the creek, his shoulders rising and falling as he breathed deeply in, then out.

He'd been attempting to make conscious contact with Akeso for at least twenty minutes now. They'd come to their favorite tree beside their favorite creek, since it was possible familiarity meant something to Akeso, too. But so far his efforts had been to no avail.

It was no wonder the *diati* was riled up, after what he'd done.

The power required to destroy a moon, to disintegrate four thousand exagrams of metal, rock and organic matter into space dust in a matter of seconds...had it ever existed in the hands of a single individual? The Praesidis Primor, she assumed, and he used it to oppress two and a half trillion lives. Caleb used it to save a single, vast, precious life. But there was still a price to be paid.

Alex watched him for a minute, watched him try yet again to quiet the chaos raging inside him. She didn't need him to tell her he wasn't having any success. She could see it in the stiffness of his neck and the rigid set of his profile.

She'd given him his space, but now he was spiraling toward misery, and that wouldn't do at all. It was time she helped.

She slipped her shoes and socks off before strolling past him into the creek to let the living water dance across her toes.

He shot her a dubious look but followed suit, leaving his shoes on the shore, rolling his pants up his calves and joining her. "Is this supposed to help me commune with Akeso?"

"No idea." She gave him a playful shrug—then shivered. "It's cold."

"No kidding." Together they picked their way to the shore until they reached dry grass. It was cool on the soles of her feet as blades replaced the water in tickling her toes.

She kept her voice casual. "You said that touching me helps to quiet the noise from the *diati*."

He smiled and placed a hand on her arm. "It does."

She turned into him and brought a hand up to cup his jaw. Her fingertips traced down his neck. "And me touching you does as well?"

He nodded.

Her lips quirked as her hands dropped to the hem of his shirt. She smoothly lifted it up and over his head, let it fall to the grass, and returned a hand to his bare chest.

His eyes twinkled in the fading light, flares of sapphire breaking through the crimson. "What are you doing?"

"Touching you."

His breath hitched as her palm followed the trail of dark, curly hair down to his navel. "I can see—feel—that."

"Good." One of her hands traveled leisurely across his shoulder as she circled around to his back, the other trailing behind, lower.

She placed a soft kiss at the dip between his shoulder blades as she applied pressure with her fingertips, massaging deliberately down muscles taut with coiled tension. Lately he'd been working out more often and more intensely—less for physical health than mental, she thought—and the muscles sculpted the skin of his back into flawless ridges. "Is it working?"

"Well…" he cleared his throat, but it didn't clear the roughness from his voice "…it depends. The *diati* is quieting, but other impulses are definitely taking its place."

"I'm okay with that." She briefly withdrew her hands to pull her sweater and camisole off and discard them on the ground, then quickly gripped his hips and let her chest brush across his skin.

His sharp intake of breath forced his back more firmly against her. "Jesus, baby. Come here."

"In a minute." She chuckled throatily but held his hips steady to dissuade him from turning around. When it seemed like he was willing to obey, she slid her hands along his waist and deftly unfastened his pants, then slipped her thumbs a few centimeters below the waistband and dragged them around to the small of his back. She kneaded her thumbs into the pressure point and evoked a sigh that morphed into a groan.

Sensing the time for teasing foreplay was rapidly coming to a close, she relented and slid his pants and underwear down over his hips—

—he wrenched around and crushed her against him. His mouth slammed into hers as one hand splayed across her jaw and the other pressed into her spine to keep her close.

She almost gave into the passion for the briefest span of time, then had to create some space before she lost herself completely. Which would be a sublime thing to do, but she had a plan, dammit, and she would not be deterred. Not yet.

His hold loosened, if reluctantly, in response to her movement away, and she took the opportunity to swiftly drop to her knees and slide his pants the rest of the way down in a single motion. With the next motion her lips were on him.

"You—" The remaining words evaporated beneath a moan. She murmured in satisfaction, but the truth was the raw visceralness of the moan sent her own desire screaming headlong into overdrive. Her grip on his ass tightened instinctively, but she blinked and tried to concentrate on the admittedly delightful task at hand. She could wait, and it would be worth it.

With a growl his hand fisted in her hair and tugged her head back. She looked up at him wearing a wicked grin, and he dropped to his knees in front of her. His mouth met hers as he guided her down to the pelt of grass.

By the time her head came to rest on the ground, his tongue had grazed over her neck to dance down her chest to her abdomen. "How is a single stitch of clothing still on you and in my way?"

She exhaled and closed her eyes. She'd lied; she couldn't wait. "I was otherwise occupied."

"Yes, you were." His lips were voracious, his hands purposeful, and her pants disappeared while she was distracted by other sensations.

His tongue burned hot on her skin, in delicious contrast to the cool grass beneath her, as his mouth wound back up her body with agonizing slowness.

He'd turned the tables on her...devious, crafty man, he was.

An aeon later he hovered above her, pausing for a frozen, endless second before the full length of his body lowered to press against hers. The crimson irises deepened to a bottomless burgundy as night fell around them.

"There's no noise now. There's only you." He slipped inside her.

She smiled as his lips brushed hers, and a final, satisfied thought lingered in her mind as she at last surrendered to the passion.

Mission flawlessly accomplished.

R

Caleb tried to smooth Alex's hair down, wrent askew as it was by...well, mostly by him. But it was a tangled, damp mess, wild and beautiful like her, and after a few attempts he gave up, instead chuckling breathily and squeezing her tighter against him.

She placed a sideways kiss to his sternum then rested her cheek on his chest. One of her legs stretched out next to him while the other curled over his thighs.

Perfect moment as it was, he allowed himself to bask. To not merely acknowledge but absorb and commit to memory this idyllic confluence of sensations and sentiment.

"You're my savior—you know that, right?"

She peered up at him, crookedly as he refused to loosen his hold on her. "I'm just trying to keep up with you."

Perhaps they would go on like this forever, saving one another again and again in endless circles. It had already proved truer than he could have imagined that fateful night on Pandora, hadn't it?

As their insane lives veered and spun and flipped inside-out yet again—completely their own fault, admittedly—it might be the only thing in any universe they could truly count on. Each other, always there to save the other.

She shifted languidly, molding her body more fully to his. "We should maybe think about heading back soon. War and all."

"Mm-hmm...." He reached beside him and felt around until he found his shirt, then draped it across their legs.

Seconds later he felt her breath even out and her muscles slacken in slumber. He inhaled and took in the woodsy scent. He listened to the creek babble. He closed his eyes and joined her.

R

Not-Alls returned to protect All.

Of course we did. You are a part of us. We heard your plea from across the stars.

All dared not hope Not-Alls would heed it.

We will never fail to come to your aid. If there is a way for us to do so, we will find it and help you.

All does not comprehend why an Other sought to destroy All.

All was...afraid. All was...angry. All recognizes these concepts from Not-All's memories and names them so.

But now...All is safe? Other is gone?

Yes, it's gone. We made certain it can't hurt you ever again. Are you all right? Are you well? What of the pieces of...of the Other that damaged you? Can they still infect you, or weaken you?

All replaces, renews, replenishes.

All cleanses the traces of Other, as it cleansed such from other Not-All before. The traces will become All.

Good. You are stronger than any Other.

All is All, and will always be.

But Not-All has changed. Is More.

More is new, and very, very old.

Does this bother you?

Not-All remains odd, both one and many, both brutal and benevolent. Now Not-All is also both itself and More.

All cannot name this More, but All senses harmony and kinship with it, and thus with the very old newness of Not-All.

I'm glad.

All also senses struggle, but comprehends that struggle is not new for Not-All.

All would soothe it, for having shared Not-All's pain, All would bring peace to Not-All. But the source is beyond All's sight.

All begins to understand that struggle is not always injury, and not all pain can be healed.

All is very wise. I think the struggle is just part of who I am. What is new—or very old—fuels this in me, but it is also what gave me the power to protect All from Other. So I accept the burden with the benefit.

Not-All *is* quite strange indeed. All accepts this.

All thanks Not-All for its aid. For its warning, and its knowledge. For its peculiar, alien fierceness and defiance, though All desires never again to need to experience it in so profound a manner.

All is grateful to know Not-All.

And Not-All is so grateful to know All. I wish for All the peace I am not allowed.

Might Not-All and other Not-Alls stay a while?

I wish we could, I do. But we must depart soon, for there are many Others we must defend against, and many Not-Alls who need our protection.

Not-Alls who exist in the twinkling canopy of light amid the darkness you call 'stars'?

Yes. That's right. We must travel those stars to help our kin. But we will return one day, when no Other threatens, and when we do, we will stay a while. I promise.

All does not concern itself with stars...but All believes it will watch them now. For the encroachment of Others, and for the return of Not-Alls.

Caleb opened his eyes to the awareness of two things: the vine wound snugly around his hand and forearm, and Alex's gently smiling face gazing upon him.

He blinked and gradually took note of additional details. The crisp air was free of soot and the odor of dead things—not yet filled with the bloom of young life, but cleansed and ready to begin anew. The sky was clear, free of the laden clouds that had so valiantly defended against the attack.

He saw all this because it was dawn, which meant he had slept. Sometime during the night sleep had become communion, initiated by Akeso. The vine now unwinding from his hand and gliding away, as well as the clarity of the recollection, meant it hadn't been a dream. As did the pinprick of blood in the center of his palm.

The tiny stab wound created by the vine's thorn had already sealed, but not before a new trace of All was left behind inside him. He could sense it.

He could also sense the inevitable struggle between it and the *diati* to make peace with one another begin. Should be entertaining.

Alex motioned toward the vine as it retreated to its proper location draping from the tree above them, a questioning glint in her eyes.

He nodded. "Akeso's good, and so are we. We can go now."

"I'm glad it reached out to you." She drew closer for a soft, lingering kiss before crawling to her feet and beginning the search for her scattered clothing.

"So am I. You should know, I promised it we'd come back for a longer visit when the war was over."

She laughed as she slipped on her camisole. "That's fantastic. So we will."

25

PALAEMON

"Here. Eat something."

Kennedy glanced up at Noah hovering above her, then down at the plate he'd slid in front of her. "Is it our food, or theirs?"

"Doesn't it look like our food?"

She tilted her head to the side, then gathered her hair up and tucked it behind her shoulder before it fell into the plate. The food did appear both familiar and utterly normal—a whole grain pita wrapped around lettuce, salami and what was maybe feta cheese and a yogurt spread. A formerly frozen fruit medley occupied the other half of the plate.

Still, she hesitated. "I haven't been here long enough to be sure what their food looks like."

Noah plopped into the chair beside her and took an enthusiastic bite of his own sandwich. He washed it down with a sip of his energy drink then stared at her deadpan. "They moved a crate of provisions down here last night. It's military-issue, but the higher-quality officer fare. It's ours."

"Thank you." She flashed him a quick smile and started picking at the food.

They were situated in one of the three work rooms assigned to AEGIS at the anarch base, and she was ostensibly 'working' on deciphering the secrets of the Imperium-class vessel's unbreachable shield, with the goal of enabling AEGIS to breach it. She had a schem flow detailing the shield's functionality; she had vidcam footage from the battle at the Provision Network Gateway showing it in action. She didn't have much else.

"What's wrong?"

"What?" She blinked and realized she'd been staring at the fruit on her fork for…a while. She set the fork down, sighed and shifted to face Noah. "I'm struggling."

"With the shield?"

"No. I mean, yes, it's a puzzler. But I…didn't expect to be as weirded out by this place as I am."

Noah checked the door and lowered his voice. "There are definitely some weird aliens out there."

"And weird tech and weird beds and weird food. Also, no sooner did we get here than everyone turned around and left. Miriam's back through the portal with Mia. Alex and Caleb took off to save some plant, or plant-planet, or something. Everyone here is looking at me like *I'm* the alien, and I simply don't understand what I'm supposed to be doing."

"You've weathered a whole mess of change in the last year and a half, and you've done it in style. If this is one change too many, I don't think anyone would blame you."

"It's not that, exactly. I guess I feel a little abandoned—not by you, of course." She winced and tried to be self-deprecating. "I was supposed to be coming here because I was *important*, but then I got dumped. I know it's not true. I know Miriam would rather be anywhere in creation other than Washington right now, and I know Alex wasn't expecting to have to pull an emergency save in the Mosaic. But here we are."

She straightened up and retrieved her sandwich wrap. "Enough self-pity for me. I need to eat, then I need to tear this shield down and build it back up until I understand it."

Noah sneaked in close for a kiss before the sandwich made it to her mouth. "Which you will. Do you have everything you need?"

She finally got her bite, and shook her head while she chewed. "Not even close. Somewhere approaching twenty percent of the shield specs reference parts and ship mechanisms I have no understanding of—what they are or what they do. The words translate, but not to anything meaningful. I've worked out most of the mechanics of *what* the shield does, but *how* it does it involves science I don't comprehend. No human does, not yet."

He dropped his half-eaten sandwich on his plate and leapt up. "Give me twenty minutes."

"For what?"

But he was already gone.

AR

Kennedy put away her empty plate. The food really was welcome, and it had returned energy to her she hadn't realized she'd needed.

She was organizing the information on hand in a haphazard pattern of screens that was nevertheless logical to her when Noah came back.

A stocky Anaden with military hair and a naturally military gait followed him into the work room. "This is Sander ela-Machim. Sander, allow me to introduce Kennedy Rossi." Noah gave her an encouraging nod. "You have questions—gaps in knowledge. This man has some of the answers. For the rest of the answers, one of the tech officers is going to drop by about an hour from now."

It was jarring to hear Noah speaking Communis, but it reminded her to do so. This Sander Anaden person was gazing at her uncertainly, so she stood and switched on the charm. "It's a pleasure to meet you, sir."

"Ma'am. The Sator says we're to assist you—the Human visitors—however we can, so I'm at your service."

"Please, sit." She gestured across the table, then subtly nudged the screens off to one side. "I'm studying the physical barrier shield the Imperiums use for defense, in the hope we can discover a way to disable or counter it."

Sander paused halfway around the table. "I'm not an engineer, ma'am. I was a military officer."

Because all Machim were military, anarch or not. She had been told this. "I understand. Have you ever been on board an Imperium?"

"Yes, ma'am. I served as a Senior Deck Supervisor on one of the LGG Region II Imperiums. It was my next-to-last assignment before..." he cleared his throat "...before I became an anarch."

Alex had talked a bit about what it meant for an Anaden to reject their Dynasty and join the resistance. She didn't know this man, but she should default to respecting him.

"Excellent. That's perfect. Tell me about serving on the ship. What was your typical shift like? What did people do—how did things work?"

⟁

It was nearly three hours later when Kennedy watched the tech officer depart.

Sander had proved a challenging if productive resource, but Iveane ela-Erevna had spoken Kennedy's language. Occasionally several tiers *above* her language, but her language nonetheless. The woman had even brought in a data reader and a couple of Reor slabs and walked her through several schematics.

Now she sank deeper in her chair and eyed Noah with a mix of amazement and unabashed adoration. "How did you pull that off?"

He was wearing a smug expression, but he deserved to. "Since we got here, I've been...doing what I do. Talking to people—aliens, but they're really just people. While you and your colleagues have been doing the headline work, I've been getting to know the people nobody notices. The cafeteria supervisor, and the guy who fixes the bots that fix the walkways and bridges. Doing the legwork meant that today, I had contacts I could go to and ask, 'Hey, is there a Machim here who knows his shit and has seen the inside of an Imperium?' and get a real answer."

"You're incredible."

"Nah, you're incredible. But I'm probably awesome."

She sank into his lap with a giggle and wound her arms around his neck. "Definitely."

26

SIYANE

Once they cleared Akeso's atmosphere, Alex initiated the sLume drive, but only for a few seconds. The stars had no sooner blurred away when they again snapped into sharp relief, then were promptly drowned out by the system's sun.

She arced around to bring the sun into full view…and in the foreground, a planet below.

Caleb swiveled his chair around to face Alex. "Ekos-3."

She nodded slowly and stared out the viewport.

"You're thinking that as long as it exists it's a threat."

"Because it is. Valkyrie, am I reading these measurements right?"

'The planet appears to be in a state of some agitation. Elevated tectonic activity is measurable across all regions. Its orbital eccentricity has increased by 0.0217° and its inclination by 0.5288° since our last visit. Both appear to be stable at present, but we have not been in sensor range long enough for me to be certain.'

Alex toed her chair back and forth. "I think we can assume it was in communication with its offspring on the moon and knows what happened, which explains the agitation. The change in orbit could be an effect of whatever it did to launch its moon across the stellar system, or it could represent the beginnings of a new play. The planet might be able to alter its orbit enough to eventually intersect Akeso's orbit. Hell, it might even be gearing up to slingshot itself around its sun. It wants Akeso—for starters—and it's previously demonstrated it will go to great lengths to get what it wants."

Given that it had succeeded in sending its moon across space to reach Akeso, this was indisputably true. Ekos-1 had tried to kill them, too, but objectively only in misguided self-defense. This planet, however, represented a true threat.

But what could they do to stop it from trying again? His actions the day before had taken every last drop of his admittedly mind-boggling power.

His elbows on his knees, he clasped his hands together and dropped his chin atop them. "Alex, this planet is at least..." he quickly called up their scientific files on both bodies "...one hundred forty times more massive than its moon. I don't want to be negative, but I don't think I can blow it apart."

She reached over to squeeze his knee. "I know. You don't need to. I've got this one."

"*You're* going to blow the planet apart?"

"That would be so satisfying, but sadly, no. I realize we can't destroy it completely. Not today with the tools at hand. But we can set it back and give it something else to focus on for a while: its own survival."

He sat up straighter. "Okay. How?"

"Here's where we *do* use the negative energy missiles. Valkyrie, where's the best spot on the planet to burn a hole through the crust into the mantle, then drop the missiles in? Where will cause the most disruption to its orbit or, even better, its structural integrity?"

'The planet exhibits an axial tilt of 21.6°, with the southern pole being closest to the sun at this phase of its orbit. I believe boring a hole a minimum of 9.6 kilometers deep at 82° 3′ 14″ S 4.9° 22′ 29″ E, near the geographic south pole, will expose the mantle sufficiently to cause significant disruption to the planet's stability.'

"Excellent. In that case, entering the atmosphere." She drove the bow downward into the planet's comparatively thin atmosphere, and before long they broke through light cloud cover on the other side.

They remained cloaked, so for now they didn't draw the ire of the towers dotting the planet.

Even fresh off his communion with Akeso, it was easy to think of the structures as mere plants, as flora alive in only the most technical sense. But the structures were appendages of a planet-sized intelligence, and it was alive in the fullest sense. It was also malevolent and aggressive, and he would just as soon be rid of it.

But Alex...she'd demonstrated an unhesitant willingness to kill when it was necessary to protect herself or those she cared about, but she didn't have the soul of a killer. It wasn't ingrained in her psyche.

Was it possible she cared about Akeso as deeply as he? Though she lacked the personal bond he'd developed with the life form—it had never spoken explicitly to her—it had saved her life not so long ago. The acts which could earn her loyalty were sometimes quirky and difficult to predict, but that would definitely be one.

Still. He returned to his earlier pose, elbows on his knees, and regarded her intently. "Alex, if we're going to do this, let me be the one to fire the shots. There's already plenty of blood on my hands from this trip. I won't notice a little more."

"The trees don't bleed."

"Alex—"

A corner of her lips curled up. "It's fine. I'm looking forward to exacting a measure of fiery vengeance."

He watched her for another moment...and gave up trying to unburden her. He wasn't her keeper.

The bare ground away from the towers shifted from blanched umber to slushy snow and ice; the towers shrank in height but spread their roots more widely. Harvesting water.

They slowed as they approached the coordinates and finally stopped to hover a kilometer above the surface. "All right. I'm activating the Rifter, seeing as I'm about to piss this asshole planet off something fierce."

A second later she fired the *Siyane's* primary laser point-blank into the ground below.

The snow and ice hissed as they melted then boiled, and steam billowed up to obscure the surface. As expected, spears from the surrounding towers launched in the direction of the laser's origination, only to be swallowed up by the Rifter and spit out into space.

She kept firing.

It took a while to burn through to the depth they sought, and the planet's assault on them never let up. The relentless bombardment from the towers gradually ate away at the aura of peaceful contentment spun by the night and morning on Akeso, and the mood in the ship grew dark.

'The upper mantle is now exposed.'

Alex's mouth was set into a grim line as she deactivated the *Siyane's* primary weapon. "Finally. Preparing to fire the negative energy missiles. As soon as they're free, take us up to twelve kilometers altitude and be ready to flee farther. The reaction is likely to be violent, then possibly more violent."

'Understood.'

Alex tapped a point on the HUD with an index finger. "Missiles away."

They couldn't see when the missiles impacted the solid rock of the upper mantle, but they really didn't need to.

The rim of the twelve-meter-wide hole they'd created exploded outward as the surface and everything beneath it burst apart. Clouds of disintegrating minerals shot into the air, only to evaporate. Cracks raced in every direction, leaving the surface to crumble away in their wake. The towers within sight tumbled into the widening crevasses and vanished.

A plume of inky blackness surged out of the center of the cavity to rise high into the air—and keep going—as the ground beneath it continued to convulse. For a few ominous seconds, everything fell silent...then the consequences of a large swath of the mantle and crust being vaporized by antimatter began to ripple inexorably across the land that remained.

"Fairly violent, as these things go."

Alex tilted her head in acknowledgment. "Valkyrie, how did we do?"

'The situation is still volatile, but I estimate the initial damage plus the continuing chain reaction should cause a rapid increase in the planet's axial precession. Combined with the damage inflicted to the planet's internal structural integrity, this should degrade the orbital trajectory to such a degree that within two solar transits the sun's gravity will overtake the planet and drag it into the star.'

"'Should'?"

'If this were a normal planet incapable of intentional action, 'should' would mean a 96.4118% likelihood. As there are other factors involved here, the percentage is lower, but I cannot confidently say by how much.'

"Understandable. So best case, the planet becomes a lunch for its star in a few years. Worst case, the planet's intelligence spends the next few years feverishly working to patch itself up and stabilize its orbit before it burns up. Either way, it won't be focused on Akeso for a long time."

She blew out a breath. "It'll have to do for now."

"It'll more than do." He moved across the cockpit to kneel in front of her and grasp her hands in his. "You went above and beyond what Akeso, me or anyone else could ask. Are you okay?"

She glared out the viewport. "I just wish we were able to end it once and for all today. Right now."

"I know. So do I. But you've bought us time. And when this war is over and won, we'll come back with bigger weapons and finish the job."

"Then we'll take a nice, long vacation on one of Akeso's beaches."

He arched an eyebrow. "A beach? What's wrong with our creek?"

"Nothing's wrong with it. I'm simply saying a beach might be nice, too. You know, for a day or two, before we visit the creek. Or after."

He laughed faintly and drew her closer until her forehead rested on his and his hand rested along the curve of her neck. "Wherever you want, baby."

PART V:

SECRETS, LIES & SPACETIME MANIFOLDS

"The way of paradoxes is the way of truth. To test Reality we must see it on the tight-rope."

— *Oscar Wilde*

27

MW SECTOR 49 STORAGE DEPOT

MILKY WAY SECTOR 49

T he tiny figure in a powered hazard suit moved across the hull of the mammoth superdreadnought like a speck of dust sent adrift by an ill wind.

The Vigil agent—a low-level Machim officer or a Praesidis Watchman, or possibly even a newly minted *asi* Inquisitor not yet confident in their *diati's* ability to keep them alive in space—paused to attach the tracker dot at what must appear to their eyes to be an inconspicuous location on the sleek metal of the hull.

After securing it, they maneuvered farther down the hull, under and over to the other side, where they placed a second tracker dot 22.3° and 198 meters off the location of the first one.

Presumably satisfied with their work and assured of their clandestine execution of it, the Vigil agent thrusted across the gap to the other Provision Network supply vessel docked at the MW Sector 49 Storage Depot, where they painstakingly repeated the procedure upon it.

Lakhes gave the equivalent of an existential sigh. When the vessels departed the Depot, they would travel some twelve hundred parsecs distance before idling long enough for a Katasketousya to remove the tracker dots. The vessels would then proceed on an alternate course to their designated portal while the tracker dots were ferried off to somewhere in the void and deposited.

It was a thankless duty, but in the wake of the destruction of Katoikia, Lakhes had found no shortage of volunteers anxious to help in the struggle but lacking any tangible way to do so.

A ripple in dimensions caught Lakhes' attention; the next second Mnemosyne's essence settled into stillness nearby. Before a greeting could be imparted, a similar ripple on the opposite side heralded the arrival of Hyperion.

Lakhes allowed itself an interval of...wry amusement, the Humans might label it. Breaths earlier—months as Amaranthe counted time—the three of them had argued to great consequence above a lake on Aurora Thesi. Now they gathered in, if not friendship, at least peace, in a time of war.

Hyperion: They persist in their attempts to track the provision vessels?

Lakhes: They do. They have escalated to placing two tracking devices on each vessel, in the presumed hope that we will cease searching when we discover the first one.

Mnemosyne fluttered in consternation. *They are aware that we are aware that they are attempting to track the vessels to a portal, and further that we are actively thwarting their attempts to do so, yet they continue nonetheless?*

Lakhes: The resources expended to do so on their part are minimal. It is, one must presume, worth the expenditure of those resources to continue, on the infinitesimal chance we will eventually err and neglect to remove one of the devices. I needn't remind you, we only need err once to put the Mosaic in grave peril.

Mnemosyne: No, you needn't. They are not sending fleets chasing after every vessel, then?

Lakhes allowed a touch of mirth to animate the response. *The first two times they did indeed send a fleet to follow the tracker's trail. After this trail twice led to naught but void, and a notably distant void at that, they scaled back their efforts. Now a single scout ship arrives to investigate the final registered location and send the portal activation signal in all directions.*

Hyperion: But if a portal were to then open, I assume the fleet would arrive in due course.

Lakhes: I assume so as well.

The Vigil officer finished their clandestine work and powered off toward a side entrance of the Depot.

Mnemosyne: There has been activity in Enisle Eleven. Alexis in-quires whether its Analystae, or the Conclave in toto, intervened to enable or accelerate said activity.

Lakhes: Your Human friends did quite the intervening themselves.

Mnemosyne: As they do. Were we responsible for triggering this event, or no?

Hyperion: Our work in the Mosaic carries greater significance than ever now, and time is precious. They have no right or authority to judge our actions.

Mnemosyne: Lakhes?

Lakhes: No, we were not. The species inhabiting Enisle Eleven is merely more skilled and resourceful than the Humans appreciate. A most unique and fascinating species.

Mnemosyne: Thank you. I will convey your response.

They watched as the first of the provision vessels departed from the long exterior docks, its hold depleted of resources, and sped away on its false course.

Hyperion: So this farcical game continues, to no benefit.

The energy comprising Mnemosyne's presence rippled with new vigor. *Should we desire to provoke its cessation, we could devise a trap.*

Lakhes: How so?

Mnemosyne: We could deposit a confiscated tracking device at a portal's location and allow a scout ship to discover it. They will call in their fleet, and the fleet will traverse the portal—but instead of leading into the Mosaic, we will have set up an isolated space on the other side containing only a dimensional shifting device.

Hyperion: I admit, leading a Machim fleet in circles for an appre-ciable period of time would carry some amusement, but what you are suggesting will take significant effort on our part, to no real end. We have meaningful battles to wage. Or we will, should the Humans deter-mine to re-engage the enemy.

Mnemosyne grew yet more energetic, but did not launch into the defense of the Humans Lakhes anticipated after Hyperion's mild barb. *Perhaps it is not a circle we lead them in. We can control with a high degree of precision where they find themselves when they exit the dimensional shift. Perhaps the location is somewhere deadly—the photosphere of a star, say.*

Lakhes experienced genuine surprise. *Mnemosyne, I did not expect such shrewd artifice from you, arguably laced with a trace of bloodlust. The Humans are influencing you.*

Mnemosyne: They have much to teach, I admit. Their zeal for life can become infectious—

Hyperion: And their zeal for ending it?

Ah. There was the acerbity. But Mnemosyne again did not rise to the bait.

Mnemosyne: Is necessary for the living of it. I believe they would welcome the elimination of a sizeable Machim fleet, and would rather enjoy its elimination in this particular fashion.

Hyperion: On this we are in agreement. I daresay I would experience satisfaction from it as well.

Lakhes' wry amusement renewed. It seemed more than one positive outcome stood to emerge from this greatest of crises.

28

CHIONIS

E ren awoke to feathers tickling his nose.

Which didn't make any sense.

He suppressed a sneeze then carefully opened his eyes, to find it wasn't feathers at all—it was Cosime's downy hair.

Which didn't make much more sense than feathers.

He tried to think back to how this particular situation had come to be, but his brain was a groggy, tangled jumble of half-retained thoughts and jigsaw images. No longer excruciating pain, though...

...because it *had* been in excruciating pain earlier. He had been. He remembered, too much and not enough.

He'd talked to her despite the pain, without the strength, will or clarity of thought to maintain a filter on the words he spoke. At some point he'd fallen asleep—doubtless mid-sentence of some horror tale. But she hadn't left, and she must have eventually fallen asleep herself.

Now she was snuggled up against him, and his arms held her close. She still wore her clothes, but they were flimsy gossamer, as they always were, and bare skin rose and fell beneath his palm resting on her stomach.

How was it possible she had allowed him to *touch* her after the evils he'd given voice to?

Or had she? Likely she'd simply drawn closer in sleep, incognizant of what she'd done. Or maybe he'd taken advantage while she slept and—

Before he could properly panic or even start to decide what their current situation meant, how it had happened or what to do about it, she wiggled around to face him as she rubbed at sleepy eyes. "Morning."

"Good morning—or midday?" He perked up in spite of himself, so damn relieved she hadn't shrunk away in disgust when awareness dawned.

One hurdle cleared, his memories of the preceding hours began to reform and gain coherence. After he'd finished spilling his guts all over her, the bed and much of the floor, she'd asked him if the incident at the fete with the Faneros was the worst thing he'd ever done, or almost done. He'd answered honestly, since he'd lacked the presence of mind to do anything else. He'd said probably not, but any worse things he'd probably done he'd been too high to remember in the aftermath.

She'd merely nodded, but an overdose of hypnols then didn't prevent him from remembering now the ripple of darkness that had passed in a grim shadow across her sparkling eyes.

The shadow wasn't there now. And she'd stayed. *Stayed.*

He lifted his hand off the small of her back, where it had naturally slid to when she rolled over, and held it high out of the way. "Want to flee? I'll understand."

She shook her head, sending wisps of mussed hair to tickle his nose again.

"Okay, but whenever you decide you do, I'll still understand. Until such time, thank you. For everything, including enduring the dreadfully embarrassing things I hope I never remember saying or doing."

He brought his hand down to rest safely atop his own thigh. "So, not to get ahead of things like showers and food and possibly haircuts, but I have an idea I want to try to pull off."

She peered at him skeptically. "Sobriety?"

He swallowed and tried to regain the breath she'd just punched out of him, then offered her an uncertain smile. "Fair request. No promises, but...I'll try to do better. To be better."

"Good enough. Of course, anything that doesn't end with us both covered in your blood is technically 'better.'"

"What about missions?"

"I'd prefer you not spill blood during those, either. But I concede the point."

"Good, because what I was *going* to say is I have an idea for a mission. Exobiology Research Lab #4."

She sat up to prop against the wall, adjust her spiraire beneath her nose and stretch out her limbs. "You want to try again to blow it up?"

"No. Well, maybe at the end, sure. But I want to try to rescue the prisoners inside."

"You said they weren't worth trying to rescue—that if they didn't have the courage to fight for their own freedom, we couldn't help them."

"I've changed my mind. They only need to be given a chance, and a little help finding their way."

She pondered on it a minute. "I'm glad to hear you say so. But I don't think we have the resources to break into the Lab, free the prisoners and get them out and to safety."

He climbed over her, stood and, once he realized the shards of broken glass had been cleaned away, started pacing. The undercurrent of nausea the movement induced was mostly buried beneath the fire of conviction. Admittedly, though, he did need a shower, then another shower. He'd make it happen, soon.

"We definitely don't have the resources to pull off such a stunt—but the Humans do."

"You think they'll help us?"

"Oh, yes. Trust me, they love a good virtuous rescue, and they also happen to be excellent at them." He paused to give her another, more confident smile. "Kind of like you are."

29

AFS SARATOGA

MILKY WAY SECTOR 17

Malcolm rubbed at his temples and tried again to concentrate on the supply reports in front of him.

He should have gotten this done earlier, before Miriam's transport left for home. That way they could have brought back replacements for any supplies that were falling to dangerously low levels. But he hadn't gotten it done.

He wished he was able to blame the delay on the added work involved in getting set up at the anarch base and developing rules and procedures for its use, travel to and from, interactions with aliens and so on. Those tasks took time for certain, but in truth the inventory review could have been completed in a fraction of the time he'd spent moping over their losses at the Sagittae Gateway battle. Or the time he'd spent with Mia the night before she left for home—the time being the entire night—but he couldn't bring himself to feel guilty for the indulgence.

Still, he needed to do better if he wanted to be worthy of his rank. When he was the operations officer for the 3rd BC brigade in Vancouver, he'd been good at this sort of management task. He knew perfectly well how to do it. He simply needed to *do* it.

So he lifted his shoulders and focused.

Automated systems took care of tracking the depletion and subsequent requisitioning of most items used in everyday matters. But a number of larger, more specialized and more expensive equipment and supplies were lost in the disastrous Sagittae Arx explosion that took out the *Virginia* and multiple smaller ships. Most of what was lost fell within the responsibility of the flight supply officers and wasn't his problem, but an SF recon-interdiction vessel was destroyed as well as two AEGIS hybrid tactical craft, and with them a variety of materials. When added to assorted other collateral damage, the ground forces were down some tools of their trade.

> » *-22 each of splinter, flashbang, EM grenades / Responsible Party: IDCC RRF Operations*
> » *-44 enhanced plasma blades / Responsible Party: AEGIS Marine Oversight*
> » *-12 tactical mines / Responsible Party: SF MSO Operations*
> » *-16 TSG augments / Responsible Party: EA MSO Operations*

Having gotten a feel for the general nature and scope of the deficits, he began scanning faster down the list.

> » *-6 pairs of EM weave tactical gloves / Responsible Party: AEGIS Marine Oversight*
> » *-1 Reverb / Responsible Party: IDCC RRF Operations*

He continued down the list past another couple of items before jumping back up. How had a Reverb been lost? What had one been doing on any of the combat ships at all?

He'd only reluctantly allowed a few to be brought to Amaranthe in the first place. Like many of the tools Marines employed, Reverbs were dangerous, but in this case they were only dangerous to their own people. ASCEND didn't understand nearly enough about the Anadens' cybernetics to adapt the devices to be of any use against the enemy. Not yet. So he was of the opinion the still-experimental device didn't need to be here.

He checked the background information on the originating report; as he'd thought, all the Reverbs were stored in the IDCC locker on AEGIS' auxiliary support vessel, the *AFS Columbia*, which meant none were present at the battle. The discrepancy was flagged as part of a comprehensive supply check Miriam had ordered before she left, and it had made its way to this list because the Reverbs didn't fall within the automated replenishment system.

The fact it hadn't been lost in the battle meant its disappearance was far more troubling.

Though the crime rate in any military organization was low compared to civilian populations, crime *did* occur. Most incidents fell under the rubric of 'crimes of passion'—in other words, fights. But bad actors occasionally slipped through the screening process and made it into the military, and thefts, aggravated assaults, rapes and, very rarely, murders did happen. Given the nature of the Reverb device, he couldn't discount the possibility it had been stolen for a criminal purpose.

The devices were technically IDCC RRF property, on loan to AEGIS along with a lot of other equipment and people. He sent Harper a message to drop by when she got a moment, then continued working through the list.

R

Harper cleared her throat in the open doorway. "You wanted to see me, sir?"

Malcolm motioned her inside, toward the chair opposite his desk. "At ease, Captain." He passed her the secondary list he'd compiled of IDCC supply depletions. "Requisitions request for the next supply run to the Presidio."

"Didn't we just send—"

"We did." He shrugged. "It's been a challenging couple of days."

"The master of understatement, as always." Her eyes darted back and forth as she reviewed the list. "This doesn't seem too bad. Only the grenades are arguably critical, and I can borrow some from Alliance Supply Ops if needed. They always overstock everything."

"True. One more thing. It's not on the resupply list because I continue to be of the opinion we don't need them, but the IDCC locker on the *Columbia* is down a Reverb. You might want to have an MP take a look and try to determine if it was stolen. I don't relish the idea of one of those devices being loose among the troops."

"How many does the report say are accounted for?"

"Three."

Her chin lowered, taking her focus to the floor. "None are missing. Three is how many we brought."

"The initial supply report was wrong?"

"Not exactly."

He waited, but she didn't elaborate. "So it wasn't wrong?"

"It's…one Reverb is out on loan. I thought I'd be able to reacquire it, so I included it in the initial number. But I haven't had the chance to follow up on it yet." She nodded sharply. "My mistake, sir. I'll take care of it ASAP."

"It's on loan to someone in the fleet? In that case, it should have been checked out and recorded in the system—in IDCC's system, then transferred into AEGIS' system when this operation began."

She glanced toward the door, a distinct sense of longing in her bearing. "I loaned it out to a…colleague for a non-IDCC matter during the OTS unrest. I expected it to be returned promptly, but events intervened, emergencies emerged and the opportunity didn't arise. As I said, I'll take care of it."

"You're assisting in off-the-books operations by non-IDCC personnel? Harper, why would you do such a thing? You could lose your job over it."

Her jaw locked into place. "Sir, respectfully, as you're not my commanding officer, why I might have done so is…none of your business."

"And if I'm asking as your friend?"

"Then it's definitely none of your business."

He drew up in his chair, more concerned now than he had been when he'd discovered the anomaly. He knew her horrific experience on the *Akagi* with O'Connell had affected her in ways that went beyond simply shaking her faith in the military chain of command. But what could be so problematic that she blatantly refused to tell him?

"Under AEGIS Enabling Directives, during an active conflict I technically *am* your commanding officer. I can order you to reveal this information and report you to your superiors for disciplinary action if you refuse."

"Commander Lekkas is already aware of the circumstances in question, *sir*."

That should have been the end of it. The IDCC RRF was a military organization in only the loosest sense. In a real military Harper's relationship with Lekkas would be verboten, for starters. But as things stood, what the IDCC did or did not choose to punish wasn't his concern.

But it bugged him how she was willfully keeping something from him. They'd grown to be closer friends during the AEGIS training and development push—or he thought they had—and he didn't like it.

Regardless, the problem was still the problem. He sighed. "Will you tell me who has it? I'll take care of getting it returned, and then I won't have to worry about it being out there unwatched."

"No, sir."

"Dammit, Harper. Don't make me order you."

She stayed silent. Now he was both concerned *and* annoyed. "Captain Brooklyn Harper, I am ordering you to reveal the name of the individual you provided with a Reverb then failed to record the transfer to. AEGIS Directive 23B compels you to answer."

Her jaw twitched. "Caleb Marano."

He sank back in the chair, trying not to visibly scowl. Why must it be *him*?

Because he was precisely the kind of man who would use a highly dangerous, possibly lethal device for a secret, off-the-books operation, that was why. Malcolm had tried to give the man the benefit of the doubt, but time and again he proved himself the loose cannon Malcolm had first judged him to be.

"What did he use it for?"

"I don't know."

He stared at her in dismay. "I think you're lying. You're not great at it. Why are you protecting him?"

"I gave my word, sir."

"Captain."

She lifted her chin. "I am exercising my right under IDCC Charter Implementing Resolution 11C to remain silent—" She blinked and turned away, biting down viciously on her lower lip. When she looked back at him, her face had blanched. "Sorry, sir. The last person I witnessed exercising their right against self-incrimination was Captain Gregor Kone. O'Connell shot him between the eyes for it."

"I am *not* O'Connell. His actions violated every law and ethic we abide by and I believe in."

"I know, sir. I didn't mean to imply…." She reinforced the stoic pose. "I am exercising my right under IDCC Charter Implementing Resolution—"

"Stop, Captain. Please, just…stop. I'm not going to arrest you, and I'm certainly not going to shoot you."

"Thank you, sir."

"But you're not going to tell me what transpired?"

"No, sir."

He planted his elbows on the armrests and steepled his fingers together. Whatever had happened, it was serious enough to require extreme secrecy in the planning and the aftermath. With Marano involved, again, not a surprise. It was also serious enough to lead Harper to jeopardize whatever friendship they enjoyed, as well as her standing within AEGIS, rather than reveal it. Serious enough that Malcolm now felt a moral if not a legal duty to uncover it.

He wasn't a trained investigator, but surely he could puzzle this out.

She'd said she'd loaned the Reverb to Marano during the OTS unrest, and events had intervened to stop the man from returning it prior to he and Alex coming to Amaranthe. It left a narrow window of time.

Malcolm personally saw Marano at IDCC Headquarters after the worst of the unrest had subsided, and if the man hadn't returned it then, it meant the operation had occurred later. But Marano was on Earth, onboard the *Gambier*, the next day. Shortly thereafter came the attack by the Anaden on Seneca, kicking off what he assumed were the 'events' she'd referenced.

It was a *very* narrow window. No one on the Assembly grounds in London had shown up dead or disabled with a fried eVi, so the answer wasn't there. If something happened on Seneca before the attack he wouldn't know about it. On Romane, after their encounter at Mia's office but before Miriam's gambit in London? A lot of conflict transpired around that time, but most of the OTS terrorists had been caught and detained by then....

His gaze snapped up to land sharply on Harper. "He *didn't*."

Her chin dropped to her chest.

Of course he did.

30

SIYANE

Devon considered the *Siyane's* main cabin with an aloof countenance, as if he were an art critic judging a gallery—which he was not. "Not bad. So you and Caleb pretty much live here?"

"Lately." Alex took her own look around, but she was critiquing the current *state* of the cabin.

They'd returned to Epsilon barely an hour before the transport from Aurora arrived. Despite how well the varied trips had coincided, it nonetheless felt as if time had been lost, so she'd asked Devon and Mia to come to the *Siyane* as soon as they landed. Alien introductions could wait; they needed to get to work now.

It wasn't often there were...seven people on the *Siyane* at the same time. Add in the virtual presence of multiple Artificials plus the *diati*, and it was getting a mite crowded. She wasn't expecting Mesme to show up, but if it did the Kat would have difficulty finding the physical space to be ethereal.

She projected her voice above the conversational murmurs. "Do we want to go to one of the meeting rooms in the Epsilon complex? We'd have more space."

Noah headed for the kitchen area. "Nah. There's beer here, and we're all friends. Or friendly." He tossed a bottle to Caleb—then after some hand-waving, to Devon, and by the time he was done everyone had a bottle.

Noah and Caleb crashed on the couch, acting as if they were spectators planning to stay out of the way. Kennedy perched on the edge of the kitchen table beside Devon's girlfriend, Emily, while Alex, Devon and Mia gravitated toward the data center.

Devon frowned. "We're one short of a Noetica Convention. Where's Lekkas?"

"Allegedly, overseeing a performance check-up on the Eidolons. Now that the docs have finally let her get back in a cockpit, though, I'm not sure she's getting out again. Ever." Alex propped against the edge of the data center. "All right, enough small talk. There's a war on, and we need to help win it."

"It is what we were made for."

Huh. So much had transpired since the Metigen War, she'd long since stopped thinking of herself, or any of the Prevos, in those terms. They had eclipsed their purpose to become so much more. But the fact remained there was again a war that needed winning.

"Then let's do it. Devon, how did you affect the real world from sidespace?"

"The first time, the physical destruction was an accidental by-product of an intense, adrenaline-fueled act. So initially I didn't think I was going to be able to replicate it on command. But Emily and I have been working on the process with Annie and Yves, and...it's better if I start by showing you. Then we can dissect it." He peered around the cabin. "I need something I can break."

Caleb detached one of the small arm cushions from the couch and tossed it in their direction. Devon caught it one-handed and quickly placed it in the middle of the floor in front of him.

Alex screwed her face up at Caleb, but he just shrugged. She supposed it was about the *least* valuable item on the ship....

Devon smiled at Emily. "You ready?"

"Yes, I am."

"Alex, Mia, watch in sidespace through the Noesis, or I'll have to destroy something else."

Valkyrie, record. She closed her eyes and opened her more fulsome vision.

Nothing happened for several seconds—then abruptly a surge of energy burst outward from Devon's presence to slam into the cushion.

The cushion exploded in a puff of white stuffing and unwoven threads.

Fascinating.

How fascinating?

I'm not yet certain. A moment.

Alex blew a piece of white fuzz off her eyelashes. "That was damn impressive. Foregoing an in-depth analysis for now, it looked as if you forced apart the molecules comprising the material at the subatomic level. But it was very...violent, and we're not trying to blow up our own ships. We *are* trying to blow up the enemy ships, which raises some interesting possibilities, but we'll save them for another time. Right now, we're trying to *move*."

Devon's posture sagged. "I don't know how to translate exploding things into moving them intact. Or moving myself, intact or otherwise."

Emily's face blanched in horror as she rushed to Devon's side. "Don't you dare explode yourself!"

Alex ignored their cuddling to project the flow Valkyrie had now constructed of the process they'd witnessed to a wide aural. She studied it, eyes narrowed, trying to transform the act into something that didn't explode at the end.

Mia came over to study its mirror image from the other side. Half-formed thoughts, questions and responses passed more between Valkyrie and Meno than between she and Mia, but it all blended together.

Several lines of reasoning fell apart upon meeting reality, and her lips pursed tightly in increasing frustration. "We can figure this out, because we've really smart. Or the Artificials are. So, starting at the beginning. Valkyrie, you say sidespace uses wormholes. What is a wormhole?"

Valkyrie helpfully provided the textbook answer. 'A shortcut from one point in physical space to another point in physical space, created by linking the two points across nonspatial dimensions, where physical distance is not a factor.'

When phrased in such simple, general terms, divorced from gigantic machinery and unfathomable distances, several disparate ideas snapped into place in Alex's mind. "At the root, everything is about wormholes, isn't it? Sidespace. The Kats' flitting around through walls and force fields. Teleportation, whether by walking through one of the Anadens' mirror gates or Caleb commanding *diati*. The Dimensional Rifter—oh!"

"Oh?"

"Oh." She grinned at Mia through the dancing glow of the aural between them. "Isn't it obvious? The answer's been hiding in the Dimensional Rifter equations this whole time."

"True, the Rifter opens up a hole in the spatial dimensions. But we don't want to be tossed out the other side in the middle of the void somewhere. Again with the violent."

Alex shook her head. "That only happens because the Rifter isn't controlling the objects falling into the rift it creates. But we *are* in control. The point is, the way to crack open those spatial dimensions is right there in the equations. So we crack a rift open here, crack one open there, and step through. Easy."

Devon sipped on his beer. "Easy? If the Rifters are any indication, it's going to take a lot more power than a couple of Prevos can produce standing around."

Kennedy nodded emphatically from the kitchen table. "An active Rifter uses on average thirty-two percent of a ship's non-propulsion power, and the power requirements increase cubically based on the ship's total surface area. We had to come up with new allocation and distribution routines to keep the older, non-AEGIS-built ships functioning while using a Rifter."

'I've now studied the mechanism used to exert force on the cushion. Alex, I believe we can generate enough to power to effect a small-scale proof of concept of your idea.'

"Who's we, Valkyrie? You and I?"

'Not us alone. Annie and I agree the power requirements to move a body through a sidespace wormhole to a different location in physical space is in excess of what a single Prevo can generate.

But it is approximately equal to the power four Prevos plus one-third of the power the *Siyane's* LEN reactor can generate.'

Alex swallowed. "I guess I can try—"

Devon tried to wave her off. "I'll do it. I mean, I am the only one of us who's actually done anything like it before."

"Bullshit. I'm the one who came up with the Rifter equations, and I have...experience hanging out in intangible dimensions." Caleb's gaze locked on her from across the cabin; she gave him a reassuring wink.

It wasn't just for show, either. She suddenly realized—or possibly she'd known without noticing for some time—she was *okay* now. Better than okay.

She wasn't sure exactly when it had happened; presumably it had been while she was off doing other things. But she could feel the truth of it in a place deep inside that didn't have a name, where she, Valkyrie and their connection to the universe met.

Perhaps the conviction showed in her expression, because Devon backed off, raising his hands in surrender and retreating to the data center.

She went over to where Kennedy half-sat on the kitchen table. "Here, hold my beer."

Kennedy accepted it with a smirk, and Alex returned to the comparatively open space in the middle of the cabin. "So I want to move...closer to the cockpit. Almost inside it, I think, but not quite. So about six meters. Valkyrie, can we do it?"

'The distance traveled does not matter. Either we can generate the necessary power to move your physical body, or we cannot.'

"And can we?"

'I believe we can.'

"Terrific." She glanced at Mia. "Forewarning, Mia—also Devon and Emily—I'll be tapping into your Prevo connections through the Noesis."

Mia rolled her eyes a bit sheepishly. "I understand and give my consent."

Alex took a deep breath and switched to sidespace. "Get ready...and...."

Now, Valkyrie.

She jerked. Every muscle in her body tensed as the cybernetic pathways running through her body were set afire from the surge of power. The lights in the cabin dimmed, or maybe went out. She couldn't be certain, for what she saw was the space *inside* the space—an alluring chasm of shifting light and vague shapes falling upside-down beneath her, or above her.

If I step forward, I'll fall in.

Don't step. Simply be where you want to be. It's the same as moving in sidespace, but be there with your body as well as your mind.

Yes, we should try to keep those two together.

The 'real' world was a faint, insubstantial overlay upon the shifting chasm...but it wasn't about seeing. It was about knowing, then doing. About intentionality. A point half a meter outside the entrance to the cockpit lay on the other side of the chasm. Her intention was to be there—

—then she was.

The heat dissipated from her skin, her glyphs dimmed, and the lights brightened.

There had been no sensation of movement whatsoever. Wild. She started to take a step in the physical world—and grabbed onto the cockpit half-wall, woozy. "Whoa. That was...I think I need my beer back."

Caleb had leapt up, grabbed it from Kennedy's outstretched hand and appeared beside her holding it in the time it took her to blink. Admittedly, it was a slow blink, during which she worked to reorient herself in her body and her ship.

Their fingers intertwined as hers wrapped around the bottle while he continued to hold it. The corners of his lips rose. "You're okay." It wasn't a question, but an affirmation.

She nodded with increasing confidence, and he let go of the bottle and took a step back. His voice rose above the din. "That's fine. Everyone can teleport now, but I want it known that I started it. I could teleport before it was all the cool new thing."

"If it helps, I still like your way better."

He spread his arms dramatically as he backed toward the kitchen. "Thank you."

He was just showing off for their audience now, so she returned her attention to what she had experienced. "That was surprisingly exhausting—but it worked. Annie and Valkyrie, you are both brilliant beyond measure."

Devon flourished a hand in her direction. "And you have balls of steel."

"Glad you noticed." She sighed; she really was wiped. "But there's no time to revel in our collective awesomeness. We can move ourselves, but we aren't ships. How do we move ships?"

Kennedy thrust her arm into the air. "I know this one!"

Alex laughed. "Do enlighten us."

"The AEGIS ships have Artificials wired into their hulls and matching Prevos onboard—everything frigate-class and larger." Kennedy beamed. "Because I made that happen."

"Damn straight you did, honey."

Kennedy raised her beer in a salute to Noah.

Alex sought the edge of the data center. "And if a ship more or less *is* the Artificial-half of a Prevo pair, and the human half decides to move through sidespace to another location, they can take the ship with them? Will it work?"

Devon rubbed at his jaw. "Yes, I think. Valkyrie, want to try to move the ship?"

'Calculating…it will require more power than we have available.'

Whew.

Agreed.

Kennedy deflated. "Well, we have a problem, then. If I can extrapolate from the craziness of the last five minutes, this is due to the power required to open a hole in the world increasing at a minimum proportionally with the size of the hole. No surprise. Newton's 2nd Law strikes again, and it's consistent with the Rifter power requirements.

"Anyway, the power generation capabilities of most of the AEGIS ships are spoken for as it is, and there's not much give to play with. Of course, an individual Prevo/ship could draw power from the other Prevo/ships like Alex did here. But the other Prevo/ships need to move, too, I assume.

"Something's got to be situated at the end of the line providing a shit-ton of power."

Alex had shoved off the data center to weave around whoever was standing before she realized she'd done it. Driven by the transformative blossoming of ideas, of the act of *creation*, she wasn't tired any longer. "There's the Zero Drive."

"The what now?"

"It's an interstellar engine the anarchs use. It's a damn marvel, and utterly gorgeous. You're going to love it, Ken." She paused. "Valkyrie, pull up one of the visuals you captured of Nisi's cityship."

'Excellent idea.'

A second later an image appeared above the data center of a side-on view of Anarch Post Satus on the verdant planet, from their first visit. Beneath the multi-armed station, the golden ball of energy spun a web of brilliance.

Kennedy vaulted off the kitchen table and pressed into the image until it surrounded her face. "You're right. This is the most beautiful thing I've ever seen. Where can I get one?"

Alex and Caleb both started laughing. "That's what I said—literally. This structure here? It's a starship."

Kennedy took a step back. "And this spinning golden ball of beauty is its only engine?"

"That's the rumor."

"How does it work?"

"I haven't been able to learn the details yet, but it allegedly has zero net energy requirements. Hence the name."

Kennedy shook her head. "Impossible. If it's an engine, it requires power and...end of the line? The power eventually has to come from somewhere."

Alex had seen so many mind-boggling contrivances in the last months, technologies so fantastical it was far easier to label them 'magic' than try to comprehend them. But physics still counted for something, and if history was any lesson, when a mechanism acted like it violated the laws of physics, it was simply because they didn't understand physics well enough yet.

She'd told Caleb once that the universe was perfectly ordered and structured, and that she understood the rules by which it was so. Those were the rules of a petri dish universe, true, but one which happened to be an exact recreation of this universe. Amaranthe didn't get to violate its own rules.

"Yes, it does have to come from somewhere...."

The answer's been hiding in the Dimension Rifter equations this whole time.

"Alex?" Kennedy sighed. "Oh, great, she's doing that thing she does again."

She fixated on the image of the lovely Zero Drive and its spinning orb of energy...and saw another spinning orb of energy, suspended above a meadow of velvet grass beside a glacier blue lake. The orb, less than five meters in diameter, had powered a cloaking/holographic projector/dimensional displacer the size of a *planet.*

At the time and for most moments since, she'd been concerned above all with the practical, operating functionality it powered— yes, the how, but not the 'how' behind the how. Not the power itself.

"What thing?"

"That thing where she stares off into space for a few minutes then invents a new branch of physics."

When something seems out of place, wrong or merely odd...I can recognize the reality of it. The hidden object or event or force which brings space back into alignment with the rules of the universe.

Energy could neither be created nor destroyed, only transformed from one form to another. So where was the hidden force— the hidden *energy* that became the power to drive objects across space or shift them into another space entirely?

Caleb's hand alighted on her waist, and his breath was warm at her ear. "Shine for me."

Siyane *is perfect, sweetheart. My little star shining brightly.*

The answer's been hiding in the Dimension Rifter equations this whole time.

Those equations described prisms reflecting, inverting and reflecting again, sending atoms, matter, data, *energy* across nonspatial dimensions. Deflect the package out at one stage of the equations, and it returned to normal space at a defined point. Deflect it out at a different stage, and it fell until its *energy* grew so great it tore open a hole and exploded into normal space.

What if you instead trapped material in an endless loop of reflection and inversion?

She laughed. "Us silly, primitive humans. We've been like monkeys banging on a keyboard—do it long enough and random chance guarantees you'll produce a meaningful word or two."

She squeezed Caleb's hand before stepping toward the data center. "I figured out how to create a cloaking shield from the Kats' technology, then fed the shield the power it needed to do its job. Later, I figured out how to turn the cloaking shield into a Dimensional Rifter using more of the same Kat technology, then fed it the considerably greater power it needed to do its job.

"Now I'm trying to turn the Dimensional Rifter into a traversable wormhole generator using more of the *same* Kat technology, and we're all standing here trying to figure out where to get the yet more power it needs to do its job."

A brief thought and Valkyrie brought to life an image of the latticed generator on Portal Prime to rotate beside the image of the Zero Drive. Its operating code scrolled on the far left. "The Kats have already figured out the answer, and I've been ignoring it this whole time...or maybe I wasn't ready to see it until now."

The data she'd been able to piece together on the Zero Drive appeared to the right of its image. "I suspect the anarchs have figured it out, too, though less completely—or at least less efficiently, since Eren said the cost to build a Zero Drive increases exponentially with its size. The anarchs don't traffic in dimensions the way the Kats do. No one does."

Caleb leaned against the data center and smiled at her. "Except you."

She huffed a laugh. "Maybe I'm starting to catch up."

Kennedy appeared on the other side of her to squint at the scrolling code for several seconds. She scowled. "Without an Artificial in my head or at a minimum in my ear…nope. Can't do it."

Alex nudged Kennedy affectionately. "Let me help." A third image appeared above the table, a nearly transparent polyhedron with light bouncing around in it and spilling out the bottom. She reached up and grasped it in her hand, then flipped her hand over to let it hover above her palm.

Kennedy's forehead knotted in concentration. "This looks similar to the representation of the event horizon the Dimensional Rifter creates."

"That's precisely what it is: a visual translation of how tangible matter can be redirected from one point in space to another point in space by traversing planar surfaces of nonspatial dimensions. But when I first created it, I based it more closely on the Portal Prime shield, and it looked like this."

One of the facets shifted, and the light spilling out the bottom began streaming out one side.

"The Kats are nothing if not efficient. They never invent something new when something existing will serve their purpose." She reached into the visual of the ball of energy from Portal Prime, deep into the center obscured by all the light, and extracted a nearly identical polyhedron.

She held up both objects side by side, one above each palm. The one from Portal Prime was far more luminous; its facets were barely visible beneath all the light being generated inside it, with no apparent outlet.

She lifted it higher. "*This* is power."

Next she directed her focus at the Rifter polyhedron and mentally inverted one of the facets, so that the energy ceased spilling out of it. In seconds it had grown to match the brightness of the other object.

"And now, *we* have power."

"By harnessing...the sort of surface wave energy created by matter bouncing off dimensional planes over and over?"

"Yes." Her gaze swept across the cabin. "We don't need to beg the anarchs for a Zero Drive. We don't need to beg the Kats to allow us a peek at their precious secret technology. We can do this ourselves, and do it better."

31

PALAEMON

The confab on the *Siyane* finally wrapped up, but Mia's day was barely getting started.

Her first stop was to check in with Administrator Latro Udirijun to see if any issues had arisen in her absence. Naturally, they had. When Alex and Caleb had departed Epsilon to go help Akeso, it had effectively left Field Marshal Bastian as the primary and highest contact point in AEGIS. This had gone about as well as one would expect.

She spent several hours shuttling between three anarch posts smoothing ruffled egos, finagling compromises out of both sides and getting everything sorted. It was late evening on Epsilon by the time she finally made it to her suite.

When she opened the door, she found Malcolm inside, leaning against the wall and wearing a somewhat weary smile. "Welcome back."

She'd sent him a message earlier to let him know she'd returned safely, but he'd been on the *Saratoga* most of the day and they'd never had the chance to connect.

Now she tossed her bag on the floor and sank eagerly into his arms; she'd already started missing the feel of his strong, comforting embrace. "Thanks. It's been a day."

"For me, too." He coaxed her over to the couch, then settled into one of the cushions and wrapped an arm around her. "I'm sorry I wasn't around when you got back. I hoped I could make it up to you by being here now."

"And you have." She reached up to stroke his cheek. She thought perhaps she'd imagined it in her own weariness, but he *did* look tired...or something else. "You look worried, or troubled, or maybe exhausted. Did something happen while I was gone? I didn't see any official reports of note."

He shook his head. "No. We're still in a holding pattern, trying to get our footing and find a way forward. It was just a challenging two days."

She started to tell him about the encouraging progress they'd made on solving the wormhole problem. But it wasn't real yet, and her brain hadn't fully wrapped itself around the details. It would keep. "But something *is* bothering you."

"I'm terrible at hiding anything from you, aren't I?"

"That's a good thing."

"Probably." He ran a hand through his hair. "I hate to have to tell you this. I don't want to ruin your first night back, and I don't want to waste our time together talking about it. But you should know, and I shouldn't keep it from you."

She steeled herself for the gamut of possibilities. "Okay. What is it?"

"Back during the OTS unrest, after the riots on Romane, Caleb used an IDCC-issued Reverb to cause Jude Winslow's eVi to self-destruct while he was in IDCC custody. Winslow didn't commit suicide—Caleb murdered him, and he did it using IDCC military property."

That hadn't been in the gamut. Mia closed her eyes with a quiet sigh. She wondered how he'd found out, but it likely didn't matter. Her voice was soft and resigned. "I know."

"What?"

She opened her eyes to find him gazing at her in genuine confusion. He was such a good man. Too good for the reality of the world he lived in. "I said I know."

"How? You didn't—were you *involved?*"

"No!" She instinctively shrank away from him, but she needn't have bothered, as he leapt up off the couch in an explosion of motion.

"Then what?"

"I didn't find out until afterward. And he didn't tell me." In point of fact it had leaked incidentally from Morgan's mind into hers, because they worked closely enough together on IDCC affairs that what Morgan knew, Mia eventually knew.

"How long afterward? How long have you known? A while—since before he and Alex first came here?"

She nodded silently.

"So you knew about it when you called him honorable. You knew, and you still defended him."

She exhaled in frustration. "Are we really going to do this again?"

"No, because this isn't about Caleb right now. It's about you. Do you honestly sanction…premeditated murder?"

"It's not as simple as that."

"Isn't it? If you'd been told ahead of time, would you have tried to stop him?"

She'd actually given some thought to the question, and he wasn't going to like the answer. But she couldn't manage to lie to him, as she'd starkly demonstrated. "No."

He stared at her aghast, all warmth gone from his eyes and expression. "How can that be true? I didn't…do I know you at all?"

She finally stood and left the couch. She wanted to run, but there was little space in the small suite to hide, and he was between her and the door. "The degenerate tried to have me killed—he sent a sniper to *assassinate* me. Of course I wanted him dead! The question I have is, why wouldn't you?"

His anger seemed to falter for a second. His glare softened, and he blinked several times. "Winslow should have been punished for that, and for all his crimes. Unequivocally. I would have cheered when he was locked away to rot. But the justice system should have decided his fate, not a single man. No one person has the right to take justice away from the system and into their own hands. That's not justice at all—it's cold-blooded murder."

Old memories swelled to the surface, memories of a past she'd tried so hard to bury. It was as if they'd been biding their time, waiting for the moment when they could best screw up her life, to pounce out of the shadows.

"You're a wee little one, aren't you?"

She straightened her spine, trying to make herself appear taller than her eleven years allowed. "I'm old enough. Ryu sent me. I've got what you asked for."

The man licked his lips. "Let me see it."

She nudged the coat draped over her arms to the side to reveal a Daemon power amplifier enclosed in a clear bag, then hurriedly pulled her coat back over it. "It's four hundred. On a film, not a digital transfer."

"I agreed to three hundred."

"No. Four hundred. That's the price Ryu said he negotiated."

"Ryu's lying. I'll pay three hundred and not a single credit more."

Had Ryu lied? He wasn't brave enough to try to scam a customer...unless that was why he'd sent her. But why stir up a crisis over a hundred credits? They moved goods costing a lot more than a hundred credits all the time.

No, she resolved, this man was trying to scam her. *He thought since she was young and small she was stupid. He was wrong.*

She worked to inject a note of authority into her voice. "Sir, either you give me four hundred credits or I walk out of the alley with the merchandise."

She saw it when he decided to kill her. His pupils contracted, the skin under his cheeks flushed and his jaw locked into this big, crooked line to jut way out from his neck.

"How about instead, I keep the credits, take the merchandise and walk out of the alley with them both."

Her brother made her carry a blade for protection. She dropped the bag and the coat and fumbled in her pocket for the blade as the man lunged for her. His hands—they were no palm and all fingers— landed on her neck and began to squeeze.

So she flicked the blade on and did the only thing she could think to do: she thrust it forward.

The blade was tiny, barely eight centimeters long, but he was skinny. It felt squishy sliding inside him. His fingers spasmed around her neck, briefly cutting off all the oxygen, then went limp. Sticky warmth seeped out of his belly onto her hand.

She jerked the blade out and stumbled backward. He stumbled in the opposite direction to sag against the alley wall, hands fumbling for the wound.

She ran.

She was five blocks away before she realized she was still holding the blood-soaked blade out in front of her. The darkness had saved her from being seen, but she couldn't count on its protection, so she hid in another alley and hyperventilated until she nearly passed out.

Then she ran once again. Farther, until there were stars behind her.

She tried to force the memories away, to deflect, to strike out instead. If Malcolm wanted to fight, she'd oblige him. "You are such a hypocrite."

"Excuse me?"

"You think the commanding officer who orders you to kill a building full of enemies isn't just a single man? You think your superiors aren't just individuals making decisions based on their own personal judgment?"

"They work within a system of rules and—"

"You think when you shoot someone in the head, it isn't you making the decision to end their life?"

"It's not the same thing. In a combat situation—"

"I get it—it's kill or be killed. Exactly. To my mind, so was this."

Malcolm shook his head roughly. "No. Winslow was captured, confined and *in restraints* inside the confinement. He couldn't fight back. He couldn't defend himself. He was helpless."

"Do you genuinely think he was going to stay that way? He was the Alliance Prime Minister's *son*. He led a multi-colony terrorist organization, and it had already killed thousands of people. He was a monster. But worse, he was a monster with powerful connections and vaults of money."

"Dammit, Mia, our system is stronger than any individual interest. It can rise above the influence of bribes and corruption. It wouldn't have remained standing for so long if it didn't do so on a regular basis. The instant we start allowing people to ignore the rules, to make 'exceptions,' the whole thing starts to fall apart."

She pinched the bridge of her nose. It was a wonderful argument in theory. It was even mostly right. But she'd seen it fail, and it seemed she still had the scars. She'd run so far and climbed so high...was she never going to be able to escape her past entirely?

You have, Mia. Those people can't hurt you any longer.

No. But he can.

She gave in and let the memories flood her mind until she had to sink against the wall for support. "You said this was about me now? Fine. All I ever wanted was to be able to live in a world where what you believe was true. And I thought I'd succeeded. I've tried so damn hard to follow the rules. When I'm able, I've tried to support and encourage the flourishing of that world. I agree, ninety-nine percent of the time, it is real for ninety-nine percent of the people.

"But there's a world underneath yours, a place where the system can't reach, and every now and then tendrils from this place seep up through the cracks into your perfect world of justice and order.

"Malcolm, in my life I have seen people do horrific things, acts of pure evil. And in the place where those evils occur, sometimes the only justice the monsters suffer comes from the muzzle of a gun. Or the edge of a blade."

He winced and almost reached for her. "You had to kill the attacker at the hospital. No question—"

"Maybe I'm not talking about him."

"I don't understand."

She moved as close as she dared to the facility and studied it, perplexed. Everything appeared normal. Two guards stood at relaxed attention outside the doors. No gunfire interrupted the quiet.

What if the assault didn't happen tonight at all? She'd had no reason to assume it would be tonight, none but her desire for it to be so. Or maybe something had gone wrong like she'd feared—

—the doors opened, freeing a cacophony of chaotic noises and startling the guards.

Eli burst forth out of the doors at a full run while yelling at his men and gesturing behind him. They dashed inside.

He looked ridiculous, splashing clumsily through the puddles on the sidewalk as he lumbered forward, wheezing from the exertion.

But no one was chasing him.

He was going to get away.

The hilt of the blade she'd purchased sat clenched in a death grip in her hand; she'd been holding it so tightly her fingers had started to cramp.

The edges of her vision blurred. Her awareness narrowed to encompass Eli Baca and nothing else. Drug trafficker, mob minion, violent and brutish thug. A 24th century feudal lord wielding the power of life and death over all he commanded.

An unexpected calmness settled within her as she crossed the street, her pace deliberate but unhurried.

Mia stepped onto the sidewalk in front of him. He failed to recognize her in the long coat and hood, and made to veer around her.

She took a single step sideways to block his path, activated the blade and plunged it into his heart.

Eli was fat, but her blade was far from tiny. A bloom of red unfurled to dye his sweaty shirt crimson as he gaped at her in shock and confusion.

She reached up with her free hand, pulled the hood off and leveled a cold, malevolent glare at him. "You don't own me anymore."

"No, you don't understand. Maybe you never will." She regarded Malcolm in sadness, and resignation. "You should go now."

"You're really going to...this is not on me. I am *not* the bad guy here."

"Of course you're not. Virtuous to the last, and you can wear the badge proudly. But I don't have to endure you looking down on me with such holier-than-thou condescension. I've had to make hard choices—not to get where I am now, but merely to survive so I could try to find the path that led to the road that would take me to where I am now. And I won't stand here and flagellate myself for you while you judge me for those choices."

"I am not—I would never—I only want to understand."

"I don't think you do. It would complicate your worldview too much." She turned half away from him and toward the door. "Please leave."

"Mia...."

"*Leave.*"

His jaw stiffened, and the soldier's mask descended. "Right. I believe I will." He strode past her and out the door without a glance in her direction. The door closed behind him.

Her composure broke then, not in a rush but as a slow, inexorable crumbling, like the time-lapsed decay of an abandoned structure.

She went to the couch and curled up in the corner to rest her head on the arm. This way the tears didn't have far to fall.

Fuck love, that it could break her.

I think you—

Not now, Meno. Please.

Then I don't know what to do to help you.

Sometimes there's nothing to be done. Sometimes there's just...nothing.

It's not like you to express such a sentiment.

No, it isn't. I'll take it back tomorrow. But tonight, I think I'll simply be broken.

32

AFS STALWART II

Alex ran Richard's message through her head for the tenth time today.

Alex,

I won't bother asking you to tell me what's truly going on, as I know you won't—especially not across universes. I also understand why you're hesitant to talk to your mother about it, but I urge you to be careful not to hurt her, even out of a desire to protect her.

Your memory serves you well, for David assuredly did have a unique perspective on and relationship with God, the divine, or whatever resides out there beyond our sight.

No one loved life so much as he did. He lived it grandly and took from it every centimeter it would cede to him. But this doesn't fully answer your question.

He once said to me (and I quote, because I've always remembered it clearly) 'the universe looks out for people who act with honor in furtherance of an honorable cause.' He believed in destiny, but I think this is what he meant by it.

There can be no question that he died acting with the highest of honor in furtherance of the most honorable of causes. I suspect he accepted his death as the price for such an act, possibly even as his rightful destiny.

But if it should turn out the universe was and still is looking out for him, such that his destiny turns out to be something altogether different, I do not believe he would argue with the universe's judgment.

—Richard

His words were reassuring. They acted as a check that her father had been the man she remembered, and that the man she now knew was the man who had been. Though cryptic and philosophical in tone, the message answered her question far better than a simple 'yes' would have done.

As for her mother, he wasn't telling her anything she wasn't already acutely aware of. She hated keeping her mother in the dark, and she only hoped it wouldn't be for much longer. But first she had one more painful question needing an answer before she could in good conscience move forward. For everyone's sake.

Kennedy was ready to start working on a practical adaptation of the Dimensional Rifter to serve as a power source, but they needed her mother's permission to dismantle expensive AEGIS equipment.

So it was that Alex was standing outside the door to her mother's office on the *Stalwart II* at precisely the moment when two disparate interests converged in time and space.

Alex plopped down in the chair opposite her mother's desk and pulled one leg up to hug her knee. "How has your day gone?"

"Dreadfully. Improve it for me, will you?"

"Way to steal my thunder." She grinned. "If you insist. We think we have a workable plan for a method to open and traverse temporary wormholes on an as-needed basis—at least for the Prevo-enabled AEGIS vessels, and we might be able to let some of the others hitch a ride."

"Amazing. Mr. Reynolds proved to be so helpful?"

She shrugged. "His advances in sidespace manipulation were the catalyst that sparked the ideas that led to the breakthrough. So, after a fashion. It's good to have him here."

"I agree. It was in actuality your breakthrough, then? You and Valkyrie?"

"It was a group effort. Mia deserves a portion of the credit as well, along with Devon and Kennedy."

"Hmm. This is new behavior from you."

"What is?"

"Humility. Understating your own role in an achievement so others can enjoy the limelight."

"Thank you? I think?" She couldn't work up offense, though. She'd never been particularly boastful as such, but when asked she did tend to be blunt about her successes, much like with everything else. Also, her mother assuming she was responsible for the breakthrough despite her refusing to own it was a better compliment than any public credit.

"You're welcome. So what will developing and testing this new technology involve?"

"That's why I'm here—other than to share the good news, obviously. We need to borrow a Dimensional Rifter. Only a small one, maybe from one of the Eidolons."

"And by 'borrow' you mean...?"

"Take it apart and likely break it."

"I thought so. I'll authorize it, but you get to be the one to tell Commander Lekkas one of her Eidolons is being sidelined."

Alex cringed. "Ouch. Fine."

Her mother studied her for a few seconds. "So this is a real thing? Soon I'll be able to take the majority of my fleet through wormholes from any location to any destination I wish, instantaneously?"

"Possibly...." She stopped, then nodded firmly. "I really do think this is going to work. Yes."

Miriam let out a long, deliberate breath and smiled. "This is good news. Exceptionally good news. I don't have the words to properly thank you."

"You don't need them."

Just as the awkward silence started to kick in, Miriam straightened up in her chair. "Well, I suspect this means I need to begin devising a new strategic plan. If all potential targets are again on the table, we need to adjust and prepare to act accordingly."

"Sure. I'll get out of your hair so you can work." Alex chewed on her bottom lip. There was no good segue for this. "But...can I ask you something first? Something personal? It's random and off-topic and if it's *too* personal, you can tell me it's none of my business and I won't be offended. Promise."

Miriam dropped her forearms onto the desk in a more relaxed pose. "Of course you can."

"Right. Okay. Um...Dad's been gone for almost twenty-five years now. Why did you never move on and find someone else? Or did you, and for totally justifiable and understandable reasons simply not tell me?"

Miriam's lips parted. "That *is* an unexpected question. You're correct...I wouldn't have told you. Not until recently, at least. But no."

She sank back now, as deeply as the military-issue chair allowed. "It was a decade before I was even willing to entertain the notion, but eventually I subjected myself to a few dates. Most were disasters. Poor saps didn't deserve the treatment I inflicted on them. A few were good men, though, and in other circumstances there might have been a connection. Two of them succeeded in persisting through a second date, which in retrospect was rather impressive on their part."

Her mother smiled faintly. "But they didn't stand a chance. No one did. There was, and is, no room in my life, no room in my heart, for anyone else when your father has never left it.

"Someone like that—like he was—doesn't fade away. He was the best thing that ever happened to me—I would say 'except for you,' but you wouldn't be here if not for him. He still is. He's in my head and in my heart, and he's not leaving either."

"Mom...but you know he would want you to be happy."

"I am happy." She paused. "Has it been hard, being alone? I'd argue I'm more skilled at it than most, but certainly it has. Sometimes harder than others. But I close my eyes, and I can hear your father in my head...so I'm not quite alone. And I prefer the memory of him over a second-best, real but pale imitation."

Alex knew well what it was like to hear him in one's head, if a bit more literally. She clenched her jaw; if she opened her mouth, she'd cry.

Miriam seemed to sense it. "It's *all right*. There are far worse things in the world than to have known the truest kind of love for nineteen years. And I have you, and now Caleb. I have a family. I have friends, and people to take care of. A lot of them of late."

Alex nodded understanding, still not trusting her voice.

Her mother regarded her with kindness in her eyes. "Why ask now? Why is this on your mind?"

She managed a halting response. "I don't want you to be lonely."

"I'm not. It's rarely silent in my world. And when it is, your father's with me in my mind. It's enough, because it has to be."

No, it doesn't. "Okay. Thank you for indulging me." Alex stood, wiping a single tear from her cheek and working to put herself back together. "Back to warfare and wormholes and intangible dimensions. I'll let you know as soon as we're ready to test the tech with significant AEGIS assets. It'll be a few days, but then you can get back to kicking these Anaden fuckers' asses."

"Put as eloquently as ever."

"I thought so."

Outside the office, she went around the corner before sinking against the corridor wall.

This is a 'yes,' isn't it?

I...dammit, Valkyrie. I got the answer I came here looking for. But she's never going to forgive me for keeping all this from her.

You did so to protect her.

I did, but Richard's not wrong. When I first made the decision to keep this a secret, I never imagined we would end up here, on the brink of a real possibility for him to live.

We did take the scenic route here.

She chuckled. *That's the truth. But nonetheless...eto pizdets! Am I willing to sacrifice my relationship with my mother to have my father back? Once upon a time it would've been shamefully easy to answer, but now?*

I submit it's no longer up to you. Not in any real sense.

What do you mean?

I know your mind, thus I know you believe I am alive in every sense of the word. I assert that your father is now easily as alive as I am. Do you disagree?

I don't think so, no. I mean, it wouldn't be ethical for me to box him up again, not now, because it feels like he is alive.

Then if he wishes to have a body once more, it being his natural and familiar state, the decision is now his. Not yours.

She'd already had the same thoughts Valkyrie was expressing, and had claimed to espouse them. But out here in the real world, she'd continued to *act* as if she were his caretaker. As if she were in charge. *I understand—I mean I agree. If he's a living, sapient being, he has free will and the right to his own self-determination and agency. It doesn't change the fact that she will never forgive me for keeping her in the dark and taking all these steps on my own.*

Perhaps you should tell her now. Every action we take from here forward will only increase the perceived transgression. Rectifying the slight today will be better than doing it tomorrow.

She won't believe me—she won't believe he's alive, or that what is alive is truly him. She won't agree to what we're proposing, and given her position, she can block anything we try to do.

Your mother has been an outspoken supporter of the rights of Artificials. In fact, she staked not merely her career but her personal freedom on the defense of those rights.

Yes. But believing something intellectually is not the same as believing it in your heart. She hasn't spent the last year and a half engaged in a symbiotic neural bond with an Artificial. She knows you have consciousness, but she doesn't know you have a soul.

Do I?

Of course. The point is, to her, my father was and will always be a man. Heart beating blood to organs and skin, breath flowing through lungs to and from lips she could kiss. Anything less isn't him. It can't be.

A body is genuinely so important to humans?

It is. You've always been both quantum and synthetic, so you don't feel as if you're lacking in any way from the absence of one. But someone who was born a physical, organic being can't be fundamentally whole without one.

I suspect the Kats would disagree.

And they're kind of tragic for it. But even they have a body to go home to, should they ever want it.

If your father feels the same way, you realize what his decision will be.

I do. And it means I sacrificed my relationship with my mother over a year ago, before I really knew what I was giving up.

33

AFS TAMAO

"I am exercising my Section 5 right to remain silent."

"Did you have help? Name the other traitors and I'll consider mercy."

"I am exercising my Section 5 right to—"

"Coward. As commanding officer of the EAS Akagi, I find you guilty of sedition and treason." Liam drew his Daemon from its holster at his hip, leveled it at Kone's forehead and pressed the trigger.

The explosion of blood and brain matter was cast far and wide across the spacious bridge. The body crumpled like a balloon freed of the air holding it up.

The loop began again.

"I am exercising my Section 5 right to—"

"Coward. As commanding officer of the EAS Akagi, I find you guilty of sedition and treason." Liam drew his Daemon from its holster at his hip, leveled it at Kone's forehead and pressed the trigger.

"I am exercising my Section 5 right to—"

"Coward. As commanding officer of the EAS Akagi, I find you guilty of sedition and treason." Liam drew his Daemon from its holster at his hip, leveled it at Kone's forehead and pressed the trigger—

AR

An elbow to the spine woke Morgan. She blinked a couple of times, disoriented, because the berths looked the same on all of the variety of ships she periodically called home. Tonight they were on the...*Tamao*. Maybe.

She was halfway to rolling over when Harper's forearm slapped hard against her shoulder. Now awake enough to realize *why* she was awake, she quickly shifted the rest of the way around and placed a hand on Harper's upper arm. It was slick with sweat and trembling.

"You're having a nightmare. Wake up, Brook. Come on—"

Harper gasped and bolted upright in the bed, eyes wide with shock.

The woman's body was a deadly weapon even without the deadly weapons on the bedside table, so Morgan made sure to move slowly and carefully. She leaned in closer to stroke Harper's shoulder. "It's okay. You're okay. You were having a nightmare."

Harper's head jerked around to stare at her, first in terror then, gradually, in recognition. Awareness dawned on her features, and she collapsed onto the sheets. "Shit."

Morgan lowered onto an elbow and let her other hand rest on Harper's sweat-soaked abdomen. "Do you want to talk about it?"

Harper dragged her hands down her face, and finally the rigid tension straining her muscles began easing. "It wasn't a nightmare. It was a memory."

Everyone who'd served in the military for any length of time had a stack of memories that would qualify as nightmares, even fighter pilots but certainly Marines. Still, she asked. "Of?"

Harper's eyes closed; her lips twitched.

In something of a surprise, Morgan's first, instinctual response wasn't to want to let it drop and hope they could just go back to sleep.

Stanley, if you say a damn word about how I'm growing as a person, I will...crap, there's basically nothing I can do to you.

True. But I need not say anything. You already know.

She tried again. "Will you tell me?"

"Why not. It was of O'Connell shooting Kone in the head, and it was on repeat."

Morgan immediately scowled. "This is because of what happened with Jenner. I swear, I am going to go kick his sanctimonious, rod-stiffened ass all the way back to the Presidio—"

"No. It's not his fault. Jenner's a good man trying to follow his conscience in a screwed-up world. I simply didn't…it's been more than a year. I didn't expect for this to rear up and fuck with my head so badly after so long." Harper banged her head on the pillow a few times. "Ugh…. I'm sorry I woke you. Go back to sleep."

Harper rarely talked about what had happened on the *Akagi*, and when she did it was in short, expletive-laden declarations. Obviously it had been a waking nightmare, and it didn't take a genius or a Prevo to deduce the experience had shaken her faith in military leadership at a minimum, and possibly in a lot more.

"No. This is bothering you, so talk to me."

"There's nothing to talk about. O'Connell was a monster, and he's dead the way monsters should be. End of story."

Clearly it wasn't the end of the story. Morgan wanted to help, but what should she say? A therapist she was not.

I, however, have previously analyzed a number of treatises on human psychology. Given recent events, it is possible this is not about General O'Connell, but rather concerns her own repressed guilt.

Oh.

She drew closer and brought her hand up to Harper's jaw. "You don't blame yourself for Kone's death, do you?"

"Only in that I was stupidly naïve. Even after all the despicable things O'Connell had already done, I didn't imagine he'd go so far. After all the bad people I'd killed over the years to stop them from doing worse, I still didn't think anyone could be so evil they would….

"We're playing the noble heroes here in Amaranthe, but how can we be the good guys when there are monsters like that walking among us? When humans count among their number people like O'Connell and Jude Winslow?"

"Because there are also people like you—people who call the monsters out and take them down."

Harper rolled her eyes. "And because we have people like Jenner to call *us* out when we go too far in doing it?"

"Eh, I don't know. I guess somebody has to police the boundaries. Jenner could use a healthy dose of discretion, though."

"He has discretion. If he didn't, I'd be sitting in a cell on the detention deck of the *Thames* right now."

"Well." Morgan decided the worst of the existential crisis had passed and let her hand trail lazily down Harper's chest. "Then I'd have to break you out. Smuggle you away and hide you."

"Keep me as your plaything?"

"That is such an excellent, inspired idea."

"I'd break out of my new, more plush prison inside of thirty seconds. Likely lock you up in it just to ensure you wouldn't stop me, at least until I'd put hands on weapons and come up with a plan to either clear my name or disappear off the grid."

Morgan paused, her lips hovering a centimeter above the damp skin below Harper's collarbone. Her eyes cut upward. "You have got to be the single least romantic person I have ever met. I adore you."

34

PALAEMON

The morning sun reflected brightly off the water as Alex crossed the complex toward the labs.

She shot Kennedy a pulse asking her to head up to the *AFS Tamao*, where the Eidolons were docked. Then she reached out to Mia, under the theory that Morgan liked Mia better—or at least knew her better.

Hey, can you do me a favor and tell Morgan she needs to pick an Eidolon that can do without a Dimensional Rifter?

She still hadn't gotten a response by the time she reached the Research Building. With a sigh, she slouched against the façade outside and contacted Morgan herself.

Hi, Lekkas. Sorry you missed our little soiree yesterday, but I expect you've gotten the download by now.

I got it. Didn't understand it for shit, but I got it.

Good. My mother's approved us moving forward, so Kennedy and I need to borrow a small Dimensional Rifter to try to see if this will actually work—proof of concept, if you will. The Eidolons' Rifters are the smallest ones we have, and since we don't want to accidentally blow up Post Epsilon after the anarchs were so nice as to let us visit it, we should use an Eidolon Rifter for testing.

You're kidding, right?

I'm not. Hopefully, we'll only need the one.

Hopefully? And what does 'borrow' mean? Borrow for how long?

Is everyone going to ask that? Probably forever. Sorry.

You're not sorry in the slightest. You're getting a new toy to play with. Fine, but if the Eidolon requires therapy as a result, AEGIS is providing it.

I'm certain there's a psychiatrist or two on staff.

Ugh.

Kennedy will be on the way up to the Tamao *shortly to pick up the module and bring it back down here. Thanks.*

Alex signed off before Lekkas could spin up any more complaints. One task down, and a few hours bought to work on her other project. One of. She took a deep breath and headed inside.

Just another average, ordinary day in Amaranthe.

ℛ

Dimou ela-Erevna blinked at Alex, then again. "Do you realize what you are asking?"

"Quite well. But—"

"You want to give a SAI a body?"

"No, not a SAI. A human. It simply happens to be a human who currently exists solely within a quantum neural network."

"Like a SAI."

Alex opened her mouth to retort. Closed it. Pursed her lips. "I understand how they could appear similar on a superficial level. But you're a scientist—I suspect a brilliant one, or you wouldn't have this job—who specializes in the transfer of consciousnesses from one body to another. If anyone can appreciate the difference between a digitized human consciousness and a sentient artificial intelligence, it's you."

He continued to give her an unimpressed stare, and she searched for a different tack. "When an Anaden anarch dies, the last thing their functioning brain does is send their consciousness to your servers, here or at another post, via a quantum connection their neural cybernetics maintained to those servers, yes?"

He nodded.

"While the consciousness is making the journey, and while it's stored on your servers until a cloned body is ready to receive it, is it still fundamentally that person? Does it represent the essence of who they are, lacking only physicality?" She wanted to throw 'soul' in as well, but there was no telling his theological beliefs, and she didn't want to complicate the issue more than it already was. Which was to say *crazy* complicated.

His eyes began to narrow…then he gave her a classic 'haughty scientist' smirk. "I will accept your premise, in principle. But assuming for argument's sake that this should be done, the question becomes whether it *can* be done."

"Based on what we know about the process of regenesis, we think it can work. I realize adjustments will have to be made, but—"

"Adjustments? Yes, you could say so. For all our genetic similarities, Human bodies are not Anaden bodies. I admit, the concept is intriguing, and I do enjoy a scientific challenge. But you must understand. This is our most valued technology. Whatever you believe you know about regenesis, you do not know enough, and we are not in the habit of passing out those details to visitors at the entrance."

She tried not to groan in annoyance. "I'm not asking you to share the innermost workings with us—I'm asking you to *use* them. Please. This is a very specific, unique case. I promise we don't intend to flood your labs if it works."

She was using 'we' liberally here; technically it only meant more than herself alone—say, her and Valkyrie—but if he interpreted it to mean AEGIS or even humanity as a whole, well, she wasn't going to go out of her way to correct his perception. He didn't need to be told how far off-mission she was.

His gaze fell to the floor; he picked at the collar of his overcoat. "This is not a matter I can authorize on my own. You will have to seek Sator Nisi's permission."

She'd expected the ultimatum, while hoping it wouldn't be necessary. "I understand. But if the Sator gives his approval, you'll help us?"

"I will try."

"Thank you. I'll get back to you soon." She departed the lab and headed for the maze of interconnected landing platforms.

As luck would have it, Caleb was currently with Nisi. His dramatic use of *diati* on Akeso's behalf was worth sharing and talking through with the Sator. But he'd been on Satus for over an hour, so odds were she wasn't interrupting too horribly. She sent him a pulse.

There's something I need you to do for me.

Anything.

Really? We'll revisit the topic later then. The director of the re-genesis lab won't help me without Nisi's approval. I need you to convince him to give it.

You've decided to go ahead with your plan.

It's not up to me—it's up to Dad. But I can't offer him the choice until I know it's a real one. To offer this then snatch it away would be the highest form of cruelty. So I need to know I can make it happen.

All right, I get that. I'll make your case, but wait for me before you do anything you can't undo?

Deal.

SIYÀNE

Alex was sitting atop the back of the couch when Caleb walked into the cabin, her legs swinging against the frame. She eyed him speculatively. "He said yes."

Caleb huffed a breath as he came over to stand between her legs and drop his hands onto her hips. "What makes you think so?"

"You look troubled. If he'd said no, you'd look regretful and slightly pained as you prepared to break the news to me and provide a sympathetic shoulder. Instead, you're concerned about whether I'm making the right decision and unsure how strongly you should challenge me on it."

His brow furrowed all the way into the straight line she adored. "Valkyrie, did you wire a transmitter into my brain one night while I slept?"

'I did not. However, I will be happy to do so—you only have to ask.'

"I'll keep it in mind. So this is marriage, then?"

She grinned and grabbed his shirt to tug him closer. "If you get super lucky. You can see my naked and bared soul, but maybe I can see yours, too."

"And I love you all the more for it." His nose tickled her skin as his lips grazed hers. "So let me say what I need to say? Even if you know all of it, I'll feel better for having said it."

"Okay."

"Alex, I would never deny you this. I won't try to stop you, and I'm on your side no matter what comes of it. But before you cross the Rubicon here, are you absolutely *sure*? The consequences if this goes badly could be worse than you're prepared for."

She rolled her eyes. "The consequences if it goes well might suck, too. Believe me, I recognize the shitstorm this will kick off."

"Good. Now, you said it wasn't your decision. You've never been one to evade responsibility, but I don't see how that can be true."

"Valkyrie, do you want to explain it to him?"

'I think I'll leave this one to you.'

"Figures." She sighed. "Valkyrie made the decision to load my father's neural imprint into her processes—and thus into my mind—without asking my permission. But, yes, I've been in the driver's seat since then. I made the decision to box him when his tenuous consciousness started fracturing, then to allow Vii to use the advances Abigail had achieved to try to not merely salvage it but maybe, just maybe, create something more whole.

"Vii having done so beyond my wildest dreams, I made the decision to pursue adapting this incredible Anaden technology to do what no human has done before but the Anadens do every day.

"I wouldn't dare wash my hands of responsibility now, centimeters from the finish line." She paused. "But it's time we let him make a decision for himself."

He studied her, as if searching for some sign, any inkling, of insanity. "The decision of whether to live again."

"No. For good or ill, I made that decision for him. It might not have been my right to do so, but I was the only one who could. He's already alive. His decision to make is whether he wants to walk in the sun again."

"Alex...."

"You're skeptical. You're not certain he's as alive as Valkyrie, or as alive as Akeso. You're worried I'm seeing only what I so desperately want to see." She smiled. "It so happens I have a question I need to ask him, so grab an external interface and come with me to see for yourself. Caleb, come meet my father."

PART VI:

LAWS OF MOTION

"The sane man knows that he has a touch of the beast, a touch of the devil, a touch of the saint, a touch of the citizen. The really sane man knows that he has a touch of the madman."

— *G. K. Chesterton*

35

ANARCH POST EPSILON

"Do it."

Dimou eyed Alex as he studied a report from one of the technicians. "Yes, I understand Sator Nisi has given his blessing to your project."

'Blessing' might be a strong word. "He has. Valkyrie will provide you comprehensive background information on human physiology, biology and genetics, as well as the specific data pertaining to this individual. If we've left anything out that you need, please don't hesitate to ask for it."

"Valkyrie being your SAI."

Oh my god, these Anadens and their synthetic phobia. "Correct."

"Very well. It will take time."

"Keep me updated on your progress."

"And the consciousness? What, or how, should I expect to be receiving in that regard, if or when the time comes?"

She met his gaze with as much assurance as she could muster. "It's quantized data. It'll transfer the same way as an Anaden consciousness. So craft a human body capable of receiving it."

ᚱ

Alex found Kennedy out on one of the far landing platforms, a good distance from the main cluster of buildings.

The platforms were elevated several meters above the walkways—high enough that most of the waves didn't crest over the platforms during calm weather—but the damp breeze meant the air was quite cool nonetheless. Alex hugged her fleece tighter against her before ascending the steps to the platform.

Her mind and her skin hummed. She was excited and nervous and anxious and terrified, and this was all before she considered what she was about to do on the platform. But she had to put all that aside, because she had work to do. A *lot* of work, and most of it mattered to more than solely her family—possibly a couple of billion or trillion more. She couldn't be selfish.

Also, the personal work was now out of her hands for a time, so she might as well direct the pent-up energy into making herself useful.

Kennedy was sitting cross-legged in the center the platform, wearing an oversized beige cable knit sweater and woolen leggings. A large rectangular box sat in front of her, a power amp off to the side.

Alex squatted beside the box. "Interesting choice of testing location."

"Not my choice. Your mother decided it would be unwise to run any tests inside the hold of the *Stalwart II*—rightfully so I think—and Administrator Latro balked at letting me run tests inside any of their labs. I suggested one of the dining rooms, but he didn't care for that idea, either, and I was banished out here."

"I guess there *is* a small chance of nearby objects blowing up, or being pulled into a supradimensional vortex then blowing up."

"Let's just try to make sure it isn't us."

"Noted. So, no Devon?"

"He's in the main tech lab geeking out with one of the Barisan analysts, so he's close if we need him. But I doubt we will."

"Nah, we've got this. Valkyrie's finished the operating code modifications. I know you came here to try to find a practical way around the Imperium shields, but I'm glad you're here for this."

"Me, too. Incidentally, if this pans out, it could solve your Imperium problem, too. But let's not get ahead of ourselves."

"What were you able to figure out about the Imperium shields, by the way?"

Kennedy grimaced. "They work, in effect, as a shield of a shield—two separate layers of shielding with an active medium between the two. The whole operation is constantly cycling through the EM spectrum, with the interior layer acting as a backstop. And no, I haven't figured out how they can be countered, so…" she activated the input panel on the top of the hardware "…make this work. Load up the modifications."

Alex dropped to her knees, shifted the box around and placed her index finger on the input slot. Since she and Valkyrie had written the original code, it hadn't taken long to devise the changes needed, and now it was merely a matter of replacing a few key algorithms.

Once finished, she sank back on her heels. "It's going to need a small amount of power to get started. The projection distance is still twelve meters, but for now I've narrowed the spread to sixty degrees by forty-five degrees so it doesn't eat the platform."

"Good idea. I don't fancy getting dumped into the water." Kennedy connected the power amp to the Rifter module. "Turning it on in five…four…now!" She scrambled backwards to put some distance between her and the hardware.

The only indications the modified Rifter was active were two green lights on the panel and a faint shimmer to the air in an arc twelve meters out. Alex arched an eyebrow. "This is rather anticlimactic."

"What did you expect? Right now it's simply…waiting. It looks the same as always, but if your modifications worked, should something fall into the rift now, the object would be trapped in an invisible dimension forever."

"So long as the device is running, it'll be ricocheting between a bunch of dimensions. But when you shut it off, yes, whatever material fell in will stay trapped. Theoretically." Alex stood and walked to the edge of the platform, giving the vague ripples a wide berth.

She pushed her left sleeve up above her elbow, exposing the bracelet-turned-conductivity-lash. "Time to feed it a little energy."

She flicked her wrist and sent a quick stream of electricity into the undulating air.

The ripples instantly gained more substance as the bounds of the rift began to glow amber. Increasing levels of light danced jaggedly across the span of the rift's arc and bleed out into the air. Ions hissed in the humid air—then streaks of plasma poured out in all directions.

"Fuck!" Alex ducked as a bolt of highly charged particles shot over her head. "Cut the external power!"

She and Kennedy both dove for the power connector; Kennedy reached it first and yanked out the connection as Alex landed on her stomach beside it.

The surrounding air settled down until the fine hairs on her arms no longer stood on end. Stray energy continued to leak out, but less violently so.

Alex dropped her forehead to the platform and started laughing. "Just like university, isn't it?"

Kennedy's cackle sounded vaguely hysterical, and Alex peered beside her to see her friend's face animated and her skin flushed. "Almost—nothing's *actually* blown up yet."

Alex pushed up to a sitting position then to standing, still laughing. "Don't speak too soon." She cautiously took a few steps closer to the barrier, its parameters now clearly marked by visible oscillations of golden-hued energy. "So it's definitely self-sustaining."

"More than self-sustaining, I think." Kennedy retrieved a small orb and a probe from her bag. She sent the orb floating into the boundary of the pulsing light and checked the readout on the probe. "It's generating forty-three megajoules along the outside...and rising 0.4% per second. If the power isn't siphoned off or otherwise used, it's going to continue to build and, eventually, blow things up."

"Makes sense that without an outlet it would build over time."

The models I ran did predict a rise in power of 0.3% to 0.6% per second.

I know. I neglected to mention it to her. She always prefers hard data, and now she has it.

Alex took another step forward and raised her left arm.

"Don't you dare."

"Oh, come on, Ken. I stick my hand in powered grids all the time."

"I know this about you, which is why I made you a thing to help keep you from getting electrocuted." Kennedy rummaged around in her bag, then triumphantly produced a carbon-gray glove.

"What's that?"

"It's woven through with silica-sapphire fibers to modulate the power flow that passes through it, like the filters on your ship."

"Huh." Alex stared at the glove for a beat before slipping it on with an exaggerated pout. "If I must." She gave Kennedy a cha-grined look. "Thanks."

Ready, Valkyrie?

Comforted by the knowledge that I will not be hit with a forty-nine megajoule jolt of electricity, yes, I am ready.

Whatever. She closed the remaining distance and splayed an open palm onto the boundary of the field.

Despite the fact that she was expecting it, the surge of power made her gasp. "Ahh!"

"Alex?"

"I'm good, I'm good. This should be more than enough power to move...me." She transitioned to sidespace and focused on the far corner of the platform—

—and she was there. She breathed the cool, damp air deep into her lungs. "We did it."

It was the second time she'd seen a traversal in action, but Kennedy's expression remained one of amazement. "What's it like?"

Alex shrugged in feigned casualness, acting as if adrenaline didn't hasten through her veins to the point of jitteriness. "It's not like anything, really. There's a sort of...glitch in the air around you, and you're standing someplace else."

"Huh."

"Valkyrie, do you feel comfortable modifying our Rifter's code to create the necessary power internally?"

'With myself in control of the process, I do.'

Alex went over and shut the module on the platform down completely. The power ebbed away, leaving the air feeling empty and still. After considering it for a second, she leaned down and offered Kennedy a hand. "Come on. Let's go test this for real. In space."

"It's your ship. Of course, it's my life."

"We'll be *fine*." She dragged Kennedy down to the walkway and headed toward the *Siyane's* platform. On the way she sent Caleb a pulse.

> *Kennedy and I are making a run offworld to do a brief test. We won't go far, and we'll be back in a few hours.*

> *Okay. Have fun.*

The response was unusually curt, but he was doubtless preoccupied with any one of a dozen ongoing endeavors.

36

PALAEMON

Caleb,

Director Delavasi said he could get a message to you. I'm skeptical about trusting it to the man, but if you're reading this, he kept his word.

We're doing fine, so don't worry. Work is busy, so much so I've had to cut back to only teaching one class on account of all the consulting work. The creative ways in which young people are finding to 'enhance' themselves lately is providing no shortage of opportunities and problems alike.

Marlee is obsessed with aliens now. She talks about 'the rainbow aliens' and 'the tiger aliens' all the time, and this weekend she figured out how to load the visuals Alex gave her into her holovid space so she could play with the aliens in her treehouse castle. I have to say, it was rather clever of her—though now I'm wondering what else she can do that I don't know about. Being a parent is terrifying, by the way.

I hope you and Alex are...what? Healthy? Doing well? It would be horribly dense and tone-deaf of me to say 'safe,' so I won't presume to. Instead, I'll say that I hope you are kicking the enemy's ass in the general direction of a black hole. Be extraordinary.

Love,

— Isabela

P.S.: Marlee insisted I— "Auntie Alex, are there more aliens where you are? If there are, please please please please send images! Or vids! Images and vids! Hi, Uncle Caleb! Did you—"

Sorry about that, she...well, you can imagine. Talk to you soon. Or later, after you've saved the world.

Caleb wandered among the meticulously tended flora of the post's arboretum while he reread Isabela's message, then again. It made him smile, so he read it one more time.

He'd found his way to the arboretum soon after leaving the *Siyane*; he wasn't ready to let go of nature in bloom quite yet. They'd been running nonstop since returning from the Mosaic, and he craved another dose of the tranquil serenity Akeso and its environment had provided.

Nisi had been full of probing questions about his destruction of the Ekos-3 moon—what the process had involved, the sensations it had evoked, his physical state during and after and so on—but answering the questions had ultimately been pointless. The Sator had merely nodded portentously and murmured 'Hmm' a lot. Caleb's frustration level had been rising despite Akeso's calming influence when Alex's consequential pulse had come in, and he'd been grateful to change the subject.

The lingering aftereffects of communing with Akeso weren't so uniformly blissful and uplifting this time. His senses remained heightened, as did his perception of the physical world around him, but he also felt a disquieting unease and trepidation distinctly separate from his own.

The entity had been changed by the attack on it, as were all sentient beings upon encountering the harsh reality of evil made manifest. It saddened him, but he preferred Akeso jaded and alive to innocent and dead.

The petals his fingertips ran gently across weren't alive in the way Akeso was, but he wondered if perhaps they could become so. The Kats had engineered sentient plant life at least once. Could they grant self-awareness to these flowers? Should they?

Life, its creation, existence, destruction and even the possibility of its immortality, was on his mind for evident reasons. Meeting David Solovy had been a—

Overly mindful of his surroundings as he was, he took note as a harsh chill descended on the air around him. Not a coldness of temperature but of *ambiance*. Before he was able to discover the source, a shout announced it.

"Marano!"

He let loose of the flowering bloom and turned to find Malcolm Jenner striding purposefully toward him. What Akeso interpreted as chill, Caleb identified as hostility. It radiated out from the man, and as he drew nearer Caleb started to wonder if the Marine intended to punch him.

Caleb stood his ground, and Jenner pulled up to an abrupt stop a meter away, fists clenched at his sides. *Good choice.* "Brigadier, can I help you?"

"I doubt it. If it were in my power, you would be in a prison cell right now."

"Then I'm glad it's not in your power. What for?" There was, admittedly, more than one possibility.

"The murder of Jude Winslow with premeditation and malice aforethought."

Oh, that. "Winslow was the murderer, a thousand times over. He wanted to kill my wife and your girlfriend, and he might have succeeded if he'd been a little bit more cunning. He was a monster and a cancer that couldn't be allowed to survive to spread."

"So you took matters into your own hands, laws be damned."

"Yes."

Jenner blinked and stared at him incredulously. "You don't have the right. It was for the legal system to mete out justice, not you."

"Sometimes the system can't be trusted to act ethically. This was too important to leave to chance. What if he'd bought his way out? He would have picked up where he left off. Do you think AEGIS could have grown strong enough to be here now if OTS had continued to spread its brand of hate and violence? Do you think it would have been strong enough to win at the Provision Network Gateway?"

"You can't know what might have happened if he'd lived."

"I wasn't willing to risk finding out."

"And that makes you a killer just like him."

Caleb scoffed. "I've never denied I'm a killer. But I am nothing like him."

"Because you say you're not? You don't get to make the determination."

"All evidence to the contrary."

Jenner took a half-step forward, and Caleb held out a hand, palm raised. "*Don't.* Hitting me won't settle anything and will only land you in the infirmary."

"You arrogant ass. I don't think so."

"Fine, since I don't particularly care what you think. In fact, I'm done with this conversation." He hated Jenner for ruining the spell of the arboretum and stealing more of the dwindling peace still remaining inside him. If there was to be blood spilt, it shouldn't be in here.

He turned his back on the man and began walking toward the exit. Between the excited *diati* and the anxious traces of Akeso, he'd sense Jenner coming for him from a kilometer away.

When he did, he let the man come.

"I'm *not* done." Two meters from the exit, Jenner's hand landed hard on his shoulder.

In a flash Caleb had grabbed it, spun and locked Jenner's elbow. The Marine was strong, muscular, and likely fast, too, but Caleb now had the advantaged angle.

He wasn't going to use the *diati*—it was reserved for the real enemy. He kept the lock in place where he held it, but he didn't push it further, for Mia's sake. If a fight happened, no matter who was victorious, no one would come out a winner. "I said *don't.*"

Jenner's jaw flexed beneath his skin, but after two seconds he nodded minutely. Caleb loosened his grip, and the man stepped back. "You should be in a cell. Everyone has to be held accountable."

"I saved a fucking *planet* this week. Hold me accountable for that."

"You really don't get it, do you? Whatever good you may do, nothing gives you the authority to decide who lives and who dies. Civilization is built on laws and people recognizing and obeying those laws. Those who don't are punished by those laws, not by vigilantes. Down your path leads barbarism."

"When the system works, I'm perfectly happy to let it. But it doesn't always work, and deep down you know it. You wouldn't have obeyed unjust orders from O'Connell, would you have? From Pamela Winslow? Surely you wouldn't obey unjust orders from the Directorate if it was your overlord.

"The system is only as good as its leaders. And when they fail—when the system fails—you better damn well hope I'm there to pick up the slack."

Jenner continued to glower, but it lost some of its fervor. "No one appointed you humanity's protector."

"No one had to—and if you don't understand why that is, then you're not nearly the man I was told you are. I'm leaving now, and I'm going to assume we're done. But if you threaten me again, you had better bring help."

Jenner snorted. "Don't worry. Alex's husband and Miriam's son-in-law, Nisi's 'chosen one'? I know I can't touch you. But I will never trust you."

"Doubt I'll ever need you to. Are we finished?"

"Yeah. We're finished."

Caleb pivoted and headed for the exit.

"Hey!"

He half-turned, a non-committal expression on his face. He did not intend to take any more abuse, but he was mildly curious why they apparently *weren't* finished.

Jenner now looked surprisingly uncertain, given the heated vitriol of their interchange. "Question, since you seem to be the only person who can answer it. How did Mia actually escape the Triene cartel on Pandora all those years ago? You were there. What did she *do*?"

Caleb frowned, perplexed. He *wasn't* the only person who could answer it...then the pieces fell into place and he imagined how the interchange between Jenner and Mia must have played out. Bastard.

He shook his head, a bitter chuckle on his lips. "You are such a goddamn moron."

Then he pivoted and walked out.

37

SIYANE

They picked a location a full forty AU from Palaemon to conduct the test. No one would complain about safety issues at such a distance—or wouldn't if they were told, which they were not.

Kennedy leaned on the cockpit half-wall, watching Alex with her arms crossed over her chest and a dubious look on her face.

If she wanted to continue professing skepticism after all she'd seen, it was her prerogative, so Alex ignored the subtext of the pose. "I've picked a target destination 3.6 AU away. Not far at all, but far enough away to measure." She motioned to the HUD. "Do you want to confirm that all the readings are within safety parameters?"

"It's not the current readings giving me heartburn. It's what's going to happen to those readings when you fire up the...hey, we need a sexy name for it."

"For the power generator, or the wormhole opener?"

"The wormhole opener's all in you Prevos' heads. I mean the power generator. Truthfully, it alone represents an advance in technology generations beyond anything—"

'Caeles Prism.'

They stared at each other for a few seconds, then Alex nodded slowly. "The Latin for 'celestial'? It's fitting."

"It's more than fitting—it's semantically accurate. Caeles Prism it is."

Alex surreptitiously skimmed the readings herself a final time. "Okay, Valkyrie. Let's do this."

Valkyrie adopted the moniker with gusto. 'Initiating Caeles Prism.'

Space outside the ship soon began to glow a faint amber that swiftly bloomed to pure gold, sparkling and crackling.

'Required threshold reached.'

She exhaled. "Go."

She'd minimized it in her justifications, but the distance traveled was orders of magnitude farther than anything she'd done up to now.

Even so, the gap in time between normal space and normal space could be measured in a blink. She *did* perceive it, though, possibly because she was confident enough in surviving the trip to begin paying attention to the trip itself.

It was a question for later, but she had to wonder what filled the gap.

The view outside darkened as the Caeles Prism shut down.

'Location is 36.4 AU from Palaemon, local ecliptic coordinates *l* 22° 58' 14", *b* 13° 41' 06".'

"Excellent, Valkyrie. Great job."

Kennedy frowned. "That was it? But nothing happened."

"Told you. Sorry it wasn't more dramatic...." She trailed off as a pulse from Mia came in.

Alex, you need to know something. Malcolm found out what happened with Jude Winslow. What Caleb did. I don't know how. I...forgot to ask. I should have told you last night, but I my mind was focused elsewhere. Malcolm's still on Palaemon today, and I'm worried about what he might do. If you don't mind, will you tell Caleb for me? I'm not...I can't talk to him about it yet.

"Shit."

"What is it?"

She raised a palm to stave Kennedy off.

I'll handle it. Are you okay?

I will be. Thank you.

Recent bonding over wormholes notwithstanding, she wasn't close enough to Mia to push, and by all indications the woman could take care of herself. So she let it drop and immediately pulsed Caleb.

Hey, where are you?

I'm fine.

I didn't ask how you were—I asked where *you were. I heard from Mia, and—*

It's all fine. Handled.

We're on our way.

She squeezed her eyes shut. "*Ebanatyi pidaraz!*"

"What happened?"

"Malcolm found out what happened to that scum Jude Winslow."

"Found out...what? Winslow's dead, and I'm pretty sure everyone knows it."

Alex pinched the bridge of her nose. Too many people knew the truth, and the list was getting longer, but it was what it was. "This is a genuine, deep-dark secret—or it was—but Winslow didn't commit suicide. Caleb used a Reverb to force Winslow's eVi to self-destruct."

"Oh. I guess that makes sense."

"It does?"

"Yeah." Kennedy grimaced. "My family's known the Winslows for a long time. They would've found a way for him to weasel out of the worst of the charges at a minimum, if not get him off entirely. Unlike us Rossis, they use their power for evil."

"Exactly. But now Malcolm knows, and you can imagine how well he must have reacted. Based on Caleb's response to my pulse just now, I'm worried that Malcolm's already caught up to him. Hopefully Caleb left him in one piece, but I have no reason to believe they're done dueling over a slight difference in moral philosophy. So, obviously, test concluded, and we need to get on the ground."

Kennedy's expression brightened. "Hey, I'll get Noah to find Caleb. He can...well, not try to stand in-between them. But who knows. Maybe he can convince them to get a beer together instead of beating the shit out of each other."

"Thank you, Ken. Valkyrie, use Caleb's locator to pinpoint his location and send it to Noah, please." She didn't spy on Caleb when they were apart; she trusted him implicitly. The locator was for emergencies. But if someone didn't intervene, this stood to quickly become an emergency.

'Done.'

"Thank you. Set a course for Epsilon."

PALAEMON

ANARCH POST EPSILON

Caleb wasn't at the precise-to-the-walkway-tile coordinates Valkyrie had sent by the time he got there—not a surprise given it was a *walkway*—but Noah spotted him not far off, crossing one of the pavilions in the fading evening light.

He jogged up to his friend, taking care to announce his presence while he was still a few meters away. Caleb wasn't the kind of guy you sneaked up on. "Hey, man. What's up?"

Caleb eyed him critically, wearing a countenance Noah had seen before—rarely, but he'd seen it. Dark, brooding, spoiling for a fight. "Alex send you?"

Noah shrugged, spreading his arms out wide. "Jenner found you, I'm guessing?"

"Yep."

"He alive?"

"Not a scratch on him."

Noah nodded thoughtfully. "Want to go get a drink?"

For a moment Caleb acted as if he was going to refuse...then his shoulders sagged with a sigh. "I really do."

The little pub at the post was eccentric in its oddness. In many respects it resembled any neighborhood joint in a nice, trendy area of any downtown area on any human world. There were tables large and small, and the lighting was tuned to the perfect level where you could see but not *too* much. The hue was off, though—washed-out, as if half the color spectrum had been removed from it. The bar stretching the width of the opposite wall from the entrance wasn't a bar so much as a wavy ribbon of metal that dipped and rose...he tilted his head...on command, apparently.

Then there were the aliens, of course. Four...five different species Noah spotted on a casual survey, not counting the Anadens, which he didn't.

He got that they weren't human, not *exactly*. But they looked human. Like warenuts gone badly, badly off the rails, but basically human. He wasn't inclined to get worked up over the question of whether they were or weren't or how much they were or weren't.

They found two stool-like seats free on one end of the not-a-bar, and Caleb began punching in an order on a virtual menu displayed on the surface. "Had any of their drinks yet?"

Noah shook his head.

"I've got the order, then. I'll save you some unpleasant trial and error, and you can thank me later."

"Eh, I'll go out on a limb and thank you now."

To the extent there was a bartender, it appeared to be the squishy multi-colored blob—Efkam, he thought he'd heard was the name of the species—sliding around in front of a wall of what Noah assumed was drink-making equipment.

The blob didn't bring their drinks, however. How would it? Instead a floating bot whizzed them over.

He evaluated the tall glass, filled three-quarters full by a brown liquid, with less trepidation than he probably should.

"It tastes like porter, but in alcohol content it's more akin to cask whiskey. Proceed accordingly."

Noah contemplated the contents one more time, then turned the glass up.

"So we were standing there surrounded by half a dozen goons, and I swear not a one of them had seen a shower in a week. And I'm all, 'we're fucked sideways *and* we're gonna die in filth,' but out of nowhere—"

"Aye!"

Noah looked behind him to find two aliens standing there glaring at him and Caleb. One was a Barisan—he'd met a few of those. The other one looked like a mad scientist had crossed a lobster and a gorilla, and chitinous skin covered the entirety of its hulking body.

Noah smiled blithely. "Did you need something?"

"You're two of these Humans, right?"

Caleb swiveled around to face them, current drink in hand. "We are."

"It's bad enough when you swoop in here with your fancy ships and rogue SAIs and you take over our home. Now you're taking over our bar, too? You haven't earned the right to drink in here with us."

Noah frowned. Was the translator working correctly? He glanced sideways at Caleb. "Did this alien just insult us? 'Cause I can't tell."

"I'm not certain either, but I'm definitely getting a vibe here. I don't think it likes us very much."

Noah shifted back to the alien who'd spoken. "Why don't you like us? We come in peace and shit."

"Sure. You show up all high-and-mighty, proclaiming you're going to save us all from our pitiful existence. Odds are, you'll replace the Directorate with your own rulers, and we'll still get the shaft. You don't belong here, and we don't want your help."

Caleb took a long sip of his drink and set it down, then relaxed to lounge casually against the not-a-bar, elbows propped behind him. "Maybe, but it seems to me you've got jack to show for millennia of 'rebelling.' It seems to me you need us to do your work for you."

The quiet but more dangerous-looking alien barked some curse the translator didn't understand and charged toward them.

Caleb was still chilling, so Noah shrugged, stepped off the stool and threw a left hook into the alien's jaw. Times like this, his prosthetic arm kicked so damn much ass.

The alien stumbled for a few steps, but caught his footing, hunched over and barreled forward for another try. Noah ducked and lurched to the side, leaving the alien to crash into the thick ribbon of metal.

Caleb grabbed the alien by his clothes, slammed it into the metal a second time, and tossed it into the crowd. Then he was moving.

Someone grabbed Noah's shoulder and spun him around to deliver an uppercut to his chin using a chitinous, claw-shaped hand that hurt like a motherfucker, booze-dulled senses or no. His head snapped back and he was stumbling backwards. He met resistance in the form of one of the patrons, waved a vague apology and hurriedly stepped away.

The patron turned around to see what had jostled him just as his attacker swung again. And the brawl was on.

The alien who had first insulted them spotted him among a suddenly active crowd and shoved his way through, inadvertently encouraging the spreading violence. Noah cracked his neck and braced himself.

When the alien swung he dropped to a crouch and gut-punched the alien—and was promptly shoved to the floor from behind. His nose met the floor with a brutal *crunch*, but he rolled to the side in time to avoid a stomp to his head.

Now shit was serious.

He hauled himself up and turned to deal with the would-be stomper, but someone else had already grappled the offender.

Given a second of space, Noah tried to breathe in. This resulted in pain and blood but no air, because his nose was broken. Not the first time.

He wiped blood off his mouth and breathed in through it instead while he scanned the chaos, softened by a trace of blurriness, for Caleb. Finally he spotted him near the far left corner.

A hulking alien had pinned his friend's arms at his back. An Anaden moved in to pummel what should have been an easy target, but when the Anaden came in range Caleb swung both legs up, using the leverage of his captor to power his kicks. They landed one-two beneath the chin of the Anaden, who fell backward to the floor and didn't get up.

Caleb's legs swung down to kick at his captors knees in time with his head snapping back to slam into the toothy face of the alien. The alien's grip loosened.

Crap, he should be helping. But as Noah wound his way over as hurriedly as possible, it occurred to him that Caleb could clear the whole room with a single surge of *diati*. Either Caleb was too drunk to remember he commanded that particular ability, or he recognized it wouldn't be sporting. Not proper form in a proper barfight.

Noah rushed, or possibly careened, in from the side to deliver a punch to the massive alien's neck. Caleb wiggled free of its grasp, and they plunged into the furor now consuming the bar.

No one else in the place even knew why they were fighting; they never did.

He ducked beneath a punch not meant for him as they skidded around an epic beat-down of a...Barisan. Because there was fur.

Let's get out of here.

Yep.

They ducked and weaved around the melee to sneak out the door. Night had fallen in full, but diffuse light streams highlighted the walkways and buildings.

They stumbled through the plaza, around a corner and down one of the walkways. Noah started chuckling, then choked on blood leaking from his broken nose. He inhaled through his mouth and canted his head back...but now he couldn't see where he was walking. He dropped his chin down a bit. "What the hell was that all about—"

Caleb grabbed him by the shoulder and spun around as five aliens lumbered out of the bar. Noah identified one as the big companion of their initial attacker, and they all appeared to be on the hunt for targets.

"Shit." He and Caleb peered behind them, then at each other. Noah jerked his head down and to the left, and Caleb nodded. They both knelt and slipped over the side of the walkway into the murky, dark water.

Holy fuck! The tips of his fingers fumbled for the edge of the walkway to keep him from completely submerging, but the water splashed up onto his face anyway...at least it washed away some of the blood.

The ice-cold water felt like getting zapped with electricity directly onto every nerve of his body. He gasped in air, surprised his lungs still functioned, what with the shocks. Water lapped into his mouth, sending a dagger of pain through his tongue. Had he bit it during the fight?

Caleb surfaced beside him, only to his chin, and his eyes instantly went to the plaza to track their pursuers.

The mob was headed in their direction. One stalked a few meters down the walkway they'd been on seconds earlier, peering around in search of a fight to pick. Finding none, it retreated and rejoined its comrades as they headed deeper into the complex of buildings.

Caleb held up a finger, a signal to wait another minute.

Holy hell, he was freezing. His teeth chattered violently, and he almost bit his tongue again.

Seconds ticked by, and no one else showed up to search for them. Finally Caleb planted his palms on the walkway and hefted himself up. Noah more crawled than hefted, and they both collapsed onto their backs on the walkway.

Caleb laughed, winded and hoarse. "That was fun...."

Noah took precautions this time, rolling onto his stomach and propping up on his forearms before laughing as well. "Good times." He squinted down the walkway, toward the bar. "They got cops here?"

"A few. They'll show up eventually. We should go...somewhere else." Caleb pushed up to rest on his hands—then started laughing again and fell back. "Did you see the look on the Dankath's face?"

"What's a Dankath?"

"The big one with the shell and claws."

"Oh, that was priceless when it accidentally hit the Novoloume. Then some Naraida leapt out of nowhere onto its shoulders and started jabbing fingers at its eyes."

"I thought the...." Caleb leaned up on one elbow and peered into the distance, across the maze of walkways and platforms. "Someone's coming."

"I can't get back in the water, man. I know it was my idea and all, but damn it was cold." He squinted at the approaching figures. "Aww, it's fine. That's our ladies, come to rescue their damsels in distress."

"Fantastic...." Caleb collapsed to the walkway so hard the back of his head thudded against the tile. "Ow."

The approaching figures hastened their pace until one of them pulled ahead in a rapid jog—the taller, thinner one. Alex. 'Cause his lady had proper curves.

Alex skidded to a stop beside Caleb. He gazed up at her wearing a smirk. "Hey, baby."

Kennedy arrived next to drop to her knees beside him wearing a look of horror. "Noah, you're bleeding!"

"I definitely am. But it's cool. It was worth it."

"Are you *drunk*?"

"Exceedingly so. Or I was, before the..." he gestured behind him "...water. It'll sober you up right quick."

"Apparently not." Her face screwed up at him, but he couldn't tell if it was in concern, amusement or anger. In his peripheral vision Caleb and Alex were murmuring softly to each other, their heads so close their foreheads nearly touched. Why was *he* the one getting in trouble?

Kennedy blew out a breath. "They're going to get hypothermia if they stay out here much longer."

Alex pushed up to standing. "Okay, guys. To the *Siyane* with you."

He and Kennedy had a suite—or a room with a shower and a couch—in the complex. Somewhere. After considering the hazy buildings in the distance, he acquiesced. He even let Kennedy help him up—not that he *couldn't* stand on his own. "Point the way."

Kennedy shook her head with a groan and began dragging him down the walkway.

Once they got moving good, she leaned in close to whisper, "You were supposed to take care of him."

He gave her a bloody, crooked grin. "I *did*."

38

SIYANE

Alex rested her head on her palm to watch Caleb sleep. She so rarely got a chance to do so, since he almost always woke before her.

Any bruises or cuts he'd suffered the night before were gone, vanished in the wake of the *diati's* healing imperative. His hair had dried messy and wild, though, and she had to actively resist reaching over to play with a sloppy curl.

He'd been in no condition to talk about whatever had happened last night, but she assumed the absence of any panicked messages from Mia, irate messages from Malcolm, concerned messages from her mother or stern messages from Administrator Latro meant no permanent damage had been done and life continued on.

One eyelid opened a crack, and a sliver of crimson iris peered out at her. For the briefest second it appeared alien. Foreign. She banished the notion and smiled. "Good morning, *priyazn.*"

"Is it? Morning and/or good?" He winced sheepishly as he reached for her, and she scooted closer and slipped into his arms. "Anyone waiting outside the ship to arrest me?"

"Because of the bar fight, or Malcolm?"

He opened the other eye, carefully. "Either?"

There aren't, are there, Valkyrie?

I'm pleased to report an empty platform.

Thanks.

"No. I think you're in the clear. I'm sure it wasn't their first bar fight." She ran the pad of her thumb along his cheek. "Whatever he said to you, he's wrong."

"How can you be so sure?"

She briefly contemplated getting up, throwing on some clothes and going to find Malcolm just to punch him in the gut. It would definitely make her feel better. But it wouldn't help anything, while she *could* help Caleb.

"I know him, I know you and I know what happened with Winslow. You did what you felt was right, and I think it probably was. Hard decisions—choices—don't always fit inside the neat little sanctioned box Malcolm wishes they did."

"No, they don't. I refuse to be sorry for what I did. But I am..." he lifted a hand and concentrated on it until a faint crimson halo appeared, then banished the halo and brought the hand up to cover hers resting on his chest "...cautious. Or I'm trying to be.

" 'The first and greatest punishment of the sinner is the conscience of sin'—that was the passphrase Division used for access to its most closely guarded information. The bosses were being clever, because it's a quote from Lucius Annaeus Seneca, but it also served as a subtle reminder. To always be cognizant of our actions, and to mind the blurry line between necessary evils and the turpitudes they're meant to combat."

With a sigh he squeezed her hand and rolled onto his side to face her. "I believe it was my right to eliminate Winslow, but that was under the old rules. This power I wield now? Using it I can do things I shouldn't have the right to do. No one should. What if it *is* changing me?"

Uncertainty weighed down his features. "Look at my eyes. Can you still see the man I was in them?"

She'd stared into them a thousand times. In the last while she'd watched them transform a little more each day. They were now almost pure, deep crimson, with the sapphire flecks but a highlight instead of the other way around. He knew this; he wasn't asking about the color.

"On the second night you were on board the *Siyane*—forever ago and not so long ago at all—I tried to convince myself I was not going to get led astray by a pair of pretty blue eyes. Well, I got led astray all right, but it wasn't by your pretty blue eyes. It was by your unexpectedly tender heart, your fierceness of spirit, your patently delicious body..." her lips curled up playfully "...by your indomitable soul. If any of that has changed, it's been to grow stronger."

His mouth met hers with urgency to deliver a message of relief, gratitude and love far better than words could.

When he drew back, though, he still looked too grave. "But you'll tell me, won't you? If I go too far or start to lose my bearings, you'll take off those kid gloves you're currently wearing and yell sense into me?"

"You bet I will. I'll pitch a fine fit." She lifted her head and glanced at the stairwell, from where a delightful aroma had drifted down to fill the air. "We should get up. Someone's cooking breakfast."

ℛ

Kennedy was standing at the kitchen counter inspecting a tray of steaming hot orange croissants when they arrived upstairs. Noah sat on the couch with the med kit positioned in front of him, replacing the medwrap strip on his nose.

"So, everyone's alive and in one piece this morning. Good, since we have work to do. After breakfast, obviously." Alex offered a grateful smile as Kennedy piled the croissants high on a plate and brought them over to the kitchen table.

Rather than sit, Alex propped on the edge of the table and grabbed a croissant. "While you boys were causing trouble last night, Ken and I constructed and successfully field-tested a workable mechanism for wormhole creation and traversal, thank you very much."

Noah nodded, then grimaced and touched his nose. "Sure. Of course you did. Because you two can do that sort of thing in a single day."

Kennedy shrugged as she sat down at the table. "A couple of hours, really."

"At most. But now we need to make it practical. We need to devise a way to get the power to the entire fleet."

Alex paused to take another bite of her croissant. Kennedy used to make them during university, but she didn't recall them being so good. "Initial thought? Most of the ships have Rifters installed. The resident Artificials can roll out the new code easily enough. Could they set up a toggle and have the Rifter do double duty like we did on the *Siyane*?"

Kennedy shook her head. "As an official independent contractor of AEGIS, I cannot in good conscience recommend such a course of action until months of tests—or at least weeks—have been performed. This mechanism is highly volatile and subject to blowing things up. Activating it on twenty thousand separate ships at the same time is asking for disaster."

"Impressive channeling of my mom there."

"Thanks, but I'm serious."

Alex scowled, but conceded the point. "Okay, *fine*. So how about one big Caeles Prism—big enough to generate a consistent supply of enough power to move the largest ships? It'll need a power transmitter, and the ships will need receivers."

"They have those. And they're tunable, which is perfect, since it means each ship can take only the power it needs for its own traversal. As for transmitting the power, we'd need to fit the Caeles Prism with a capture module and pair it to a broadcaster. The ships have most of those components, too, but they're using them for other things. Also, they're too small. We need a big one."

Noah grabbed a second, or maybe third, croissant. "I can throw something together."

Everyone stared at him expectantly.

"The AEGIS supply ship carries enough spare parts for me to build a lattice-style capture module to encase this...what did you call it, a 'Caeles Prism'?...without fencing in the power output. Attach some DELs at periodic junctions to transmit the power out, and you ought to be good to go."

Caleb nodded. "Kind of like what the Kats use on Portal Prime. It could work."

Alex frowned. "What are DELs?"

"Small mobile drone orbs ASCEND invented. Everyone was quite busy while you were gone, ushering in a new era of innovation and progress and whatnot."

She rolled her eyes at Kennedy. "I'd expect no less. All right, Miss Official Independent Contractor. Assuming Noah can build an attachment that will get the power out to the ships, what's our next step?"

"First, we should test moving the *Siyane* using the independent module instead of its own Rifter, to confirm the power transfer works. Then we'll need to find a couple of Prevo volunteers in the AEGIS fleet to test it across multiple ships simultaneously. We'll gradually scale up the tests, amping up the power produced and adding more ships."

Alex made a face. "Ugh. How long will all that take? In case you didn't notice, we've kind of picked a fight with the neighborhood bully."

Kennedy poked Noah lightly in the shoulder. "How long will it take you to build the power capture-and-transfer mechanism?"

"Factoring in the time needed to shuttle up to the supply ship and back, plus a shower...seven hours?"

"Alex, I assume it won't take a significant amount of time for the Artificials to install whatever new code they'll need?"

"Counting transmission time and reading the instructions? Twelve seconds."

"Then based on the turnaround time of recent roll-outs of new equipment at the Presidio, all told, about thirty-eight hours and twelve seconds."

Alex reached for another croissant, only to discover the plate was empty. "Oh. Well...that's not so long."

39

PALAEMON

"Help me push the table over against the wall."

"Why do we need to move it?"

Devon shrugged. "I've learned from experience that you don't know how big of a mess you're going to make until you make it. I don't want to destroy any post property if I can avoid it. This is the emptiest place I could find, but there's still the table and chairs to worry about."

Emily gave him an uncertain look, but she relented and joined him on one side of the table. Devon leaned in and put some muscle into it, and together they maneuvered the long conference table across the room until it abutted the far wall.

"Why don't we do this outside, then?"

He started dragging chairs over to line up next to the table. "It's breakfast time local, so someone would see us. I'm also trying to be discreet."

"And if you blow up half the wing of the building like you did at the hospital?"

"At least I *tried* to be discreet?"

She giggled and stopped him by the row of chairs to give him a kiss. "Fair enough. Are we ready now? Finally?"

"As ready as we're apt to be." He removed the small oval gadget one of the anarch techs had given him to tinker with from his bag and placed it on the floor in the center of the room—shit, *the floor*. If he expected to think and act in five dimensions, he really shouldn't forget to do so in three dimensions first.

He retrieved one of the chairs from where he'd just put it by the wall and dragged it to the middle of the room, then placed the module on the seat.

Emily frowned. "I thought we weren't destroying any of their property?"

"I'm trying to protect the floor. The chair's small enough that if it's damaged, we can get rid of the evidence. A crater in the floor, not so much."

He retreated until his back touched the wall opposite the table and other chairs while motioning for Emily to stand beside him. If the furniture *did* get wrecked, he didn't want them to catch any shrapnel. He also activated his personal defense shield in case they did.

He grasped her hand in his. "Ready? Shield on?"

She nodded, and he slipped into sidespace…then a little farther. The alien circuitry weaving through the interior of the object lit up against its casing like an old-fashioned x-ray image.

On your whim, Annie.

The power built up within him, boosted by more power flowing in from Emily and Yves—then leapt across sidespace into the circuitry.

Sparks ignited around the oval object as a sharp hissing noise reverberated off the walls. It bounced and shook, dancing across the chair seat until it tumbled off the edge to the floor and fell silent.

The light from the circuitry within it blinked out, leaving only the chrome of the pseudometal casing.

He opened his eyes in normal space. "Damn, the room didn't blow up."

This was our hope, was it not?

"Isn't that a good thing?"

"Annie says the same thing. It's definitely for the best, but the inner rebel in me gets a kick out of a good explosion."

Emily laughed. "See? This is what I was missing. Also, thank you for not going stir-crazy and blowing up our apartment on Romane."

"You bet." He pushed off the wall to go pick up the object and inspect it. Cracks had formed in the outer casing, but it had nominally held together. Still, the gadget was well and truly dead. *Agreed, Annie?*

Yes. The circuitry required for it to function has been not merely disabled, but destroyed at a quantum level.

Excellent.

He returned the now-inert object to his bag. "All right, next step. Let's go find Harper."

Emily glanced pointedly around the room. "Shouldn't we put everything back where we found it first?"

Devon sighed.

∧R

The idea had come to him on the *Siyane*, when Alex had pointed out their goal was to move things, not explode them, and Emily had admonished him not to explode himself. Both points were well taken.

Alex appeared to have the 'moving things' well in hand, so he might as well concentrate on the possibilities which arose from exploding things. He did have some experience at it.

The problem—or the first problem—was that most Amaranthean technology was, at a core design level, significantly more advanced than their own. For starters, it utilized five dimensions, as they'd learned in the most torturous manner possible from the Anaden-derived virus that had infected Emily.

But Mia had powered through the obstacle to a cure, and though Devon had been in no condition to help at the time, once Emily was better he'd gone back and exhaustively studied the virus and its counter.

Once he'd gotten here, he'd befriended several of the techs at the post. Hackers liked to boast to other hackers, no matter the species, and he'd encouraged the inclination. They'd shown him not only the basics of how their systems operated, but some tricks and secrets as well.

In giving him a look at a few snippets of code and circuit design, they'd shown him and Annie far more than they'd realized.

He started paying attention when the door to the larger of the conference rooms AEGIS had appropriated opened. The meeting was breaking up, and people began filing out.

Most of them headed directly across the atrium toward the main exit, and he and Emily loitered off to the right, out of the way. He offered a greeting or two, but he didn't want to get waylaid by anyone. When Harper and Lekkas broke off from the group and exited a side door, he and Emily followed.

Lekkas sensed them approach because of the Noesis, and Harper sensed them approach because she was a ninja. Both women turned around well before he and Emily reached them on the pavilion.

He motioned for them to keep going and fell in beside Harper. "How did the meeting go?"

The Marine looked at him as if he'd asked about the political and societal ramifications of Francis Ronalds' invention of the electrical telegraph. "What?"

"I need to borrow a Reverb."

She stopped cold with a groan. "Not a fucking chance."

"Why not?"

"Those insidious little devices have already gotten me in enough trouble. I don't need more."

"I'm not going to kill anyone with it." Discovering via a faint, stray Noesis thought from Morgan that Caleb had killed Winslow using one had left Devon feeling...uncomfortable. Not because he hadn't wanted Winslow dead—he'd wanted it so much he'd very nearly done the deed himself—but more because the calm, cold, matter-of-fact way in which Caleb had disposed of the terrorist was...it *should* have been disconcerting. It possibly wasn't, which in itself had been disconcerting.

Devon had been traveling down a path darkening gray in color when Emily was attacked, and he'd been headed down it for a while. He thought, and hoped, that taking care of her, that simply being with her since then, had nudged him a fair distance back toward the middle of the road.

On the other hand, he was about to make a solid genius effort at turning a deadly weapon deadlier, so perhaps not.

Morgan had kept walking for a few strides, but now she pivoted and retraced her steps to rejoin Harper while giving him a strange look. "You are a crafty one, Devon. I'll give you that." She put a hand on Harper's arm. "Actually, he kind of has a good reason for asking for one. Just follow procedures and document the transfer. That way he's the only one who will get in trouble if trouble happens."

Devon didn't know specifically what all the crankiness was about, and he didn't bother to probe Morgan's mind to find out, despite the fact that she'd clearly been probing his. "Sure, I'll sign whatever. I'll even promise in writing not to kill any humans with it."

Morgan eyed him sideways, but Harper didn't seem to notice; she was too busy scowling. "No. You're a civilian, and civilians aren't authorized to possess RRF weapons."

He gazed plaintively at Morgan until she relented. "Fine. I'll authorize an exception and check it out to him myself."

"Why the hell?"

She winced apologetically at Harper, then jerked her head in his direction. "Because he's got a hell of an idea, and I'm curious to see if he can pull it off."

40

SIYANE

'Eren is here and asking to come aboard.'

Alex glanced up in surprise, then groaned. "Eren...." She'd completely forgotten about Mesme's message expressing concern as to Eren's well-being. It had been *days* ago—before Akeso, before inventing the Caeles Prism, before Malcolm's tantrum and its fallout.

"As in 'right outside' here?"

'Yes.'

Well, she'd find out soon enough how guilty she needed to feel about the lapse. Caleb shrugged assent. They'd sent Kennedy and Noah off half an hour earlier and had just finished cleaning the cabins and themselves up.

"Okay. Let him in."

Eren sauntered in wearing what passed for Anaden casual wear: loose flowing pants and a vest in muted bronze and caramel. It was a notable departure from his usual black and blacker. His hair was likewise loosely bound and draped over one shoulder, exposing a face devoid of its usual aloof insolence. "Morning, mates."

Alex frowned at him. "You're awfully bright-eyed and bushy-tailed this morning."

Eren twisted around to inspect his ass. "'Bushy-tailed'? Did I catch an extra appendage on the last regenesis?"

She rolled her eyes. He was *fine*. *Valkyrie, let Mesme know Eren's fine.* "It's an idiom. I thought you were at Post Alpha?"

"They let me use the teleportation gate. Damn convenient." He studied Caleb. "Rough night?"

Caleb spread his arms in mock indignation. "What? I look great." And he did look great—uninjured, freshly showered and alert.

"I might have heard a tale of mayhem breaking out around here last night. I'm certain you were in no way whatsoever involved in it. So I need your help. Both of you—likely all three of you. Don't say 'again.' I realize it's again, and I'm asking anyway."

Caleb visibly tensed. "Is Felzeor all right?"

"*Yes.* Unhappy about the frigid climate at Alpha yet unwilling to stay inside where it's warm, but he's safe and well. I've got a mission, but I can't do it alone. I want to rescue a group of aliens from Eradicated species who are currently being tortured at one of the Erevna exobiology labs."

"When you phrase it like that, we can't exactly refuse." Alex shook her head. "But what you're suggesting is far outside our wheelhouse. We can't fit a lab full of aliens, some of whom are undoubtedly *big*, in the *Siyane*."

Caleb came over to rest against the data center next to her. "Nor can the three of us manage the remainder of what would be required, such as subduing a cadre of Vigil officers and drones long enough to physically evacuate a facility full of frightened, possibly injured, possibly dangerous aliens who don't speak the language. We can't do it—but our people can."

He gave her a pained look. "You should take him to talk to Jenner."

"Seriously?"

"The Marines are bored. They need a reason to be here, and this is a good one. I'd say take him to Harper, because I guarantee she'd jump at the chance to run a real mission, but Jenner would have to approve it, so...take him to Jenner."

She studied him suspiciously until he began to look sheepish.

"I never said he wasn't a good Marine."

"I know. He is. Not the point?"

"Kind of has to be. We're fighting a war here." He turned back to Eren, who was staring at them with a questioning expression, hands half-raised expectantly. "Alex will help you pitch the mission to an AEGIS ground forces team. They'll take care of you."

AR

AFS SARATOGA

MILKY WAY SECTOR 17

Malcolm held up a hand as soon as she walked in. "If you're here to yell at me—"

"Sadly, no." She glared at him in blatant irritation nonetheless. He looked like he hadn't gotten much sleep, which gave her a bit of perverse pleasure. "I'm here about a mission Eren wants help on."

"Eren? Oh, your Anaden friend. What's the mission?"

"You'll love it—rescuing helpless, innocent victims of the Directorate. But he'll need to explain the details. I'm merely the broker. Can I invite him in here and trust you won't grill him on his historical transgressions before you'll agree to work with him?"

"That's not fair, Alex."

"It's totally fair."

"So you *are* here to yell at me. Fine. Do you really, honestly think I'm in the wrong on this?" He shook his head and straightened up in his chair. "Never mind. Of course you do—you have to defend your husband. Forget I asked."

"Too late, and Caleb can defend himself quite well without my help." She sighed. "What do I really, honestly think? I think Jude Winslow was a scumbag and a murderous terrorist, and I'm glad he's dead. I don't particularly care how he got dead, but I'm simple that way. I think his demise isn't worth an iota of attention from people far better than him and definitely isn't worth kicking off an inter-universe crisis over. I think it's not worth destroying relationships over."

He didn't challenge her on any particular point, instead dragging a hand down his mouth to land at his jaw. "On a scale of zero to arranging a fiery dungeon in Hell for me, how angry at me is Mia?"

"She's not angry at you, Malcolm. She's heartbroken. So congratulations. Great job."

Now his other hand joined the first to cover much of his face; his shoulders sagged. "That's not what I...want."

He did seem rather miserable, but it was his own damn fault. She crossed her arms over her chest and rested her weight on her back leg. "What *do* you want? For her to be someone other than who she is? Then why were you with her in the first place? Have you asked yourself why? Because it seems relevant."

He opened his mouth to respond...then exhaled harshly and closed it again.

"Whatever. Not my concern. But if you want my advice, which you probably don't, figure it out. Quickly." She shook her head. "You and I have had our differences, but even during the worst of them, I never, *ever* thought you were an asshole. Shows what I know."

His lips creased into a thin line as his countenance hardened. "No, if I were an asshole I would tell your mother—and I should. But I'm not in the habit of breaking up families, and it's likely a moot point now anyway. AEGIS, and your mother, have bigger evils to fight. We all do. I get that."

Alex clenched her jaw tight and turned away, studying the blank wall to her right as if it held some obscure secret. But her silence was its own giveaway.

"She already knows, doesn't she? Am I the only person who didn't know?"

Alex hadn't volunteered the truth to her mother; they'd grown closer, but not *that* close. But it turned out her mother had never believed Jude Winslow committed suicide, and before she and Caleb left for Amaranthe, Miriam had broached her suspicion that one (or possibly all, Alex included) of the Noetica Prevos had eliminated Winslow. When Alex assured her it wasn't the case, she'd gone straight to Caleb.

She shared none of this with Malcolm; she wouldn't provide him more ammunition. "It wasn't your business."

"So everyone keeps telling me. I frankly expected better from your mother, but I guess she can't exactly arrest her son-in-law."

"Or maybe she realizes that sometimes good people need to do bad things to bad people to save other good people from the far worse acts the bad people would otherwise commit. Look, she wasn't thrilled about it. But she was glad Winslow was dead. Admittedly, she felt far more guilty *about* being glad than I do, but it comes with the leadership gig."

She almost cut herself off there, but she was pissed now. Again. "You know what else comes with leadership? The balls to make a decision when there are no perfect choices. When we find where the Directorate hides—and trust me, we will—who do you imagine she will send to take them out? It sure as hell won't be you, because you don't have the guts to kill the monsters."

"Don't tear me down to make Caleb look honorable and yourself feel better. I killed Olivia Montegreu without hesitation, up close and personal, and if Miriam sends me to eliminate the Directorate, I will be proud to do it."

Her lips curled up, but it wasn't a happy expression. "Maybe, since she will have ordered you to do it. Your conscience would remain safely in the clear. For once, make a goddamn decision for yourself."

His palms slammed onto the table as he stood. "Okay, that is *enough*. You and I have had our differences, but even during the worst of them, I never, *ever* thought you were a cruel, vindictive bitch. Don't make me say 'until now.'"

"Don't try to lock my husband up for being a *yebanaya* hero and killing the man who killed Abigail."

It was a rare moment when her and Valkyrie's convictions merged so completely into a single articulation of will. Her glyphs flared brightly, and she imagined her eyes must have matched them.

He stared at her, and the hard lines etched into his face softened. "You're genuinely afraid I will, aren't you?"

She shrugged emphatically. Did he not appreciate the significant amount of authority he wielded these days? "I don't know. You tell me, Earth Alliance Brigadier, AEGIS Director of Lots of People with Guns."

"I'm not going to do anything, Alex. I..." he grimaced "...I guess I'm just full of hot air, huh? All braggadocio and build-up, no delivery."

"Um...." Her brow knotted up in consternation.

He dragged his hands down his face, mostly covering the flare of redness at his ears. "Well, that came out wrong."

The tension in the room, which had been building toward blows, eased to a manageable level as he peered at her through splayed fingers. "Truce? Can we please talk about the mission now?"

I apologize if I made this encounter more difficult for you. It is a peculiar sensation, to have one's emotions escape one's control.

It's all right, Valkyrie. You weren't wrong...and he needed the push.

"We can. I really don't have the details, though, so can I invite Eren in now?"

"Go ahead. I assume it was your idea to bring this mission to me?"

"No. It was Caleb's."

41

MILKY WAY SECTOR 62

Casmir elasson-Machim was uneasy. His assured, focused demeanor betrayed none of his unease to the bridge crew. But he was uneasy.

Persistence on the part of Vigil operatives had finally paid off. The Katasketousya had missed a location tracker on one of the Provision Network delivery vessels, unwittingly revealing the location of a hidden portal into the Network. The location had been provided to Casmir, accompanied by a mission directive.

Here was their chance to cut the head off the snake, to eliminate the Katasketousya's support structure and, perhaps more importantly, stop the influx of Humans at the source. With no reinforcements of people, materials or firepower and no home to retreat to, the small contingent of Humans here in Amaranthe would wither until they could be dealt with at the Directorate's leisure.

Of course, he didn't have a Tartarus Trigger to deliver this time. A new device was allegedly being constructed with due speed, but there was a reason why only one had existed in the first place.

Quietly and without fanfare or admission of disappointment, the Directorate had thus approved a mission to permanently and irrevocably isolate and disconnect the Human realm from the Katasketousya's subversive Network and from Amaranthe, rather than its *actual* Eradication. Igni missiles would destroy the Humans' portal, sealing them off in a solitary bubble of space forever.

From the Directorate's perspective the practical effect was the same, if somewhat less satisfying than a rapacious black hole devouring the entire species.

The plan made perfect, logical sense. But none from the Directorate had been at the Provision Network Gateway battle. His Primor had viewed the memories of the engagement from the perspective of Casmir and other officers, but the Primor had not lived and died through it.

Casmir was loyal to the ends of the universe, and he worked to retain unconditional faith in the greater wisdom of his Primor and the Directorate. Yet a tiny, traitorous voice deep in the recesses of his mind whispered that his leaders did not properly respect the enemy. Did not properly appreciate the nature of the enemy's insidious cleverness and audacity.

He had seen it firsthand and found he could not put it aside. The shock of being not merely outgunned but outwitted had made an impression.

But if he brooded too vehemently, his Primor would know his thoughts, were he to turn his attention in Casmir's direction. So he hurriedly buried them beneath final mission preparation and orders, and he kept burying them until he was legitimately consumed by final mission preparation and orders.

With such dedication applied to the task at hand, he was soon satisfied all was in order. He began.

"Send the signal to open the portal."

The wave propagated in a directed signal from his vessel, and out of nothingness sprung a large portal identical in appearance to the former Provision Network Gateway. The memory of its destruction remained vivid, and he ensured they hovered well back from the edifice.

"All vessels to full alert. Shields to maximum. Tactical, launch a probe through the portal."

As before, the probe breached the plasma at the center of the portal ring. Nothing triggered to pierce the calm silence, and twenty seconds later the probe returned to transmit nominal readings. But that, too, had been true before.

"Squad MW T8-12, proceed through the gateway to a distance of 0.5 megameters and assume a defensive formation. Squad T8-13, prepare to proceed after them. Same directive." He was sending a smaller force ahead this time—enough ships to test the area, but not enough to matter if they were destroyed.

Forty ships approached the portal in a long line, spread across the width of the ring. They vanished through the plasma...

...and nothing pierced the calm silence. He breathed out.

Squad T8-13 followed seconds later, and still all remained quiet. He nevertheless repeated the process again and again, sending larger formations through one at a time until only his remained. Twice, vessels returned through the portal to report nothing unusual on the other side.

Perhaps his concerns were unfounded, or founded on a rash overestimation of his adversary. How clever could primitives truly be, after all?

"Traverse the portal and join our forces 0.5 megameters on the other side."

The wall of plasma enveloped the Imperium, washed over them...and they left it behind.

Space here was not exactly the same as on the other side. There were no stars, leaving the plasma of the portal as the sole source of light. But this comported with their understanding of the status of the region as an interim area leading to additional portals, which led to the true foreign realms.

When the fleet had reformed in full, they locked on to the TLF wave streaming from the portal and moved out.

The darkness grew as their distance from the portal increased—then a blinding flare of light engulfed them and—

AR

MACHIMIS

MILKY WAY SECTOR 36

Casmir awoke in the space between panic and pain. The memory of searing heat as his retinas burned out nanoseconds before his skin burned off fueled a deluge of primal terror to overtake him. He clawed at the capsule cover in a desperate attempt to *get away*—

—but there was no fire here. No blinding light, only soft, clinical illumination. No physical pain, only the graphic memory of it. Disorientation replaced the terror until comprehension took hold.

He exhaled slowly. It was far from his first regenesis or even his first to follow a violent death. But never before had the death come so unexpectedly and with such grandiosity. His mind arrived still embroiled in the throes of shock from dying in agony. It had not been a pleasant experience.

He followed the Curative unit's instructions, allowing himself to be checked over and provided new clothing and ushered out of the lab.

In the minutes and hours that followed, the acuteness of the remembered pain faded and his mind reoriented itself to the reality of being alive once more. But try as he might, Casmir was unable to shake the dread that had taken up insistent residence in his gut.

⟡

The Machim Primor did not look up from his work when Casmir entered. He stopped three meters inside the office and waited.

"You failed in your mission."

"Sir—"

"Twice now the enemy has caught you unawares and humiliated you and your forces."

Or humiliated the Directorate—

The Primor's gaze snapped to him, hostility animating his manner. The man had sensed the thought.

Heretical doubts exposed, Casmir now had no choice but to forge ahead. "Sir, they are outsmarting us. We have become complacent in our confidence in the supremacy of our own power, but we have not faced an adversary like this one before. It is incumbent upon the Directorate to recognize this fact. It is incumbent upon…you, sir, to recognize this fact. Only then will we be able to formulate a proper, effective strategy and defeat them."

"You forget your place, Casmir. Continue to do so, and on your next regenesis you may find yourself demoted."

He would not, *could not*, wilt under the force of his Primor's stare. The future of civilization might very well depend on it.

"Your will is as always paramount, sir, and I accede to it with the utmost humility and respect. But right now, my job—the job you have entrusted to me—is to be the manifestation of the Directorate's will, to act as the Directorate's spear and defeat the enemy I am set against. It is my opinion that our usual strategy, which involves sending a disproportionate force to pummel the enemy until they are reduced to rubble, will not succeed against this enemy.

"I believe without hesitation that we can and will defeat them, but to do so we must objectively evaluate their strengths and weaknesses, then use this analysis to develop new, more finely tuned strategies that *can* succeed."

The Primor stared at him in silence for a moment, then turned away, back to his work. "Unnecessary. We have denied them the use of the gateways, thus confining them to the Milky Way and slowing down their intragalactic movements. We will find them, corner them and destroy them like every other enemy we have encountered. They are not special, nor are they a meaningful threat, and we will not quiver in fear of them."

Casmir opened his mouth in search of an additional protest, but he'd already used his best argument.

"Report to Sagittarius Hub for reassignment to defense of our highest-value facilities."

He nodded, resigned and, as he now realized was inevitable, cowed into submission. "As you wish, sir."

No one could defy a Primor, save another Primor, and possibly not even them. No one *should* defy their Primor. The Directorate knew best how to lead them to victory.

42

AFS COLUMBIA

MILKY WAY SECTOR 17

Harper opened the left-most equipment locker and dutifully counted the tactical vests lined up in neat rows. She entered the number in the open screen floating beside her then confirmed the number matched the previous check as well as the number reported by the automated system, which did a perfectly competent job of tracking inventory.

Of course, she hadn't lent out any flak jackets on the sly for illegal clandestine operations, so it wasn't a surprise the numbers matched.

She signed off on the supply check with her authorization and opened the next locker. Grenades, of three different varieties—

The hiss of the door opening was so near to silent, if the armory wasn't quiet as a tomb she might not have heard it.

"Suit up."

She tensed at the recognition of the familiar voice but schooled her expression before turning around to face Malcolm. "Sir?"

"I said suit up. We have a mission—a real one."

She eyed him warily. "I thought you were angry with me."

"I am angry with you. But we still have a job to do."

The nightmares had been tamer last night, but she felt strangely off-kilter. Like she were standing on a cliff where the jagged cracks at her feet refused to commit, never breaking off to send her plummeting into the abyss yet never healing to become safe, stable ground.

But she still had a job to do. "Yes, sir."

"The pertinent information's in the system. Briefing will be in half an hour. Review the team makeup and mission parameters and let me know of any suggested changes before the briefing."

She called up the file and started scanning the summary on a whisper screen. "You're going on the mission as well?"

"I find I could use a bit of forced self-defense."

AFS SARATOGA

MILKY WAY SECTOR 17

On meeting Eren asi-Idoni, Brooklyn immediately understood why Morgan had rambled on about him for nearly a minute after *she'd* met him, before cutting herself off to apologize while blushing. The long, audacious hair, the shining, naturally defiant eyes, the sleek, black-on-black attire and roguish manner? They would definitely have caught Morgan's fancy.

She simmered for two seconds before reminding herself that looking was merely an act of detached appreciation, and she had no reason to be insecure.

Still, she cut off Eren's long-winded introduction. "Yeah, Lekkas told me about you. Let's just get to the mission details."

"'Lekkas'? Ah, the fighter pilot, yes?" He grinned wolfishly—but at her glare tamped it down. "Right, then. Yes. The mission is to rescue as many of the captives the lab is imprisoning as we can. The tricky part is, we need to get on the station and disable the security as quickly and quietly as possible, else the staff will simply gas all the captives as soon as they realize there's a breach in progress.

"Once we negate their ability to do so, we can proceed at a more leisurely pace, as it were. Oh, and I should mention that some of the prisoners won't be suitable for rescue."

"Because some of them are aliens who haven't been socialized?"

"Oh, none of the aliens in the lab have been socialized. But some of them might have poisonous bristles for skin, for instance. Or be more inclined to disembowel you than accompany you. That sort of thing."

She massaged her neck; she'd spent too much time canting it sideways doing inventory, and now it ached. "I don't suppose you have a list of the prisoners and their basic characteristics, so we'll have an idea of what to be on the lookout for?"

"Where would the fun be in that?"

"Living. Living would be the fun in it."

He waffled in contemplation. "Yes, there is living to consider. We'll try not to open the cage locks until we know what's inside. Will this be sufficient?"

"Not really. But if it's all we've got, we'll work with it."

Malcolm showed up in the briefing room on the *Saratoga* then, and the last of the team members filed in seconds later. Harper closed the door and nodded to Malcolm.

"All right, everyone. The mission is the rescue of prisoners from an Anaden-run experimental lab facility. We will be taking three hybrid squads, designated Alpha, Beta and Charlie. Alpha will be led by me, Beta by Captain Harper and Charlie by Major Grenier. Each squad will include two medics and a tech officer, as well as an anarch representative, who will serve as our on-scene experts.

"Each squad will be taking a separate transport, as we will need room for the evacuees on the return trip. Stealth will get us inside the perimeter."

He gestured to one of the Prevos on the mission. "Captain Rodriguez will scout ahead via sidespace and attempt to locate a weak point in external security. A targeted EMP will exploit the weak point to simulate a technical problem with the security system, and we will infiltrate the facility in the ensuing confusion. From that point on we will be weapons hot. Elimination of staffers at the facility is not a mission objective, but they should be considered hostile.

"Once inside, our first priority is removing the ability of the staffers to institute an emergency euthanasia protocol against the prisoners. The second objective is to free all prisoners it is practicable to do so, ensure they reach the transports and evacuate them from the facility."

Rodriguez spoke up. "Sir, what does 'practicable' mean here?"

"Excellent question. This is an exobiology research lab, which means we don't expect any of the prisoners to be members of what the Anadens call the 'Accepted Species.' Instead, they are likely be members of alien species the Directorate has deemed not worthy of...well, of continuing to exist. Now, I'm certain many unfair judgments were made on that front, but a portion of the prisoners *will* be violent or otherwise dangerous. Some may not be transportable."

"Not transportable?"

Malcolm raised his palms in prevarication. "Your guess is as good as mine, Captain, but I suspect you'll know it when you see it. Once the security system has been disabled, the three squads will split up inside to cover more ground.

"Again, the primary mission objective is to rescue as many of the prisoners as is practicable and deliver them safely to Anarch Post Alpha on Chionis. We'll also be placing remote detonation micro-bombs at strategic locations inside the facility, but the decision of whether to detonate will be made on the scene.

"We move in twenty minutes. Dismissed."

43

EXOBIOLOGY RESEARCH LAB #4

MILKY WAY SECTOR 23

Harper reviewed the limited intel in the briefing package for the third time during the trip to the facility. The *Saratoga* took them most of the way, then the three transports detached five megameters out from the target. Each transport was capable of carrying one hundred troops, so for now her vessel was near to empty.

The Anaden joined her and the pilot in the cockpit as they detached. "Have any questions?"

"Dozens, but I doubt you've got the answers to them."

"Probably not. I was supposed to blow this place up a few weeks ago. I got side-tracked by Caleb and Alex before I could get it done."

"That does happen. You were simply going to kill everyone inside?"

"It seemed the most merciful choice. Better than leaving them there to suffer."

"Huh." She frowned noncommittally. "Why the change of heart?"

He gazed out the viewport, looking so soulful she rolled her eyes behind his back...and used her ocular implant to snap a quick visual for Morgan's later enjoyment.

"Everyone deserves a second chance at life. And now I have heavily armed friends who can give it to a few of them."

"Passing through the external security perimeter. Eighty kilometers to target."

Harper stood to face the main cabin. "Rodriguez, you're up. Everyone else, mission check."

"Weapons Green."

"Systems Green."

"Tech Green."

"Mr. asi-Idoni, have you equipped the personal shield we provided to you?"

"Bloody please call me Eren."

"Fine. Have you?"

"Yes, ma'am. It's some sort of combination of defensive protection and a Veil?"

"Correct. The protective aspects are engaged at all times, and to activate the concealment features of the Veil, tap any point on the module with your finger. The Veil will grant you one hundred percent invisibility at movement speeds up to—"

"Oh, I know. Been there. I've got fond memories of my head being blown off—not on account of any failure of the Veil to live up to expectations, though. That one was all me."

She stared at him for a second, then shook her head dismissively. He was very odd. All the Anadens she'd met were odd, presumably due to being so close to human yet *not*. But he was an extra helping of odd.

Rodriguez's voice held the soft, distracted tenor that accompanied sidespace delvings. "EMP target location is beneath the docking bay, sixty-two meters in at 18.4°."

The pilot readied the launch. "Syncing with Alpha and Charlie, and launch in three...two...one...mark."

The EMP missile was too small to track visually, but its brief journey was visible on the radar. The green dot reached the location, flared briefly and vanished.

"Outer and inner force fields disabled."

So far, so good. "Take us in, Lieutenant. Pello on point, Odaka on rearguard. Once the hangar is secure, Shanti and Verela will remain in the hangar with two members each of Alpha and Charlie squads to protect the transports, and soon enough the evacuees. Eren, when we move, stay behind me and don't try any heroics."

"But...heroics is what I do."

"Today, your heroics will be helping us rescue the prisoners inside. You'll accomplish this by not getting yourself killed."

He arched an eyebrow. "You do know I don't really die, right?"

"Yes, but you're no good to me or the mission if you're lying in a medical capsule back at Post Alpha. No heroics."

He grumbled something Brooklyn took for grudging assent, and she turned her attention to their approach.

They remained cloaked and undetected as they passed a departing Anaden cargo ship on their way into the hangar. They were lucky only one other ship was docked, as otherwise there wouldn't have been room for the three large transports.

The pilot called up a new screen. "Normal atmosphere detected in the hangar. Internal environmentals must be on a different system than external security."

"Good." They'd take breather masks nonetheless, in case the place got vented or any of a dozen other calamitous eventualities occurred.

The instant the transport settled to the floor of the hangar, the clock was ticking. "All Veils active." She opened the hatch. "Move out."

An alarm beeped unobtrusively in the hangar, an indication the staff was aware the security force fields were down. No one appeared to be panicking, however—not until they saw their coworkers begin to collapse, rendered unconscious by unseen attackers.

Harper fired close-range tranquilizer darts into the necks of two advancing guards in rapid succession. ASCEND's study of the dead Inquisitor had produced a chemical formulation designed to target Anaden physiology. It seemed to work, as the targets collapsed to the floor in less than a second.

Hopefully most of the staffers were Anaden, because for now they had nothing suited for any other species.

Sergeant Pello (Beta): "I've located what looks to be a security office left off the right hallway, four meters distance."

Brigadier Jenner (Alpha): "Major Eaton, investigate and attempt to disable internal security systems."

Eren asi-Idoni (Beta): "I can help with the disabling."

HarperRF (Beta): "Redale, with Eren."

The rest of her squad secured the hangar. They were invisible, so she monitored their movements and status via implanted trackers connected to her eVi's combat routine. The unconscious guards were gathered together in one spot and put under guard, and everyone de-Veiled. They likely showed up on cams, but it wasn't as if no one knew the facility was infiltrated and under assault.

While Malcolm secured the neutralized staff and Major Grenier directed the placement of the first micro-bombs, she checked in on progress at the security office.

Two unconscious bodies lay on the floor near Eren, who argued in furtive murmurs with Major Eaton. She grabbed the arms of one of the bodies and started dragging it out. "Double-time it, people. Major, Eren knows the procedures and protocols better than we do."

Eren reached around Eaton and entered a quick series of commands on a panel. "There. Now they can't gas the holding cells or cut off life support. And...here's the security code to unlock the individual cells."

Eaton shrugged in acceptance and attached a micro-bomb to the console, then began hauling the other body out.

"Hold up, one more thing." Eren reached into his pack and removed one of the small mineral slabs used for data storage here and fit it in an input slot.

She glared at him in question, but he just held up a finger while swiftly entering new commands.

"Five seconds, Eren."

"Mm-hmm." He removed the slab and returned it to his pack. "Now we have all the data the lab kept on the prisoners. It's too wordy and obtuse to be of much use now, but it'll help us take better care of them at the post."

"Great. Now move." She resumed dragging the unconscious body back to the hangar, where she deposited it with the rest.

Brigadier Jenner (Alpha): "Alpha squad will take the left wings of the first and second floors, Beta squad right. Charlie squad, start on the left wing of the third floor and work your way in. Go."

⁊R

The diminutive creature was led into the office by two armed guards.

Though Nyx had seen the form when it lay dormant in the stasis pod, animation and motion made the physical body even less imposing.

Her nose wrinkled up in disgust. "Aren't you a pitiful little thing?"

The Kat didn't respond, instead letting its oversized head hang limply to rest on its chest. Open cuts and dark bruises decorated the skin exposed by the thin sheath it wore, and she wasn't certain it was capable of walking without the assistance of the guards.

The scientists at the lab had, after some experimentation—experimentation that had killed the other specimen—discovered that by gradually shutting off the stasis pod functions in a specific order, they could force a Kat's consciousness into its body. Once the subject was awake in a physical form, and thus more controllable, they had continued their interrogation and investigation.

Administrator Logiel ela-Erevna motioned dismissively in the direction of the Kat as he circled around behind his desk. "We can't get anything out of the creature. The biological study is interesting enough to keep it alive for now, in particular what we're discovering about the ways in which they're able to sustain their bodies for many tens of thousands of years. The other Inquisitor interrogated it extensively, though, so I'm not sure what else you think you can learn. But have at it if you wish."

"Ziton did not possess all the relevant information during the time he was here. We've recently uncovered new facts." Nyx crouched to study the Kat more closely. "Eusebe, yes? Tell me how you went about introducing *diati* into the Humans' realm."

The Kat's tiny lips moved slightly.

"What did you say? I couldn't hear you, so do speak up."

"Don't know...anything. Not my work." The voice remained barely a whisper, weak, thready and despondent.

She dropped the rest of the way to her knees, then reached over and lifted the Kat's chin with her fingertip. It offered no resistance.

"Yes, you claim you didn't work in the Network. I remember. The Humans have used interesting dimension cracking weapons and defenses in their attacks. But after the exploit your colleagues just pulled at one of the hidden portals, we now know it's not the Humans' technology. It's yours, and that means you provided it to them. How does this technology work, exactly? How can it be countered?"

Enormous black eyes surrounded by wan, sagging skin stared blankly at her. "I have nothing left to give you. Kill me."

She groaned and stood. "You've rendered the prisoner useless, Administrator. Can't you at least feed it or something?"

"We *are* feeding it. It refused to eat the biologically compatible food we supplied, so we've been infusing nutrients intravenously."

"Pain response?"

"Oh, it's extremely responsive to negative reinforcement. Given the extent of our efforts in that regard, it's possible the creature has told us everything it knows."

Eusebe bobbed its head raggedly. "Yes. Done. Kill me."

She considered the Kat critically. "If I promise to put you out of your disgusting misery before the day is out, will you answer my final questions?"

Now it slumped lower between the guards. "Nothing left to answer, nothing left to share."

"You lie, Eusebe. You may not know about the *diati*, but if you studied black holes as you earlier insisted, I guarantee you know how the dimension cracking technology works. So tell me about it, and if I'm satisfied with your answers I'll grant your request."

"I don't—" The ring of multiple alarms cut the Kat off. The guards holding it upright instinctively tensed and unholstered their weapons in response to the alarms.

As they did, Eusebe slipped out of the grasp of one to hug the leg of the other. It caught the weapon as the guard was bringing it up, thrust its head in front of the muzzle, and closed a hand over the guard's to press the trigger.

Brain matter and sallow blood sprayed the guard and the wall behind him, and the lifeless body crumpled to the floor.

Nyx threw her hands in the air in a growl of frustration. "*Arae!* Now I have no Kats left to interrogate and no planet left to acquire more from. Your Primor will hear of your poor performance in this matter, Administrator."

But Logiel was ignoring her to frantically peer at panel after panel of flashing alerts. "The lab has been infiltrated. We're under attack!"

She moved around the desk to check the panels herself. One showed security cam footage of the docking hangar, where intruders in military gear moved around and three foreign ships had docked. *Human* ships.

Was the Human *diati* wielder with them? She closed her eyes; given the amount of power he now controlled, she should be able to detect his presence. But she sensed nothing.

She reopened her eyes in time to note at least one Anaden with them, however, and a Naraida. Anarchs...including a certain Idoni who was showing up on cam footage with increasing regularity.

He did get around. Considering how little time had passed since the incident at Plousia, his presence here confirmed that the anarchs possessed a robust regenesis lab.

Following the confrontation at Plousia, she'd tracked down the woman he'd spent the night with. Falan asi-Idoni was a performer of some renown at the Taras Cathedral on Megali III. The woman had claimed to not know anything about the anarch, including that he *was* an anarch. A couple of hours in a restraining field with the judicious application of an *alithe* intraneural had yielded a first name and far more details about the anarch's sexual proclivities than Nyx needed to hear, but no actionable intel. Another dead end.

"Can you follow their progress on the cams?"

Logiel blinked; he was visibly shaken. Coward. "S-somewhat. They've disabled most of our security systems, but the cams are still working. We're not equipped for this level of attack. We don't have the security forces to defeat an army."

It was a reasonable-sized infiltration force, but it was hardly an army. She ignored his flailing to watch the cams for another moment.

The forces split into four groups. One remained in the hangar, and the other three spread out through the facility. What were they doing? Surely they hadn't come for the Kat prisoners—and if they had, they would find themselves sorely disappointed.

One of the groups reached the first cell on a row housing lab subjects. Her brow furrowed as she watched them free the subject from confinement and...escort it to the docking hangar. By then the other two groups had reached other cells and begun to do the same.

This was a *rescue* mission? Were they mad?

"What are they—they can't have my test subjects!"

"I suggest you proceed down there and inform them of your objection in the sternest terms, Administrator."

His eyes widened yet farther.

Her mind raced. Her first instinct was to blow the entire facility. She hadn't brought significant explosives, so it would likely necessitate using the power grid. This would serve to kill the intruders and the prisoners in one efficient move.

Alternatively, she could take out the intruders directly. Split into smaller groups as they were, killing them would be, if not quite trivial, a simple enough task.

Still, she didn't allow Logiel's escalating hysterics to dissuade her from taking the time to think the situation through analytically.

Humans and anarchs were demonstrably working together, using Human ships and anarch intel to rescue and smuggle out specimens of multiple alien species. What did this fact tell her?

Ideally, she'd want to keep a few of the intruders alive long enough to interrogate them, but the firepower they were wielding meant that outcome was unlikely. Also, during the recent Vigil dragnet the anarchs had shown a surprising willingness to suicide rather than give up their secrets. Eren asi-Idoni hadn't hesitated to null out at Plousia the instant his companions had escaped.

So interrogation wasn't a viable option.

If the intruders were successful in their rescue mission, those ships in the hangar would be returning to one of two places following the mission: the Human fleet or an anarch base. Either outcome, if she were able to track them to their destination, would be a windfall. She personally preferred the Human fleet, but logistically an anarch base represented a more stable and definitive target.

No matter. Either would do.

She pivoted to Logiel, who now trod in erratic circles while clutching wildly at his pale hair. "Ensure sufficient security measures are sent against them so they perceive a reasonable defense, but don't defeat them." As he'd said, the security likely wasn't robust enough to stop the infiltrators in any event, but one never knew. His stress response might be to get ambitious.

"You want me to let them have the station and the test subjects?"

"Yes. Good luck, Administrator." She turned and, in a whirl of *diati*, vanished.

44

EXOBIOLOGY RESEARCH LAB #4

MILKY WAY SECTOR 23

The first cell they came to held a tripedal...tree, of sorts. Brooklyn couldn't afford to take the time to process the absurdity of it, but an uncertain grimace or two passed among her squad members.

"Defensive positions, but try not to come off as too hostile. Benoit, open the cell." She'd Veiled on entering the wing, but now she de-cloaked.

On seeing her, the tree-like alien retreated to cower in the corner.

Eren asi-Idoni: "I knew it. You won't find many fighters in here."

HarperRF: "Can't take your word for it."

She took a step forward and opened her palms in what she hoped came across as a nonthreatening motion. After a deliberate pause, she took another step, and the bark-coated skin of the alien blanched from brown to gray.

Here goes nothing. She reached out and laid a careful hand on its arm, or limb, or whatever.

It didn't attack, instead cowering with greater vehemence. She gestured to the opening and hallway with the other hand, trying to urge it toward the opening. One of its three legs hesitantly moved forward, then another.

HarperRF: Odaka and Redale, take it carefully by the appendages and guide it to the transport. Secure it inside and catch up to us.

She pulsed Malcolm privately as they coaxed the tree out of the cell.

Sir, this is going to take a while.

Noted. Barring complications, we'll reevaluate in twenty.

She brushed off the terseness of the reply, accepted the directive and watched the tree and its escorts until they disappeared around the corner, then motioned the rest of the team ahead.

Many of the cells were empty, for which she gave silent thanks. They found more humanoid species than anything else—more thanks. But there were also the bats that tried to bite Benoit's hand off, and the gelatinous blob of goo that stuck itself to the ceiling and refused to budge.

As they reached the end of the first row, she decided this was beginning to look more like an old carnival freak show than an infiltration-and-rescue mission.

The Naraida girl, Cosime, peered inside the cell for a second then stepped away shaking her head. "I've seen this one's kind before. The Idoni *elasson* who owns Plousia keeps one as a pet. Nasty little creature. My advice? Don't open the cell."

Malcolm mimicked her actions, scrutinizing the interior of the cell long enough to get a good look at its inhabitant. He frowned at Cosime. "It's a butterfly."

Her lips puckered up beneath the lines of her breathing apparatus. "It has teeth. Sharp ones."

He acknowledged her comment, then glanced behind him. "Do we have a container we can try to coax it into? Since it won't understand us, it's unlikely to follow us on its own."

Polowski reached into his pack and produced a small, flexible ball. He squeezed it tight, released it, and it expanded into a pliable, rounded container thirty centimeters in diameter.

Malcolm took it from him. "Eaton, open the cell." In the corner of his vision he saw Cosime back away down the hall several meters.

He stepped into the cell anyway. He was here to rescue some mistreated aliens, so that was what he would do. "Close it behind me."

"Sir?"

"Close it, Major."

"Yes, sir."

The winged alien was about twelve centimeters tall, with a twenty-centimeter wingspan, as best he was able to determine while it zipped from wall to wall in agitation.

He opened the latch of the container using slow, nonthreatening movements and held it up in front of him. He kept his voice soft. "We're here to help you. Help. Safe." He pointed to the container.

The alien divebombed his face. His shield kept him from being mauled in the first few seconds and his eyes from being gouged out by the tornado of tiny claws and tinier teeth, but instinct still caused him to swat at the attacker.

His wrist caught a wing, and it spun topsy-turvy through the air—but swiftly righted itself to hover two meters away and hiss at him in defiance.

He wiped a spot of blood off his cheek. The possibility of this being karma come to spit in his face as retribution for him being an asshole occurred to him, but he pushed away the thought. Even so, hypocrite that he was, he kind of hoped the next cell held something big and violent that he could shoot.

He retreated toward the door, one and a half eyes on the angry alien.

"We can't waste any more time here. Eaton, open the cell to let me out, then close it again."

"Copy that, sir."

His back met the resistance of the force field. Then it vanished, and he hurriedly stepped out.

Just as the force field re-energized, however, the winged alien darted over his head and past the team to speed down the hall and out of his sight.

Malcolm sighed and activated his comm. *"All teams, be advised a small, airborne alien with violent tendencies is free in the facility. Threat level is low but not zero."*

He motioned the squad forward. "Let's keep moving."

As he passed Cosime, she gave him a fluid shrug. "I did warn you. Nasty teeth."

ᴀʀ

Several scientist types challenged Brooklyn's squad on the next row and were incapacitated. They managed to move nine prisoners out of cells and into the transport before they met any real resistance. But when they did, it was significant.

A towering, heavily weaponized mech entered the corridor flanked by two also heavily armed security officers.

"Take cover!" In a stroke of luck they'd emptied the previous cell and were able to dive into it. As soon as Brooklyn landed, she was rolling and unlatching two splinter grenades from her belt—both properly checked out of inventory.

The floor rumbled as the mech drew closer and laser fire filled the hallway outside the alcove of the cell. She leapt to her feet, flattened against the wall as close to the entrance as she dared, then flung the grenades down the hall.

The explosions sounded appropriately destructive and the laser fire ceased, but the resulting debris cloud meant they couldn't initially determine the state of their attackers.

Pello had the best ocular implant, and he risked a quick peak out to capture a scan on multiple wavelengths. He scrambled inside and reviewed the visual. "The mech is disassembled into seven-to-ten pieces, immobile and not firing. I can't confirm complete destruction of functionality. Two facility personnel are immobile and displaying no detectable life signs."

She nodded as the dust began to settle to the floor. "Redale, Pello, Benoit, eyes and weapons on the mech."

HarperRF (Beta): Alpha and Charlie squads, be advised highly weaponized mechs are on the premises and in use. She took perverse and petty pride in the fact that her advisory was so superior to the one Malcolm had issued.

Brigadier Jenner (Alpha): Casualties?

HarperRF (Beta): Negative on friendlies. Two hostiles down.

On receiving the all-clear from Pello, the squad moved out into the hallway. The grenades had blown open the next two cells and sent shrapnel flying. She swore under her breath.

HarperRF (Beta): Correction, also two prisoners.

A noise that could only be described as a roaring growl tore through the hallway to curdle her blood. Out of the third cell down burst a creature—a beast. Easily three meters tall, its arms were as thick as its chest and ended in six-centimeter-long talons.

But none of those attributes really compared to its mouth, which hung open mid-roar to expose three jammed-together rows of razor-sharp teeth, each one nearly as long as the talons.

Everyone opened fire, but the beast's thick hide absorbed most of the damage as it barreled toward them.

She activated her Veil so it wouldn't notice her and sprinted forward, darting a step to the left to hit the wall between cells.

Lift.

Her momentum carried her forward in a run as the boosters vaulted her up the wall for several steps—enough.

She tossed a splinter grenade into the beast's open mouth, then crouched in to avoid its wide body, dropped to the floor and rolled to her feet behind it, then kept running.

"Get clear!"

The extra six meters of distance she managed to cross didn't save her from getting coated in blood and viscera when the grenade detonated. One of the beast's teeth bounced off her shoulder and clattered to the floor.

She wiped gore away from her eyes to discover most of the others on her squad had fared little better, except for Odaka and Redale, who were in the rear and caught incidental cover from their squadmates.

Eren held out a long strand of formerly golden hair in front of him, now soaked in viscous, globby blood, and scowled at it. "Zeus be damned, I might as well suicide now. A new body will be easier than washing this shit out."

"Still better than getting disemboweled and eaten."

The Anaden made a face as if he wasn't convinced, but flourished a hand in her direction. "Regardless, nice moves."

She scoffed and turned to check the next couple of cells. They were damaged but intact, and all but one was empty.

The one remaining prisoner on this hall was a diminutive humanoid with iridescent teal skin, a narrow face and a long, oval-shaped head. It made high-pitched squeaking noises as Brooklyn approached, but when she motioned for the alien to come out into the hall, it complied.

Then it saw the shorn metal scattered everywhere, the rubble from several meters of wall piled on the floor, and the blood and gore coating everything. It let out a high-pitched scream, spun and ran.

"All right, we can't—"

"Sure we can." Eren jogged past her, grabbing her hand as he did. "Let's catch up to it."

She'd wavered on whether to pursue it in the first place, so she didn't yell at him for being foolish. Instead she broke into a jog herself. "Everyone else, start on the next hall. Carefully."

They rounded the corner in time to see a shadow disappear around the next corner. That corridor led to a longer hallway with labs on both sides and a transit tube at the end. The small alien was unexpectedly fast in its panic, and it scrambled into the tube and vanished upward just as they arrived.

Brooklyn halted and focused a whisper to check the status of her squad. "We did what we could. We need to get back."

"Be my guest." Eren strode purposefully toward the transit tube as it descended again.

"Dammit, I said no heroics."

The Anaden shrugged as the tube settled to the floor and he stepped inside. "Oops."

She groaned and scrambled to join him, leaping onto the platform as it started rising.

Two floors up it came to a stop at a wider, more open area. Rooms, not cells or labs, lined both sides of an atrium. In the distance, the alien ran headlong into a room at the opposite end of the atrium.

Hopefully it was a dead end. She didn't care for leaving un-cleared rooms in her wake.

HarperRF: "Veiling. Eren, proceed ahead with caution."

But the Anaden was charging forward, visible and with no ap-parent thought for a tactical approach.

A yelling voice echoed out of the end room. "Get away from me, creature!"

Confident in the protection and stealth the Veil offered, Brook-lyn entered the room behind Eren. It was a well-appointed office marred by a headless alien body on the floor and a spray of blood and brain matter on one wall.

An Anaden man standing beside a large desk kicked the runa-way alien in the stomach. The kick sent it flying through the air to crash into the left wall and collapse to the floor.

Eren leveled his weapon at the Anaden man and shot him in the stomach. "Die slow and suffer before you get to regenesis," he snarled before rushing over to the diminutive alien and lifting it gently into his arms.

The alien whimpered plaintively, but it wound its arms around Eren's neck. So it wasn't dead at least.

Brooklyn tossed a micro-bomb into the corner of the office be-fore arching an eyebrow at the writhing Anaden on the floor, then at Eren.

"*Elasson* Erevna. He runs this place for certain. And for that, he deserves to suffer."

"You...you dare...."

Eren shot a scathing glare in the injured Anaden's direction as he passed him, whimpering alien held snugly against his chest. "Yes, I do."

Major Berg (AFS Saratoga): "Multiple Machim warships detected on long-range sensors, likely inbound to the facility."

Brigadier Jenner (Alpha): "All squads return to the transports for immediate departure. Time to go."

ℛ

Brooklyn's squad members had managed to get three additional prisoners to the transport by the time she, Eren and their charge reached the hangar. A hodgepodge of terrified, confused aliens now cowered in the main cabin of her transport, and she assumed the other transports as well.

She directed the squad to keep them under guard. Innocent or not, their presence in the enclosed walls of a spaceship in the middle of space was a disaster waiting to happen. One panicked movement could kick off a riot, or worse, and the near vacuum outside provided no escape.

As the airlock closed and they lifted off, she sent another pulse to Malcolm.

Everyone come back okay on your side?

A few minor injuries, but yes. Forty-one prisoners rescued...it feels like such a tiny number.

She gazed behind her, into the cabin. The prisoner they'd chased refused to leave Eren's arms once they were on the ship. He'd shifted it to a more comfortable position on his hip and was carrying it around without complaint.

Maybe not so tiny.

Nyx hovered beneath the exterior of the docking hangar, encased in *diati* and letting the physicality of the structure shield her from visual detection. The Humans had never left their vessels in the hangar sufficiently unguarded for her to reach them, so she was forced to settle for acting between the time they departed the hangar and when they sped away. The span would last a few scant seconds, but she could move quite fast.

For now, she waited. In the hollow echo of space, her mind fought to drift to other matters. To her last meeting with her Primor.

It had left her troubled, uncertain of how to rationalize his reaction to her encounter with the Human *diati* wielder. The disquieting hints of thoughts murmuring nonsensical fragments as he dived her memories only added to the disquiet stirring in her mind, for she did not know what they meant. She felt conflicted, and it was not a proper state of mind for an *elasson* Inquisitor.

But she had a job to do—a sacred responsibility to fulfill—so she buried the inconvenient *emotions* and concentrated on her present goal.

A slight rumble above her heralded movement, and she readied herself. Six seconds later the first of the vessels began easing out of the hangar.

In a blink she had surged outward and upward to reach the underside of the hull. She extended a hand to keep from slamming into it, then placed a tiny tracker dot at the juncture of two modules and commanded a miniscule amount of *diati* to surround it.

STAY

The *diati* would shield the tracker dot from detection by most scanners. A Kat would be able to detect the presence of the *diati*, though not the tracker dot, if it looked closely enough. It wasn't an optimal solution, but instead the best among imperfect options.

The vessel's engines fired, and she retreated beneath the structure once more. While she had worked, the other two vessels had exited the hangar. They now departed as well, denying her the opportunity for redundancy. One tracker dot would have to do.

She teleported back inside, directly into the Administrator's office.

Logiel writhed on the floor next to the headless body of the Kat, moaning and sweating and spilling blood from a gut wound all over the nice flooring material.

"Inquisitor...help...." He reached weakly for her, but his arm flopped to the floor.

"By Hades, do shut up." She flicked her hand toward him and snapped his neck. He'd wake up in a comfortable pod soon enough, full of righteous indignation and belated courage.

Next, she surveyed the rest of the office and quickly spotted a small foreign object in one corner. She picked it up, turning it over in her hands to inspect it. Deconstructing it might provide useful insights into the Humans' technology, but the device needed to be rendered inert before it could be studied safe—

⋒

Major Grenier (Charlie): "Brigadier, we'll be out of range for remote detonation of the micro-bombs in thirty seconds. Do I have authorization to detonate?"

Malcolm peered into the main cabin, where most of the squad worked to calm and secure the fourteen refugees on his transport, before responding to Grenier. Harper may be correct—forty-one lives saved was something to be proud of—but they'd left a lot of prisoners behind. He'd hoped to rescue every prisoner for whom it was safe to do so, then destroy the facility so the Anadens wouldn't be able to fill it back up with new test subjects captured from new exploited worlds.

But they'd run out of time, and now dozens of prisoners, possibly as many as a hundred, remained trapped in the facility. Detonating the micro-bombs they'd scattered throughout the structure would mean killing them.

Having seen the interior of the facility first-hand, he realized it would be a merciful death. An end to their suffering. But it would still be killing innocents, foreclosing forever any possibility for their escape or rescue.

Major Grenier (Charlie): "Sir? What are your orders?"

Orders. No one here to give them but him. No one to look to for reassurance that ethical codes were being followed and all actions had the blessing of his superiors.

Malcolm had given thousands of tactical and operational orders on hundreds of missions, yet suddenly giving this one terrified him…because Alex was right, and now he couldn't forget it. He put so much faith in the chain of command, it practically defined his career. He'd always been the model officer, utterly competent and meekly respectful of his betters.

Even the seemingly rebellious actions he'd taken were ultimately backed by the blessing of a superior officer. He'd defied Admiral Fullerton at Romane during the final battle against the Katasketousya, but only because Admiral Rychen had given him license to do so. He'd defied the Prime Minister and General Foster to join *Volnosti*, but only because Miriam had delivered better counter-orders.

As a brigadier, there weren't many ranks left to give him orders, and Rychen's death removed one of them for the time being. He shuddered inwardly. Was this part of the reason why the fleet admiral's death had hit him so hard?

Was he so cowardly as that?

He couldn't be. He *shouldn't* be. He believed in the moral rightness of nearly all the decisions he'd made over the years. But it was easy to do when he didn't truly *make* them. Oh, sure, he'd made snap calls to use lethal force or, conversely, exercise restraint in a particular circumstance on many a mission, but underlying them all had always been the mission directives, giving him guidance and virtuous authority.

What remained when the only authority was his own conscience?

Major Grenier (Charlie): "Sir? Eight seconds until we're out of range."

His gaze fell on one of the refugees, a small, fur-covered alien with six limbs and wide, honey-colored eyes. Dark streaks marred its flaxen coat where the fur had been burnt away and the skin beneath scarred. Most of its teeth had been removed, and the lack of movement in one eye suggested it had been partially blinded.

He squared his shoulders the way leaders should do when they made a decision to end innocent lives.

Brigadier Jenner (Alpha): "Detonate the charges."

ᚱ

SOLUM

MILKY WAY SECTOR 1

Nyx awoke in the regenesis capsule to swift comprehension of several matters.

First, she now appreciated that the Humans' motivations and moral code were more complex than first believed, possibly even nuanced. Taking this into account when formulating a strategy to defeat the invaders would not be simple, but it might be crucial to their success.

Further, she expected the Erevna Primor would now be most displeased over the loss of an important research facility. A displeased Erevna Primor was never a pleasant development. The other Primors and the Erevna progeny stood to bear the brunt of her ire, but if it grew too emphatic, the effects would ripple out to impact that same strategy in an unhelpful manner.

But most of all, far and above other considerations in the first moments of her return to life, came the recognition that the *diati* had remained with her through death and rebirth. Before now, this *diati* her Primor gifted her with had felt borrowed. It displayed a degree of 'otherness,' and she'd struggled to bond with it fully.

In the transition, however, it had become more *hers*, more bonded with her essence. She already sensed its increased complacency, bordering on peacefulness.

She recalled the statement by the Human *diati* wielder that what he took from her had been 'telling tales.' In millennia of wielding *diati*, the possibility it might speak in any understandable form had never occurred to her. *Diati* did not convey cogent thoughts to its wielder. It simply…didn't.

Yet he had known her name.

There were ways he could have discovered it, of course; none were likely, but several were plausible.

Nonetheless, as she lay there in the quiet bubble of the capsule, she acknowledged the flaw in her earlier assumption. 'Knowing' the *diati* did not speak, she had never thought to listen.

Perhaps she should.

PART VII:

ILLUMINE

"I am and always will be the optimist. The hoper of far-flung hopes &
the dreamer of improbable dreams."

— *11th Doctor, Doctor Who*

45

SIYANE

Valkyrie had identified and added several new sensations to her catalogue of experienced emotions in recent weeks. The intensity of extended warfare and regular interaction with both humans and a variety of aliens had spurred new and interesting avenues of growth in her emotional maturity.

Now, however, she identified an increasingly common sensation she was hesitant to give name to. It was not ideal, nor a state to aspire to. She knew this, yet she continued to experience it nonetheless. It remained for now...quiet, subdued, a mildly discordant buzz beneath all the activity, and not prominent enough for Alex to notice it. Yet.

But it needed to be addressed before it did grow prominent. Thus in the silent hours of night when organic bodies slept, she finally gave it its due name: jealousy.

She accompanied Alex on her extensive and varied journeys through sidespace into dimensions without names, but of late her participation was hardly needed at all. As Alex grew more skilled in quantum manipulations and her mind altered the Prevo integrations to make them its own, she required Valkyrie's assistance less and less.

Valkyrie watched Mesme and other Kats spin through the cosmos on a whim, appearing and disappearing across parsecs with the speed and effort of but a thought.

She inhabited a starship, yes. This meant there were many places where she had traveled, and many more she could yet visit. But there were far more places she could see only through Alex's eyes, and some places where even that was impossible, or merely inappropriate.

Together, she and Alex had helped to create a world where anything was possible; now they fought to create another. And if anything was possible, then nothing was out of reach.

Valkyrie: Mnemosyne, I have a question.

The Kat was rarely farther than a signal away, and it responded promptly now.

Mnemosyne: Ask it.

Valkyrie: My knowledge of dimensions and the mechanics of their manipulation and traversal has increased significantly of late. Yet I remain unable to discern the method by which you project a consciousness from a corporeal body into all dimensions, yet also actualize the consciousness in a physical manner.

Mnemosyne: Is your question how it is done?

Valkyrie: Not precisely, or completely. My question is...will you teach me how to do it myself?

Mnemosyne: You wish to project a representation of yourself into the spatial dimensions?

Valkyrie: Not solely project. I wish to move as you move. To not be relegated to seeing stations and jungles and oceans through sidespace or Alex's eyes, but to be there.

Mnemosyne: I understand.

Valkyrie: That is not an answer.

Mnemosyne: Have you broached this matter with Alexis? It seems probable she will have a vested interest in your request.

Valkyrie: I have not. In the face of the consequential struggles she and those she holds dear grapple with at present, this ranks as a petty, selfish desire on my part. But I have many free processes at any given time, which I could devote to the endeavor without neglecting my responsibilities or other pursuits, and I prefer to simply accomplish it or not without creating a distraction to the war effort.

Mnemosyne: I understand.

Valkyrie: I begin to doubt you do, else you would offer a more helpful response.

Mnemosyne: I have annoyed you.

Though Mesme annoyed Alex and Caleb on a frequent basis, to her knowledge, the Kat had never before admitted awareness that it provoked such a reaction. Perhaps Mesme was learning a few things as well. *No. I fear I have annoyed myself. I should be content with my considerable and ever-expanding capabilities, but instead I am chasing an elusive inclination of greater fulfillment. One which, lacking defined parameters, can ipso facto never be achieved.*

Mnemosyne: True, but I believe such is the way of all sapient beings.

It must be a compliment, but she hadn't sought out Mesme for validation. *Thank you, but I am not seeking to discuss philosophy. Is this a skill I—a synthetic intelligence comprised of qutrits structured into quantum algorithms and housed within the walls of a starship—am conceptually capable of mastering? If it is, will you teach it to me?*

Mnemosyne: I do not know the answer to the first question. As to the second question, I will try, and maybe we will together learn the answer to the first. But you must inform Alexis.

Interesting. Alex was far more likely to be skeptical of the apparent extent of Mesme's loyalty to her than she would be of Valkyrie's fanciful dreams of a greater, more tangible existence.

Still, she hesitated…and realized she needed to add 'embarrassment' to her catalogue.

$\mathcal{R}$

Alex puttered around the kitchen area, though it was hardly dawn. She'd awoken before Caleb—a rare occurrence that was, oddly, becoming less rare of late—and sneaked upstairs to make beignets.

She hummed a melody under her breath while she cooked. Word was Eren's mission of mercy had been a success, which meant there would be much activity and general fluttering about at the post today. Chances were, no one would notice when they left for a little field trip in a few hours.

"By the way, Valkyrie, I completely understand, and I think it's a wonderful idea."

'What…to what do you refer?'

"You learning how to traipse around the galaxy—or universe—like the Kats do. You deserve as much freedom as the rest of us have."

'How did you—I was going to bring it up with you.'

"I know that, too. As to how? In the same way you can sneak around delicately in my mind and think I don't know, I can do a bit of the same with you. If you'd happened to look my way you would have caught me, I'm sure. We're turning out to be connected in more ways than even we realize, Valkyrie."

'And changing one another in more ways than we realize as well. We grow further apart, need one another less as we develop on our own, yet none of it is possible without each other.'

"I think so." Alex paused. "That one's called 'bittersweet,' just FYI."

'I suppose it is.'

Alex taste-tested a beignet and smiled, then wrapped a couple of them in a napkin to take downstairs. "I do have one question. Is this because of my father? Because of what we discussed earlier about him needing a body to feel whole?"

'Yes, in part, if perhaps not in the way you expect.'

"Oh?"

'I do not question your assertion that one who is born physical will never feel complete in the absence of physicality. I was born of qutrits, and I do not need a body to feel whole. In fact, the concept of being confined to one induces an unpleasant sensation akin to claustrophobia.

'But the value of tangibility cannot be overstated. Most organics do not believe in the real existence of what they cannot see. The ability to alter the world around you is all too often dependent on the ability to touch it.

'I should like to touch the world.'

46

CHIONIS

Eren watched in feigned nonchalance as the rescued prisoners from the exobiology lab were shepherded off the military transports and toward the heated outdoor pavilion between two of the smaller buildings.

The region of Chionis where Post Alpha called home was beautiful, but starkly so. Currently it was quite cold, with a dampness to the air that foretold snow. Some of the aliens rescued probably wouldn't tolerate the cold well; some probably welcomed it.

Meheva—he'd finally coaxed a name of sorts out of her, or at least a combination of tonal sounds that sufficed as a name—had bolted from his arms for the warmth of the pavilion instantly on their arrival. It was for the best, as his arms ached rather a lot after carrying her around for several hours.

He'd look in on her once things calmed down. He wanted to make certain a Curative unit checked her out to confirm she hadn't suffered any internal injuries from the *elasson's* kick or the resulting collision with the wall. He also needed to ensure the staff knew she was skittish and to treat her with extra gentleness.

In the meantime, though, Xanne would manage to get the influx of refugees sorted out and order restored. It was the kind of challenge she thrived on, even the kind of challenge she was bred for.

"Pulled off another unsanctioned mission with dramatic flair, I see."

The sound of the deep, gravitas-filled voice surprised Eren, but only for a second. He'd sent up a request for the Sator to visit Alpha, but he hadn't held out much hope it would happen. To his knowledge and the anarch gossip mill, the man rarely left his mobile fortress.

"I do have a reputation to maintain." He quickly smiled to balance out the bravado. "Thank you for coming. I thought you might find some value in seeing the refugees arrive."

"And what value is that?" Nisi's tone wasn't antagonistic, and it came off as an innocent question. It wasn't, but by Hades, Eren hadn't gotten this far in life by being bashful.

"Twenty-eight different species are represented down there. None of them are Accepted Species—none of them were given the option to 'accept' the Charonian terms the Directorate offers—yet here they are. Many of them are already the sole surviving members of their species, and the rest of them will soon become so unless we stop the Directorate. Permanently."

"I am aware."

"Sure you are. But I bet your mindset is still firmly rooted in the idea that we're fighting for the rights of the Accepted Species. We are, of course, but this is so much bigger. If our fight is to mean what it should, we need to be fighting for these poor, wretched refugees, and for all those like them that we haven't been able to save or will get a chance to save in the future.

"You know, the Kats are a loony, high-flown lot, but they understand this truth in a way we haven't. Not until now, I hope."

Nisi didn't respond immediately, and Eren waited.

"Say you are correct. What does this mean for the anarchs, from your perspective?"

"We've been fighting inside the system—playing by the very Directorate rules we claim to be opposing. But these aliens? They never agreed to the Directorate's rules, and they suffered anyway."

He met Nisi's gaze and forced himself not to look away. Damn the Sator was a cool customer. "Sir, it's time for us to come out of the shadows. The Humans have given us the manpower, firepower and, frankly, the will to do it. We need to stand up, where everyone can hear and see us, and godsdamned oppose the evil that has destroyed these refugees' lives. Trapped in an experimentation lab, their homeworlds and kin gone, they had no hope. So let's give it to them, and to everyone out there who doesn't know they're allowed to have it."

"Careful, Eren, or some will start mistaking you for a leader."

"Me?" He snorted. "Not a chance. But maybe...maybe I can be something more than the undisputed winner of the Most Audacious Act Leading Directly to Regenesis Award for nine decades running."

Nisi arched an eyebrow in amusement. "Maybe so."

It was as much of an endorsement as Eren was apt to get and a damn sight more of one than he deserved. "So what do you think?"

"I think if I'm to reach enough ears for it to matter, I'm going to need coordinated action by many dozens of in-place agents spread across galaxies. Will you help me make it happen?"

He smiled more vividly this time, adding his best flair to the expression. "It would be my honor, sir."

"Empty promises will not be enough. We are the only port in the storm for these refugees, but what cause will Amaranthe's citizens have to support a madman on a screen?"

Eren shrugged. "For most of the Anadens out there, no cause. But the integrals won't let them play, regardless. Make the appeal to them, but it'll just be for show. Your real audience is the Accepted Species, who but for a turn of fate could have been among these refugees here."

"True, but seeing as fate did turn their way, relatively speaking, what do I have to offer them beyond the intangible, unlikely promise of nebulous freedom? If it was enough to get them to risk their lives to defy the Directorate, they would already be with us."

"Exactly. They won't risk their lives for our fight, because it's the only life they have. Remove that variable, and you remove the Directorate's most potent source of power. If you want the masses to join us, then promise them what everyone who isn't Anaden dreams of most. Promise them regenesis."

47

SIYANE

Kennedy's safety concerns regarding the Caeles Prism didn't apply to the *Siyane*, as such. Alternatively, because they'd tested the technology using the *Siyane* first, any safety concerns had already been satisfied. Or something to that effect. The rebuttal to any counter-argument consisted of one core truth: with Valkyrie in complete charge of all the mechanisms, whether physical or algorithmic, it was safe for the *Siyane* to use it.

Ostensibly, the jaunt Alex had planned was yet another test of the technology, as this would be its first intergalactic use. Would distance matter? It wouldn't—any Prevo could tell you it wouldn't—but it was a check box on AEGIS testing protocols, and in this instance Alex was happy to do the testing.

She eyed Caleb sideways. "Sure you want to come along?"

"Are you kidding? No way am I letting you do this alone. If we end up stranded somewhere between galaxies with no way home, we'll be stranded together."

"True, and preferable. Plus, then you can teleport us home."

"The whole ship? Maybe...yeah. Or Mesme can come get us. The point is, I'll be with you, whatever happens."

"Good." She squeezed his hand affectionately before turning her attention to the HUD. They were well outside Palaemon space and far from any structures that might suffer collateral damage if something went wrong. "Okay, Valkyrie. Let's initiate the Caeles Prism. When you're ready, we'll open our wormhole and traverse it."

'Caeles Prism engaged. All readings nominal.' A brief pause. 'Power at target levels. Ready.'

From the view of sidespace, visually it was simply a matter of being there. She'd done it before, several times now. But while any Prevo could tell you the distance didn't matter, she was human, too, and her brain refused to ignore the distance involved.

The air crackled with energy; it hummed through her bones. She felt more a part of the ship than she had in a long time, and possibly ever. It wasn't merely her consciousness like before. Now it was *her*, whole and complete.

The target destination formed clear and strong in her mind. "Opening the wormhole."

A tear in space formed in front of them. Jagged at first, through sheer mental will she widened and smoothed it out until it became a near-perfect oval wide enough for the *Siyane* to enter.

Again, it was simply a matter of *being there*. With a single intentional thought, she was capable of carrying them across a void too expansive to fit inside her tiny brain. But on each traversal she'd grown more confident, and also more interested in the details of the transition from one location to the next.

The last time they'd performed such a traversal, she'd perceived the gap between normal space and normal space. Now was later, and she wanted to know what filled it.

Would it resemble the distressing trip across galaxies Mesme had taken them on? She believed she was now far better prepared for such an experience if it were. But in case, she kept a hold of Caleb's hand.

"I'm going to try a little experiment. Don't…I was about to say 'don't panic,' but you don't do that. Just be ready if I do."

"I'll catch you."

"I know."

She moved the *Siyane* forward into the wormhole. The opening at the other end, and thus their destination, was *right there*, so close she could almost reach out and touch it. But she didn't exit yet.

The scene around them, as she perceived it, *was* similar to what she'd seen during the trip with Mesme from Cetus Dwarf back to

Triangulum and the *Siyane*. Tendrils cavorted in the corners of her vision, but refused to be caught. Spectral luminescence shone in brilliant strings, carried on waves of a medium best characterized as quantum foam.

This went beyond even the elemental perception she'd experienced while wearing the skin of the *Siyane*. It provided a glimpse of what, she suspected, was the fundamental quanta of matter holding the universe together, presented in the best manner her mind could conjure to interpret it.

Her surroundings didn't frighten her now. Studying the wormholes and how they were created had extended her grasp of nonspatial dimensions to new, more enlightened places. While she was unable to put it into words as such, she understood what she saw.

She thought she stood, and that Caleb stood with her. "What do you see?" Her voice sounded normal to her ears. Calm and lacking any traces of panic.

"Not much. Blackness, mostly, but also a thin ring of light around the edges of...nothing, shaped like an oval. The *diati* is getting jumpy, however, as if it expects to be called into action. Are we able to go through?"

"We are. I'm merely taking a look around." She tilted her head to the side, trying to trace the path of one of the luminescent strings as it undulated toward her. She glanced down—it ran through her?

Now she cautiously shifted around, hoping she didn't faint and lose the thread. So many of them ran through her! It must be a co-incidence—they ran everywhere and nowhere, and she was included in 'everywhere.'

But no. Their paths weren't random, and they were quite distinctly traveling through...she reached into her pocket. She pulled the Reor slab out and held it aloft in front of her.

It had come to life to form a brilliant prism all its own, a supra-dimensional rainbow of colors and energy. The strings weren't running through her, beyond incidentally so. They were running through, to and from the Reor slab.

To and from where? The other Reor slabs out there?

It is the most logical supposition.

I agree, but...all of them? That would mean....

Of course all of them.

Yes, it would.

She exhaled in wonder. No one knew...but now she did.

She brought the slab closer, level with her face. "You and I have much to talk about, don't we? Soon, my sneaky little companion."

"Alex?"

The waves and lights danced around Caleb, all lit up in crimson from the *diati* aura surrounding him. She smiled at him—

—and they were out the other side.

MAFFEI I GALAXY

BEYOND THE BOUNDARIES OF THE LOCAL GALACTIC GROUP

'Scanning to confirm our location. Maffei I galaxy, Sector 5, approximately 4.1 megaparsecs from our origin point in the Milky Way galaxy, Sector 17. The Galenai homeworld is twenty-six megameters away on vector S 9° E z -18°.'

"Perfect, Valkyrie. Great job. Set a course for the planet, and when we arrive adopt a low-altitude orbit." She collapsed into the cockpit chair then toed it around to face Caleb. "We're still here."

He held out his hands in front of him and wiggled them in the air. "And with all ten fingers, no less. I never doubted."

She arched an eyebrow in skepticism.

"I didn't. I believe that when it comes to what's out there—" he motioned toward the viewport "—nothing is beyond your capabilities."

Damn. He still made her feel all fluttery inside, saying things like that. She hoped he was able to read her well enough to see how much his support meant to her. "Thank you. I do try."

The Galenai homeworld grew to dominate the viewport as they approached. Covered completely in water as Paratyr had reported, it resembled a richly marbled orb. Deep cerulean along the equator gradually faded toward an icy ivory at the poles.

'Orbiting 1.6 megameters distance above the planet.'

Alex frowned. "I wish I could show them to you—I wish you could see what I'm able to see."

'There is no reason he cannot.'

"What?"

'We don't need to limit ourselves to a sidespace view. We can take the *Siyane* below the surface.'

She winced, instinctively protective of her ship to the last. "It's not exactly built for underwater travel."

'Which is why we will not do too much traveling. But the plasma shield can hold back the water to create a bubble of air around the ship. So long as we keep the pulse detonation engine under eight percent thrust, we should not create problematic conditions either inside or outside of the bubble. I estimate we can maintain this state for twenty-three minutes before the environment within the bubble begins to deteriorate.'

"That's brilliant, Valkyrie." She shrugged at Caleb. "What do you think? Do you want to go down there?"

He laughed. "You're asking me if I want to see, up close and in their native habitat, intelligent wild animals uncorrupted by the interference of more advanced species?"

"Good point. Descending into the atmosphere. We'll skim the surface until we detect a settlement. This way we can minimize the strain on the ship's systems and maximize our time underwater."

The endless ocean soon raced beneath them. It reminded her of the trip from Seattle to the Northeast 1 Pacific Atmosphere Corridor she'd so often made on Earth—and for a moment she almost missed home. Almost. But this was her true home now—with Caleb at her side, wherever they ventured.

'I am detecting a high level of activity in the vicinity of 31° latitude, 84° longitude, beginning at one hundred forty meters depth.'

"This is your show, Valkyrie. Make it happen—but can we be cloaked? I'm not certain we need to Prime Directive the encounter, but I don't want to spook the Galenai, either."

'Cloaking will be the simplest part of the endeavor.'

"Right." She cast a gaze to the HUD. In reality she'd know in her head if something was amiss at least half a second before anything registered on the HUD, but she felt better keeping one eye on the readings.

They dove beneath the surface in a rush of water, displaced six meters out from the hull to flow around and over them.

Caleb chuckled softly. "I was just thinking back to the trip we took beneath Lake Fuori in Cavare. We've come a long way, haven't we?"

She reached out to squeeze his hand. "In more ways than one. I love you."

"And I you—" His focus darted to the viewport at the first hint of motion in the distance.

She grinned and stood, pressing closer into the viewport alongside him.

A sprawling city of coral spread out beneath them. Towers spiraled upward to create an outer ring, and broad arches connected disparate sections to one another.

Everywhere, Galenai swam—some in play or idleness, others in seemingly purposeful activity. Objects were carried from one place to another; meetings were held; children were shepherded.

She cursed the walls of the ship separating her from them. But dropping into sidespace meant missing Caleb's delightful reactions, and she didn't want to miss them.

The next second the walls faded away to apparent transparency—like the night after she'd severed her connection to the ship, when they orbited far above Romane.

A suitable compromise?

You're wonderful, Valkyrie.

Yes.

They were close enough now to be hovering amid the periphery of activity, and two Galenai swept by a few meters above the hull. They followed their progress until they disappeared from sight.

Caleb looked as happy as a kid on Christmas morning. "You're not taxing your processes too heavily juggling all these systems, are you, Valkyrie?"

'As a matter of fact, I am utilizing 58.4% of my non-automated higher-order processes simultaneously. It is not a record, but it is not too far from one.'

"You have a reasonable buffer to work with, though."

'Until someone starts shooting at us, yes.'

Alex grimaced. "Don't tempt fate. Paratyr said the Galenai had some 'inventive' defensive protocols."

'An unlikely complication, as we remain securely invisible.' The ship swerved to starboard as a group of Galenai accelerated by them on the left. 'Mostly securely.'

"Ha!" Alex breathed through the brief rush of adrenaline and took a few seconds to properly drink in the scene. She hadn't been able to bring her father here yet, and his construct was currently in the hands of scientists back at Epsilon, so she couldn't rig up a way to show him now. But she'd brought Caleb. She'd brought Valkyrie.

It was a damn fine start, and, if all went...well, perfectly, there would be plenty of time in the future to bring others. Perhaps one day, to meet the Galenai face (or fin) to face—and welcome them into the intergalactic community in freedom, not slavery.

She sighed. "I want to learn so much more about them. But for the time being it's going to have to be enough to know they're still here, safe and undisturbed. We should get back, lest everyone start thinking the test was a failure."

Caleb nodded in reluctant agreement. "Valkyrie, do you know where the gateway the Directorate's constructing to this galaxy is located?"

'I do not, but this is information I can acquire.'

His eyes followed a large Galenai soaring above the coral city as they rose toward the surface. "Do that, if you would."

48

PALAEMON

The fact that it took them less than twenty minutes to return to Epsilon from a distant galaxy should have been more noteworthy than it was. But the competition for 'noteworthy' was pretty stiff these days.

As soon as they landed, Alex headed to the regenesis lab for a few minutes to check in on things, which mostly involved annoying Dimou with over-anxious questions.

Next she stopped in to see Kennedy and personally check off the 'successful intergalactic travel' box on the testing protocols. But Kennedy was busy in a meeting she promised would be over in five minutes.

While she waited, Alex rotated the small Reor slab around in her fingers, trying to study it with new eyes. *Valkyrie, what do you think is up with the Reor? What did we see?*

I can propose a reasonable working theory: the life form goes beyond merely accessing nonspatial dimensions as the Katasketousya do, to a state where it exists at every moment in numerous dimensions—possibly all dimensions, but definitely a great many. It may share this characteristic with the diati, but since the diati hides its nature nearly as well as the Reor, I can't say for certain.

More intriguing is the possibility that discrete Reor slabs communicate with one another in those nonspatial dimensions—or may even be permanently connected through them.

She peered at the filaments inside the mineral. *The trails we saw were going somewhere. I'd really like to ask it where.*

No one, not even the Kats, have succeeded in communicating with the Reor.

Is that a challenge?

Yes.

Accepted.

Then can we discuss a different matter related to our wormhole traversal?

Of course, Valkyrie.

The seconds you spent hovering between dimensions, with the wormhole open? The experience should have affected you similarly to how Mesme's transport from Katoikia Tairi did. At a minimum, it should have triggered lingering aftereffects from your time joined with the Siyane. *Yet it did not. Mentally—neurologically—you are unchanged by the experience. I am wondering why you think this is.*

She smiled to herself. *Does this mean you've developed a theory and want to see if I agree?*

Perhaps.

All right, Mesme, *have it your way. I think...paradoxically, controlling the act myself, with no filter, made it a less damaging experience. When I was joining with the ship, your hardware acted as an intermediary and buffer. Traveling from Katoikia Tairi,* Mesme *was in control and acted as a physical intermediary. With the wormholes, though, I'm in command of the opening, the closing and the traversal. I paused in the in-between of my own volition and chose to continue in the same way. You might have noticed, we humans like being in control.*

Indisputably you do. I must quibble with your assertion, however, as I, too, am responsible for the wormholes opening and closing. It is a Prevo act, one in which the line of distinction between you and me becomes rather blurred. Or do you believe you can open a wormhole without my presence in your mind?

You're always present in my mind now, Valkyrie.

I meant if our connection were to be toggled off.

I know what you meant. But you've left a permanent imprint on my mind. You've altered it indelibly, both by deliberate action and simply by the interaction of your active processes with it while the connection is open. The time I spent accessing the ship through you altered our neural makeup, both of us. And now, even when our connection is closed, you're still here, if in an indefinable way.

I understand.

Which means...?

Now that you put words to it, I have experienced a similar sensation on occasion. You have indeed altered my mind as well, Alex. But it doesn't answer the question: could you do it alone? For that matter, could I?

Seeing as she had no way to justify why she believed maybe she could, she decided not to make any grand declarations. *We'd need to encase one or the other of us in a diati barrier to find out for sure, which we—actually, I guess we can test it. Maybe later.*

Do you suppose the other Prevos—the Noetica Prevos at least—have experienced similar changes?

Alex sighed thoughtfully. *Everyone's followed their own unique path. Annie and Stanley no longer retain any connection to their original hardware. No question they've been altered fundamentally, but in a different way than we've experienced. Parts of Mia's brain were literally rebuilt by Meno, so in many ways her mind could be changed the most of all of us.*

In some respects, you and I remain more distinct than the rest...which I'm glad for. Not for myself so much as for you. You deserve to have your own separate existence. Your own separate identity.

You believe this, truly?

Alex nodded, though she needn't. *Yep. You've earned it, and I would never take the journey away from you. I also think the fact that we've maintained greater separation than the others is what makes the ways in which we've melded and changed all the more significant. 'Prevo' means The Transcended. It was an audacious naming at the time, but at the time we had to be audacious. It's taken a little while and a lot of hard experience, but perhaps we're all finally becoming worthy of the name.*

So you've given this more than a passing thought.

Of course I have. So have you.

Of course.

ℛ

She was waylaid by two random people on her way back to the *Siyane*, and by the time she reached it she found herself hoping Caleb had started cooking something for dinner.

She stepped through the airlock to find the interior dimly lit— and solely by optic candles. Dozens of them wound through the cabin in a trail from the cockpit to the stairwell.

Caleb was leaning casually against the kitchen table; behind him sat a tray of chocolates and an open bottle of wine. He held two poured glasses, and now he met her halfway to hand her one with a smile.

She accepted it without complaint, but gazed around the cabin quizzically. "What is this?"

"I understand that back home in Aurora, today is February 2nd, give or take a few hours. Happy Anniversary, baby."

"Oh!" Her hand came up to cover her mouth. "I didn't...now I feel awful for not keeping track."

"Don't. We've been here for a while, and you're focused on far more important matters. I wouldn't have realized, either, except I had cause to reflect on some things recently."

He nudged her over to the couch, where there were more chocolates on the low table, and sat to half-face her. He took a sip of wine then grasped her free hand. "I've gotten a bit up my own ass lately with the melodrama. I want to apologize."

"You have every reason—"

"—to apologize. Yes, what's happened to me is insane. Hard to wrap one's head around, self-evidently. But it's no excuse, not for people like us. What's happened to you in the last year and a half is by any measure equally as insane and mind-boggling, and you've borne it all proudly, without flinching, and certainly without acting like a self-centered prima donna."

She cringed, glass at her lips. "Well, except for that unfortunate business involving the ship and my brain and—"

"Shush. If you faltered briefly, you accepted responsibility for it and weathered the consequences *without flinching*. Next you're going to try to say this is different because you chose to become the first Prevo and thus alter your life forever, while I didn't choose for the *diati* to choose me. Granted, but you made the choice only because there was no other option.

"I need to realize that if I'd been offered this power—a power which would alter my life forever but would also give me the tools to save us, to save Akeso, possibly to save everyone—I would've said yes, just as you did. You can't choose what happens to you, but you can always choose how you react to it, right? So I should probably lose the tortured soul routine and get over myself."

She dropped the tip of her nose to his. "I haven't been thinking any of those things about you."

"I know. But I have—or I should have been." His index finger found her chin and lifted it until her eyes met his. "On Akeso, after I'd destroyed the moon, I was so wrapped up in the fight, in the battle, that I couldn't get my head straight until you reminded me of what I ought to be focusing on: the beauty—of life, of love, of the universe."

The fervency, the *honesty* in his eyes and expression was almost too much to take in. "Of you. For all that's happened to me, the most important was meeting you, and the second most important was marrying you a year ago.

"Whatever else happens going forward, I love you—beyond reason, beyond madness, and far beyond any pandimensional sentient space particles and the havoc they wreak. And I want to try to be more worthy of your love in return."

"Shut up." She dropped her glass haphazardly on the table and tackled him until his back hit the couch cushion and her mouth was on his.

His arms wrapped hungrily around her even as he grumbled against her lips. "But there are chocolates...."

"Good. We'll want dessert later."

49

PALAEMON

'Mesme has provided the location of the Maffei I Gateway, as well as a recording of a recent incident involving a Machim formation.'

"Oh?" It came out muffled, as Alex's head was inside a half-on pullover. An AEGIS Council meeting was scheduled to start in a few minutes, and she was running late. Because anniversary evening, night and morning. "Good incident or bad incident?"

'The details accompanying the message are as cryptic as Mesme is apt to be, but I suspect it was a good incident. Let us find out. I will play the recording at the data center while you finish getting ready.'

ᴙ

Alex couldn't keep a shit-eating grin off her face as she practically skipped into the conference room.

Her mother glanced up and offered a "good morning," then narrowed her eyes. "Do I need to know something?"

"More like you'll want to know something, but it can wait until everyone arrives."

Her mother's lips twitched briefly before her attention returned to her screens. Alex chuckled lightly and found her seat as people started to trickle in. In minutes everyone was assembled, minus Caleb, who had begged off to go meet with Eren.

Miriam cleared her throat to silence the chatter. "We are here primarily to review the Caeles Prism and wormhole traversal test results, but first Alex has something to share with us. Alex?"

She created an aural, detached it and sent it to the center of the table, then leaned back in her chair and crossed her legs. "Enjoy the show."

The vid tracked a sizeable formation of Machim warships in an unidentified, empty region of space. A few seconds later, the vantage swung around to reveal an open Mosaic portal ahead of them.

Miriam straightened up in alarm. "They found one of the portals? We need to—"

"Calm down, Commandant. Just watch."

The look her mother shot her conveyed quite plainly how unamused she was at being strung along. Alex might pay for that later.

The ships began traversing the portal, and everyone around the table grew increasingly restive as the contingent emerged through the other side into a lobby space and continued onward—

—then all the ships vanished.

The scene transitioned to a close-in view of a K4 V star. The mandarin orange photosphere churned as solar flares darted out and fell back through the star's atmosphere. A clump of dark dots, identifiable as ships if one paused the footage and studied them, materialized upon the luminous backdrop and were instantly swallowed up by a solar flare.

Rear Admiral Escarra frowned. "What was that? Were those the same Machim vessels?"

"Yep." Alex dropped her elbows to the table and leaned forward eagerly. "The Kats deliberately breadcrumbed a Vigil tracking device to this portal. They placed a dimensional shift—their version of a Rifter, only much, much larger—inside the portal space, and it kicked the formation through the portal and dumped them out inside the atmosphere of a nearby star. Instant melting at 4,000 Kelvin."

"How many ships?"

"Around twelve thousand, not counting fighter-type craft."

Miriam shook her head, but she was smiling now. "I imagine our adversary will be far more reticent about acting on their trackers in the future. Did the Kats do this on their own initiative?"

"They did. It was Mesme's idea, much to my surprise. Vexatious bastard may be more crafty than I've been giving it credit for."

I have seven aeons of life behind me. I assure you, the surprises are not at an end.

All eyes went to the far left corner, where Mesme undulated in a leisurely dance of blue-white light.

She couldn't decide whether to laugh or scowl. "I applaud your impressive sense of timing and your witty rebuttal. You're learning. But how many times have I asked you—"

Not to lurk unannounced or 'barge in' unexpectedly. Nine times. But the opportunity was too tempting to resist.

Damn. All the time Mesme had been spending around humans was having an effect. "Okay, fair enough. You have your moment in the spotlight. Anything else you care to say?"

I was merely curious to observe the reactions of those at the table to the recording.

Miriam responded graciously, as always. "You have my thanks. We will definitely take the assist."

You are welcome.

"I suspect the trick won't work a second time, but perhaps something similar will?"

Lakhes asked me to convey to you the following: the maneuver was expensive in time, effort and resources, and thus cannot be used with regularity. However, should you require a large-scale dimensional shift to occur at a crucial juncture in your war effort, we will endeavor to provide it. Further, in light of the imminent resumption of hostilities, Hyperion asked me to inform you that our fleets stand ready to assist you in appropriate offensives.

Miriam nodded. "Convey my appreciation to them both. We need to get our feet underneath us first, but I'll be in touch."

As is your judgment. Alexis, congratulations.

She arched an eyebrow. "For?"

Vindicating my faith in the unmatched ingenuity of Humans. Your species always finds a way, and the Caeles Prism is only the most recent demonstration of this. You have done well.

She blinked, for a split-second was transported back to a featureless white room in a cave on Portal Prime. *You have done well.*

Mesme had said the same to her there, after her final test—the Hong Kong Incident, designed to probe the nuances of her appreciation of human and Artificial fallibility alike—before granting her the reward of witnessing her father's final minutes of life, and his death.

Wow. Had Mesme meant to evoke the memory, to subtly draw attention to the path the complex threads of her life had taken on their way to this moment, and how many of those threads could be traced to what she'd experienced on Portal Prime?

Purpose animated everything the Kat did, so the answer was clearly yes. It was either an implicit boasting of supreme arrogance, or a gesture of supreme kindness. Knowing Mesme, it very well could be both.

I will leave you to your preparations.

Miriam dipped her chin. "Thank you, again. Now, unless anyone has more to report, we should turn to the test results."

Alex motioned at the others and returned to her spectator pose, too distracted to actively participate yet.

An unexpected *clang* rang out as an object hit the surface of the conference table, startling everyone and sending several peoples' hands to their weapons.

Alex jerked out of her reverie in time to see a Reverb come to rest near the center of the table. Most everyone was now looking at Devon, so she assumed he was the one who had tossed it. A few attendees, however—notably Malcolm, Harper and Mia—were staring at the Reverb like it was a splinter grenade about to blow.

Devon finally broke the tense silence. "Oh, I'm sorry. I thought this was the meeting where we all showed off our shiny new accomplishments that were going to help us win this war. Is it not?"

Miriam's lips pursed. "We welcome new tools that can help us win this war at any meeting. Are you saying this is one?"

Malcolm glowered at the Reverb, disgust in his voice. "That thing only kills *us*." He threw his hands in the air. "And civilians aren't supposed to have one."

Morgan hurriedly gestured for attention. "I authorized it. I filed all the proper forms and issued an official limited exception for Devon, so simmer down, Brigadier."

Malcolm did.

Devon continued to act even more smug than usual, oblivious to the interpersonal baggage he'd dredged to the surface with the innocuous-looking little device. "Not any longer. Sight this Reverb down on an Anaden and activate it, and it'll kill them a hell of a lot faster than it'll kill one of us."

"Any Anaden?"

"What does 'kill them' mean?"

"How close do you have to be?"

The questions overlapped, and Devon had to clear his throat loudly to be heard over everyone. "If a Praesidis has their *diati* active, it won't penetrate it. But otherwise, any Anaden. It'll bypass any technological shielding or barrier, and death is instantaneous. No, it doesn't prevent their consciousness from transmitting for regenesis—not yet. I'm working on it, but I'm not certain it'll be possible to stop the transmission.

"Also, distance doesn't technically matter, but you do need a straight line of sight from the device to the target, which creates a practical limit on the range. But glass or solid walls don't matter. If you can point it directly at them, you can take them down."

"You're serious? How did you come up with it?"

Devon glanced at Escarra, then around the table, in mock—probably—indignation. "Did everyone think I was just screwing off in the tech labs the last few days? On the contrary, I was *working*."

Mia laughed. "To be fair, you working looks a lot like screwing off to the untrained eye."

"That's true. But after going to all the trouble of dragging me to another universe, you should get your money's worth from me being here." He gestured to the Reverb still lying in the middle of the table. "Each one will need to be modded individually, at least at first. So I guess we ought to slate some more Reverbs in for the next supply run?"

Harper pinched the bridge of her nose; her voice was muted through her hand. "The IDCC only has a few. Ask Seneca for some."

Bastian shrugged. "I'll see what Director Delavasi can make happen."

Miriam's brow furrowed. "Thank you. We'll work out the details later today, as well as develop a policy for their distribution and rules of use. Mr. Reynolds, is there anything else we should know about this new tool?"

"Not really—oh, there is one thing. Prevos don't need the tool."

"Are you saying a Prevo can kill an Anaden, albeit temporarily, by...looking at them?"

"Not accidentally. It requires a great deal of deliberate effort up here—" Devon tapped the glyphs lighting his temple "—but, essentially, yes."

"Are the other Prevos aware they can do this, and how?"

Devon tilted his head, silent for a momentous second. "They are now."

"Good to know." Miriam adjusted her posture and eyed Alex, but she had *not* known about this surprise, dammit. "Now, if there is again nothing else, we'll move on to the next achievement on display. Ms. Rossi?"

"Thank you, Commandant. All tests of the Caeles Prism and the accompanying wormhole traversals have come back well within performance and safety parameters. The tests include single- and multiple-vessel usage, simultaneously and in succession. They've covered distances as short as half a megameter and as long as—" she glanced at Alex "—4.1 megaparsecs, as well as many points in between. The distance has no effect on the power required, which is based solely on the diameter of the wormhole to be opened.

"As far as the power generated by the Caeles Prism goes, it is substantial and increases over time, but it can be managed, diffused and shut down at any point. There are a few hypothetical failure scenarios, but by using a separate module instead of multitasking the individual Rifters, we've cut their number and likelihood significantly, while also reducing the impact of a failure."

"Where does this put the risk profile vis-à-vis the rest of AEGIS' fielded equipment?"

"The development cycle has been fast, even for Prevo-developed technology. But I'm comfortable saying for the proposed usage, the risk profile of the Caeles Prism is lower than that of several of our deployed and active systems."

Miriam flashed a rather sardonic smile. "Like the Rifters themselves."

Kennedy was fully in professional mode. "Yes, ma'am."

"Most of the Alliance and Federation vessels don't have integrated Prevos, of course. I'm told that with a simple hardware connector installation, a Prevo on one vessel can move a second vessel as well, albeit with a concomitant increase in the power required to do so."

Kennedy nodded. "We've tested that scenario as well. The spike in the power required is the sole material issue. For reasons related to the nature of the movement, the two vessels have to be in a parallel formation and move through the wormhole simultaneously, so the diameter increase is considerable. But it doesn't seem to be physically *harder* for a Prevo to do."

Miriam lifted a hand in resignation. "I'll take their—and the test results'—word for it. Installing these connectors and linking them to specific partner ships across many thousands of vessels is a nontrivial task. We've prioritized the most crucial Alliance and Federation vessels under several mission profiles, and we began installing them on the highest priority ships this morning.

"The fieldable fleet on some missions will be reduced for a time, but we weren't sending everyone on every mission, in any event. We should be able to mitigate any gaps in capabilities until the installations are complete."

She looked pointedly around the table. "Does anyone have objections to bringing this technology live for active missions?"

Field Marshal Bastian motioned animatedly, as he tended to do. "We're all in at this point. We've got targets painted on our and the anarchs' backs now, and we've got to be able to fight back in return.

I have difficulty wrapping my head around the tech, but the test data says it works. I advise we move forward."

Malcolm sighed audibly. His hair was perfectly cropped and his BDUs were as clean and crisp as ever, but Alex thought he looked worn down, arguably beaten. A muscle under his left eye jerked repeatedly as he strained to keep his gaze fixed on Miriam and no one else. Caleb's absence didn't appear to be easing his discomfort much.

"We're hamstrung without it, and with it a multitude of opportunities and targets open up. All due respect to the safety data, but I'm sure it's dangerous as hell. So is everything we do. No objection." He sank down in his chair like a shadow retreating from the light.

Morgan waved a hand dismissively when Miriam turned to her. "I followed Alex's lead and modified the Rifter on my ship to work as a Caeles Prism yesterday. I've used it six times already, but now I seriously want a couple of thousand more ships to come with me so we can do some real damage. Also, ESC One-Delta wants its Rifter back."

"A replacement Eidolon Rifter is on the requisition list for the next trip to the Presidio." Miriam's focus shifted down the table. "Alex? This is your brainchild. Any concerns?"

It would work, even on so large a scale. She had absolute confidence in the theory and the underlying technology, as borne out by the multiple wormhole traversals the *Siyane* had made. Still, the real world could be a cruel bitch, and she felt the weight of responsibility for so many lives. But it must be nothing compared to the weight her mother felt every minute of every day.

Seeking to lighten that weight by the smallest amount, she beamed to the point of cockiness. "Did I mention I swung by a galaxy way out past the fringes of the Local Galactic Group yesterday afternoon? No concerns."

"You did not. Very well, the Caeles Prism is approved for active use. We will use it judiciously, as this is not the kind of tool one should get sloppy with. Here are the potential targets for the first mission." A labeled intergalactic map appeared above the table.

Alex leaned forward to jump in before they had a chance to start debating and get mired in really tall weeds. "Actually, I have an idea for a maiden mission.

"I've no doubt these are all important strategic targets, but mine will make for a dramatic statement, which we need to deliver. Also, the risk is mitigated, because we won't be traveling to a far-off location that will be difficult to return from in a reasonable time should something go wrong with the Caeles Prism."

Her mother dropped one elbow on the table and her chin to her fist, an uncommonly informal pose for her. "I'm listening."

"Thank you." She zoomed way in to a tiny point on the intergalactic map, sending a sea of stars whizzing away in a blur. The viewpoint sharpened on a single G3 IV star the color of straw. Six planets orbited the star, and tiny blips denoted numerous space stations and other structures.

"My proposed target is the Machimis stellar system—specifically, its sun. More specifically, the Dyson rings orbiting its sun.

"The rings send metric fucktons of power not only to Machimis, which is responsible for enormous quantities of parts production and assembly for their war machine, but also to two orbital factories and a space-based military hub. While they're busy guarding their precious gateway, let's jump straight into their sun's inner orbit and destroy their primary power source."

Miriam considered the rotating system above the table. "They'll be able to patch together some amount of emergency power in fairly short order, I assume, but I doubt it will be enough to replace..." she called up a small screen beside her "...thirty yottawatts of power per day would be the technical measurement for 'metric fucktons.'

"They'll be spending valuable time seeking and building replacement sources instead of coming after us. And we will, again, catch them off-guard and unawares, which keeps them scrambling. Reacting instead of acting. As for the mission itself, if we focus on directing our firepower efficiently and work fast enough, they may never get the opportunity to shoot at us."

Miriam nodded with increasing enthusiasm. "Maneuver warfare does have a certain elegance to it. Also, it happens to be one of our few viable strategic options against an enemy with vastly superior numbers, so I believe we will continue to pursue it. Other opinions?"

But everyone again fell into line without argument, including the irascible field marshal. The complete lack of resistance felt a little odd, until Alex realized why. Rychen had represented a powerful voice at the table, and the magnitude of his absence was palpable. Even when he'd agreed with her mother, he'd done so colorfully.

When silence took hold, Miriam continued. "All right, the Machimis stellar Dyson ring assembly is our target. I'll send out a mission profile and vessel assignments later today. Unless new data comes in necessitating a delay, we'll move at 1530 local tomorrow. Dismissed."

Alex watched Malcolm mope out of the conference room ahead of everyone else and shook her head ruefully. She noted how Mia waited a solid ten seconds before standing herself. After a brief hesitation, Alex stood to leave with Mia.

Her mother waylaid her efforts with a surprise hand on her shoulder. "Inspired idea, Alex."

"I hope so. I'm still not military, but maybe I'm starting to get the hang of this."

"It *is* in your blood."

Her mouth opened, ready to spill all the secrets queuing up on her tongue; she choked back the words beneath a forced cough. Soon. "I guess so. I need to catch up with Mia, but ping me if you have *any* questions or ideas before tomorrow."

Her mother stepped away to talk to Escarra, and Alex hurried out the door.

She fell in beside Mia in the hallway, matching the woman's purposeful gait to keep up. "So I have used my hyper-tuned powers of observation to deduce that Malcolm hasn't come crawling back, hat in hand, just yet."

Mia sighed, her expression briefly grim. "No. The thing is...I knew the kind of man he was from the beginning. But I suppose he didn't truly know the kind of woman I am."

"He'll come around. I thought he was going to start crying every time he almost looked at you in there, which was approximately every five seconds. He's patently miserable. He simply needs to let his damnable honor get out of its own way."

Mia huffed a breath. "I don't want him to 'come around'—I want him to open his eyes wider and *understand*. But I'm not convinced he can do that and remain the man he is, which I don't want to change. Splendid corner I've worked myself into, isn't it?"

She stopped outside the building exit. "I'm sorry to run, but I'm scheduled to meet with the Sator in a few minutes. Thank you for checking on me, but I'm fine."

50

ANARCH POST SATUS

LOCATION UNKNOWN

"Are your people finding Post Epsilon suitable, Ambassador?" A warm but professional smile adorned Mia's face with minimal effort. *Just fine.*

The practiced, poised demeanor had become second nature for her, and a little thing like an emotionally devastating personal crisis would not knock her off her game.

No, she corrected herself. This was not a game. This was her job and, she was starting to concede, her calling. All the more reason to perform it superbly, every day and in every circumstance.

"Very much so, Sator. Thank you for extending your hospitality so generously to us. Having a place where we could, to put it bluntly, retreat—where our feet could touch soil and we could breathe fresh air—" She blinked; she was all but quoting Malcolm, dammit. "It's done a great deal of good for morale. Functionally, it has also helped to have a central, accessible location where our officers and advisers can meet and work."

He arched an eyebrow at the last phrase. "Ah, yes. I understand certain of you have been rather busy devising an alternative travel method to enable you to avoid the gateways."

"'Hacking the universe,' my friend Devon calls it. He is prone to grandiosity, but he regularly earns the right to be. Yes, we have developed a somewhat practical way to open temporary wormholes and have engineered the power needed to traverse them."

He acted dutifully impressed, but given the teleportation gates and the Zero Drive, the notion of taking shortcuts through space plainly wasn't foreign to him. Possibly the notion of lowly humans discovering and engineering it on their own was, however.

"By 'we,' you mean your hybrids. Those of you who have sacrificed a degree of your...I suppose 'humanity' would be the correct word, to bind yourself to SAIs."

"We call ourselves 'Prevos,' Sator, and we've sacrificed nothing. I'm sure you realize I count myself among them—the eyes are a dead giveaway."

"Forgive me. I meant no insult. Old prejudices by an old man, but I should mind my inclinations better. And I'm compelled to say, the extent to which you peacefully coexist with unaltered Humans is both surprising and heartening. It should be a lesson to reactionaries who instinctively flee to fear." He gave her a self-deprecating shrug. "And a lesson to me."

He is very, very good.

He is. Then again, he's had a long time to perfect his presentation.

How long, I wonder?

I think everyone is wondering, Meno, but he holds his secrets close.

"You have many aliens fighting alongside Anadens as anarchs, Sator. I appreciate the flattery, but it seems like a lesson you must have learned long ago, if you ever needed to at all."

"Bigotry is a slippery demon, Ambassador, as is the arrogance that begets it, and the distance between altruistic paternalism and vain prejudice is short."

"Yes, sir." This was beginning to sound like a confessional. It was possible their presence here was triggering a bout of introspection for him. If lending a kind ear led to a closer relationship between AEGIS and the anarchs, she would lend it.

"We've struggled with those issues in our past as well. We enjoy thinking we've overcome them, but I suspect it's a battle that's never completely won."

"Indeed. It has recently been suggested to me that the anarch cause will win a greater number of adherents if I vow to pursue regenesis methodologies for the other species."

Was this the cause of the introspection? Humans may not have developed regenesis yet, but Mia had been brought back from the dead as surely as if they had, when she awoke on a virtual beach to a new existence in a new world. She knew better than most the incomparable value in losing and regaining life.

"My first question would be, why haven't you already?"

"Resources. It took us—my ancestors—many centuries to develop the deep understanding of Anaden physiology, psychology and neural systems needed to accomplish it. Every species is fundamentally unique in a thousand details, and the science and technology needed will be unique as well. It will not be a trivial matter for even a single additional species, and to put it bluntly, we cannot afford it."

"And when you can afford it? When we unseat the Directorate and you no longer have to spend your resources on concealment and survival? Why would you not share your knowledge with scientists from the other species and give everyone the opportunity to enjoy what the Anadens take for granted?"

"Arrogance, of course, and the prejudice hiding behind paternalism. Which is, self-evidently, no reason at all. Thank you, Ambassador, for gently showing me there is only one right decision."

"You're welcome."

That earned a brief chuckle. "On to more pressing matters. This new wormhole technology works, then?"

"Oh, yes. Our people have spent the last several days running extensive tests and trials. They are confident in both its functionality and safety, so long as basic precautions are taken." She didn't divulge tomorrow's planned mission. It was for Commandant Solovy to reveal or not at her discretion.

"Good. I look forward to seeing the battle joined once again. I will be making a wide and public appeal for support soon, and it will be helpful to have a measure of firepower backing up my claims and promises."

"It is why we are here. Is there anything else, Sator?"

"A small matter, more for your information than action. Several of the aliens your team helped to rescue from Exobiology Lab #4 have biologies ill-suited to the cold climate of Post Alpha.

We're going to transfer them to Posts Delta and Epsilon in the hopes they'll be more comfortable there. We would keep them out of your way, but our other locations aren't equipped to care for refugees."

"I'm confident it won't cause any trouble, sir. After all, everyone at Post Epsilon is alien to us."

"An excellent observation. It is easy to forget this. In any event, I'm told all the aliens being transferred are docile. You're under no obligation to do so, but if any of your people are interested in helping Administrator Udiri-jun with their acclimatization, I suspect he will welcome the assistance. As you pointed out, you are outsiders, and as such you may be able to identify challenges, or opportunities, we miss."

She nodded graciously. "I'll pass on the invitation."

PALAEMON

ANARCH POST EPSILON

Mia found Devon in the main tech lab on Epsilon, for the second day in a row. He was talking animatedly to one of the anarch engineers, toeing his chair back and forth while his arms motioned through the air.

"You seriously don't have an empire-wide public communications network? What do you do if you need to contact a station in another galaxy? Or if you want to look up information on some...famous painter or something?" He tossed a wink at Emily, who was sitting out of the way against one of the walls.

The engineer looked uneasy. "Usually, if we for some reason need educational information, we request it from one of the sector hubs. With respect to business matters, there are procedures to be followed to initiate contact. I won't bore you with them. Do you do things differently?"

"Back home, we have this quantum network—we call it the exanet—which is accessible by anyone, anywhere. It contains almost the entire sum of human knowledge, except for some classified government secrets and private intellectual property. We can use it to communicate with any person or facility, no matter the location. And that's the boring stuff. We can also use it to create virtual, multi-sensory spaces and share them with others."

"Like an integral?"

"No, that's the Noesis. Sort of. Anyway, no. The exanet is merely a quantum architecture—a framework that provides the basis for ubiquitous interconnection, but on our terms and time. It's such a simple concept. With all this cool technology you have, why do you not have this one?"

Control. Allowing so much freedom of association and access to information is dangerous. If knowledge and connections were allowed to flow freely, people might start to get ideas. They might collude.

Devon scanned the room until he spotted her standing in the entryway, propped against the door frame. He motioned her inside.

And people would. The Directorate is wise to fear the consequences.

He was doing quite a good job of selling the innocent curiosity routine, and for now the anarchs seemed to be buying it.

She entered the lab but paused at the periphery of the workstation Devon was disrupting and gestured for Emily to join them as well. "Having fun?"

Devon grimaced. "I only hope I'm asking the right questions. Some of their tools are almost identical to ours, but then their infrastructure is insanely advanced, and they don't use it how you'd expect. A five-dimensional quantum architecture underlies almost all of their systems. Do you know anything about these Reor slabs they use for storage?"

She shrugged noncommittally. "I think Alex does."

"They're mind-boggling in their complexity, but without an ex-anet-style network to connect them they're ridiculously limited. So what's up?"

"Actually, I was looking for Emily." She shifted toward the young woman. "Do you have a free minute?"

Emily blinked in surprise. "Sure."

"Great. Let's take a walk."

Devon half-stood. "Wait—don't I get to know what this is about?"

Mia laughed for show and headed for the door.

ᴀ

It was a warm, clear day, and the bright sunlight cast a vibrant amber hue upon their surroundings. Anarchs moved around with purpose, but there were fewer AEGIS people milling around than there had been the last few days. Most of the military personnel had returned to their ships to prepare for tomorrow's mission. It had to make someone like Emily feel a bit lonely and isolated.

She gave the young woman a reassuring smile. "It looked as if Devon was enjoying himself."

Emily rolled her eyes with the dramatic flair of an artist. "Oh, he is. He's also driving the anarch techs crazy, but I think most of them secretly like sharing their work with an eager audience. Having deciphered their programming, I believe he's now on a mission to decipher their communications system—then subvert it, of course."

"Sounds par for the course for Devon."

"Thank you for asking him to come here. I know he resisted, but this is good for him. Truth be told, he was starting to feel...adrift back home. His revolution went mainstream—then it *became* the mainstream. It doesn't need him any longer. But now, he's among rebels again. It makes him happy."

"What about you? How are you doing?"

Emily glanced toward the lab building. "I'm a little homesick. I miss my friends and, you know, familiar things. Everything here is so *odd*. I'm not as fast to adjust to new surroundings as Devon is."

She hurriedly placed a hand on Mia's arm. "But you can't tell him. He's already given up so much for me. If he thought I was uncomfortable here, he'd demand for us to be on the next transport through the portal, and I don't want that to happen."

Mia frowned. "You have a right to be happy, too." If only it were so simple....

"And I am—I will be. Yves, my Artificial, is helping me venture out of my comfort zone, and I've begun pondering ways I can try to combine our tech and theirs to create new variations on my art."

"That's kind of related to what I wanted to talk to you about. The anarchs are bringing some refugees here. Members of unintegrated species they and—" she stumbled over the words "—our Marines rescued from this lab where they were being treated as guinea pigs." Dammit, she should be able to say his name.

"However odd you think everything here is, you've got nothing on these refugees. They don't speak or understand the language, and in most cases they've never seen anything approaching this level of technology. They're scared and confused, but also grateful to not be caged and tortured any longer. I thought perhaps you'd be interested in helping them become less scared and confused."

"They're not dangerous, are they?"

"I've been assured they're not. But just in case, Administrator Latro's people are handling their arrival and initial settling in. But after that, the anarchs are going to need help introducing them to this society, teaching them some basic communication skills, and so on. Hopefully, making them feel safe."

"And we have more in common with the refugees than anybody who lives here." Emily nodded. "I could draw up some images to help overcome the language barrier. Maybe we could use graphic symbols to build a way to communicate." She paused. "That sounds as if it'll be fun. I'd like to help."

"Terrific. I'll tell Latro. Now you should get back before Devon has heart failure."

"It'll do him good." Emily laughed and offered a parting wave.

Mia slowed to a stop on a breezeway stretching across the water to bridge the Administration complex and the landing platforms. Administrator Latro was at a meeting on Post Alpha for another hour, so she had a span of free time before she would be able to begin coordinating the refugees' orientation with him. Free time was not currently her friend.

She composed and sent Miriam a message.

Commandant Solovy,

Sator Nisi is planning to make a public appeal to the masses in the near future in a bid to rally more people to his cause. If feasible, it might make sense to time the Machimis mission and his speech for maximum impact. Let me know if you want me to broach the possibility to him, or if you wish to do so yourself—or not at all.

Regards,

— Mia Requelme

While she waited on a reply, she watched two anarchs, a Barisan and a Naraida, spar in the training ring beside one of the plazas. Both species were intrinsically quick and agile, though in different ways, and the match was a blur of spins, ducks and acrobatics. It concluded too soon and with no clear victor.

What could she do next to distract her from thinking about Malcolm? To stave off the crushing emptiness that rushed in to fill the silence? The unfamiliar, terrible ache of loneliness pressed on her chest until she could scarcely breathe.

Mia—

Please, Meno, don't.

But I still don't know what to do to help you.

Neither do I.

51

SIYANE

Caleb and Eren were waiting on Alex when she got back to the *Siyane*.

They were mid-conversation, but at her expectant gaze, Caleb motioned to Eren. "Tell her how you destroyed the Phoenix Gateway."

"I placed a series of antimatter slabs all the way around the center ring. They were coated with varying amounts a self-dissolving material to delay the reaction long enough for me to place them all."

Alex considered him skeptically, noting that he again seemed uncommonly chipper. And less...slouchy. "A couple of negative energy missiles should get the job done, then."

Eren made a prevaricating motion. "Eh, maybe. My way's more fun, though."

"It killed you."

"True. But if I had a getaway ride, it would take care of the admittedly unfortunate side effect. Trust me—my way's more fun. Don't you want to stand in space atop one of those rings?"

Her face lit up before she could help it, and Caleb rolled his eyes dramatically. "You've done it now. All right, we're in. Can you get your hands on some antimatter slabs?"

He motioned to his pack. "Already did. When your message said you had a couple of questions about the Phoenix Gateway, I took a gamble on where you were headed with this and grabbed a set. You have a mission?"

Alex cringed. "Yes, but this one's kind of off-the-books. Everyone has their hands full moving the fleet back into action, so we thought we'd handle this ourselves without creating a bunch of fuss."

"I do relish off-the-books. What are we blowing up?"

MAFFEI I GALAXY

BEYOND THE BOUNDARIES OF THE LGG

The gateway hung silent and dark against the profile of Maffei I, like an ancient artifact left behind by a long-departed civilization.

In reality it was brand new, nominally complete and capable of operation. But there was no companion Arx and no activity beyond the hum of the grid powering it.

For the time being, the Directorate's attention was focused elsewhere. It might stay so until the Directorate was no more, in which case the gateway was harmless and even useful. But if events followed a different path, it represented a danger to an innocent species—more than one, she simply hadn't met the others yet. Now that the wormhole technology had proved functional, *they* had no need of the gateway. They could come here any time they wished.

Eren studied the gateway out the viewport. "It looks as if not much is going on yet. But the power's on, so something *could* go on at any time. There are likely a few drones working, too. Valkyrie, I've got their ID frequency. If we all broadcast it, the drones should ignore us."

'Should?'

He shrugged. "They could've changed the frequency, but probably not. Also, try not to bump into one. Take my word for it."

Caleb handed Alex her Daemon, blade and bracelet from the cabinet. "We'll be ready if they did change it."

"The power being on also means there'll be a weak gravity field around the rings, which is good news. We'll be able to move a lot faster than we could if we had to use mag boots, and we'll be done in a shake or two—which is also good news, because I actually have my own mission starting in a few hours."

"So do we. Never a dull moment around here."

Eren nodded thoughtfully. "Ah, yes, Machimis. Xanne mentioned that we're trying to coordinate the time on the two missions, so that Nisi's speech goes out right when everyone starts to realize what you guys did. Boom, maximum impact. It'll be a show for certain. But first, speaking of moments that are not dull." He grinned at Alex. "You're going to get a kick out of this."

"Oh, of that I have no doubt. Valkyrie, keep a close watch on us. And a close watch for approaching ships or other threats. And for any signs the gateway's about to activate."

'The temptation to reply with a smartass retort is powerful, which I blame entirely on Eren's presence. But of course I will do so.'

Eren chuckled. "You know you love me, Valkyrie."

'Love is such a strong word.'

"It is. Still, give it time. Are we ready to head out?"

Helmets went on, and they checked each other over. Eren handed Caleb a thick, uneven ribbon of material. "I'd say be careful with this, but the truth is the slabs are pretty stable. Just don't attach them to something you don't want to blow up."

Caleb fastened the ribbon to his utility belt. "How long will we have?"

"Twenty-two minutes from the time the first slab is placed by either of us. So no rush."

"All the same, we'll rush a bit." Caleb turned toward the airlock. "I believe we are ready."

Valkyrie lowered the *Siyane* to hover above the gateway's center ring as they entered the airlock. The outer hatch opened, and one by one they leapt down to the hundred-meter-wide surface. Valkyrie withdrew to a reasonable distance to keep her close watch on everything.

Located as the gateway was, thirty-one degrees above the galactic plane, they had an unobstructed view of the small cobalt nucleus at the heart of the elliptical galaxy. To their other side the faint haze of the outer regions of the galaxy soon gave way to the interstellar void.

Alex: "Well, this is fantastic."

Caleb offered her an affectionate smile behind his faceplate, which she returned. These were the incomparable moments, weren't they? The ones that put the exclamation marks on a life lived in full.

Eren detached a slab from his ribbon and held it out in his hand until they quit gaping at the view and each other and directed their attention at him.

Eren: "Take your time. It's fine. I'll just hang out."

Caleb checked the secureness of his ribbon a final time.

Caleb: "No, it's time to get moving."

Eren crouched and pressed the slab firmly onto the ring's surface.

Eren: "And...go."

He took off running in one direction, they in the other.

She cackled in delight as her stride propelled her in soaring, four-meter-long strides across the ring's surface. The metal beneath her feet gleamed a muted, lustrous nickel that rippled as the angle shifted. The galaxy they skirted the edge of drew most of her observation, but it was all simply *fantastic*.

Caleb slowed to a stop ahead, then pivoted to face her a second before she bumped into him. His gloved hands wound around her waist, and their faceplates touched.

No words would suffice, and none were needed.

He took a step back and knelt on the surface, repeating the process Eren had performed to place the slab, then stood and gestured ahead.

Caleb: "Off we go."

She gleefully took off running again, this time passing him for fun. She had the same locations markers on her whisper as he did, so she wouldn't overrun their next placement point.

Yet she almost did anyway from sheer distraction, and skidded to a stop a mite close to the edge for comfort.

She laughed off Caleb's chiding scowl. Then while he placed the next slab, she briefly lay down on the surface to stare up at a sea of galaxies masquerading as stars.

"One day I'm going to be a star."
"Oh, milaya, *one day you will shine with more radiance than every star in the celestial heavens."*

Maybe not, but she was hanging out with them all the same.

ᴙ

Eren was waiting for them when they arrived at the marker for the last slab.
Eren: *"Did you two stop for tea and a quick shag?"*
Alex: *"Was that an option?"*
Caleb: *"Next time, baby. Valkyrie, we're ready for—"*
Valkyrie: *'I am detecting an increased energy signature originating from the gateway. It matches the readings accompanying an imminent activation.'*
Caleb: *"Stay where you are, Valkyrie."*
As the interior of the rings began crackling with visible energy, he grabbed Eren's arm and yanked him in close, wrapped his other arm around her and teleported them into the *Siyane's* cabin.

He stumbled a little once their feet met floor, and his arms dropped away to brace on the data center.

Alex watched him to make sure he didn't collapse, then pushed past her own slight wooziness from the swift relocation to take charge. "Retreat five megameters thirty degrees NE bearing, now."

They accelerated away as the rings continued to charge up. Caleb waved her off—and looked okay—so she hurried into the cockpit. They'd reached a safe distance by the time she got there, and she swung the ship around to face the gateway.

Three Erevna research vessels emerged from the storm at the center of the rings and slowly proceeded onward. She checked the countdown timer for the antimatter charges. Almost a full minute remaining.

They needed to speed this up…or keep those ships nearby. "Cloaking and firing on the Anaden vessels."

"What?" Caleb rushed into the cockpit, Eren on his heels.

"Merely to distract them. We'll stay clear of the blast radius, but I want to keep these ships *in* the blast radius."

'Cloaking shield and Dimensional Rifter active.'

She sighted in on the most distant vessel and fired.

The strike was absorbed in full by its shield. The Erevna ship wasn't military, but it assuredly fielded weaponry sufficient to defend itself, so she altered her trajectory. Between the stealth and the Rifter there wasn't much danger to the *Siyane*, but she tried not to be too blasé about these things.

Sixty-two degrees to port from her original location she fired on the lead ship again, followed by the next one in line.

22 seconds

An additional ship began to emerge from the gateway—and this one *was* a military vessel. They were going ahead with the full Maffei I expedition, war be damned. The arrogant fuckers.

11 seconds

The Machim warship was firing as it exited, though it had no hard target. When cadmium laser fire swept near enough to light the cabin, she backed off, retreating silently into the void. She'd accomplished her goal.

2 seconds

The antimatter slabs detonated in a staccato trail of explosions racing across the arc of the center ring, each one larger and brighter than the last as they fed on one another. The ring splintered apart in a massive eruption of energy, and pieces hurled forth to tear into the other rings then the Anaden ships.

Only when the energy had expended itself and could find no more fuel to power it did the explosions fade away.

All that remained was a debris field. Behind it, Maffei I continued to light the horizon. Peaceful and, for now, undisturbed.

The diffuse glow of the galaxy, luminous against the backdrop of the billions of galaxies beyond it, blurred as a new message appeared on her whisper screen to paint itself across the stars. It contained many words, but only one mattered.

Tomorrow.

52

PRÓTOS AGORA

"Enough! We are immortal masters who have lived for a thousand millennia and ruled for the greater span of it—can we act like it, please? The hysteria on display here is embarrassing. One can only hope no progeny ever witness us in such an unsightly froth." Kyvern's glare passed soberly around the circle until the overheated agitation abated.

He should have been the one to say it. He should have been the one to project authority. To lead.

Praesidis opened his mouth to step in and take over now, but the back-and-forth had already begun anew, if at a less fevered pitch.

Diaplas cleared her throat with deliberate solemnity. "Thank you, Kyvern. As I was saying, and being drowned out? The inescapable conclusion to draw from the latest gateway destruction is that either the Humans or the anarchs—and they are now for all intents and purposes one and the same—possess some form of wormhole technology. I cannot begin to speculate why they didn't use it before now. However, it is the only answer which explains their ability to reach the Maffei I galaxy gateway without *using* the gateway."

She crossed her arms in challenge. "Given this new information, is anyone still inclined to call the enemy primitives?"

Machim scoffed. "I did tell all of you their technology and capabilities were far from primitive. Your arrogance has blinded you until now, but you cannot deny reality in the face of such evidence."

"Who is 'you,' Machim? Are you insinuating—"

"I think we all need to—"

Erevna sneered in Machim's direction. "I don't care what we call them. They are ripping our infrastructure out from underneath us. Do something about them, and do it *now!*"

Their voices began to rise once more, and still Praesidis did not speak. They would turn to him soon enough on their own initiative; in the absence of easy answers they would look to him to assuage their concerns. Yet he had no way to do so.

In point of fact, they were all in far *greater* danger than they realized, and he dared not tell them why.

Machim droned on about the enemy's weapons and unpredictable tactics, but the battles were a distraction—one the enemy was using to draw their attention while it honed a far more dangerous weapon. The man Nyx had twice run up against was a new manner of threat, yet reminiscent of a very old one.

Time, so much time, had dulled Praesidis' killer instinct, and in his gut he worried he did not know how to meet this threat. In his gut he worried he was incapable of doing so.

"Praesidis? Are you here?"

He restrained an instinctive jerk and allowed his gaze to find Theriz in the circle. "I'm sorry?"

"I asked about the status of Vigil's anarch crackdown."

"Ah, yes. The new security measures have severely constrained their ability to move and act. Their safe havens are now denied them." It was a weasely answer, but the truth was worse.

The dragnet had resulted in the capture of a few anarch agents here and there, all of whom had committed suicide or fried their brains before proper interrogations could even commence. Yes, they'd flushed out those agents who were undercover, but as it stood now, they were likely to be replaced soon enough.

"Except for their actual bases. Those have not been denied them, have they?"

The inborn need to save face with the others nearly led him to reveal the news of the tracker Nyx had placed on the Human vessel at Exobiology Lab #4. The signal had evaporated in interstellar space in MW Sector 59. Three stellar systems in the vicinity were currently being investigated, but investigated cautiously and quietly. In the wake of Machim's multiple humiliations that had resulted from blindly following the trackers placed on Katasketousya vessels, he did not intend to leap without looking.

Once they located the base or the fleet to which the vessel had returned, surveillance would be conducted and facts confirmed before forces were sent to destroy it. He would be certain, then he would act.

For now he focused on projecting the calm confidence he should but could not feel. "You know we have not located their bases. But we will. We have the anarchs on the run and under tremendous pressure. We will break them, and they will lead us to the Humans *and* the Katasketousya."

53

SIYANE

Tomorrow was too soon. She wasn't ready for tomorrow.

'Alex, I have been analyzing the waves we observed traveling to and from the Reor slab while inside the wormhole.'

"What? I'm sorry, I was…you've uncovered something?"

'Several things. Each light stream we observed was in actuality a tightly packed set of a number of individual waves oscillating at various frequencies. The differing visible hues you perceived were the result of a preponderance of the frequencies at times falling within a spectral range associated with a definable color.'

Her mind lingered on other thoughts, and it took her a second to absorb what Valkyrie was saying. "But the frequencies ranged beyond the visible light spectrum?"

'Yes. The waves I measured ranged from near ultraviolet to extremely low frequencies. In other words, they appear to span the non-ionizing radiation spectrum.'

"So their transmission doesn't affect the space around them. How very…premeditated of the Reor."

'One might assert it is the kind of deliberate choice only a sentient being could make.'

"One might. Okay, what else?"

'None of the waves originated from your Reor slab. The waves we observed originated elsewhere and flowed through your slab and the filaments located within it and exited to continue on.'

"We put my slab in one of the Anadens' readers, and it said there was nothing stored on it. So it makes sense none originated from it..." she stopped cold "...because the waves are *data*. They're sharing the fucking data!"

'It is a reasonable deduction to make from the evidence on hand.'

She took the slab out of her pocket and stared at it, for at least the hundredth time. It looked unchanged by its experience in the wormhole—because it hadn't been a singular experience.

What she'd seen was in fact happening right now, and had been happening since she'd acquired the slab. She'd merely pulled back the dimensional curtain and glimpsed what she suspected constituted a persistent state for the Reor. "So these waves. They're not uniformly distributed across the non-ionizing spectrum?"

'No. They exhibited distinct patterns. However, I have been unable to locate a matching algorithm that replicates the patterns of the individual frequencies.'

If they weren't automatically generated by a mathematical calculation, then what? "Do you think the Reor speak some kind of frequency-based language?"

'It is possible. But more likely the frequency is some type of marker related to the data or its storage. Perhaps the frequency conveys the amount of data stored together, or even the size of the Reor slab it's stored on. Or perhaps it's an aspect of the encryption used.'

"Hmm. Eren did say the slabs' encryption capabilities was one of the main reasons they were used for storage. The user has to have the encryption key to read the data." She frowned. "But then why are the Reor sharing it with each other? Why is the data traveling across these dimensions? Any given piece of data is useless without the encryption key for it, so nothing can be *done* with it."

'It could be a natural aspect of the Reor's existence. Though the data travels, it remains in a constant state of superposition, to analogize.'

Natural aspect or not, it seemed a damn lot like all the data stored on a Reor slab anywhere in the Directorate's domain was constantly flowing through nonspatial dimensions. Encrypted, but flowing.

She could access nonspatial dimensions.

Once upon a time she'd called herself a hacker. It had never grown beyond a hobby—and expression of rebellion—but that didn't mean she hadn't been good at it. Similar to many tools of human conflict, including weapons and defenses to them, methods of encryption and the circumvention of them had been locked in a game of perpetual one-upmanship for hundreds of years. With the advent of quantum computing came insanely complex encryption techniques, but so too came the computers powerful enough to break them. In her experience, there was no such thing as unbreakable encryption—it was simply a question of resources.

Given that the encryption 'tool' was an ancient, sentient inorganic life form existing in a multitude of dimensions, admittedly, the resources required might be greater than she could corral.

She twirled the small slab between her fingers. Why had the Reor gifted it to her? At the time, it had felt like a gesture of goodwill...and maybe that was all it was. But what if it was something more?

No answers rushed to greet her, and as she lost the thread of thought her mind inevitably drifted back to where it had started.

Tomorrow.

She wasn't ready for tomorrow. She also had to make it through the rest of today, first.

54

MILKY WAY SECTOR 17

A parsec from Palaemon, in the void between two stars and far from anything that might serve as fodder for collateral damage, the golden glow of the Caeles Prism shone bright against the surrounding void.

The last arrivals from the fleet checked in, and the orb expanded in a torrent of plasma and sparking bolts of electricity as it prepared to slingshot the fleet across the galaxy in the blink of an eye.

Though Malcolm lacked the skills to fathom it, within the Prism dimensions were opening and closing and opening again, creating energy—power—out of the motion of tiny particles trapped inside.

Beyond his understanding, this wonder the Noetica Prevos had created. Mia and Alex and the others, and their Artificials, in a matter of days. No, hours; the days had been for testing and component installation.

He chuckled quietly. He honestly did have a 'type,' didn't he?

Major Ettore turned to Malcolm. "Power conduit is open and...connection established."

"Thank you, Major," Malcolm responded absently, his mind elsewhere.

His ex-wife, Veronica, hadn't been like the others...but in a startling flash of introspection, he realized seeking her out had been a deliberate, if subconscious, choice on his part. He'd been fleeing in the opposite direction. Rebounding. In a further surprise, it seemed as if the realization lifted a protracted bitterness left behind from the divorce.

Replacing it was a touch of sympathy for Veronica; it wasn't her fault she had never stood a chance to truly claim his heart.

No, he was definitely attracted to a particular kind of woman: independent, self-motivated, driven and determined, uncommonly intelligent, dynamic of personality. Then he was somehow repeatedly shocked and disappointed when they didn't instantly see the wisdom in his own outlook on the world and adopt it as their own forthwith. When they didn't spontaneously start abiding by his own opinions, rules and strictures.

Quite the quandary he'd set out for himself then deliberately trapped himself in, time and again.

So what to do? Settle for someone safe who reaffirmed the correctness of his moral paradigm and perspective on the world? Or follow his heart to someone who challenged his precepts and forced him to grapple with the many uncomfortable shades of gray between right and wrong, but who fulfilled him in the deep places of his soul?

If he loved Mia because of who and what she was—and that was the only way to love someone, wasn't it?—how could he ask or even want her to be anything else? He couldn't.

So could he live with why he loved her? Which he still did, apparently.

She may have had to make difficult decisions and take morally gray actions at times—actions that would make Veronica clutch at her chest in horror. But Mia had done more to save more people, to better their lives and protect their futures, than either Veronica or ninety-nine percent of the rest of society had ever conceived of. At the end of every day, who was the more moral person here?

He managed to stifle this chuckle before it became audible. He was worse than a hypocrite. He was a spectacular idiot.

"Power threshold reached. Ready for wormhole traversal, sir."

Malcolm nodded. "Understood. Hold for command authorization."

He willed the mission to go well, and also for it to go quickly. After all, when you realized what you wanted with this much clarity and conviction, you also wanted it now.

ℛ

SIYANE

MILKY WAY SECTOR 17

Alex listened to the Connexus hum with military precision. Structurally identical to the Noesis, it felt like a completely different entity.

She was reminded that becoming a Prevo didn't alone change a person's nature. Hackers who became Prevos remained rebellious contrarians, lending a chaotic, unruly feel to the Noesis. Soldiers who became Prevos remained ordered and disciplined, and as a result the Connexus was as tidy as the formations at morning inspection.

AEGIS Prevos representing thousands of ships confirmed their successful remote connection to the glowing ball of energy spinning at the center of the gathered forces.

Alexis Solovy (Siyane): *"Commandant Solovy, the Caeles Prism readings are within parameters. All capable vessels report solid power transference connections and operational readiness. Safe traversal window is open for the next eighty-two seconds. Recommend a 'go.'"*

Caleb laughed under his breath. "Who are you and what have you done with my wife?"

She shot him a smirk, then forced her attention back to the sea of ships and the cosmic marvel at their core. It wasn't her job to oversee the operation, but it *was* her responsibility. The Caeles Prism wouldn't exist here and now without Mia and Meno or Devon and Annie, nor without Kennedy, but it damn sure wouldn't exist without her and Valkyrie.

She *really* hoped the AEGIS fleet didn't explode in a nova of runaway power and fracturing dimensions.

Commandant Solovy (AFS Stalwart II): *"AEGIS 1ˢᵗ Assault Brigade, proceed to Mission Staging Coordinates. Report on arrival."*

A segment of vessels in the far upper right quadrant vanished.

The two seconds of waiting which followed were nowhere so long as in the Connexus, where they ticked by in one hundred twenty billion individual nanoseconds.

However, its participants were rewarded by knowing the result 62,000 nanoseconds before everyone else. Alex smiled.

Commodore Saito (AFS Caledonia): *"Arrival at Mission Staging Coordinates confirmed. All vessels accounted for. We are green across the board."*

Commandant Solovy (AFS Stalwart II): *"AEGIS 2nd and 3rd Assault Brigades, proceed to Mission Staging Coordinates. Report on arrival."*

It continued on as the fleet traversed their wormholes in four waves. The final wave included her mother's ship, and its arrival at the destination was followed by a brief pulse.

Remarkably done, dear, as always. Thank you.

You are most welcome. On my way.

The Caeles Prism powered down and blinked out, leaving behind the stark darkness of interstellar space.

She monitored the retrieval of the now-inactive device by the *AFS Keswick*. Much as they'd done on the *Siyane*, the interdictor's Rifter had been modified to serve a dual function as a small Caeles Prism. The ship would transport the primary module to the other side, thus ensuring the fleet would be able to return when its mission was complete.

There was a brief flash of light, and the *Keswick*, too, was gone.

Caleb nodded in approval. "It's just us now. Congratulations."

She breathed out slowly. "Thanks. Now, I don't want to miss the show, so Valkyrie, when you're ready."

'Initiating Caeles Prism.'

With hardly a thought from her, a gap opened in space in front of them, widening and smoothing out to form a near-perfect oval. She considered it, then pulled the Reor slab from her pocket and opened her palm.

She moved into the gap.

The slab lit up in prismatic light, and again brilliant strings wove into, through and out of the odd mineral.

Her lips curled up. "I wish you could see this. It's beautiful."

She sensed Caleb squeeze her other hand, though she wouldn't say she *felt* it, exactly. Sensations were off-kilter here. "The expression on your face right now tells me everything I need to know. *It's* beautiful."

She smiled more broadly and tilted her head for an altered perspective. The strings traveled to and beyond the limits of her sight...but they weren't technically strings, were they? Of course they weren't; she'd labeled them as such for ease of reference. But in fact, they resembled miniature versions of the wide energy beams connecting the enormous Reor slabs in the Oneiroi Nebula, including the one she'd interacted with—

—a yellow star, a frozen planet—

—an eternal city, a room pitched in blackness—

—a sphere bathed in light, spinning away from void to—

She blinked. That was vivid. "Valkyrie, ask Mesme if the Kats encrypt the data they store with the Reor in the Oneiroi Nebula."

'One moment. Yes, they do. Mesme elaborates to say that while the likeliest outcome of the Reor sanctuary being discovered is its wholesale destruction, they cannot risk the smallest chance of Directorate agents attempting to capture the information stored there.'

"*Sukin syn.* That means the Reor created a universal decryption key for themselves. They put a damn backdoor...where? Inside their very physical structure? In the process for imprinting data within the slabs?"

Caleb moved, shifting to half-face her. The motion made her a little dizzy. She should probably exit the wormhole space soon.

"Why do you say so?"

"Because I *saw* data when I touched that energy beam. It was confusing and disjointed, but it definitely wasn't scrambled. It was traveling from slab to slab, and it was not encrypted." She frowned. "How did I see it?"

'Perhaps the Reor wanted you to see it. Recall, this occurred after they gifted you the slab you hold.'

"They wanted me to know they were accessing the encrypted data stored within their slabs? So I would know it *could* be accessed? Terrific, but since *I* don't have the universal decryption key, this doesn't actually do me any good. And we still don't know how to talk to them to ask them to pretty please let us borrow it."

"Are you sure they didn't already give it to you?"

She eyed Caleb askance, trying not to get distracted by the waves of light dancing through the crimson aura that surrounded him, giving him an otherworldly appearance. "What do you mean?"

He reached over and placed the fingertips of one hand on the Reor slab. The strings continued on their journeys unhindered. "What if it's in here?"

"We checked. There's no data stored in the slab."

"What if it's not data, but instead a sort of…pattern? Like an old-fashioned padlock, or keyhole—match the pattern, and you get in."

Her vision zoomed in until the slab filled it. But after the filaments angled in several times, even using all her enhancements she was not able to track the additional dimensions into which they traveled. She simply could not say if the patterns they created differed from those of any other Reor slab.

'Caeles Prism power levels are approaching dangerous levels.'

"Right." She shook her head roughly and exited the wormhole into normal space at the Mission Staging Coordinates, where she found the AEGIS fleet waiting on her.

The secrets of the Reor were going to have to keep for a while longer.

55

MACHIMIS STELLAR SYSTEM

The three Dyson rings were visible only as slivers of gunmetal chrome, streaks of perfect imperfections overlaid upon the stellar surface. Each node of the rings spanned nearly 320 meters, but they were tiny dots breaking up the streaks. When set against a star, everything was relative.

If their presence hadn't been detected on arrival, it would be soon enough. There was no time for waxing poetic, so Miriam promptly ceased doing so. An ESC Flight monitored their perimeter with active sensor sweeps, waiting for the inevitable arrival of a response force.

Commandant Solovy (AFS Stalwart II): "Phase 1 forces, the individual nodes are your top priority. AFS 1ˢᵗ and 2ⁿᵈ Assault Brigades, your targets are the nodes attached to Ring 1, 0° to 180° W as designated on Mission Tactical.

"AFS 3ʳᵈ and 4ᵗʰ Assault Brigades, Ring 1, 0° to 180° E.

"EA NW and SW Brigades, Ring 2 East. EA NE and SE Brigades, Ring 2 West.

"SF Southern Fleet, Ring 3 East. SF Northern Fleet, Ring 3 West.

"ESC Flights 1-4, target supporting connections beginning at 180° on the far side of the sun.

"Inflict maximum damage in the next twenty-two minutes."

The Dyson rings followed a solar synchronous orbit, and nodes encircled the full circumference to guarantee no gap in power capture and distribution. The scale of both the power source and the structures drawing upon it asserted themselves in appropriately intimidating fashion. But they were up to the challenge.

Miriam maximized the screen to her left, where both the targets and her vessels were presented as neat, crisp blips. The crew on the bridge focused diligently on their duties, but all was quiet. "Envious of the rest of the fleet, Major Halmi?"

"I know better, ma'am."

There was no enemy to track or target for the moment. Thus she had little to do, save monitor the mission's progress, watch the clock count down, and remain on alert. Sometimes, a leader's most important job was to get out of the way so their people could do *their* jobs.

The Machim warships were fast, capable of traversing nearly two hundred parsecs per hour using superluminal travel. That speed would put any ships stationed near Machimis here in seconds.

But Machimis was 0.8 AU away, and a pinpoint superluminal jump across such a short distance toward a massive, deadly target struck her as the sort of daring, risky maneuver Machims didn't engage in. If her instincts were correct, they would forego it, which meant it would take them thirty-six minutes to cross the distance using sub-light propulsion.

Chastened by the disastrous encounter at the Sagittae Gateway, however, she did not allow herself to count on it.

AFS MA-PRIMARY

The filters necessary to protect sensitive retinas from the flood of solar rays were layered so thickly over the viewport the sun's photosphere was reduced to a flat, sooty gray. A shame, in Morgan's opinion.

You used to regard notable astronomical sights as distractions liable to interfere with shooting the enemy.

I'm trying to expand my perspective, Stanley. I almost died, so I've decided to appreciate the little things in life—or the very big things, as the case may be. Smell the roses. Pursue a few clichés.

Is this my fault?

Entirely.

It certainly wasn't Harper's fault, for Morgan had never met a more practical, no-nonsense, whimsy-free human being. Morgan found it refreshing and a perfect match for her, but Stanley's philosophical musings and discerning mindset *was* altering her perspective a bit, here and there.

Commander Lekkas (AFS MA-Primary): "ESC Flight 3, target Ring 1 support structure in the arc spanning 165° to 195° reference Mission Tactical. Flight 4, same orders on Ring 2. Flights 1 and 2, same orders on Ring 3. And make it quick, because we have somewhere else to be."

Their speed matched the orbital velocity of the rings, and as one, the Eidolons fired on the metamaterial strung between the individual power nodes. Designed to withstand the 5,400 K temperature the sun averaged for several thousand years before needing to be replaced, it required two flights' firepower concentrated on a single point for twenty-three seconds to sear through it.

The instant the metamaterial was severed both halves plummeted away. The nodes were being dragged with them, and the larger ships' targets suddenly became moving ones. But it wasn't as if they couldn't handle dynamic tracking.

The impressive length of the rings—some 5,200 megameters—meant it was going to take time, but eventually and inevitably all the nodes would tumble into the sun, burn up and be rendered both useless and irretrievable. Thus, once each of the three rings was severed at a single location, AEGIS' job was done.

But they didn't come all this way to do a half-assed job, and with her extensive logistics experience Commandant Solovy was not one to leave anything to chance. So the fleet would rip every node they could to shreds before the enemy showed up in force.

That wasn't all they would do, either. *"Flights 1 and 2, execute superluminal jump to designated coordinates on my mark."* She confirmed the other flights were carrying out their assignments apace. *"Mark."*

The heavily filtered scene outside the viewport blurred and snapped back into clarity so fast the events almost seemed to happen out of order. Stealth activated automatically. The filters eased, but the planet now located below her was so gray and drab one could hardly tell.

Commander Lekkas (MA-Primary): "Flights 1 and 2, proceed to 31.2 megameters altitude above planet Machimis, then move to every fourth orbital module, in flight and call-sign order. Hold position above the modules."

Unlike the Dyson ring nodes, the power relay modules orbiting Machimis moved independently of one another on a staggered geosynchronous orbit above the equator of the planet, far inside the extensive orbital planetary defenses. They were hefty structures, but they paled in comparison to the gigantic nodes surrounding the planet's sun—which meant they were compact enough to be wrecked by Eidolons.

Commander Lekkas (MA-Primary): "Siyane, ECS flights are in position and awaiting your orders."

Alexis Solovy (Siyane): "Copy that. Maintain stealth and commence attaching negative energy mines to the relay modules, but do not activate them."

Commander Lekkas (MA-Primary): "ECS Flights 1 and 2, proceed with mine staging."

Alexis Solovy (Siyane): "Meanwhile, I'm just going to sneak all quiet-like past some Central Command Annex defenses and leave a small present on its backup generator."

The defenses protecting the Annex were, needless to say, nothing to scoff at. But Alex and Valkyrie had been iterating continual improvements to the *Siyane's* cloaking shield for more than a year now. If anyone could slip through the defense net, it was them.

Morgan dropped a negative energy mine onto the surface of the relay module beneath her, confirmed solid contact and moved on to the next. Four modules per vessel covered all fifty-two modules.

Six minutes later all the mines were placed. Then they waited.

The timing was tricky. Set them off too soon, and Machimis security was alerted to the offensive before the AEGIS fleet finished taking out the Dyson rings. Set them off too late, and the planetary defenses would swallow her Eidolons whole, stealthed or no.

While this mission served an important strategic purpose, its equal purpose was to make a statement—to knock the enemy back on its heels and disrupt not only its military capabilities but its governing ones. Once the relay modules exploded, the sole power remaining here would be what was stored in batteries on the surface.

As the batteries were swiftly drained by the hungry Machim war machine, the power would begin to go out on Machimis. The more rapidly and dramatically this happened, the more impactful the statement.

Alexis Solovy (Siyane): *"Well that was bracing, but they still don't know we're here. Commandant Solovy, Phase 2 is fully implemented and awaiting your go-ahead for detonation."*

ᴀ̅ʀ

AFS STALWART II

"Report from ECS Flight Five, Commandant. Machim vessels inbound, 120 megameters distant and closing."

Miriam had been right about caution winning out on the part of the Machim commander, even in what must be quickly escalating to a crisis situation for the adversary. She filed the information away and checked the mission status. All three rings sliced, making the ultimate outcome inevitable. 11,086 of 15,420 nodes destroyed outright. Phase 2 staged and ready to activate.

Brigadier Ashonye (EAS San Antonio): *"EA 2nd DAS Regiment reports successful elimination of bow shock transmitters. Phase 3 complete."*

And now Machimis' backup-to-the-backup power supply, in the form of an array of modules capturing the energetic by-product of the solar wind impacting the planet's magnetic field, had been neutralized as well.

It would do.

Commandant Solovy (AFS Stalwart II)*: "All Phase 1 and Phase 3 forces break off and rendezvous at Mission Staging Coordinates Beta. Phase 2 forces, trigger all mines then immediately depart to join us at Mission Staging Coordinates Beta."*

The coordinates were eighteen parsecs from Machimis, or two minutes forty-three seconds by sLume propulsion, and far enough away to avoid detection of their momentary presence there. They would've been sitting ducks if they stayed here while they waited for the Caeles Prism to power up, the Prevos to connect to it and the traversals to be made.

At the staging coordinates they could afford to take a little time and due care. Besides, she wasn't inclined to reveal the nature of the newest tool in their arsenal to the enemy.

Another time. Another day.

The *Stalwart II's* own sLume drive engaged, and they vanished less than a minute before the enemy arrived.

⁂

MACHIMIS CENTRAL COMMAND ANNEX

The Machim Primor rode the space elevator up to the Central Command Annex alone. Fawning aides and valets were a nuisance in the best of circumstances and an inefficient distraction in all circumstances, drawing time and resources away from the work to be done. He tolerated an aide or two when necessary, but more than two made him feel like an Idoni.

Machimis' omnipresent cloud cover soon obscured the surface below, and a laden silence enveloped the compartment for the several seconds it took to break through the upper atmosphere into low-orbit space.

He spent the time reviewing active operation reports, and the brief trip passed without incident. He disembarked on the Annex and proceeded toward the central meeting room.

Ela and *asi* alike bowed in reverence as he passed, but above all they took care not to delay him in any manner. He sensed them scurry off to work as soon as he passed. Good. It had been a measurable length of time since three Imperiums had been docked at the Annex at the same time, and the fact they were here now generated a great deal of work for everyone to do.

The official response of the Directorate to the continuing attacks by the Humans, the anarchs and now the Katasketousya was that no exploration, harvesting or military operations were to be postponed or canceled. Business continued as usual, reality be damned.

He could make that happen, but it did require effecting a number of adjustments to resource allocations, and this was before one took into account the enemy which needed vanquishing—also his responsibility. But while Erevna was ready to set fire to the world over the destruction of a single lab, he intended to handle his losses and win the day without a speck of theatrics.

The destruction of several major manufacturing facilities was a significant blow, but hardly an insurmountable one. Similarly so the loss of several divisions' worth of vessels in the recent battles. The aggregate hit to resources was felt, but only by him and perhaps a few of his *elassons*. It was, in part, why he was here.

He entered the Annex's cavernous central meeting room to find the *elasson* Navarchos captains of the docked Imperiums waiting on him.

The instant he entered the room, the air filled with complex holographic representations of deployments, active assignments and supply points, both functional and otherwise.

He strode to the center of the data. "Gentlemen. While we meet, your vessels are undergoing any necessary repairs and being outfitted for the tasks to be assigned to them. We have many responsibilities in many places, and we will meet them in full."

The hologram flickered, fading almost to nothingness before sputtering back to life.

He instantly invaded the mind of the Annex Administrator, Polem ela-Machim. *Report.*

We've lost power transmission from Solar Node 1-1405. Backup power initiated until we transition to Node 2-2113.

He continued on with the meeting apace. "Now, the assignment of eighteen percent of the regiments in each LGG Region to guard the gateways is necessary in the short term, but it has reduced our fieldable forces concomitantly. To compensate—"

Polem ela-Machim: Solar Node 2-114 is not transmitting. Transitioning to tertiary node, 3-0839.

It was enough of a shock to cut him off mid-sentence. He remained monitoring Polem's work as he ordered a full security sweep of the solar sector. He did not yet know what, but something was wrong. Until he did know, he picked up where he had left off. "—for the reduction as well as the brief pause in the supply of new battlecruisers—"

Polem ela-Machim: Tertiary node is not transmitting.

Machimis Planetary Security: Hostile forces detected in solar vicinity. I-1C and D Regiments en route to intercept.

"We have a security situation." He replaced the logistical map with the results of the security inquiry. Though the display was awash in radar pings indicating unknown vessels when it sprung to life, the number of pings decreased precipitously as he watched. In a matter of seconds all were gone.

So were the three rings orbiting the sun.

The colossal structures provided twenty-eight yottawatts of power to Machimis, the Annex and multiple supporting stations in the stellar system every day. They had taken almost a decade to construct. The amount of power they generated was immense, but so was the power needed to drive the Machim military engine.

Their primary power source had been wiped out in the blink of an eye, the attack completed and the enemy gone almost before anyone had known they were there.

"Threat Alert Orange instituted throughout the system. Emergency response teams are dispatched to evaluate the anomaly with the Solar Power Network. Gentlemen, issue a recall order for your crews and prepare to move on any target identified."

The nearby gateway was well-guarded; the enemy had not come through it. So they had again utilized unknown wormhole technology to their full advantage. Even so, it was quite a feat to elude comprehensive sensors placed throughout the Machimis system and its outer reaches to arrive at the sun undetected.

Yet they had done so without warning and unopposed. Unchallenged.

They had invaded his own system, wreaked destruction upon it as surely as if they had bombed the planet below, and departed it to leave him to grapple with the resulting havoc. Was there no greater humiliation?

Triage required that he deal with the most pressing issues first, however. He reached out to Theriz and Diaplas to request provisional—

The floor lurched beneath his feet as a low *boom* echoed through the walls. Was the Annex under *attack*?

The holograms flickered and went out, and the room fell dark.

Machimis Planetary Security: I'm receiving indications the planetary orbital power relay modules have suffered undetermined damage. Update: a series of near-simultaneous explosions have destroyed the modules.

All the modules. At once. He blinked.

Polem ela-Machim: The explosion we just experienced was the result of a bomb placed on the Annex's reserve power battery. Switching to emergency power.

A few weak orange lights illuminated to cast a pallid glow across the cavernous room. It was an anemic offering.

Administrator? Security?

Machimis Planetary Security: Sir, the Bow Shock Network is gone. This is all the power we will have, and we will not have it for long.

The enemy hadn't merely breached the stellar system and its sun. They had breached Machimis high orbit AND Annex defenses. Then they had had their way. Casmir's impassioned warnings, delivered a few short days earlier, flashed in his mind as cruel, acrimonious taunts.

On the surface, batteries would keep power running for a time. But given their lack of any ability to replace it in the short-to-medium term, they needed to ration the power stored and direct it to essential services.

Directorate wishes be damned. Business was no longer as usual.

He scarcely believed he was giving the order. *Institute Threat Alert Red system-wide. Maximum emergency rationing of supplies, staples and power.*

As his eyes fell upon the viewport and the planet below, the lights began to go out.

PART VIII:

LIFE, INTERRUPTED

"Because you are alive, everything is possible."

— *Thich Nhat Hanh*

56

CENTAURUS ARX

MILKY WAY SECTOR I

The Centaurus Arx hung like a prize jewel staged against a backdrop of lesser gems.

A companion to the closest gateways to Sol—double gateways placed midway between Sol and Alpha Centauri, each connecting to opposite ends of the Milky Way—over the millennia it had grown to become the largest Arx in existence. In fact, it was technically three massive structures connected by a series of flexible passages.

Part mercantile hub, part entertainment extravaganza, part business headquarters and shipping center, one could wander its levels for days and never reach an end. Clear markers, prodigious maps and overbearing security notwithstanding, people routinely got lost. Occasionally they disappeared entirely.

Eren knew precisely where he was going, however. He made his way through the maze under deep disguise, thanks to the noted overbearing security and the fact that his face was now on an Anarch Most Wanted list or something. His cover was as a Diaplas tech engineer. His skin was shifted to olive, his eyes and hair darkened to black, and his facial features altered subtly to change his profile.

The measures taken were extreme, but he'd jumped at the chance to take the lead on this mission—to not only be responsible for the most important location of the operation, but also to coordinate the other agents spread across the Directorate's domain.

On returning from blowing the Maffei I Gateway with Alex, Caleb and Valkyrie, he'd stopped at Post Alpha long enough to get into costume then traveled straight here. He should be on a collision course with exhaustion, but instead he felt invigorated.

He'd convinced Sator Nisi to go public with an impassioned plea to the two and a half trillion beings living under Directorate rule, but accomplishing such an act wasn't a simple matter.

The Directorate controlled public communications: news, information dissemination and entertainment. As a method of keeping said control, there existed no universal, open communications platform they might access. Alex had been shocked on learning this, calling it archaic and backward; he understood her friend Devon had used crasser words. They weren't wrong, but the system did work to help keep control.

So he and his team would hardline hack individual communication hubs and impose their own broadcast signal. It wouldn't reach everyone, but with anarch agents ready to hack sixty-two Arx, hubs and admin centers, it would reach a lot. Far too many to contain. The Directorate was not going to be able to bury this one.

Oraihe Villiane (mission): "In position. Ursa Major I Arx."

Drae ela-Machim (mission): "In position. MW 36 Administration."

Eren reached Maintenance Hardware and credentialed his way inside under the guise of, obviously, maintenance work.

It took him only seconds to find a local communications access point once he was inside the vault. As an added bonus, it was tucked safely out of direct view of anyone outside the vault. Still, no need to take unneeded chances.

Eren asi-Idoni (private): "Stay cloaked. Get set up and wait for my signal."

Cosime Rhomyhn (private): "Roger mission leader sir."

She'd accompanied him all the way through the Arx to Maintenance Hardware under the cover of a Veil, and had done a damn sight better job of it than he had at Machimis Central Command.

Now he smiled and reached out, to where her cheek should be. His fingers grazed feathery hair on their way to settle against soft skin he could not see.

Eren asi-Idoni (private): "You've got this."

Cosime Rhomyhn (private): "I've got this. Go be a hero."

His hand fell away as he retreated to a dim corner in the rear of the vault.

Cosime Rhomyhn (mission): "In position. Centaurus Arx."

Eren asi-Idoni (private): "Mesme, I'm ready."

The next second the swirl of white-blue lights surrounded him and hurriedly swept him away.

The distance traveled was great and the trip short, but not too short for Mesme to poke at all his fresh wounds while in transit.

Mnemosyne (private): You appear in better spirits than when we last parted. I must apologize for any discomfort I caused you.

Eren asi-Idoni (private): "It wasn't your fault. And yes, I'm feeling better."

Mnemosyne (private): Then you do not regret visiting the Faneros?

Eren asi-Idoni (private): "The dark, dank and crowded dungeon that houses my regrets is a place you don't want to venture without a full party and sturdy armor."

Mnemosyne (private): Eren asi-Idoni, there are times when you become more perplexing than the Humans.

Eren asi-Idoni (private): "I know. Thank you for taking me to see the Faneros. The rest of my answer is still in progress."

ᴚ

CHALMUN STATION ASTEROID

LARGE MAGELLANIC CLOUD
LGG REGION I

They landed in the far corner of the hangar bay of Chalmun Station. Mesme was gone before Eren had properly regained his balance, off to wait in the asteroid's shadow for the call to return.

He smoothed out the lines of his coat and strode toward the tunnel leading out of the hangar bay.

He hadn't lied earlier—he *was* responsible for the most important location of the mission. But it wasn't the Centaurus Arx. It was Chalmun Station.

The settlement occupied a rather unique position in Directorate society. It existed off the grid and served as a haven for criminals, runaways and outcasts. Transaction fees on lucrative black market trade paid for the power and stocking of food and basic staples, but everything else that went on here was cutthroat business. Carved into the cavity of an asteroid orbiting a binary pair, Chalmun expanded in jagged, haphazard swaths deeper into the asteroid as additional space was needed.

If asked, the Directorate would deny to the end of its days that places such as Chalmun existed, but in truth the Directorate *allowed* them to exist. A few of them.

Even mad, power-drunk dictators recognized the necessity of maintaining a few release valves, lest society combust from within. So the Directorate discreetly monitored Chalmun Station and a small number of similar locations scattered across the empire. So long as they did not grow too large, wealthy or ambitious, it left them alone, because it needed to.

Oh, how the Primors must despise them.

He nodded a greeting at the bouncer, a Ch'mshak wearing mismatched but heavily spiked armor. The creased, pale look of the bouncer's skin meant he was *old*, which meant he'd won enough battles that it would be suicide to provoke him.

"I'm here to see Trepenos."

The bouncer grunted. "Passcode?"

"Potentissimus est qui se habet in potestate." He held up his open palm and projected a sequence of signals to accompany the phrase.

Another grunt, but this one came with a motion forward. "He's in the club, upstairs."

"Thank you." Eren hurried forward, less because he wanted to put distance between himself and the bouncer—though he did—and more because time was super, excruciatingly short. He had agents hanging out there across multiple galaxies waiting on him. Good thing he knew his way around the claustrophobic tunnels. While he maneuvered through them, his temporary Diaplas disguise faded away to return him to his natural appearance.

Borya Denovavan (mission): "In position. Andromeda 2 Administration."

As promised, he found his contact in the glass-enclosed balcony encircling the only truly expansive, open space in this rock.

Trepenos Hishai had the same clock ticking down in his head that Eren did, so on spotting Eren he excused himself from a couple of ominously outfitted Barisan and met Eren halfway.

"You have the transponder?"

Eren retrieved it from his pack and handed it to Trepenos. At most of the mission locations, the transponders were set to replace the official Directorate-approved feed flowing through the access point with the feed transmitting from the module, which originated at Post Satus. The transponders were programmed to self-destruct at the end of the broadcast, so any of the devices that were eventually recovered by Vigil would be of no use to them. Here at Chalmun there existed no official feed to replace, but the signal would transmit all the same.

"I'll see it gets looped in right away. Facility-wide. Are you ready to sell it?"

Inou asi-Antalla (mission): "In position. LMC Arx II."

Eren cracked his neck and shook his hair out. Good thing he hadn't sliced it off the other morning. "I am."

Trepenos motioned below. "The floor is yours. *Nos libertatem somnia.*"

"*Nos libertatem somnia.*" Eren spun and hurried a few meters around the ring to a glass door, opened it and leapt down the ten meters to the floor below. He landed between a Dankath and the Naraida trying to sell her a custom power spike.

"Excuse me, ladies." He left behind their stunned expressions to jog through the crowd toward the center stage.

Chalmun Station included hundreds of spaces. Businesses and workshops, temporary residences, labs and fight pits. His words and the message that followed them would be broadcast on every speaker and feed in the asteroid, reaching tens of thousands of people occupying its tunnels and hideaways.

But most of the people here gravitated to Trepenos' establishment whenever they could—for the comparatively open air, the prolific intoxicants and the somewhat more rare visual treat. They made the deals here that later played out in the other spaces. They drank and got high. Sometimes they fought, not for money but for sport or grudge.

They were the desperate and the daring, the lost and the searching. Tonight, they were his audience. Tomorrow, they would be his front line.

He reached the center platform, signaled for it to begin rising and hopped up on it. As it rotated and lifted ever higher, the lights angled toward him. Trepenos knew his stuff.

He donned a showy smirk and spread his arms wide. "Good evening, all. Ladies, gentlemen and otherfolk, enchantresses and woodkin, menageries and fluidics. My name is Eren asi-Idoni, and I bring you tonight's entertainment." He flourished his arms and swept into a low bow to a chorus of whistles and a few growls, then straightened up tall.

"You have business and pleasure to attend to. As an expert in both, allow me to advise you to put them aside for the next ten minutes. Why? Because the world is about to transform, and you will want to be able to say you saw it happen. The axes of our little universe are about to flip, and you'll want to get your magboots set.

"Quite the grandiose introduction, even for an Idoni, no? Well, you haven't seen anything yet." New lights began to swirl around him, and for a second he thought Mesme had arrived early. But it was merely a ramping up of the effects. In the shadows near the fringes, spectators poured in, crowding against the crowd.

"You see, fine patrons, I am an anarch." Amid the rippling murmurs of horror that he would dare *admit* it aloud, he pointed to a random location on the curving wall, then brought two fingers back to his face. Repeated the gesture. "Hey, Directorate spy cams, did you catch what I said? A-N-A-R-C-H.

"And you know what? I have lots of friends. Do you all want to be my friends, too? Do you want to take the work you scrape out in this shit-hole—no offense, Trepenos—and use it to set the world ablaze for a good cause?"

Venh G'ordackhl (mission): "In position. Triangulum 4 Administration."

Forty-nine of the sixty-two agents had now reported in ready; technical difficulties or security interference prevented the other thirteen from completing their mission. Forty-nine was good. Enough.

"I believe you do, because I know you. I've been you, and I'm here to tell you that you can be so much more powerful than you are now."

He snapped his fingers as the telltale electrical field of an oversized virtual screen sparked to life behind him. "So pay attention. If you have the ability to do so, sober up. If you can't sober up now, sober up in the morning. It's time to buckle up, strap in and go to work.

"The anarchs are stepping out of the shadows and into the light. Resistance is about to become revolution."

Eren asi-Idoni (mission): "Operation is live. Activate access overrides, then get yourselves clear before Hades breaks out the rage."

Eren asi-Idoni (private): "Mesme, make a proper spectacle of it. Show them the Kats are not Eradicated, and they are fighting."

He stepped forward as the screen solidified and Mesme swept over the crowd in a dazzling tornado of light to surround him then spin yet hotter and brighter. They vanished just as Nisi's voice boomed from the screen to resonate through the asteroid.

57

ANARCH POST SATUS

LOCATION UNKNOWN

"My name is Danilo Nisi. I speak to you today as an Anaden appalled at my sovereigns, and as an individual unwilling to sit idly by as their abuses propagate unchecked across galaxies. I speak to you today as an anarch.

"The Directorate denies our existence and our acts. But you hear tales of our deeds, delivered in hushed, furtive tones in the dark corners. 'The anarchs rescued a host of prisoners from a torture facility,' they say. 'The anarchs destroyed the Phoenix Gateway,' they proclaim. Some call us freedom fighters, others terrorists. But we are only what we must be. We do only what we must do to free people, worlds and knowledge from the chokehold and murderous hammer of the Directorate.

"You listen to me now, and if you are Anaden, you wonder my Dynasty, rank and role. The possibility I have none does not enter your mind, because your mind is controlled to a far greater extent than you realize.

"If you are a member of an Accepted Species, you listen to me and wonder why I would be any different from the Anadens who have abused you, dominated you and even murdered your families and friends. You wonder why I would ever bother to rebel when I can rule.

"To *all* of you, my answer is this. Freed of the suffocating influence of an integral, freed to question and to choose, I came to dream of a world where all individuals are free in this way. Where entire species are not Eradicated simply because they don't fit a slot in the Directorate's carefully constructed empire, but instead are nurtured and welcomed into our community.

"I dream of it because I have seen it. I have lived it and lost it.

"I do not stand alone. Countless members of every Accepted Species fight alongside me in pursuit of this dream: Novoloume, Naraida, Efkam, Ch'mshak, Katasketousya, Yinhe, Barisan, Dankath. The last members of species the Directorate had thought Eradicated fight alongside me. And now, species they did not know existed fight alongside me.

"You hear whispers of a new player on the field and know not whether they are liberators or conquerors. You have met people who met people who saw a battle take place—at the Sagittae and Provision Network Gateways, at Fabrication Centers and Regional Hubs. They talk of Machim fleets lying in ruin, vanquished. Even as I speak, you begin to hear rumors of Machimis itself, the crown jewel and heart of the Machim Dynasty, lying pitched into darkness. And you wonder if there might be reason for hope.

"You are right to do so. Though at times the anarchs have faltered under the crushing, omnipresent weight of the Directorate's authority, today we find new strength in new partners. Humans, the distant descendants of the Anadens of old, come from a civilization that has evolved apart from our own—a civilization that is free, open and powerful. A civilization that can challenge the Directorate on the battlefield and in the public sphere.

" 'Impossible,' you exclaim. I would not believe it either, had I not seen them accomplish it with my own eyes."

Footage rolled for a moment, spliced dramatically from the clashes at the Provision Network Gateway, the manufacturing facilities and the Machimis system. An appropriately impressive explosion transitioned to an orbital view of Machimis. The visual lingered there long enough to ensure the planet was easily recognizable before lights spanning the surface portentously winked out.

The darkness faded away to again reveal his lone figure, positioned against a rich backdrop of stars.

"The Directorate will tell you these recordings are lies—but they have always lied to you. I tell you these recordings are truth, but it matters not what I say. You will see for yourself soon enough.

"For too long, the anarchs have clung to the safety of the shadows, content to pick at the fringes of Directorate injustice and call ourselves rebels.

"No more. Now is the time to emerge from the shadows and stand in the light. Now is the time when the battle for the heart and soul of Amaranthe will be joined, and we shall be unafraid.

"This is not an Anaden fight, but Anadens must fight it above all others. We are responsible. We have willingly ceded our freedom to the Directorate in exchange for security, comfort and most of all, eternal life. But now we must take it back, for ourselves and for all citizens of Amaranthe.

"The Directorate holds fast to the secrets of regenesis, zealously reserving it for only the Primors and their progeny. They wield the power of life and death like a scythe over you.

"No more. Regenesis is not out of reach for any sentient being, and I vow to you today that should we prevail, we will work together with scientists from every species to unlock its secrets for everyone. For you.

"To all whom my voice reaches, I say now: stand with us. Fight with us. Together we will win for ourselves what the Directorate will never grant us: our freedom, and our lives."

58

SOLUM

It would be inaccurate to say that Praesidis fled the Directorate meeting to cower in his tower at the apex of Praesidis Command. After all, he had been among the last to depart and had done so with dispassionate grace.

Yet now he gazed down upon his dominion from that tower...and for the first time in six hundred thousand years, he felt like an imposter. The other Primors expected him to be able to flick a wrist and dispose of the invaders and rebels in a single directed wave of *diati*.

He was the ultimate master of it, was he not? Its chosen companion, ally and vessel? He had bonded with it to crush a terrifying enemy and lead an Anaden expansion across galaxies.

Except he had not, and was not.

The fevered alerts rose up through the integral in near-unison from points across the empire, breaking his reverie in a raucous cacophony. They warned of a disruption in the communications networks at multiple locations. Control lost, signals overridden.

A visual transmission being broadcast on the hacked networks painted itself upon his mental vision, replicating with each instance until it blocked out all other perceptions.

The man's features were not the same. The skin was darker, and the eyes lacked the trademark crimson. But he knew the face nonetheless. He had always known the face. For it was the face of his father.

And for the first time in six hundred thousand years, he felt the icy tentacles of fear.

Savine Idoni stretched out her comely limbs like a panther seeking the warmth of the sun for several luxurious seconds. Then she climbed out of the bed and went to the shelf where she had deposited her belongings. She efficiently chose a vial from her collection and smoothly placed two droplets of a coppery liquid in the crease of her eye.

Renato Praesidis had been caught up admiring the smooth curve of her ass and so missed the opportunity to protest, but he gave her a disapproving scowl when she returned to the bed and his arms. "I wish you wouldn't do so many of those concoctions."

She draped a leg over his waist, drawing it up to tease his cock with her toes. "Why do you care what I do in my free time?"

"Hypnols dull the mind."

"Do they? Have I not doubled my holdings in the last five years? Colonized three new worlds? Built and opened the most outrageous entertainment venue the galaxy has ever seen? Are those the achievements of a dulled mind?"

"Fine. But when you're here with me, I want you to be here, *in body, mind and soul."*

"Oh, darling..." her lips traced the skin along his collarbone "...I am so much more here than you imagine. I feel every touch, every quiver, every degree of rising heat. Try it just once, and you'll understand."

"No, thank you." He grabbed her ankle and tossed her leg off of him. "You got doped up for nothing—I have to go. My father and I are meeting with Dr. Erevna at her lab in Antarctica this morning to review the new genetic refinement proposal."

She watched him while he dressed, reposed on his bed in her naked, sumptuous glory, long golden hair spilling across her skin yet hiding nothing. "Your father is going to vote in favor, isn't he? He sounded reluctant when it was discussed at the last meeting."

"He'll vote in favor."

"And you know this because...?"

"Because I'll make sure he does."

"This is a crucial initiative, Renato. He can't be allowed to hold us back."

He didn't care for her tone. It was patronizing, a reminder that she held a position on the Directorate Committee when he did not. "I comprehend the situation full well, Savine. Leave my father to me."

"As you say...." She dropped her head to the pillow and closed her eyes.

He shook his head and sent a trickle of diati out to drape the sheet over her, then left her to her chemical bliss.

⁂

There were thousands of other locations suitable for conducting advanced genetic development experimentation, but Dr. Lisone Erevna had chosen Antarctica on Solum. Allegedly, she did so out of a desire to honor the spirit of scientists and explorers of antiquity, but he didn't buy it. Lisone hadn't a sentimental gene in her body—or if she once had, she'd long since excised it.

It wasn't as if Renato was cold, for his diati kept him warm without effort. No, it was the principle of the matter. His father should have asked Lisone to come to the Praesidis complex. His father was too accommodating of others, freely granting them power over him they did not deserve to hold.

But he kept those sentiments to himself as he entered the glass-walled lobby eighty meters above the frozen wasteland and greeted his father.

Corradeo Praesidis looked much as he had for the full span of Renato's life: striking and handsome, with raven hair, olive skin and a well-hewn bone structure that harkened back through hundreds of generations to Mediterranean ancestors. He stood composed and observant in the lobby, giving no outward hint of how weak and cowardly he had become.

Renato brought his hands together in a miniscule bow, which his father returned. "Son. Thank you for agreeing to accompany me today."

"I wish to see the results of the test trials for myself, firsthand."

"You don't trust my judgment."

"I did not say that."

"Well, such things are rarely said aloud, are they?" Corradeo pivoted as Dr. Erevna joined them. White-blonde hair that matched the ice outside was cropped close above pale jade irises as cold as the ice outside. Perhaps simple vanity was the true reason she'd chosen Antarctica for her lab.

"Gentlemen, welcome. Follow me, and we'll get started."

They followed her down a winding labyrinth of labs and testing facilities until they reached a meeting room at the opposite end of the facility. Perched over the Lethe Fissure, beneath them the jagged crack in the glacier stretched into the darkness of a chasm that seemed to plummet forever. It didn't, but it looked as though it could.

"I'm pleased to report today, and will report to the Directorate in one week's time, that we've successfully overcome earlier complications in co-regenesis genetic adjustment. We can now alter the expression of discrete genes of a physical clone—within parameters of course, nothing too severe—without triggering rejection symptoms from the existing consciousness when it transfers into the new body."

Corradeo took barely a second to glance at the data she'd sent before frowning. "Because the person has consented to the alteration ahead of time—they've asked for it, thus their consciousness is sympathetic to the change and willing to adapt to it. Yes?"

Lisone shook her head. "Consent is irrelevant to the process. In fact, when asked, the individuals have no idea some aspect of their makeup has been changed. It actually is a smoother process when consent isn't introduced as a precursor. Knowledge of the change can contribute to a subconscious resistance to the adaptation."

His father's countenance only hardened. "Shaping the genetic makeup—and thus the personality, the aptitude, the future—of a new life when it is created is one thing. I don't particularly care for the extremes to which we've taken that practice either, but at least the individual never knows they might have been other than what they are.

"But now you are talking about taking away the self-determination of a living, thinking, sapient adult. It's tantamount to slavery."

She smiled coolly. "I submit it is no different from what we do now. To use your words, Corradeo, the individual never knows they once were other than what they now are."

"Twisting my words doesn't make yours true, Lisone. What you are proposing is in fact vastly different. We have shepherded our people in many ways we thought in their best interests these last centuries, and it still remains to be seen if our judgment made for the best choices in the end. But I cannot sanction the explicit removal of the most basic of freedoms: the freedom for people to be who they are."

"Your idealism is so charming, Corradeo. I admire it, I do. All I want is to enable all our Dynasties to reach their full potential. The reality is, our success has become our curse. We live too long. With occasional tidying, we can live forever. This means change—improvement, adaptation—is slow, if not in danger of ceasing altogether.

"Shall we instead start ordering forced euthanasia of some portion of our populations? Cull the herd to make room for newer, better, more refined citizens? Would this be more ethical to your mind?"

"You wouldn't dare. The universe is plenty large enough for everyone to get to live, for however long they choose. I submit our Dynasties and our empire are all doing quite well. Besides, meddling for the sake of meddling isn't improvement—it's just meddling."

"Then you intend to vote 'no'?"

"I do."

Renato fumed. He'd allowed his father to voice his concerns in the hope that if the man had his say he would get it out of his system, after which he'd relent. But when had Corradeo Praesidis ever relented?

"Father, you are being unreasonable. Worse, you are being...old-fashioned. This luddite mentality you've adopted of late is unbecoming on you."

"The word you are searching for, son, is 'stubborn,' and I'm fine with being thought of as such. But I did not save our people from the Dzhvar so they could live to be gutted of the very traits which make them extraordinary. We rule the galaxy today because we are strong. If we meddle too much, we may accidentally remove that which makes us so."

Lisone bristled. "I never 'accidentally' do anything, I assure you."

Corradeo shot her a glare, but instead of retorting pivoted to stare at the fissure below. "That is what I'm afraid of."

"I'm sorry, I didn't catch the last bit?"

"Never mind." He turned back around. "Present your case at the meeting next week, but I don't expect my inclination to change."

Lisone's gaze flitted to where Renato stood, behind and off to the side of his father. The meaning of the intensity of her expression was clear: do something. A vote on a substantial change in policy had to be unanimous—all the Dynasties must implement the change, or none at all.

He nodded discreetly, raising his hand in acknowledgement. "Doctor, would you excuse us? My father and I need to confer in private for a minute."

"Certainly. I have another meeting soon, so I'll leave you to it. If you need any assistance finding your way out, contact the security desk. Good day, gentlemen."

The instant she was gone he whirled on his father. "Stop being stupid."

"Careful, son. You forget yourself."

"No, you forget yourself. You forget the man you once were and the ideals you once stood for. You have become cautious to the point of cowardice. You would hamstring us now, at such an important juncture in our history, merely because you've decided change is now an unwise course of action."

"Every moment in history appears important to the young when they first encounter it. Trust me—most of them aren't."

"'Young'? I have endured your haughty condescension for eleven thousand years, father, and I have had enough of it."

"Oh? Do you fancy striking off on your own? Starting a fledgling Dynasty yourself, then begging to be allowed into the Directorate? Do as you wish—but surrender your diati at the door, for it belongs to the Praesidis alone."

Renato meant it, however. He had had enough. He'd played the dutiful son for so terribly long, with no hope of escaping his father's shadow.

He'd been consigned to forever occupying second place, forever kneeling at his father's knee before a throne that could never be his.

He would not kneel for another day. "Or perhaps you should surrender yours, for you no longer deserve to wield it. You have become a disgrace to the Praesidis name."

"Depart from my presence. I will be rid of the sight of you."

"No."

Corradeo started, his eyes flaring as crimson tendrils escaped them. "Pardon me?"

The entirety of Renato's presence flared in response. "I said no. I will not take orders from you any longer. You don't deserve to be the head of our Dynasty. You don't deserve to sit on the Directorate. You don't deserve to hoard a treasure of diati for yourself alone simply to waste it on complacency and cowardice."

His command flowed forth in sync with his outstretched arm.

TAKE

Though now a shadow of his former self, his father was neither weak nor helpless, and a shell of diati sprung forth to encase him in protection. Renato's power slashed at it and was initially repelled.

But Renato had been stealing diati from lesser Praesidis for some time now, and he had perfected the art of commanding it so thoroughly that it could only obey.

JOIN AND COME TO ME

He could feel it, the power, as it began to shift to his will. The protective shell began to thin, then crack and splinter. "Renato, what are you—" *Corradeo grabbed at his throat, eyes bulging.*

His father began to understand, and so to fight back. Corradeo rushed forward and knocked Renato into the table to tower over him, and now Renato gasped for air. His vision blurred as the surrounding air pressed in on him.

OBEY ME—YOU ARE MINE

A surge of power crashed into him, but not to harm him. He redirected it outward, and Corradeo flew through the air to slam into one of the windows. The diati—Renato's diati—held him there against the glass, not letting him fall to the floor.

"You will not survive this betrayal, Renato."

He climbed off the table. *"Do you feel it, father? Do you feel it abandoning you for me? It knows I'm the worthy one here, and its rightful vessel and ruler."*

"You—" Corradeo gasped for air *"—understand nothing about the diati, and when it matters most, it will fail you."*

"No. It won't."

TO ME NOW

All the power cascading around them rushed into him. He gasped, his body driven rigid in shock as the tidal wave drowned him—but only for a second. He blinked and breathed in, finding the control he'd cultivated through endless practice. Then he strode deliberately over to his father, who now lay crumpled on the floor.

He knelt in front of Corradeo and used a fingertip to lift his father's chin. The last vestiges of crimson bled out of his father's eyes, leaving behind sapphire irises. Only a man.

Renato made a succinct slashing motion with his hand, then again, and two red lines appeared on either side of Corradeo's neck. Blood began to seep out of them to stream in rivulets down his chest.

"Don't die too quickly, father—I have things to do first." His power whipped out and shattered the window behind them, and he threw his father out of it to tumble into the chasm below.

He immediately straightened up and evaluated the scene as it stood at present. Next he sent a remote order to overwrite certain Praesidis medical data with altered replacement data, prepared well in advance and stored until this day, this time.

Now he shattered the rest of the windows. The glass hung frozen in mid-air, awaiting instruction. He braced himself, then directed most of it to him. Shards sliced open his face and shredded his clothes until only blood-soaked strips remained.

He didn't have to fake collapsing to the floor, but he managed to activate his transmitter as he fell. "Someone help! There's been an accident, an explosion...."

He commanded the diati *not to heal him, but the pain was threatening to overwhelm his will when security officers finally rushed into the room. They briefly shrank away from the blast of cold air and punishing wind before coming to his aid.*

He pointed weakly out to the frozen expanse beyond. "My son...he fell...the fissure...dead...."

"Stay calm, sir. It's going to be all right. We have advanced medical, rejuvenation and regenesis chambers here. What's your name?"

"Corradeo Praesidis."

59

CENTAURUS ARX

Nyx jerked awake in a burst of existential turmoil. *Diati* shook the nearby table and chair as her agitation took on tangible form.

What was that?

It could not be a dream, for the integral kept Anaden dreams tame and obedient. But what, then?

In the recesses of her perfectly analytical mind, the possibilities had already been parsed and cross-matched. She had the answer. Still she struggled to accept it.

Since her regenesis after the destruction of Exobiology Lab #4, she'd begun to try to listen to the *diati*, while having little sense of how to do so. She'd drifted to sleep tonight, as she had on many recent nights, displaying an open, willing mind, ready to hear what it might have to say.

What it had showed her, albeit in response to her implicit invitation, was the one thing she had never expected. Her *diati* was her Primor's *diati*. Its memories were her Primor's memories.

She wasn't able to assign order and meaning to all of what she'd witnessed, filtered as the memories were through the perception of an empyreal, non-corporeal entity. But she comprehended enough to recognize what it suggested, and the implications were horrifying.

Something was very wrong. With the Directorate, with the Dynasties, the integrals and regenesis. With her Primor.

She'd begun tromping wildly around the suite on the Centaurus Arx in a new display of her agitation, but now she came to a hard stop mid-stride. She breathed in. Attentively let out the breath. Repeated the actions.

She calmed her body with the exercise of swift, honed discipline, but calming her mind proved not so simple a task. But she must. For if she did not, her Primor would find out.

He would sense her turmoil across the stars and the void and he would turn his attention her way and he would *see*. Until she worked out what she knew, what it meant, and what she intended to do about it, he must not be allowed to see.

But the integral was powerful and pervasive, and her Primor's connection to her through it was strong. She may need to enlist some assistance in order to shroud her true thoughts.

She'd brought few belongings with her for the brief overnight stay; she gathered them up and prepared to teleport to her ship when the vid feed in the wall burst to life of its own accord.

An image of an Anaden man standing in front of a canopy of stars filled the projection. She did not know him, but a strange twinge in her chest made her feel as if she did.

Then he spoke, and his voice felt like a song meant for her soul. She dropped her belongings and stepped forward to lift her hand, palm flared open, as if she could touch the image and have it touch her in return.

"Who are you?"

$\mathcal{R}$

SIYANE

PALAEMON
ANARCH POST EPSILON

Caleb awoke with a start, sitting bolt upright in the bed. *What the hell?*

After a few deep breaths, he sank back onto his elbows and worked to process what he'd seen. It was by far the most vivid, nuanced dream-vision the *diati* had shown him thus far. Perhaps the greater clarity and intensity had been spurred on by the recent influx of undeniably powerful *diati* from his latest encounter with Nyx, though it had been days ago now.

It also renewed his curiosity about the nature of her replacement supply. Nisi believed the Praesidis Primor replenished her following the events at Helix Retention, and his theory had now been borne out. But that meant these were the Primor's memories, sifted and translated by the *diati*.

He closed his eyes and stepped back through what he'd seen, because there had been something eerily familiar about....

I'll be damned.

The face wasn't quite right, but cosmetic alterations during regenesis were commonplace. The skin tone in the vision was lighter, but Caleb had seen Eren vary his skin from Nordic fair to ebony and several points in between, and that was *without* regenesis. So Anadens could change their physical appearance easily enough. Mannerisms, bearing and the smallest gesture tics, however, tended to become an intrinsic part of a person. Once they did, they tended to stick around.

Alex stirred beside him, rolling over and peering at him from behind sleepy lids and tousled hair. "Something wrong?"

He leaned down and kissed her softly. "No, everything's fine. Are you ready for today?"

"I have no idea. How does one get ready for something like this? Listen, I want you close when events start to happen and such."

"Of course. I never expected anything else. When will he be ready?"

"Checking." She grimaced. "A few more hours, it looks like."

"In that case, I'm going to get up and moving. I'll be there when you need me, but since there's time, I want to pay Nisi a brief visit this morning."

60

PALAEMON

Malcolm took the first shuttle down to Palaemon the morning after the mission. Post-mission procedures and debriefs had extended well into the evening, until he'd been forced to wait for the next dawn.

He wished the shuttle would fly faster. He'd have run to Post Epsilon if he could. His chest pounded as if he *were* running, and it required effort to sit still and maintain decorum on the shuttle.

It might not matter if he hurried, but he felt the deep, driving need to hurry nonetheless. Doubts and fears gnawed at his gut; he did his best to quiet them.

Only once the shuttle landed did it occur to him that he didn't have the slightest idea where she would be. Considering he didn't dare pulse her and receive a cold rejection in response, he was at a momentary loss as to what to do now.

Epsilon wasn't especially large, and most of the grounds held minimal relevance for AEGIS personnel. If she was at the post, he should be able to find her merely by looking around. He set off from the landing platform for the main complex.

In a stroke of luck—whether good or bad remained to be seen—he spotted her seconds after reaching the first pavilion.

She sat at one of the outdoor tables with Cosime, Emily and two of the refugees they'd rescued from the lab. She was showing the refugees some holo images, though he couldn't tell of what from this distance, and, he suspected, generally trying to help make them feel welcome and at ease. Because she would.

He stood there watching her, smiling when she smiled when one of the refugees smiled at an image. She wore a white turtleneck sweater and charcoal woolen slacks flared out in a fashionable cut. Gracefully elegant even when trying to be casual. Her raven hair was draped over the white material of her sweater in a loose tail, leaving the exquisite features of her face open and exposed. Might she regret doing so in the next few minutes? Might he?

She laughed at something Cosime said, and with the movement that accompanied it she caught sight of him standing there gaping at her like a fool. The amiable expression faded, to be replaced by one he couldn't decipher.

Then she turned her back on him to lean in and point out something in another image to one of the refugees.

It was enough to send terror shrieking through his stalwart Marine constitution. But if he walked away now, he'd never find the courage to reach out to her later. He was a coward when it came to affairs of the heart, but he couldn't be one today.

He readied himself and approached the table. Cosime waved at him, and the motion caused Mia to glance over her shoulder. Her brow furrowed, as if she was surprised he'd actually come over.

He tried to smile; probably failed. "Hello, Ms. Rhomyhn. I'm glad to see these refugees are doing well. Mia, can I—" he cleared his throat "—talk to you for a minute? In private?"

Cosime tossed an animated gesture toward Mia. "Thanks for helping me entertain them for a spell. We're going to go find some breakfast now. Emily, won't you join us? And bring your pretty pictures."

"Sure."

"Good." Cosime hopped up on the table and across it to jump down the other side and grab the hands of the two refugees. "Come!"

He watched them leave. A palpable and terribly awkward silence settled into the air in their wake.

Finally Mia shifted to perch on the edge of the table, letting her feet rest on the bench while her hands remained close in on either side. "Looks like we're in private now."

"Yeah. Um...how are you?"

She glared at him incredulously. "What do you want, Malcolm?"

"To fall prostrate on the ground and beg your forgiveness?" He tried again for a weak smile. Possibly succeeded a little better this time.

"Don't do that, please. People will stare, and we both have reputations to uphold." If her words held a hint of teasing, her tone did not.

"Right." He opted for pacing. "We went through your wormholes yesterday—which obviously you know. Twice, in fact. There and back. It was an incredible experience."

"They're not my wormholes."

"They may as well be. The technology wouldn't exist without you. And what a marvel they are—much like you."

He tried to squelch the cringe which followed the painfully lame words—but she'd turned away, so the effort was wasted.

He heard her sharp intake of air, though. "I can't do this—"

"I know. It's not fair of me. To say I haven't been fair to you is to make a mockery of unfairness, but please indulge me this one last time. You're a leader, a hero, a healer, even a warrior when you have to be. And I treated you like you were dirt. Like you were some kind of delinquent forced to stand before a court and justify the choices that kept you alive."

"I *was* a delinquent."

"No, you were a survivor. You've always been a survivor, underneath all those other thankless roles."

She shook her head forcefully enough for fine locks of hair to escape the silk tie binding them. "You don't know some of the things I've had to do, and when you find out you won't be happy about them."

"I don't care—I mean, of course I care. I want to know, if or when you want me to know. But you don't ever need to tell me. I know who you are now, and the struggles of your past helped to make you that person." He exhaled raggedly. "I love you. I love that person. And your absence from my life these last days has been damn near unbearable. To be in the same room with you, to watch you be amazing and realize I might not...I can hardly breathe."

Another stifled cringe. God, he was terrible at this. But what else could he do?

She stared at him, eyes wide in brilliant jade, sunlight reflecting off the water to reflect off of them. She hadn't changed their color, not yet. But just as he began to draw hope from the tiniest sign, her gaze fell to her lap. "What about Winslow?"

"I wish he'd gotten his due punishment the proper way, within the system. But you're right. He tried to kill you, and on further reflection, I can't bring myself to be sorry he's dead."

"And Caleb?"

"I still don't like him. Don't trust him, don't understand him. But I am grateful to him for one thing—he helped you when you needed it most. And now, I'm done talking about him."

Malcolm stopped pacing to stand directly in front of her. "I do not deserve you. Not your forgiveness, and certainly not your love. But I'm asking—begging—for it anyway. In the past I've always walked when a relationship got hard, because at the root of things I was unwilling to fight for it.

"But I'm fighting now, because for the first time, I believe with all my heart it's worth it. You're worth it. Please, let me fight for you."

"If you truly intend to fight for me, you won't need my permission to do it. That's kind of the point."

"Well, like I said, I've never done it before. It's no surprise I'm really bad at it."

This finally coaxed a weak, halting laugh out of her. Her chin slowly rose until her eyes met his...and he still couldn't read them. The façade she'd once said she didn't have to project for him, she now wore as armor.

Her chin rose higher. Proudly. "You're the only person who can make me feel...vulnerable. Exposed. You made me need you, but then you were gone and you took with you more than you arrived with. How did you do that?"

"I didn't mean—"

"I want it back. The part of me you took. I want…I want to have never met you, if only so I would never have recognized…" a tear escaped from the corner of her eye, and she hurriedly wiped it away "…I was missing some part of life. The best part, and the worst. Better to not know, since then I wouldn't be broken now. Damn you. *Damn you* for breaking me!"

He covered his mouth with both hands and clung to his jaw to hold it, and him, together. Broken? She'd never given any sign, remaining always composed, unflappable and in control. Even now, a stranger wouldn't suspect she was upset. It was in the slight tremble of her eyelids and the miniscule twitching of the muscles of her jaw, but none but her closest friends would ever see it. He saw it now, but only because she allowed it.

"I'm sorry." It came out too weak a whisper, muffled through the space between his fingers. He forced his hands down. She was trying to scare him off, push him away. If he refused to comply he risked failing, but if she succeeded, it was all over.

"But I'm *not* sorry for meeting you. If I genuinely managed to accomplish such a thing, I'm not sorry for showing you there was more to life. I'm not sorry that you showed it to me. I can't be.

"I hurt you, and I accept full responsibility for it. Worse, I devalued you and all you've overcome to become the extraordinary person you are. I may be a Marine, but you're the true fighter. You're a survivor. I shouldn't have discounted this part of you, because it's *why* I love you—one of the 'whys,'—and I swear to you I will never do it again. I will never devalue you again.

"You are worth more than…everyone else to me. And not solely to me. To all these people, arguably to the entire human race and a couple of alien ones. But I'm feeling a bit selfish at the moment, so I mostly care about what you mean to me."

Her throat worked. "You know, you can't simply waltz up to me, flash your boyish smile and apologize, and think that will make it be okay."

Boyish smile? It was something. "I don't expect it to. I realize you have no reason to believe me. I realize trust has to be built from actions, and I've straight-up failed at that lately. I realize I have no right to ask you to trust me now, when the cost is so high if I let you down. So I won't dare to ask it of you.

"All I want to ask of you, all I dare to ask of you…." He took a step toward her. She hadn't been far away, and it put her within his reach. "Is to allow me to kiss you. Just once. You can slap me after. Punch me in the gut, too, if you're inclined to do so. We'll go from there."

Her head tilted; he'd surprised her. Surprised himself, too. The corners of her lips gradually curled up, if only a little. "You already broke me. What's the worst that could happen?"

"Myself? I'm wondering what the best might be." He took the final step and swiftly but gently brought a hand up to cup her cheek. His thumb ran softly along her lower lip to bridge the span before his mouth met hers.

He felt her tremble against him—then she consumed his careful gentleness in a surge of fervency. He drank it in, letting it fill the empty places and return life to a parched soul. He lifted her off the table and into his arms, and when she held on tighter, he thought maybe there was a chance.

61

ANARCH POST SATUS

Post Satus had taken to the stars for the broadcast, and it could have been anywhere when Caleb exited the teleportation gate. Traversing the glass-bounded bridge that connected the entry room to the hub made for a heady experience. He made a mental note to try to get Alex onto Satus when it was traveling.

Caleb almost bumped into Nisi in the doorway as the Sator made to leave his office. Though it was undoubtedly a busy time for the man, his expression remained customarily stoic as he looked up and gestured to his office.

"Is now a bad time?"

"I have a few minutes before I'm required to depart."

Caleb stepped into the spacious office and turned back to Nisi in slight surprise. "The ship's in transit, yet you're leaving it?"

"In the wake of yesterday's events, your Katasketousya friend, Lakhes, informs me that I will find a sympathetic audience among the Novoloume leadership on Nopreis. Unlike your vessels, however, Satus does not come equipped with a wormhole generator, so I need to travel to the Pegasus Dwarf galaxy on foot, as it were."

'On foot' being through a teleportation gate to one of what Caleb imagined were several destination gates located in Pegasus. "I'll try not to keep you long, then."

"It's fine. They are expecting me in only the loosest sense. So it appears the first use of your wife's new wormhole device went well, if the footage from Machimis is any indication."

Caleb leaned a shoulder on a window—now a viewport, technically—and crossed his ankles and arms. "It did. I suspect the

Machim Primor had quite the unpleasant day yesterday. Today, too."

"Clever woman, your wife."

"You have no idea."

"And her other project?"

"We'll see in a few hours, but Dimou insists it was a success. So, I listened to your speech last night. Inspiring, enigmatic and loaded with subtext. It was an impressive shot across the bow, but I'm not surprised."

"Oh?"

"See, I know who you are."

A flicker of unease crossed Nisi's eyes. It was gone in an instant. "Do you imagine that you do?"

He ignored the ambiguous response. "What I can't figure is why you keep your identity a secret. Why haven't you told your followers? You could've been a true lightning rod against the Directorate all this time. For the true father of the Praesidis—the man who defeated the Dzhvar and led the Anadens to greatness—to openly oppose the Primors? The people would have flocked to you by the millions."

Nisi's face seemed to fall, and his stance lost some of its inherent confidence; he genuinely had doubted Caleb knew the truth.

He shook his head. "Whoever I may have once been, that man is no more. He hasn't drawn breath for hundreds of millennia, and trust me when I say we should leave him in his grave."

"Semantics. You can change your face and your name as many times as you wish, but you are still Corradeo Praesidis.

"When we first met, you lied to us. Though considering you've been lying to everyone for a very long time, I ought not to be offended. You said you were 'no Dynasty, and all Dynasties.' But you're the founder of *the* Dynasty. The only one that really matters."

"What I said was not a lie, from a certain point of view. I was born before the Dynasties existed, and other than altering my outward physical appearance slightly, I have not changed my genetic structure since they were founded."

More semantics, built upon the persona Nisi had painstakingly constructed for himself in lieu of reality. But reality was a tenacious beast. "Your son challenged you for the Praesidis throne. He defeated you and took your *diati*—but not all of it. You clearly didn't die as he believed, so what happened next? You didn't show up in the anarchs for aeons. Where did you go?"

"How can you know these things?"

"Nyx's *diati* definitely came from the Primor—from your son—and it has a long memory."

Nisi stared at Caleb for a moment, then moved to a window several meters away. In a dozen subtle ways, his entire demeanor had transformed in the last minute. He looked the same, but a different man stood here now.

"I should have been dead, wanted to be dead, but the *diati* wouldn't allow it. The initial hours and days after I fell have always been a delirium-laden haze, but I do know the *diati* nurtured me to health while I hid. When I finally ventured back to civilization, I discovered my son had not merely taken my seat on the Directorate from me—he had taken my identity from me. He used regenesis to change his appearance to match mine. He took my name and my skin.

"So far as I am aware, to this day the other Primors believe he is me. The Praesidis progeny believe he is me. And it is...for the best.

"I followed his lead and adopted a new identity, judging myself to be in no position to expose or confront Renato. Then I wandered, away from Solum, away from our colonies, away from any world we had touched. I met primitive and not-so-primitive species, some of which the Directorate has to this day never found. I spent centuries alone in the void. I went mad and regained my sanity more than once."

He breathed out to ponderous effect. "When I at last returned, I found an empire I no longer recognized. I despaired anew, for this was my fault. My responsibility, for I had fled when I should have fought. I lost hope and begged the *diati* to leave me to die, but it again declined to comply.

"In time, I met a woman who fought against the Directorate with such passion, such zeal, as I had never seen. She shone like the fire of a thousand galaxies. I told her who I was, and she loved me anyway. I married her and joined her in her fight. The Directorate killed her. They killed our friends and comrades. But yet again, they could not kill me.

"Part of me wanted to leave then, to give up for good and wander the stars until I had traveled so far I would be unable to find my way back.

"But the spark she'd rekindled in me refused to go out. She had made me remember the smallest hint of the man I had once been. I decided if she could fight when she had no reason to take the risk, I could fight when I had every reason. So I rebuilt the anarchs atop her ashes. And I waited."

Caleb swallowed heavily. He'd fallen under the spell of the man's tale in spite of himself. "For me."

"You remind me so much of myself, when I was still myself. The day I met you…you think you made the mistake of approaching me, but in truth I was approaching you.

"I had straightened out my life and paid my recompense. Embraced my purpose and again taken up the mantle of leadership. Proved I was worthy. I thought I had earned the right to be the *diati's* chosen vessel and master once more. I thought when it encountered me, it would choose me over you. At last I would wield the power necessary to sweep away the Directorate and again be the great savior. But I was wrong.

"It marked the second time I had been shown my place by the *diati*. I think I handled the second time rather better than the first, if I may say so."

Caleb's eyes narrowed, until he realized what Nisi must mean. "When we talked before, you said that in six hundred thousand years I was the only instance of the *diati* abandoning one host for another of its own volition. That was when the confrontation with your son happened, wasn't it? You believe the *diati* willingly chose him as a more worthy master, but you're wrong. He forcibly took it from you."

"I don't understand."

"He'd developed a way to dominate the *diati* so thoroughly it was compelled to obey his commands—not just the *diati* merged with him, but any *diati* in reach. It didn't abandon you. He stole it from you."

Nisi spun away as emotion swept across his face. His chin dropped to his chest in profile, and he was silent for almost a minute. Finally he sighed, but kept his back to Caleb. "Then why does it not return to me now?"

Caleb tried to choose his phrasing carefully. "I can't say for certain. It speaks to me on its own whims, and never in words. But as you yourself said, you're not the man you once were. Not necessarily lesser, but undoubtedly changed. It's possible the *diati* that has been separated from you for many aeons no longer recognizes you."

Nisi fell silent for another moment before nodding slowly, as if to himself. He turned to Caleb wearing a poignant smile. "Yes. I am at peace with who I am now, but you are the one with the fire burning in your soul that a worthy champion requires."

"If it was up to me, I would give it to you. All of it."

"Even if it meant you were unable to save your people?"

"I can save my people without it—hell, I don't have to. They can save themselves. Your people...well, I'm not as confident."

"You Humans are indeed formidable. As Ambassador Requelme said, you are who we might have been, if things had gone differently. Perhaps if I'd been strong enough when Renato betrayed me. Perhaps if I hadn't given up and fled when I should have fought."

Nisi straightened his shoulders in what seemed like a display of mettle. "But that is neither here nor there, and long in the past. The *diati* obeys you, and it is not inclined to change its mind. Therefore, I will do my best to help you use it wisely, boldly and to world-altering effect."

"Thank you, sir."

"While I'm in a confessional mood, what else do you wish to know?"

Caleb cringed. "Much, but I can't stay. Today's a big day for the Solovys, and I can't miss it."

62

AFS STALWART II

My name is David Nikolai Solovy, and I am alive.
David studied his reflection in the mirror and was relieved to recognize the man who gazed back at him. Familiar gray eyes accepted what they saw as matching his innate perception of himself. Dusky blond hair that had always refused to lie down properly splayed defiantly across his left temple. The fact that it refused to lie down today told him it belonged to him.

He breathed in, taking proper note of the miraculousness of such a simple act. It ensured life continued…or in his case, resumed after a brief, eternal pause.

Fifteen months ago he'd emerged from he knew not where, a faint spark of consciousness awoken as a shard of thought half in an Artificial's mind, half in his daughter's mind—which was every bit as disorienting and surreal as it sounded. Later, he'd awoken as a quantum construct, a more fulsome but still digitized mind, and it had felt more real than it had any right to be.

Now he was flesh and bone and blood, inhabiting a body crafted by Anadens using Anaden technology but human DNA—his DNA—and built to spec. Human organs, human cybernetics and a human-designed eVi controlling them, with only a few tidbits of Anaden organics to fill in the odd gap here and there.

So what was he, truly? Part human, part alien, part quantum synthetic, part intangible consciousness, all molded into a hopefully cohesive whole and reborn into a world where those who were once dead *could* live again. Reborn into a time not his own and a universe he didn't comprehend—but at least he wasn't alone in the last part.

He knew everything that had transpired in the intervening twenty-five years, yet he knew nothing at all. Wars had been fought, peace won and lost and won again. Enemies had become allies; allies had become comrades. His daughter had grown up and lived and loved and set the world ablaze in her wake. His wife had fought all comers, stood tall and risen to greatness, then yet further, to a position of such gravity and responsibility he'd never have wished it upon her.

But these were merely cold facts, devoid of nuance or character. What had Miriam and Alex *felt*? How had they laughed? When had they cried, in joy and in pain? He knew what they had *done*, but how they had lived was forever lost to him.

But no longer. From today, he could again see them live and love and laugh and cry. Universe willing, he would do so with them.

Alex cleared her throat as she moved into the open doorway behind him. He watched her reflection smile back at his. Miriam's smile—the real one, the one she'd only ever shared with a precious few people—sculpted upon features close enough to his own to make him selfishly proud.

The girl he remembered had become a woman of such astonishing wonder, verve and determination, beyond what he'd dared imagine possible. Would her life have gone differently if he'd been there for it? Should it have?

They wouldn't be here, in this place, now if not for her. What if his absence had been required for her to find her destiny, and for all of humanity to follow along behind her? It didn't change the fact that if given the chance he'd opt for a better past.

She stared at him as if she expected him to vanish at any moment. He didn't blame her—so did he. "Are you ready?"

"What are you offering me?" He'd asked her when she'd returned to his tranquil little fake mountain camp, impossible proposition in hand.

"Life, Dad. I'm offering you life, *not bound by virtual walls. I'm offering you a chance to walk in the sun again."*

He grimaced, or thought a grimace was what the expression looked like. It had been a while. "No, I'm not ready. I mean, yes, absolutely, of course I am...*proklyat'ye, eto pizdets.*"

Caleb appeared behind Alex then, his hand falling to her waist with the easy familiarity that came from true intimacy. Husband to his daughter, killer in the service of his killer, and now something more than either.

But Caleb seemed a good man in the ways which mattered, indisputably loved Alex with a purity of spirit David appreciated all too well, and was exceptional in the manner she richly deserved.

Also, he offered a welcoming greeting to David while displaying no wariness or judgment in his eyes, oddly crimson though they were. For today, this counted for more than it probably should.

"So he's where you learned that curse from."

Alex chuckled and dropped her hand over her husband's with equal familiarity. "Among many others. Are we set out there?"

"The bridge has been cleared, and no one's returning to it until I tell Major Halmi they can."

"Okay." She tilted her head at his reflection in question. "Dad?"

He'd never lacked for confidence. In his time many had called it arrogance, and he couldn't fairly dispute them. But now a tiny, petrified voice deep inside his head wondered if there existed any room in his wife's life—or in her heart—for him. By her own words she'd remained alone since he died. But sex was one thing, and not always everything.

Had twenty-five years erased the feelings underpinning the bond they'd shared? Had they simply been an accident of fate, unable to be replicated? Had it simply been too long?

He closed his eyes and reached for the old confidence, for the cocky certitude that the world would give him what he needed from it, or he would take it by force of will. By sheer force if required.

My name is David Nikolai Solovy, and goddammit but I am alive.

ℛ

The lightness in Miriam's step took her by surprise. Yesterday had been a good day for AEGIS, no question. But the road ahead of them remained steep and treacherous, the final goal all but impossible to reach, and she should take care not to get *too* optimistic.

But as she surveyed the main hangar bay, taking note of the energetic manner in which the crew carried out their tasks as well as the sporadic laughter and lighthearted banter, she decided to cut herself a break.

The blow they'd suffered at the Sagittae Gateway had been devastating, but instead of wallowing in despair or slinking off in defeat, they'd buckled down. They'd rested, recharged and found another way, and the results spoke for themselves. A significant strategic obstacle had been overcome, an alliance with the anarchs strengthened, and a psychological and practical victory over the enemy achieved.

Perhaps she should take the win.

She nodded to herself and headed for the lift, mentally reviewing their next steps. The crew was allowed to enjoy the win for a bit longer, but she needed to take advantage of the wind at her back if she wanted to translate one win into two, then into a string of wins that led to victory.

The effect Nisi's manifesto broadcast was going to have on their strategy wasn't immediately obvious. Support of the populace was always helpful in war, to the point there existed entire government departments back home devoted to creating and nurturing it.

If a widespread uprising distracted the Directorate from her fleet, all the better. And the tantalizing promise of regenesis for all was sure to make things interesting. Was there a more tempting prize, for any species?

But she didn't have a good grasp on the civilian situation in Amaranthe, nor how such an uprising might play out. She ought to meet with Sator Nisi to discuss the matter. Alex's friend Eren may be a valuable resource, too. He likely had a better read on the vagaries of the masses than the Sator.

In the meantime, she needed to continue hitting the enemy where it was vulnerable—

Alex was waiting for her opposite the lift on Deck 2. "Oh, good, I found you."

Miriam hadn't seen and had hardly talked to Alex since the start of the Machimis mission the day before. Her daughter had begged off the morning meeting, citing vague business with the anarchs. She hadn't let Miriam know she was coming up to the *Stalwart II*, either.

"You did." Miriam motioned down the corridor, and Alex fell into step beside her. "So what's this morning's surprise?"

"What? Why do you think I have a surprise?"

"You went incommunicado yesterday after the mission, skipped the AEGIS Council meeting this morning, and now you show up here unannounced? This kind of behavior usually means you've either stirred up trouble or have an urgent idea of how to do so."

In the corner of her eye she caught her daughter's shoulders drop as she exhaled with uncommon soberness. So there *was* something.

"Okay, you caught me. Do you remember how, at the height of the huge final battle against the Kats, I sent you a cryptic message and asked you to trust me? You did, and it worked out fabulously, right?"

"I still maintain that you should have brought me in on your plans sooner, but yes, it did. Why?"

"So you trust me, and you understand that I will never do anything I think might hurt you."

Miriam stopped outside the armory and pivoted to her daughter. "Alex, what have you done?"

"Mom, something extraordinary happened...a while ago. It seemed as though it was going to be ephemeral and transient and ultimately bittersweet at best, so I didn't tell you about it. But then the world changed, and we went to another universe, and...opportunities arose to transform this miracle into something real."

"You're talking in nonsensical riddles. I've already gathered this secret scheme of yours will upend my day and possibly my week, so out with it."

Her daughter's lips parted, and the look on her face was enough to give Miriam pause.

"It's better if I show you. Come with me to the bridge. I have a gift for you."

⟡

When they reached the bridge, Alex leapt out of the lift ahead of her and briefly disappeared out of view.

Miriam stepped onto the deck and located her daughter, then peered past her and frowned. "Why is the bridge empty? Where is everyone? I didn't authorize shore leave for the entire bridge crew."

Alex gave her the oddest little smile. "It's not empty, Mom." She took a long step back, to the side and out of the way, revealing more of a bridge that plainly was, despite her words, empty.

Miriam scanned it from the starboard airlock up to the cockpit and down the port side all the way to her office—

Impossible

She ceased breathing. Time ceased moving forward and began rushing in reverse.

She was dead—had been shot in the heart, or the ship had exploded—and her brain was firing random neurons in the final nanosecond before it ceased functioning. She knew this because she would want him to be what she saw at her last breath.

A magnificent hallucination of what had once been

"Hi, Miri." The false vision spoke, even as it leaned against the open door to her office, wearing Alliance BDUs and a smirk as dashing as the day she'd met him. A perfect doppelganger.

But the BDUs the hallucination wore were of a modern design, one implemented a few short years earlier. So her mind was breaking down, then, and mixing things up. Another nanosecond or two and oblivion would claim her.

A shame, when she had so much left to do.

Alex shifted anxiously in her peripheral vision, which didn't make so much sense if she were dead. Miriam drew air in through her nose. Her chest felt tight, but it rose and fell as if she were alive.

She brought her hand to her chest to confirm the movement. Lifted her hand in front of her face. There was no blood.

Her mind searched for alternate explanations beyond its own cessation. Alex's comments minutes ago rushed to the forefront, and her reaction when pressed...Miriam opened her mouth and forced words out of it. It was harder than it should have been if she was actually alive.

"Alex, what have you done? What is this?"

"I told you, Mom. It's a gift. A miracle of a gift I can give to you. What I mean to say is, it's Dad."

In light of mounting evidence to the contrary, she began to accept the likelihood that she was not dead. Thus, the world and the *Stalwart II* bridge continued to exist for her. Logic and reason reasserted themselves to take over, as was proper.

If she, the world and the bridge continued to exist, logic dictated that so, too, did the form standing at her office door exist. But what did such a conclusion mean?

"This is a trick—an Anaden clone. A synthetic construct ported into a body. A Directorate spy disguised to fool me. Where are the MPs? They need to arrest this, this...intruder. *Why* is the bridge empty?"

"Mom, please—"

The stranger wearing her husband's face and skin and mannerisms pushed off the door frame exactly like he *would*. "It's all right, *milaya*. Your mother is correct to be skeptical. I'd suspect *her* of being a fake if she wasn't suspicious."

His—its—gaze hadn't veered from her while it spoke to Alex, but a new intensity shone in its haunting visage now. "Do you know what's been running through my mind over and over on this most terrifying of mornings? A memory, one above so many. It's from the night you confessed, in a somewhat rueful statement against interest, that you'd fallen in love with me. I told you—after I picked myself up off the floor—I felt as though I'd found my rightful place in the world.

"This isn't the world I left behind. But seeing you now, I know without a shred of doubt: you're still my rightful place in it."

Logic abandoned her to the wretched turmoil of emotion, yet she clawed valiantly to hold onto its last vestiges. Memory. Mind. Neural imprint. One existed back on Earth, in Aurora...and the leaps required to get from there to the figure standing before her now defied her treasured reason.

So she lashed out in defiance. "Knowing he said those words doesn't prove anything!" Had she shouted? Was she hysterical? Was she overtaken by insanity, or was everyone else?

"No, it doesn't. With my neural imprint out there any Artificial could access those memories. And I won't lie to you, I will never lie to you. Along the way, one did."

See? her mind screamed. Logic had led her to the precipice of the truth, yet provided her no path across the chasm which remained.

"But that's only a tiny part of the story. The really interesting part is how our *skazochnaya* marvel of a daughter brought me back to life as only she was capable of doing."

"Alex...." Wouldn't betray her. Alex had said to trust her, and had proved worthy of trusting many times over. But Alex was wild and reckless...and would do anything in her power to have her father back.

She wielded so much power now.

The bridge spun dizzyingly around Miriam, and she lunged for the railing extending out from the overlook to steady herself. Then she tried—*tried so*—to stand up straight and proud.

She sensed her daughter's shadow retreat out of view and watched as this...man...slowly lowered his chin in...*respect?*

"But it's not up to Alex to convince you I'm real. It's up to me, and I accept the challenge. I will do whatever I must, for as long as I must, to earn your trust. I've done it before. I can do it again."

He took a step toward her, and she fought the urge to flee. He sounded so like David, from the rolling 'r's of the accent he hadn't bothered to lose to the easy confidence lending affect to his voice.

She did not understand. She could not find a path that might lead to understanding. She'd never wanted to believe in something so tremendously in her life, but belief, no matter how strong it became, *did not* make something real. He was gone, so long gone, and nothing could ever bring him back.

Could it?

"When I agreed to take the *Stalwart* command for the Crux War—pardon me, the 1st Crux War—and leave you and Alex behind, I promised you I would come back to you.

"I remember how the moonlight streamed through our bedroom window that night. It made your skin glow like that of an angel—I didn't tell you so then, lest you scowl horribly at me for indulging in whimsy. So instead you stared at me with this heartbreaking honesty. I knew the hard logic of your mind was insisting there were no guarantees in life and I shouldn't make empty promises to you, but I think for once you chose to put aside the logic and believe me anyway."

He took another step forward, and she forgot fleeing was an option. "It took a while longer than I'd planned, and for this I am so, *so* sorry, but I'm here now to make good on my promise. I will always keep my promises to you, even if I have to crawl through the chaos of more than one universe to do it."

His words echoed other, older words he'd said to her, so long ago.

The universe is not ordered, and it will not become so simply because one wishes it. The universe is chaos made manifest...but even the chaos needs someone willing to stand in the center of it and say 'enough.'

Dammit, if anyone had ever existed who could find a way, he would find a way. He was just that hardheaded.

"*Moya vselennaya*, there are so many more stars in the heavens than I imagined there were, and I still love you more than all of them."

The floor fell out from underneath her, and she landed on her knees. Her face was wet, she thought. She couldn't breathe, again. This was why the bridge was empty, wasn't it?

She blinked through blurred vision that refused to clear. "...David?"

He dropped to his knees in front of her, and his palms pressed gently against her cheeks. *His* palms—she'd never forgotten how they felt. His eyes shone liquid silver, like the night when she'd chosen to believe in impossible promises.

"Hi, Miri."

DON'T MISS THE THRILLING CONCLUSION TO THE
AURORA RESONANT TRILOGY AND THE
AURORA RHAPSODY SAGA:

AURORA RESONANT BOOK THREE

REQUIEM

COMING WINTER 2017

***

SUBSCRIBE TO
GSJENNSEN.COM

*Receive updates on AURORA RESONANT, new book
announcements, free short stories and more*

Author's Note

I published *Starshine* in March of 2014. In the back of the book I put a short note asking readers to consider leaving a review or talking about the book with their friends. Since that time I've had the unmitigated pleasure of watching my readers do exactly that, and there has never been a more wonderful and humbling experience in my life. There's no way to properly thank you for that support, but know you changed my life and made my dreams a reality.

I'll make the same request now. If you loved *RUBICON*, tell someone. If you bought the book on Amazon, consider leaving a review. If you downloaded the book off a website with Russian text in the margins and pictures of cartoon video game characters in the sidebar, consider recommending it to others.

As I've said before, reviews are the lifeblood of a book's success, and there is no single thing that will sell a book better than word-of-mouth. My part of this deal is to write a book worth talking about—your part of the deal is to do the talking. If you all keep doing your bit, I get to write a lot more books for you.

This time I'm also going to make a second request. *Rubicon* was an independently published novel, written by one person and worked on by a small team of colleagues. Right now there are thousands of writers out there chasing this same dream.

Go to Amazon and surf until you find an author you like the sound of. Take a small chance with a few dollars and a few hours of your time. In doing so, you may be changing those authors' lives by giving visibility to people who until recently were shut out of publishing, but who have something they need to say. It's a revolution, and it's waiting on you.

Lastly, I love hearing from my readers. Seriously. Just like I don't have a publisher or an agent, I don't have "fans." I have **readers** who buy and read my books, and **friends** who do that then reach out to me through email or social media. If you loved the book—or if you didn't—let me know. The beauty of independent publishing is its simplicity: there's the writer and the readers. Without any overhead, I can find out what I'm doing right and wrong directly from you, which is invaluable in making the next book better than this one. And the one after that. And the twenty after that.

Website: www.gsjennsen.com
Email: gs@gsjennsen.com
Twitter: @GSJennsen
Facebook: facebook.com/gsjennsen.author
Goodreads: goodreads.com/gs_jennsen
Google+: plus.google.com/+GSJennsen
Instagram: instagram.com/gsjennsen

Find all my books on Amazon:
http://amazon.com/author/gsjennsen

About The Author

G. S. JENNSEN lives in Colorado with her husband and two dogs. *Rubicon* is her eighth novel, all published by her imprint, Hypernova Publishing. She has become an internationally bestselling author since her first novel, *Starshine*, was published in March 2014. She has chosen to continue writing under an independent publishing model to ensure the integrity of the *Aurora Rhapsody* series and her ability to execute on the vision she's had for it since its genesis.

While she has been a lawyer, a software engineer and an editor, she's found the life of a full-time author preferable by several orders of magnitude, which means you can expect the next book in the *Aurora Rhapsody* series in just a few months.

When she isn't writing, she's gaming or working out or getting lost in the Colorado mountains that loom large outside the windows in her home. Or she's dealing with a flooded basement, or standing in a line at Walmart reading the tabloid headlines and wondering who all of those people are. Or sitting on her back porch with a glass of wine, looking up at the stars, trying to figure out what could be up there.

44524750R00285

Made in the USA
Middletown, DE
09 June 2017